THE
UNVEILING
A Novel Series: Volume 2.0

K. L. COLLINS

ISBN: 978-0-9884296-2-8

Cover art: designed by K. L. Collins & illustrated by Yamen Elgamal
Cover design & graffiti art: Tamara Johnston
TheUnveilingSeries.com: designed by Tamara Johnston
                    & built by Stephen Winsor
facebook.com/TheUnveilingSeries
facebook.com/kl.collins.94

THE
UNVEILING
Volume 2.0

The works of K. L. Collins

The Unveiling 1.0
The Unveiling 2.0

Coming soon from K. L. Collins

The Unveiling 3.0
The Adventures of Zuko

For my mother and father

FOREWORD

Circa 2008. It all started at DreamWorks Studios. Kevin (or K.L. Collins as you know him) and I were assistants in our respective departments, each beholden to the whims of our bosses. To help us cope with the everyday madness of filmmaking and television, we would sometimes engage in conversations, scouring each other's thoughts about a multitude of topics. It was just the simple things, really: office politics, family, relationships and of course movies. Then, one random day, just like any other, I came across a YouTube video about this large mysterious planet called Nibiru. Now, I know the different planets in our solar system, who doesn't, right? But learning for the first time that a mysterious dark planet, larger than Jupiter, could possibly exist and might be on track to collide with earth AT ANY MOMENT (yes, the drama!) put me in the darkest funk I've ever been in. This, of course, intrigued Kevin! We had suddenly found something thrilling to research that dominated weeks of dialogue. This new curiosity led to various internet discoveries about the Grays (extra-terrestrials), Mayan mythology, Sumerians, the Anunnaki, and of course the Illuminati.

As we immersed ourselves in the subject matter, we became more fascinated with an array of conspiracies that were mind-boggling and oftentimes frightening: UFOs, chemtrails, microchips and flu shots, massive depopulation and FEMA coffins, and the list goes on… Kevin took a particular interest in parallels between the Old Testament and Sumerian mythology, which eventually became the genesis for these *Unveiling* books.

A year later, Kevin left DreamWorks and moved away. When he called me and said he was going to write a novel about a billionaire heir whose family is part of an ancient bloodline that controls the nation's politics and wealth… I knew we were in for something special. And of course, Kevin did not disappoint. The world of billionaire playboy Max Battenberg is so well crafted that I felt I was living in his shoes every step of the way. What person wouldn't want to be rich, good looking and living the life of a modern-day Indiana Jones? Volume 1.0 dropped us into the fast lane of expensive vehicles, ritzy nightclubs and beautiful men and women. Max's extravagant life eventually took a turn for the surreal when his father, Demetrius Battenberg, revealed that the blood running through their veins was more ancient than the Pyramids of Giza, and that their standing in the world had bestowed them with more power and influence than the President of the United States (POTUS). Kevin's *Unveiling* books present a world in which there is more to life than meets the eye. The story of Max Battenberg is provocative in its ability to make us question, "Could any of this be true?" For Max, the rabbit hole spirals even deeper in this second book, and he must uncover who he truly is and how he intends to make a difference in today's world.

Many years have passed since those DreamWorks days, but the inspiration Kevin and I felt during that period endures in our creative endeavors. I have recently completed my directorial debut of a feature film (about an alien invasion, no less), and Kevin has finally released this book, and a third is on its way. I hope (and believe) you will derive as much fascination and enjoyment from these books as I have.

-Alexander Murillo
Writer/Director of *Watch The Sky*
Co-creator/Co-writer of the graphic novel series *Future Proof*

Acknowledgments

The following people have all been instrumental in bringing this book to fruition: Norma Henry, Melissa Hendricks, Alex Murillo, Darryl Stephens, Char Walter, Vincent Cummings, Alma Thomas, Roger Collins, Sam Flowers, Yamen Hazem, Rick Atcheson, Tamara Johnston, Stephen Winsor, my editor Jennifer French, my father Winfield Collins and countless other friends and family who have offered their love and support throughout the process. To all of you I offer my deepest gratitude.

A Note from the Author

If you recently completed Volume 1.0 of *The Unveiling,* and the details of it are fresh in your mind, please feel free to skip directly to Chapter One, as the story of Max Battenberg picks up in this book exactly where it left off in Volume 1.0. If, on the other hand, it has been a while since you finished Volume 1.0, or if you are fuzzy on the details of what previously transpired, please continue to the following recap. Thank you — your readership is greatly appreciated.

About QR Codes...

For your convenience, a series of QR codes have been embedded throughout this book. Each one will lead to a website or a video that delves into a topic or concept addressed in the story. To provide an example, the following QR code links to The Unveiling Series website:

To access any of these QR codes, you will need to download a QR code reader on your smartphone, which can be obtained at your local app store. I hope you will find these intriguing and informational.

Previously in *The Unveiling* Series...

When we last left Max Battenberg, in Volume 1.0, he was in a livery vehicle, headed across Washington, DC from the National Archives Building. He and his father's friend, Otto Khrzinsky, had just parted ways after emerging from a secret underground installation deep beneath DC. To recap, the following events are what led to this moment:

☐ Max, a few friends, and his girlfriend, Brigitte, traveled to New Orleans for Mardi Gras. There, a peculiar psychic named Indigo Blue accused him of belonging to a worldwide system of oppression. She also warned Brigitte and his friend Ted to get as far from Max as possible, otherwise danger would befall them. Minutes later, Ted suffered a brutal attack in the crowd.

☐ Max had never believed in psychics, but Indigo's prediction coming true unnerved him. For this reason, he decided to follow her advice and travel to the Money Pit on Oak Island. Deep inside the ancient booby-trapped hiding place, he recovered the missing piece to the Antikythera Mechanism, a device that provides the user with clairvoyant abilities.

☐ Max's father, Demetrius, dispatched him to the family's traditional rite of passage, the Battenberg Initiation. Deep inside Teotihuacán's Pyramid of the Moon, he was given an elixir known as the fruit from the Tree of Knowledge. The concoction resulted in a vision that revealed the entire Battenberg clan is descended from an ancient race referred to in Sumerian mythology as the Anunnaki.

☐ Shortly thereafter, Max's father was severely injured in an explosion. As a result, Max was whisked away to a secret underground installation, where his father was convalescing. There, he was told he must replace the elder Battenberg at an important meeting for a clandestine organization known as the Rizick Group. To prepare, Max was sent to DC for training about the world's über elite and the methods that they use covertly to run the planet. On his way to DC, Max discovered a top-secret underground train network with multiple compartments that are outfitted with chains and shackles, but what on Earth were they for?

Find out all there is to know about the Rizick Group in this latest installment, Volume 2.0, of *The Unveiling* Series.

THE UNVEILING 2.0

$\mathcal{M}$ax sat in the Town Car's back seat, gripping his smartphone with the speaker on. Brigitte had been calm, but her voice now blared through the cabin.

"What the fuck, Max?"

He understood why she was aggravated, but he hadn't expected she would still be so angry. The driver glanced in the rearview mirror, while Max fumbled to switch the call from speaker to handset. He placed the phone against his ear and whispered, "Brigitte, I told you I'm sorry."

"Yeah, Max, but a dozen sorries are shit when you have to keep apologizing. You couldn't wait ninety seconds for me to say goodbye the other day."

Max stared, silent, from the livery vehicle's back seat. Days before, they were blocks from his home, where they had agreed to meet. Max had been the first to arrive only to discover a limousine blocking his driveway. Within seconds, his father's minions had whisked him inside and insisted upon his departure. He felt awful, watching Brigitte arrive just as his limo pulled away.

She, of course, had been speechless and was still smarting from the incident. "How do you think that made me feel?"

"Probably pretty shitty," Max replied. Varied landmarks of the District of Columbia shot by to the left and right as his current transport traveled down Constitution Avenue. They had already passed the White House lawn and the Washington Monument. Max turned toward the car's sidewall, trying to sound normal while keeping his voice low. "I'm being pulled so many different directions. I wish you could see that."

"I can, Max, but you've been acting strange. It seems like, just once, this baby and I should be a priority. I mean, fuck, you couldn't wait because of your father's plane, like it wasn't gonna wait?"

"Brigitte, my dad almost died; you realize that, right? What aren't you grasping?"

Silence rang out, signaling her compassion more than acquiescence. "It'd just be nice if you showed us the same concern once in a while."

Max wasn't sure if she meant herself and the baby, or her and him.

"You would've done the same thing whether your dad was hurt or not. One of these days you're gonna have to stand up to him."

"I am sorry I haven't been around... We've both had a lot on our plates lately." Max took a breath, and they listened to each other breathing on the phone. "I'm pretty wiped out. All this traveling..." He stared out across the streets of DC. "Can we talk about this later?"

This was not the direction Brigitte wanted for their conversation, but talk of his father's injuries had pulled the trigger on her guilt. "Sure." Her voice was flat and emotionless.

"All right. I'll call you after I get to the hotel."

"Sounds good. I'll talk to you then."

Max switched off the phone as the Town Car turned left on 23rd Street, heading toward the Lincoln Memorial. His spirit sank even deeper when he spotted a street blockade before them. A series of police cruisers were carefully parked in formation, perpendicular to oncoming traffic. At the intersection of 23rd and Lincoln Memorial Drive, a dozen officers stood at attention both in the street and along the curbside. The chauffeur braked, bringing them to an abrupt halt. Max looked up and saw they were only half a block from the monument of the sixteenth U.S. president. Low on energy and patience, he leaned forward to question the driver. "What's going on?"

The chauffeur narrowed his eyes, evaluating the roadblock. "Looks like a presidential motorcade, sir. It shouldn't be long."

Max leaned back on the leather seat, praying for quick passage. "Are there any detours?"

The driver diverted his eyes from the road to the rearview mirror. The start of rush hour had begun, and a row of cars already stretched behind them in an ever-growing queue. "I apologize, sir. The roadblock should've been on my schedule. It shouldn't be long. They've got the president's movements down to a science."

Max considered a peculiar irony: many regarded the President of the United States as one of the most powerful and influential men in the world. Even for a simple excursion, the U.S. Commander-in-Chief required a well-placed barricade of Secret Service and police. But Max knew a carefully guarded secret. There were others who were considerably more important than the American president. Max hadn't fully accepted that he might be one of these people, one of the world's super elite, but he was slowly beginning to grasp the possibilities.

He, of course, had no doubt that his father wielded such influence. It had been less than a week since Demetrius fell victim to a terroristic attack on one of their production plants in Brazil. His injuries had been grave. Had POTUS suffered a similar circumstance, Max wasn't so sure that the leader of the free world would have been whisked off to a deep underground hospital like the one where his father was currently being housed.

As it turned out, Demetrius had been correct about impending danger regarding their family. He had erred though, fearing for Max's safety over his own. Arrogance had prevented him from realizing that he, the almighty father, might have been the target rather than his son.

The longer Max sat in traffic, the more his mind wandered through events of late. Not only was Brigitte pregnant, but he had finally gone through his initiation. *Aliens. Shit.*

To minimize any potential threat, Demetrius had advanced the date of his initiation. Details of what transpired there had always been shrouded in mystery, not only to the world, but also to the Battenbergs themselves. What Max learned during his own induction, he still found difficult to accept. They had stripped him naked and given him an elixir to drink. The peculiar concoction contained a white powder, the byproduct of vaporized gold bullion. *White powder of gold* is what the priestess of the ceremony had called it. From what Max could gather, the elixir may have been what the Bible referred to as "the fruit from the tree of knowledge." Both Adam and Eve had been expelled from the Garden of Eden for partaking. *Was it the same elixir they had drunk?*

Of course, Max still struggled to believe anything he experienced after ingesting the bizarre blend. Could he have left his body and ventured to some faraway dimension to witness the past? *Astral projection! Seeing extra-terrestrials on distant planets?* Things like that simply didn't exist and had to be some form of hallucination: that's what he had believed, until now. Even the idea that it all took place inside of a well-known pyramid outside of Mexico City was difficult to digest.

For countless generations, the Battenbergs had remained politically and financially powerful. Their lengthy rule had been possible because of a little-known group called "Rizick," whose far-reaching tentacles extended into global politics, commerce and banking. Demetrius was one of Rizick's prominent figures, but his injuries in Brazil had temporarily removed him from the equation. He had survived, but it would likely take months for him to make a complete recovery. Owing to the serious nature of his wounds, he had instructed Max to attend the upcoming Rizick meeting in his stead. Despite their strained relationship, Max had agreed, which is why he was in Washington, DC in the first place, for intense training.

The honking of a car horn snapped Max back to reality. *Shit. Still in traffic.* They had been waiting less than five minutes when he spotted a series of presidential limousines crossing from Henry Bacon Drive onto Lincoln Memorial Circle. The black limousines, commissioned specifically for the president, were like no others. Each was outfitted with special communications equipment, presidential conveniences and, most importantly, armor. Tinted windows made it impossible to determine which vehicle in the motorcade contained the president. To Max's relief, three Cadillac Ones shot by, flanked by police and secret service vehicles.

The chauffeur turned toward Max with a satisfied smile. "It'll just be a moment, sir."

"Very good," Max replied.

The pendant around his neck contained a tiny microchip. It had been implanted in his arm just days after birth. The minuscule piece of technology was smaller than a grain of rice, but it contained some of the most advanced microscopic circuitry available in today's modern world. Demetrius had finally admitted to its existence, so Max had located it and removed it from the fleshy part of his underarm. From that point on, he had worn the tiny device around his neck in a small glass pendant. This provided him the option not to carry it, when he wished for privacy from his father's prying eyes.

Max had no clue that anyone beside Demetrius had access to

the chip, which provided detailed personal information about his location, heart rate, body temperature and other important vitals. As his Town Car edged through the opening blockade, the chip around his neck activated. The homing beacon beamed his location to a high-tech craft more than 800 miles above them in orbit. A woman Max had seen, but still didn't believe existed, had easily hacked in to the chip's mainframe. Unlike Demetrius, she possessed the technology to calibrate the microchip for sound. If and when she desired, she could easily tune in and listen to Max's conversations.

Her name was Aurelia, a designation perfectly suited to her persona. At six feet tall, she was slender yet well proportioned, like an art deco statue that had come to life. Silky blond tresses seemingly fluoresced, cascading down her back like liquid light. She stood before a large picture window, staring into the night from what appeared to be an ultra-modern living room. Sleek furnishings sparsely populated the circular, minimalist space. A perfectly smooth gray concrete floor had an oval couch on one side with a glass and metal coffee table before it. A single dark pedestal sat beside the picture window, and Aurelia had her hand resting upon it. Her mannerisms were ethereal, giving her a faery-like, otherworldly appeal.

While she stood at the window, staring into the darkness, her stocky cohort, Sutekh, approached from the couch. He was three and a half feet tall and built of sinewy muscle. When he stood at her side, his head barely reached the bottom of her chest. He stepped beside her and gazed into space, as they had done hundreds of times before. For more than a decade, they had been a team, and their sole concern was focused on one man: Maximilian Battenberg.

Sitting atop the pedestal beside the window was a unique implement that measured one square centimeter and looked to be a piece of simple tinfoil. In reality, the technology was infinitely more sophisticated. Hidden within its microfibers were small neuro-connectors and pathways that directly linked the wearer's thoughts to the ship's mainframe. Aurelia picked up the square and placed it against her right temple. Like a second skin it quickly adhered to the side of her head. Without so much as a blink, she turned to Sutekh and spoke. "Are you ready?"

He continued gazing through the glass. In lieu of an answer, he simply nodded.

"There isn't much time. If we don't go now..." Her voice trailed off. It had never been Aurelia's habit to speak about unfavorable options.

Sutekh remained contemplative. "You realize with each visit we are losing our ability to control him."

She and the small man locked eyes, pondering this new reality. She knew he was right. Weeks earlier, they had stolen into Brigitte's house while she and Max were together, presumably asleep. Within minutes of their arrival, they had lost control of the situation. Before they could sedate her, Brigitte had awakened, kicking and screaming. To their dismay, it had taken both of them to restrain her.

On top of that, Aurelia had been conscious that Max, while immobilized, had nevertheless been cognizant of his surroundings. It had become painfully clear that he was now more than likely aware of their existence. Without a doubt, their next moves concerning him would need to be formulated with delicacy.

Aurelia turned to Sutekh to let him know, "I'm bringing the ship online."

In the blink of an eye, the tiny square connected the electrical impulses of her brain to the ship's control center. Their craft, nearly 800 miles in orbit, came to life, pivoting around until the large window tilted down, pointing toward the North American continent. As she concentrated, the transport plugged into her thoughts, becoming an extension of her very being. While the change seemed infinitesimal, the ship contorted, altering its configuration from circular to oblong. Aurelia took a deep breath and exhaled as she transferred her attention to the planet below. In a moment's time, she had hacked in to the chip around Max's neck.

"He's in the Capitol."

Together, she and Sutekh tracked Max's movement as he crossed DC in his Town Car. During the brief surveillance they remained silent. When Max reached his hotel, he made a few calls, ordered room service and began to watch TV. Without warning, a sudden bout of laughter overcame him.

The man from the yoga studio, Max thought, unable to forget the stranger who had somehow afflicted him with symptoms of uncontrollable laughter and unexplained muscle spasms. *What did he do?*

The miniature device, despite having been removed, still remained quite effective at monitoring his vitals, including infinitesimal changes in body temperature that were often due to eating or drinking. Aurelia and Sutekh quietly watched changes occurring as Max erupted with laughter. Both his temperature and pulse had increased in addition to his body's electrical conductivity. The chip also held the ability to measure Max's exhaustion, which was more than apparent. He reclined on the bed and quickly fell asleep in his clothes with the TV still blaring in the background.

Satisfied that he was on his way into deep slumber, Aurelia finally spoke. "I'll clear a path and bring the ship down over his hotel." A moment later, she and Sutekh made their way toward the couch against the far wall. Even though the piece of furniture appeared solid, it unfolded into a large membrane that encircled them like a protective womb. With them both secured inside, Aurelia barked an instruction.

"Brace yourself."

For someone with average sensibilities, the interstellar craft's movement would have been nearly imperceptible, as if it had vanished from one spot and reappeared in another. But Aurelia and Sutekh had some of the most heightened senses in the galaxy. With just a thought to do so, the ship had locked onto its new position just meters above Max's hotel. Due to its astonishing speed, a path through space first needed to be cleared or an impact could occur and prove fatal. Once the proper precaution had been completed, the ship had literally slingshot itself with such velocity that the human eye would have been unable to detect it.

Within a fraction of a second, the craft had come to a standstill, hovering fifteen meters above Max's hotel. For a single moment, the mere blink of an eye, the transport was visible while its hull collected the data it needed to cloak itself. Tiny panels that comprised the exterior were each cameras and projectors at the same time. While the craft was in any given position, it could photograph and project images of what the naked eye thought it should be seeing.

Had they landed beside a tree, the craft could easily have created a mirror image of this tree, or of any landscape it was blocking from view. As such, anyone who looked in its direction, instead of seeing the ship, would see whatever the ship obscured, creating the illusion of invisibility. When traveling in areas of high traffic, the only danger involved avoiding other moving objects that were unable to perceive the ship's presence. At this point, there was no one on or near the roof, so this was not a concern.

The protective shell unfolded from around them, and reconstituted itself into the circular couch. Aurelia pulled her suit jacket aside to reveal a compact utility belt. Satisfied that all was in place, she crossed to the center of the ship.

"Let's get this over with."

Without a reply, Sutekh joined her beside a large circular portal that began opening in the center of the floor. Aurelia nodded as a soft white light shot down from the ceiling and bathed the opening in its glow. Together she and Sutekh leapt into the light and floated down toward the roof's surface as the golden beam gently buffered their fall. The moment their feet touched the roof, the light shot back up into the ship and, in a flash, the portal vanished entirely.

Although they knew the ship was there, they gazed upward into the stars, their view seemingly unimpeded.

Together, she and Sutekh hurried to the roof's entrance. There was no doubt it would be locked from inside, but this was hardly an obstacle. So far, Earth had not presented a single security measure that their technology could not bypass.

Just a few hours earlier, Max had checked in to his hotel, where he was now sleeping soundly. After a few calls to friends and to Brigitte, he had ordered room service.

He channel surfed following his meal, but quickly fell into a deep slumber. When the outer room door chirped ever so quietly, he did not stir. Its electronic lock had disengaged, allowing access to his room. Like thieves, Aurelia and Sutekh crept inside. After gently closing the door, she followed him down the short hall into the larger chamber where Max was asleep. He slumbered on his side, facing the sliding glass door to the balcony. Aurelia had always relished seeing him, and this time was no different.

In the background, an infomercial on acne skincare echoed in the room with countless testimonials. Sutekh circumvented the bed until he was facing Max. He removed a triangular red sticker from his jacket and gently placed it on Max's forehead. Assured that he was now immobilized, Aurelia opened her jacket and removed a sleek eight-centimeter syringe from inside. She double-checked the cartridge containing a purple neon solution before she turned to Sutekh.

"Is he ready?"

Sutekh gently nudged Max before reaching across to open his eyelids. Just as they hoped, Max's pupils were unresponsive. "Affirmative," Sutekh replied.

Without hesitation, she and Sutekh rolled Max onto his back, and Aurelia repositioned his head gently on the pillow, tilting Max's chin toward the ceiling. Pleased, she maneuvered the syringe into Max's nostril until she pierced the posterior wall of his sinus. Closing her eyes, she concentrated on the needed path as she angled the needle upward. In an instant, the tinfoil chip on her temple fluoresced in unison with the handle of the syringe. The eight-centimeter needle immediately began elongating until it found the optic nerve and traveled across it, passing the pituitary gland until it finally reached Max's pineal gland.

Although her eyes were closed, the tinfoil square blinked once to indicate that the needle was in position. In tiny spurts, the syringe began emitting microscopic doses of the purple solution. With each injection, the solution began eating away at a calcified shell surrounding Max's pineal gland.

"I'm nearly done," Aurelia indicated.

Sutekh quietly observed the procedure, watching as Max's fingers twitched, opening and closing into a partial fist. "You realize, very soon, we'll be unable to immobilize him."

Aurelia felt encouraged as she withdrew the syringe from Max's nostril. "Perhaps by then, it won't matter." She returned the syringe to her belt and repositioned Max in a more ergonomic posture. "Okay, let's go."

Sutekh surveyed the room to assure there were no signs of their presence left behind. In the same way they entered, they stole into the hallway, and Sutekh carefully shut the door. The last thing he heard were the words of a teenage boy on the infomercial, celebrating the clarity of his skin.

Together, he and Aurelia made their return to the roof. After they reassumed their position, the control chip on her temple pulsed and the ship's portal opened above them. The beam of soft gentle light enveloped them, and they leaped upward and disappeared into the craft. As the portal closed, all signs vanished of the ship's presence.

Aurelia approached the giant observation window and gazed out on a spectacular penthouse view of Washington, DC. "Shall we?"

Sutekh glared at her since she readily knew his response. "You know how much I hate this place. Of all our missions, this planet is by far the worst."

"I know, Sutekh. This is why our work here is even more important." In a moment of hesitation, she looked across the landscape. "I'll bring us back to observation distance."

As she had done less than a half hour before, Aurelia diverted her attention to the path needed to return them to orbit. They crossed to the couch, and it transformed again into a protective cocoon, completely surrounding them.

"Brace yourself."

The ship pulsed with energy, and the cloaking device lifted for less than the blink of an eye. In the same instant, the ship vanished, shooting into space, where it reassumed its position in orbit. The entire 1600-plus-mile journey had been completed in less than 30 minutes. When the protective membrane unfolded, Sutekh and Aurelia stared down on the small blue planet. Only from such extreme distance did it appear completely peaceful.

Without another word, Sutekh approached the center of the room above where the portal had opened. With a mere swipe of his hand, copper rods rose from the floor until they formed the skeleton of a pyramid. He entered the assembly and sat in lotus position. After a deep inhale, he relaxed, breathing out the tensions of the hour. Sutekh closed his eyes and began his descent into deep meditation.

Aurelia peeled the tinfoil device from her temple and placed it on the pedestal beside the window. Filled with trepidation, she gazed upon the North American continent, praying that their work with Max would suffice.

Some 800 miles below, Max quietly slumbered, unaware of the visitors who had joined him once again in his room. In the interior architecture of his brain, the purple solution was doing as intended, dissolving the calcified shell that surrounded his pineal gland. For more than a few months, Aurelia had been working to free the often-ignored gland from its organic prison. With the majority of the shell dissolved, fresh blood circulated causing the glandular structure to pulsate.

In that instant a form of lucid dreaming began. Max entered a state that was neither awake nor fully asleep but somewhere in between. He spotted images that seemed entirely real. At the same time he was aware of himself in bed. As the landscape of slumber crystallized around him, he saw the familiar face of Enki staring back at him.

CHAPTER 2

Enki stood in the center of his laboratory, contemplating his successes, and how many of them had grown out of past failures. It was true: he had committed a plethora of tactical errors in his command. The Nibirian Council had dispatched him to procure Earth's gold. In a few years' time, he had established a mining operation toward that goal. The extreme distance from Nibiru, however, had given him a false sense of autonomy. Without fully thinking it through, he had commissioned Eridu, a palace of extreme extravagance. The diversion of resources toward Eridu's construction had caused the production of gold to suffer. In the end, his father, Anu, and the council had both been greatly displeased. His meddlesome half brother, Enlil, had made sure of that.

In the midst of what should have been Enki's most glorious phase, Enlil had traveled to Earth in secret, hoping to point out every weakness of his mining operation. In an amazing display of sabotage, it had taken Enlil only a week to have Enki banished to the Abzu on the far southern coast. As part of his exile, he was given a workforce and tasked with creating an additional, albeit inferior, outpost for further gold extraction. While the Abzu offered none of Eridu's extravagances, Enki made sure to construct a settlement that was dignified of someone with his royal status. In the end, he had fashioned a mildly satisfying existence there.

His one saving grace existed in the results of a breakthrough made thirty-four years prior. After years of tinkering with earthling DNA, he and Ninmah had created a completely new species. Their initial genetic trials had mostly resulted in failures, yielding unusable progeny. Many offspring suffered from mental or physical challenges, or both. The spoiled fruits of their experiments had therefore been released back into the wild to fend for themselves among Earth's indigenous tribes. In desperation, they had taken their experiments to another level by coupling their own Nibirian DNA with that of the earthlings. In the end, an entirely new worker race had been born.

The hybrids, although smaller and less elegant, held strong

physical similarities to Nibirians. Enki and Ninmah both marveled that they had successfully molded a new species in their own image. To this end, their latest workers were suitably sophisticated. With minimal training, they could follow instructions to work the mines and operate some of Nibiru's more powerful tools. Over time, the newly created workforce had sufficiently impacted production, leaving the Abzu team of Igigi happy for the aid.

Desiring to further increase his advantage, Enki fervently encouraged his first grouping of hybrids to breed. The moment he felt they were of age, he ushered the females into his laboratory to inseminate them by natural or artificial means. Until now, nothing had resulted in pregnancy. Both he and Ninmah now understood that their precious new breed suffered from morbid infertility. For more than a decade, they toyed with genetic code and created other hybrids in search of a solution. In no time, the number of offspring had grown to fifty: sixteen females and thirty-two males, but not one among them had ever successfully reproduced. And though they worked day and night, neither Enki nor Ninmah had found a feasible resolution.

To work around the unfortunate circumstance, Ninmah and four female assistants had agreed to serve as living incubators. Each hybrid embryo had carefully been engineered in the laboratory and was subsequently implanted in the wombs of the "birth goddesses," as they came to be known. To economize energy and time, Enki had grouped the implantations into sets of quadruplets. In the first year, the birth goddesses delivered twenty hybrid infants. In subsequent years, Enki pushed them to collectively carry and deliver between fifteen and twenty additional progeny per year.

In reality, Ninmah and her assistants had given birth to many more, but there had been only fifty survivors. Of course, she and her birth goddesses had quickly tired of their role as conduit for hybrid life. By the end of the tenth year they had flat out refused to carry any embryos to term. Since then not a single hybrid had been conceived. The latest forty-eight, along with the first male Adamu and the first female Tiamat, was not an inordinately large number, but it was significant, and Enki had seen a material increase in the Abzu's production of gold.

In order to compete with Enlil, who was now in charge of his former operation, Enki had driven the Abzu workforce as fervently as possible. He hoped an increase in gold production could restore his status as the premier commander of Earth's mining operation. Right now, his sole advantage over Enlil resided in his hybrid workforce, something his half brother knew nothing about.

Enki found himself in the lab once again, this time with his last young female. She had recently displayed outward signs of her premiere estrous cycle. The young girl had been inseminated several days before. Both he and Ninmah were eager to learn if a pregnancy had resulted. A beeping alarm rang out to signal completion of the test result.

Enki approached the laboratory console, on edge. To have fifty working hybrids was a blessing, but he stood to further ameliorate his situation if he could increase his stable of workers. Across the room, Ninmah also heard the alarm and joined Enki at the console. Together, they lifted the indicator to observe the final result of their latest exam.

"Negative," Enki proclaimed, deflating with disappointment. "Mah, this was our last female."

Ninmah turned to face Enki, full of concern. "Please tell me you will not request that we resume as birth goddesses."

"Fifty more is all I require, over three or four years. Can you not convince your team?"

"I will not ask this of them. I, too, have delivered workers. It is draining, and the numbers you desire are unreasonable. I cannot explain why, but birthing is somehow more strenuous in this place. Certainly, you, or any other man, would find this difficult to comprehend."

"Half as many then," Enki pleaded. "At least twenty."

Ninmah stared into her half brother's face, which was masculine and chiseled, so well defined as to be beautiful. But she did not feel impressed. "Oh, how shameful you are, brother. And terribly greedy given that your goals have already been met. For months now, production here has surpassed the Eridu operation."

"But I built them both, Mah, don't you see? They are my exploits, here, and in Eridu."

"You may as well claim the entire planet then."

"Perhaps I should."

Ninmah's sarcasm was lost on Enki, so she switched to a more serious tone. "I am certain before long you will be reinstated as chief and commander. So, tell me, what is your true motivation for these additional workers?"

"You know the answer to this. You and Enlil are Ki's offspring. As the children of father's first wife, you are afforded certain luxuries I do not enjoy."

"And although you are the eldest, your mother's position places you second to Enlil," she replied. "Have we not gone over this a thousand times? When will you see that second is not a bad place to be?"

"But this is why I came here, Mah. To escape an existence in which I am subordinate to Enlil, who is my junior." Enki still felt enticed by the possibilities of what could have been. "I truly believed I could call this tiny place my own." Enki's spirits sank even deeper. "Back on Nibiru, I thought a marriage between you and me would somehow rectify my circumstance, but..." His words trailed off.

Ninmah could not mask her frustration. "How many times must I apologize? Yes, Enlil seduced me."

"And you gave in, Mah. Which maybe I, or the council, could've excused, but the two of you produced an heir." Enki struggled unsuccessfully to hide his disgust. "And so close to our wedding? Do you not see how inexcusable this is?"

"I do. And every associated shame I carry with me wherever I go. But I will not feel shame for my child, Enki. Not for Ninurta. I will not regret him, even if Enlil is his father."

Enki gazed once again at the negative test result for the hybrid's pregnancy. "It is done now. You and I shall never be wed."

"It is father's and the council's respect for you that forbids it." Neither blindness nor death could have prevented Ninmah from perceiving Enki's pain. "You know how he respects you—most times, I believe more than he does Enlil. But you mustn't blame me for your mistakes here. As lavish as Eridu is, that palace is also vulgar and disrespectful, especially to father. To construct a castle more magnificent than the one back on Nibiru, I mean, Enki, what were you thinking?"

"Just tell me you will consider reinstating your girls. I am in desperate need of this."

Ninmah always found her half brother's doggedness persuasive. "All right, I promise to think about it. We might both consider that we have defied our own laws with these hybrid creations."

"Oh, Mah, must you be so naive?"

Ninmah jabbed Enki in the side, causing him to squirm. "Tampering with these beings goes against galactic edict, you know this. We have meddled with these creatures' natural evolution. Should the council learn of this, I am certain the two of us would be exiled or even imprisoned."

Enki barked out a laugh, refusing to focus on anything negative. He pulled Ninmah into his arms. "We shall promote our decision as sacrifice, not infraction. Come, I want to show you something."

Enki took Ninmah's hand and led her from the room into the corridor. Minutes later, they hurried outside, and Enki pulled her toward a large field behind the building.

"Where are you taking me?" she asked.

"You'll see."

They rounded the corner, and Ninmah spotted a modest, oblong airship that measured 20 feet in length. The craft sat atop a sizable stone slab that served as a flight deck. She stared, wide-eyed, from the ship to Enki.

"Come, I want to show you something."

"And we must fly there?"

"Yes." Enki triggered the cockpit hatch. It popped open, and he motioned Ninmah inside. "Get in."

After they were both secured inside, the craft floated upward, and retractable wings unfolded from the fuselage like handheld fans. Enki turned the ship toward their desired destination, and they drifted silently across the grounds until a burst of speed catapulted them above the clouds. Enki continued southward until they traversed the coast above one of Earth's vast oceans. Ninmah reveled at Earth's landscape. In comparison to Nibiru, it was varied and often lush with vegetation. Beautiful, white sandy beaches stretched as far as the eye could see. Enki circled toward the east and banked until they were heading north. Gaining in speed, he and Ninmah rocketed up the coast until they headed inland. On one side, Ninmah witnessed herds of wild beasts grazing in the plains. On the other, mountainous rocky cliffs rose before them. They crossed over sandy deserts and fertile valleys. She spotted several large lakes that served as giant oases.

"Where are you taking me?"

"You'll see. Just enjoy the view. The landscape here offers so much that we never see at home."

In an hour's time, as they flew up the eastern coast, what seemed like endless green tundra eventually rose again into more mountainous terrain.

"Oh, look, Enki," Ninmah exclaimed, pointing down at the landscape. Beneath them, a large tribe of indigenous earthlings was herding animals in some kind of pilgrimage toward the north.

Enki banked around and dove toward the nomads in a display of speed. He shot over their heads, eliciting screams of fear and awe from the tribesmen and women. "I love it!" Enki screamed. "They give the same reaction every time."

During the flight, Ninmah recalled exactly why she had chosen to marry Enki. There was a playful innocence about him that made him exciting to be around. Before she knew it, they were circling a snow-capped mountain peak that looked rather treacherous. Huge boulders were stacked as if an avalanche had occurred from a higher summit. Like an ice cream topping, a sprinkling of snow capped many of the large rocks. On the sides and in crevices, however, the boulders were exposed where snow had fallen away or melted in the sun. Enki, who was an excellent pilot, slowed the ship until they were hovering above a peak. He carefully brought it down atop a rocky ledge that seemed entirely inadequate.

"My god, brother, are you sure this is safe?"

"Patience, Mah, wait till you see."

"But you are foolish. Neither of us is dressed for this."

"We'll only be a minute, I promise." Enki triggered the hatch and a rush of frigid air enveloped them. "Come on, it's this way."

They shivered as Enki helped her from the ship. She looked around, as if for courage to find their footing on the precipice. Less than eighty meters above, the mountain was covered entirely in snow that could have rushed down upon them at any moment.

"This is insane. If our ship doesn't tumble down, I guarantee we will."

Paying close attention, he led her along a path that snaked up the ledge. After forty treacherous steps, Ninmah spotted a craggy entrance to a cave. "You certainly can't think I'm going in there."

"Trust me, you'll want to see what's inside."

Ninmah gazed at the opening. "Okay…" Although hesitant, she followed Enki's lead into the cavernous opening. As they continued deeper inside, she expected increasing darkness. Instead, a soft blue glow illuminated the space. The bluish tint shimmered like an unseen light source reflecting off water. Then Ninmah spotted the items Enki had flown so far to show her. Her mouth fell open, and she raised a hand to cover it. "Oh…"

A cache of powerful Nibirian weapons was carefully arranged beside a rectangular golden box. The ornate container, referred to as the Ark, was adorned with hieroglyphs from their home planet. On each side, two powerful-looking gold eagles served as handles. Sitting beside the Ark was an item that some believed might simply be legend.

Ninmah uncovered her mouth. "The Atu-waa. I was convinced it didn't exist."

"I was too."

Shaped like a pyramid, the Atu-waa was a foot tall, crystalline and glowing. The light it cast slowly transitioned from a soft blue to a warm green. As they watched, its colors oscillated between shades of blue, green and orange.

Ninmah's mouth was agape again. "But how? Where did you find these?"

"Alalu stole them when father unseated him as Supreme Leader. He fled with them to this planet. When I pursued him I discovered his ship. Thankfully, he was absent, so I hid the items here."

Ninmah could hardly believe her eyes. She diverted her gaze to Enki. "What about the Table of Destiny?"

Enki found sheer enjoyment in every sliver of Ninmah's amazement. "I looked for it, but couldn't find it."

"Does father know?"

"Not yet."

"You realize had Alalu wanted, he could've used any of these against us? Or all of Nibiru, indeed. If the Atu-waa is real, did you—"

"I haven't a clue how to operate it. Besides, every legend says it's incredibly unstable without the Table of Destiny."

"Who else knows about this?"

"As of now, just you, me and my pilot Abgal."

"You were right to hide them, but you must bring this to father at once."

"That was my plan, but you know, Mah, timing is everything. The hybrids we created... should we have trouble, the Ark and the Atu-waa... even the other weapons will provide us the leverage we need."

"Enki!"

"Not that we would use them, Mah. If we reveal these things, we must do so in steps, when it is to our advantage."

"But father is here now, in Eridu. You must do this before he returns to Nibiru."

Enki wanted to consider the suggestion, but he wasn't completely convinced, not yet.

Ninmah glanced around the cave as the glow from the Atu-waa transitioned and she shivered. "Shall we go? I've caught a chill."

"All right." Enki placed an arm around his half sister, grabbing her in a warm embrace. "I should give them to father then."

Ninmah felt nervous laughter rising in her throat. "Each of these, individually, is too powerful to remain unsupervised. All of them here together... this feels foolhardy. What if the earthlings should find these and try to use them? Or even worse, if one of our own should find them."

"Okay, but I need time to determine the right moment."

Together, Enki and Ninmah left the cave and hiked back to the ship. Still satisfied of the location's inaccessibility, Enki fired up the engines and took to the skies.

Once they were in flight, he considered their return to the Abzu, but Ninmah was correct. Their father was still on Earth, and Eridu was much nearer to the mountain peak where the weapons were hidden. Enki could not only explore whether or not Anu was ready to lift his exile to the Abzu, but he could also visit the illustrious palace he had built. Without further thought, he turned the ship toward Eridu, knowing fully well that they would be there within the hour.

$\mathcal{N}$inmah felt thrilled once again to be in the safety of Enki's cockpit, flying out over the mountains. His secret hiding place had ultimately been well chosen, as it was terribly difficult and precarious to reach without a ship. Neither of them spoke much during the brief flight to Eridu. The surprise of seeing the cave's contents was too grand to discuss, and anything less felt too trivial for conversation.

After the brief flight, Enki dove through a large cloudbank. He hardly expected the burst of emotion he felt when he saw his former palace come into view. All at once, pride, joy and a sense of longing arose in his heart. In the thirty-plus years since his banishment, his brother, Enlil, had made changes and editions. He had erected obelisks, statues, and many sphinxes with Enlil's likeness throughout the gardens and surrounding environs.

I must tear them down, Enki thought as he shot over the palace, taking it all in. He turned to watch Ninmah, who was equally awed by Eridu's magnificence.

"It is truly splendid what you've done, brother. But surely you can see why father was displeased."

"I see nothing of the sort," Enki proclaimed with indignation. "I obliged reliable production of the ore and built a palace dignified of a king. And for my reward, I was exiled and tasked with creating yet another production outpost. This hardly seems fair."

Enki slowed the ship considerably as he circled back over Eridu, whose surrounding enclaves had spread out to accommodate the increased number of Igigi working the mines. When he banked for another pass, he spotted a figure lounging on his prized sundeck. *Was that father? Or might it have been Enlil?* Enki decelerated even more until they were hovering fifty meters above ground. When he looked down he could spot the figure more clearly, and anger bit into him like a wild animal.

Enlil was sunning himself on the royal veranda that Enki designed when Eridu was built. His half brother stood up, shielding his eyes with one hand as he gazed up at the craft. An expansive landing strip ran from the palace gate, stretching more than a mile to the west. At first, Enki intended to land there, but the sight of Enlil made him think otherwise.

"What are you doing?" Ninmah questioned. "Why have you not set us down?" She quickly scanned the grounds, but Enki banked, placing Enlil outside of her view.

To make his point, he flew directly over their brother, dipping the ship's front end to ensure there was eye contact between them. From her seat, Ninmah was certain she had missed something, but it was too late as the transport floated out of view to the other side of the château. Although it was ill advised, Enki expertly squeezed the ship onto a much smaller veranda that was not intended as a landing pad.

"That should buy us time," Enki proclaimed, "before your loving brother accosts us."

"You are so reckless," Ninmah exclaimed, shooting Enki a disapproving glare. "I knew it must've been Enlil below."

Enki popped open the hatch and grabbed hold of some scrolls in a compartment beside him. "I'm in no mood to be trifled with. We must find father before we are intercepted." He jumped from the ship before assisting Ninmah with her exit. "He will be on his way any moment." Enki flashed a mischievous grin. "But remember I built this palace. There are passageways only I know of."

Enki and Ninmah rushed into the building. Within seconds, they were in a subterranean tunnel.

"Come," Enki urged as he pulled her along, clutching the scrolls in his other hand. "Because I am technically still in exile, Enlil will no doubt try to head us off before we reach the royal chambers." Enki squeezed her hand with a smile. "I wouldn't be surprised if we were crossing paths at this very moment."

Ninmah hardly shared the grudge against Enlil that Enki bore. The former, after all, was her full-blooded brother. But she knew well that Enlil was shrewd, untrustworthy and constantly jockeying for superior position. After what felt like a long time jogging through the underground corridor, Enki pulled Ninmah into a circular stairwell. Just as she was tiring of the climb, he pulled her into a bright open hall, at which point they could hear their father's voice thanking a servant for his meal.

Anu appeared startled when he spotted his children entering

the royal quarters. "I was unaware you were expected. Am I ill-informed?"

Enki and Ninmah took in their father's lavish table setting, where an array of courses was set out, many of them still steaming. Enki, upon realizing the inopportune timing, was the first to speak out.

"I apologize, father, we were not scheduled."

"I should think not," Anu replied, barely hiding his annoyance. "Has your banishment been lifted?"

"No, father, it has not. But I thought this visit a worthy one–"

Before Enki could finish, Enlil burst into the room, completely winded. It was clear he had been running, which brought a smile to Enki's lips.

"What are you doing here?" Enlil threw the question at his older half brother.

"I have business to discuss with father before his return to Nibiru."

"But, father, his banishment has not yet been rescinded," Enlil protested, gesturing toward Enki with acrimony. "Which, last time I checked, means you shouldn't be here."

With the most condescending smile he could muster, Enki continued. "I was banished for the inadequacy of my gold production. This is why I've come this day. Must my exile continue when I've lifted the ore's production in the Abzu to levels even higher than you produce here in Eridu?"

Enlil gawked at Ninmah, helpless, full of enmity toward his half brother. "This is preposterous. I have seen no proof of such production."

Enki lifted his scrolls into view. "All of it is here, brother. And why all the vitriol? I prepared this planet's first gold operation for you to run, and now I have made an even greater operation in the south. As I see it, there is no downside to my visit."

Enki crossed to Anu and handed him the scrolls. Their father unrolled them and began to read. Enlil rushed to his side to read along. The documents were sound, with the appropriate stamps and approvals. In meticulous fashion, the Abzu workforce had documented their gold extractions and shipments.

With a great smile on his face, Enki diverted his father's attention.

"If you observe totals from the last six months, you will see that production in the Abzu has surpassed that which is produced here in Eridu."

Anu perused Enki's records with Enlil at his side. "Yes, I see. All seems to be in order." Anu looked up, both impressed and satisfied. "The council back home will be pleased."

Filled with smugness, Enki turned to his younger sibling. "You see, brother, I come bearing nothing but cheer and good news."

In the time since Enki's banishment, Enlil had only seen him twice. On two occasions he had traveled to the south to enforce his authority over Enki's operation. Still bristling with agitation, Enlil finally chimed in. "Father, when you mention this to the council, you must be sure to remind them that both operations, here in Eridu and in the Abzu, are under my authority."

No stranger to his sons' constant maneuvering, Anu already felt irritated by their power plays. "You mustn't fret, Enlil, as the facts you declare are already clear. It is true that Enki has built much of the Earth operations. This role must be acknowledged."

Enlil snatched up Enki's scrolls. "In my position as Supreme Commander, I would ask that you allow me to confirm these records."

Enki turned to Enlil with a smirk. "Do as you will, brother. I can assure all is in order."

"This is good news," Anu bellowed, "but your timing is less than opportune. I was to have my meal at this time. Enlil, you will confirm your brother's data before I report back to the council. And Enki, you and Ninmah may stay a few days if you wish. Your exile to the Abzu will likely soon be lifted."

"Very well, father," Enki exclaimed. If nothing else, he was patient, and three decades was hardly too long to wait to deal Enlil a blow.

"Now, if you permit, I will eat my meal. Should you wish to meet again, you will arrange so through proper channels."

"Thank you, father," rang out in chorus from all three of his children. They bowed, then quickly filed from the room as Anu sat down to his lavish table.

In the outside corridor, Enlil hemmed Enki up against the wall, waving the crumpled-up scrolls. "I'm not sure how you did this, but a horrible stench reeks in it somewhere. I should reassure you, I'll find out exactly what it is." Enlil pointed toward the ceiling. "Before long, I'll have you banished to that other red planet, along with that ne'er-do-well son of yours Marduk."

Without hesitation, the larger Enki snatched Enlil up and pivoted around, slamming him against the wall.

"Stop it, you two!" Ninmah screamed in a hoarse whisper, trying to keep her voice low enough to avoid disturbing their father.

Enki held his hand tightly against Enlil's neck, not choking off but restricting his air. When he spoke his voice sounded firm and controlled. "Listen carefully, Enlil. You keep mine and my son's name from your lips. Do you understand?"

Although he was rattled, Enlil stared at his brother, intent on displaying his resolve. Enki pressed harder upon his throat and continued.

"Aside from Alalu, I am the first of Nibiru to step foot on the soil of this planet. It is I who constructed this palace you enjoy. And it is I who built the operations here, and the ones in the south that you so boldly take credit for. If anyone is departing this planet, trust my words, it will be you. My records are in order, you shall see. And you haven't the faintest clue what other tricks I have in my arsenal, and believe me when I say, you shouldn't wish to know."

Enlil looked to Ninmah, who covertly nodded to confirm Enki's threat. Having seen the eldest sibling's cache of weapons, she knew exactly what kind of devastation Enki could deliver if provoked.

Enlil offered a sarcastic smile. "Might you remove your hand from my throat, brother?" he croaked.

Enki unhanded his younger brother and took a step back. Only then did either of them notice how agitated Ninmah appeared from their altercation.

"Must you two bicker so when there's more than enough to go around?"

"As I told you, this is why I alighted here. I figured I could leave Nibiru to him, but that wasn't enough. Of course he had to pursue because, for Enlil, it has no value unless I want it."

Enki's statement hung in the air between them, ringing true

like church tower bells. The silence stretched longer than it should have, for history had provided too much evidence in support of Enki's claim. Back on Nibiru, Enlil had sabotaged their union by his seduction of Ninmah. Now, centuries later, he had followed Enki to Earth to either wreck or take credit for everything Enki had built.

Finally, Enlil spoke. "Might I have a word with my sister?"

Enki wished to strike Enlil and erase the smug look from his face, but he decided there was already sufficient satisfaction in how things were going. "Ninmah can do as she pleases."

"Anything to separate the two of you," she interjected with urgency.

Enlil warmed with an artificial smile. "Nin, you're welcome to stay in one of the royal chambers of this wing." Then he turned to Enki. "If you're planning to stay, I can have a chamber readied on the other side where you landed."

"I built Eridu, I'll have no trouble arranging my accommodations."

"Very well then," Enlil responded, as he turned and led Ninmah to his quarters across the hall. Once they were in Enlil's chambers, he closed the door, leaving Enki alone in the corridor.

"What is it, Enlil?" Ninmah questioned, already skeptical about her brother's intentions.

He smiled suggestively at his full-blooded sister before continuing. "I wanted a word with you because I'm confused about something."

"What is it?"

"You and Enki are both rather skilled geneticists, are you not?"

Surprised by the question, Ninmah perceived tension creeping up her neck and shoulders. Until now, they had kept the Abzu's hybrid project secret. *Certainly, Enlil must know. But how?* She held a poker face for her reply. "Yes, brother, it is what we studied back on Nibiru. It is our area of expertise. Why?"

"All three of us share Anu as a father, but you and I also share Ki as our mother."

"So?"

Enlil stepped closer to Ninmah and softly stroked her forearm. "So... why do you think you hold such an allegiance to someone who shares half as many chromosomes as we do?"

With a laugh Ninmah removed Enlil's hand from her arm. "You are so transparent, and Enki is correct. You only want what he wants. As if his desire somehow makes it sweeter to you. We did enough damage when you succeeded in preventing our marriage. Now you make some sad plea for me because I arrived with him."

"This is not entirely true, sister. We are good together. Certainly, our son Ninurta has made us both proud."

At the mention of their son's name, Ninmah couldn't help but smile. "Yes, he has. If we're to spend so much time on this planet, perhaps we should send for him."

But Enlil was not so easily deterred from his original enticement. The upset of his day left a yearning for comfort that he believed Ninmah could assuage. He lowered his voice an octave as he stepped nearer to her. "If you're amenable to it, we can make another just like him."

"Please, Enlil, I won't be your pawn, and I don't wish to come between you and Enki any more than I have already. But you are correct about Ninurta. I will never bemoan him, even though I feel remorse that I allowed you to use me. You may want to bring him here. In the end, you might need him."

Enlil studied his sister, wondering if her recommendation arose from some maternal instinct. *Or perhaps it's something else.* "Whatever could you mean, sister?" Enlil asked the question although it hardly required an answer. He knew Enki was maneuvering for a return to power and, sadly, his older brother's first steps at returning to Eridu had been effective. *I have to get in gear,* Enlil thought as Ninmah turned and exited through the door. *There's no way he'll beat me at my game. I will prevent his return to Anu's graces.*

For the remainder of the afternoon, Enlil sat in his quarters, peeling through Enki's reports. *They all seem to be in order,* he thought, growing angrier with every page. *But how has he done this?*

Enlil had purposely sent less competent workers to the Abzu so he might compromise the operations there. Somehow, in spite of it, Enki had figured a way to extract the ore in larger quantities. As he read further through the reports, he saw his brother's triumphs on every page. *And it is I who volunteered to report back to father.* Upon realizing that he would be the one to hand Enki his next victory, Enlil threw the papers down and stormed from his chambers. *What a dreadful day,* he thought, until he spotted a stunning beauty on the veranda.

Sud was technically one of Ninmah's assistants, who had been conducting business in Eridu on her behalf. Enlil had caught sight of her just a few times before, but he had hardly found an opportunity to speak to her, since she was skillful at making herself scarce. Just shy of six feet, she could best be described as curvy and statuesque. While auburn hair was quite common on Nibiru, Sud had unusually bright strawberry blond tresses that cascaded down her back in beautifully thick curls.

I might easily draw comfort from such a woman. Enlil contemplated the option, quickly moving to head Sud off at the adjoining entrance to the veranda. When they nearly collided, Sud was quick to apologize.

"My Lord, how clumsy of me."

Enlil evaluated her from head to toe, taking in every single ounce of her beauty. Up close, Sud was even more stunning than he originally thought, with full lips, hazel eyes and flawless skin. "A creature of such beauty could scarcely be described as clumsy."

Sud couldn't help but blush even though she knew every bit of Enlil's reputation as lecherous, conniving and opportunistic. "Why thank you, my Lord."

"Tell me your name, girl," Enlil demanded.

"I am Sud, my Lord."

"You are in my sister's employ, am I correct?"

"Yes, my Lord. Lady Ninmah is my mistress."

"Very good." Enlil evaluated Sud, unafraid to display his salacious intentions. *I must have this woman,* he thought. Pulling himself together, he finally spoke. "There are papers she and Enki delivered earlier today. You must come to my chambers to fetch them."

A voice of caution arose in Sud's heart, but she was hardly in any position to refuse. "Of course, my Lord."

Enlil took Sud by the hand and led her to his chambers. Once inside, he closed the door and promptly latched it. Noticing the worry on her face, he reassured her by pointing to Enki's records. "Those are the papers there on the floor. I fear I've made a mess of them. If you could gather them, and deliver them to my father…"

At first hesitant, Sud quickly took to gathering the scrolls, so she might find her exit from Enlil's room. Enlil admired Sud's curves as she stooped to gather the reports. As she stood, he stepped near to her and took hold of the papers.

"Hand them to me, so I can make sure they're in order." As he took the records, Enlil fixed his gaze upon Sud. He was unsure if his inability to cope with such desire might be due to the intense emotions from earlier in the day. He dropped the papers on the table and grabbed Sud close. "You truly are a work of art."

Sud screamed out as Enlil pulled at her clothes. His walls were well soundproofed, but he covered her mouth to silence her nonetheless. Although she certainly hadn't invited it, Enlil began to kiss and caress her. Time seemed at a standstill as she knew what might happen if she refused the crowned Prince of Nibiru. Before her mind could adequately process an exit strategy, Enlil was upon her, forcing her to pay a dear price for his anger, envy and aggression.

A half hour later, Sud burst into Ninmah's quarters, unable to restrain her sobs. Although she had dressed, her garments were improperly adjusted and even tattered in places.

"Sud, what on Earth is wrong?" Ninmah questioned, until she spotted Enki's scrolls in her hands. Just as she suspected, Sud confirmed her account of Enlil's attack. Sadness and regret arose in Ninmah's heart, mixed with fury toward Enlil and his brutality.

Ninmah led her assistant to the bathing chamber of her quarters and washed her face and fixed her hair. "Stay here and pull yourself together. I will be back shortly."

Still sobbing too much to respond, Sud nodded in acknowledgment.

"I will deal with this, I promise. Lock the door when I take leave, and allow no one to enter until I return." Ninmah caressed her assistant's face before turning to leave. As instructed, Sud crossed to the door behind her and fastened the lock.

A moment later, Ninmah blew into Enlil's chambers like a hurricane. "How dare you take your aggressions out on my assistant!"

Enlil looked up with a smug smile. "What're you talking about?"

Unable to contain her venom, Ninmah crossed to her brother and struck him across the face. "I didn't think you capable of this variety of cruelty, but it's clear there is no limit to how far you'll go to have what you want. Well, congratulations, brother. You have now coaxed a similar resolve from me. Watch and see how far I'll go to right this injustice."

"Nin–" Enlil began, rubbing the side of his face.

"Not a word, Enlil, I don't wish to hear a word! Always you fight for what you want. Now you will watch me do so, in-kind."

Enlil watched Ninmah retreat into the corridor, wondering for the first time if he had perhaps overindulged his whims.

$\mathcal{M}$ax held no awareness of the time of day or of his whereabouts in the DC hotel. Everything had blurred into a mish-mash surrealism that didn't quite feel like either reality or a dream. He lingered in this fugue state until the knocking sounds began. Someone was banging at his hotel room door, and his consciousness came crashing back to reality.

"Max, are you in there?" It was Otto yelling from the hallway.

Max sat up and looked groggily at the clock radio on the nightstand. It read 9:45 a.m. "Oh, shit!" He glanced at the TV on the wall: a pharmaceutical commercial was running a long list of disclaimers. He jumped to his feet, mumbling as he crossed to open the door for Otto. *What the hell happened?*

This time, he had not used the prophetic Anti-k Device. Its phenomenal powers had been proven once he secured the missing element from the Money Pit. But now, despite not having used it, he had witnessed another vision of Enki and Enlil. *What's happening to me?* He swung the door open to reveal his father's friend standing there, looking puzzled.

"What's going on, Pal?" Otto asked as he thumped his watch. "We were supposed to meet forty-five minutes ago. In front of the archives."

"Shit, Otto. I must've overslept."

"In your clothes?"

Max looked down at his clothes from the night before. "Yeah, I guess." The entire night he hadn't stirred, so Max had no recollection of the blonde and her small cohort, or of the injection she had administered during the night.

Otto, who was in a suit, looked refreshed and ready to go. "C'mon, get dressed. We've got a lot to cover, and we ain't doin' it here."

Max frowned at Otto's unusual use of slang. "Give me ten minutes, maybe fifteen." Then he excused himself and hurried into the bathroom, where he quickly showered. He exited and dressed in the jeans and t-shirt he had purchased in the underground mall of New Mexico.

Otto glanced at the time; it was just after 10 a.m. "Good job, kid. You ready?"

"As much as I'll ever be." Max heard his own words and wished they sounded more convincing.

"Good. We only have a week and some change to convert you into a mini version of your dad. Let's skedaddle."

Otto and Max exited the hotel and rushed into a waiting limousine. During the ride back to the National Archives, Max glanced at his phone and saw there were no missed calls. He had intended to phone Brigitte in the morning, but he had awakened too late from the bizarre Anunnaki dream.

In many ways, Max knew he had fallen into a strange trance that left him teetering between truth and fantasy. Was the Enlil-Enki story a simple dream, or had he accessed some slice of ancient history? *But how? I didn't use the Anti-k Device.*

His girlfriend Brigitte was sure to be pissed, and he felt badly for the way things had been left between them. She had desperately wanted to speak to him in Chicago, but his father's driver hadn't allowed him to do so. Sadly, his Town Car had departed at the exact moment of her arrival. *Shit.* He still needed to smooth things over, especially because of the pregnancy. It was difficult to believe that there had been no time for them to discuss what to do about their baby. But the Brazil "accident" had nearly killed his father, and he had finally been summoned to learn of Demetrius' condition. Max had not even officially replaced his father yet, and already he was being pushed and pulled in so many directions.

Just minutes after he and Otto left the hotel, they pulled up in front of the U.S. National Archives Building. Hardly anyone knew that the archives building was just one of many entrances into an intricate underground network. Once he and Otto commandeered their own elevator, Otto input a code. Even though the elevator seemed old and antiquated, there had still been a pause where they were bathed in infrared light. In addition, a strange vibratory resonance was used to execute some form of decontamination.

Within seconds of the cleanse, they were descending at nearly 60 miles per hour into the Earth, where they had access to one of DC's deep underground installations. More than a minute passed before the elevator finally clanged to a stop. Then Max felt the elevator jerk to the left, and they were moving again, but this time horizontally. They crossed beneath a significant portion of the Smithsonian. Before Max knew it, they had accessed another clandestine elevator shaft for their final descent into the underground complex.

Finally, the elevator slowed to a cushiony stop, and the doors opened with a "ping" to reveal a long corridor. Max and Otto stepped off and the doors closed behind them. Within seconds, Max heard the mechanical groan of the elevator climbing its way back to the National Archives Building. Unsure what to expect, he turned to Otto, who took his first steps leading the way.

As they strode the length of the corridor, Max noticed the return of that uneasy feeling he had experienced the day before, like his body was reacting to stress from some unforeseen source. Unable to shake it off, he dismissed the odd sensation as anxiety at the turn of events, even if it didn't quite feel that way. He and Otto turned a corner to access another long hallway.

Because of its unfinished nature, Max found the DC facility much harder to appreciate than the glossier one he had visited in Las Cruces. Here in DC, the passageways were cold and, in places, dark and damp. Max considered the shopping mall music that played in the underground installation in New Mexico, but there was nothing like this in DC. While Las Cruces felt fresh and new, DC appeared more like a complex from antiquity. He supposed it probably wasn't so different from the ancient complexes in Egypt or the Yucatan.

After traveling through a maze of centuries-old corridors, Otto led Max into a large conference room. Inside, a couple of men were laughing, but they straightened to attention when Otto and Max entered.

Otto nodded in acknowledgment. "Good morning, gentlemen, I'd like you to meet Maximilian Battenberg. He'll be attending the next Rizick meeting in his father's stead."

The men nodded respectfully, but no formal introductions were made. Max wondered if either of them had been present at his initiation but, of course, there was no way to know. The men resembled each other in a strange way. One had hair almost as gray as Otto's only with traces of blond mixed in. The other had bushy red hair that gave him the appearance of a large Kew-pie doll. Both their complexions were white and pasty, and Max wondered if they ever went above ground. The notion that they might have instead lived like Morlocks in the underground passages of DC did not elude him.

Otto continued, "Apologies for our tardiness."

"No worries." The redhead spoke, and his voice was deeper than Max expected for a man who was so thin and pale.

"I guess we should get started," Otto suggested. "Max just completed his initiation, so he has a lot of catching up to do."

"Virgin meat," the redheaded Kewpie doll proclaimed with a large smile on his face. "So you're filling in for your dad, huh?"

"Yes," Max answered.

"Is it safe to say you are completely unfamiliar with Rizick?"

"Forty-eight hours ago I'd never even heard of it."

The redhead nodded with a playful look, giving the impression that he intended to toy with Max. "You ever see that movie 'Fight Club'?"

Max found the question odd, considering the context. "Yeah, I think so."

"You remember the first rule in that movie?"

Max hesitated, looking at Otto, who also had a strange expression plastered across his face. "Uh, don't talk about Fight Club."

"Precisely. We never talk about or discuss Rizick unless we're at one of the meetings, or in a situation like the one we're in now. Is that understood?"

"Yeah, of course."

"Like you, Rizick members are initiated by blood. Only on rare occasions are some chosen. Most of us are known for our business acumen, and we are almost never involved in overt politics. We prefer to operate in the shadows, like ghosts or phantoms, never directly heard from or seen, especially in the political arena. It's better that way. And of course, we are strategically placed across the globe."

Max turned to Otto. "Was everyone here initiated like me?"

"Absolutely," the white-haired gentleman interjected before Otto could answer. "What a ride, huh?"

Yes! Max thought, wanting to proclaim, *It was crazy.* Instead he simply nodded.

"Believe it or not, that ceremony has only existed a few hundred years. The secrecy we employ today wasn't needed before then." The white-haired man seemed lost in nostalgia. "In the beginning, our role as master was accepted, and we lived in the open as pharaohs, kings and queens."

"Until the uprisings," the redhead interjected.

The white-haired man frowned. "He can be dramatic at times. He's referring to the revolutions, some of which are going on even today, mostly in the Middle East. I suppose you could say they started to be successful in France. The fucking French... they overthrew their aristocracy. From that point on, we began to lose our edge. Country by country, the masses rose up..."

The redhead nodded. "But, of course, we knew what to do. With a lineage as old as ours, it's not like uprisings had never happened before." He crossed to a credenza against the wall and opened a cabinet to remove a binder. He placed the notebook in front of Max. "Read it when you get the chance. It's a fascinating guide."

Max opened the binder and flipped to the index. He could hardly believe his eyes. Entries like *Manipulation* and *Domination* jumped off the page in bold type. *The Fear Of God as a Tool* and *Democracy: The Conviction of Control.*

In his head, Max questioned why there was a manual for this. The words of Indigo Blue, the psychic from New Orleans, resurfaced in his head: *... the majority of us are in servitude to an intricately organized system – slaves, handing over our most precious resource. Not gold or diamonds, mon cher, I speak of our own free will.* Max could hardly believe the words he was about to speak. "I know now about the Battenberg bloodline, I mean where it comes from and everything – "

Otto smiled. "He means the Anunnaki."

"Yeah," Max acknowledged. "You said almost everyone is initiated by blood. Does that mean we're all descended from... them?"

The white-haired man hadn't said much, but he was studying Max closely. He finally chimed in again. "In theory, members of Rizick should be. Fortunately for me, this isn't always the case."

"To be honest," Otto interjected, "even those of us who are have blue blood that's been diluted by thousands of years."

"Blue blood refers to nobility, right? Does it mean anything else?"

This time, the redhead seized an opportunity to reply. "On a physiological level, the original Nibirians looked almost exactly like us, but their DNA is actually different. Their blood, in its true form, has a blue tinge to it."

The white-haired man cleared his throat before he spoke. "As tradition has it, there are 300 members on Rizick's determining council. Any decision of consequence that you hear about— OPEC prices, international trade laws, monetary concerns, the next president or prime minister—all of it's decided within that group of 300. The upcoming meeting you're about to attend, you'll be joining the other 299."

"Wait a minute," Max spoke with a nervous laugh. "Are you saying 300 people pick the president?"

"Not only him, Max." The white haired man shrugged, matter-of-fact. "Every world leader has been placed in power by us."

"So, what are the elections for, then?"

"Depends what countries you're talking about," the redhead answered. "Here, it's actually quite easy, since all true candidates are chosen by Rizick anyway."

Max peered at his instructors in wonderment.

The redhead frowned with a condescending smirk. "Read about it in the binder, Max."

Max marveled at every revelation. "What happens if Rizick's choice doesn't correspond with the voters?"

Otto and his cohorts looked amused, then Otto offered a friendly smile. "This rarely occurs, but when it does, it's simple: a scandal, an affair, some financial indiscretion. Whatever it takes to create the desired shift."

"The important thing," the man with the white hair continued, "is allowing the masses to believe that they matter and that their choices are being honored—"

"Even when they aren't." The redhead finished with a smug expression that Max didn't quite believe he trusted.

Max listened to the men and their strange stories. He pondered the U.S. elections that he remembered and muttered under his breath, "George Bush and Al Gore..."

The redheaded Kewpie doll nodded. "Gore was fully aware he wasn't our choice."

"Which is why he conceded," Max continued, "even amidst the controversy." No one contradicted him.

For several hours more, Max was apprised about upcoming elections, and his father's desires were made known to him. They discussed world banking and politics. If the Rizick Group wanted to move resources, its members simply voted on currency values and used the markets for stocks and bonds to manipulate them. Before Max could blink, it was 4:30 p.m., and they were all exhausted.

"C'mon, Max," Otto exclaimed, "we better get going. They're about to close upstairs."

Max and Otto gathered their things and wished the men good night. Minutes later, they were exiting the National Archives Building as if they had just spent a day working there, which was not entirely untrue. Otto playfully joked about Max being on time the following day. There was still an enormous amount to cover.

Max returned exhausted to the hotel and collapsed onto the bed. After staring several minutes at the ceiling, he flipped on the television. For most of the day, he had suppressed the strange laughter and spasms he had been experiencing. With each passing minute, Max could feel his anxiety dissipating from the day's teachings. He pulled out his cell phone, which he hadn't checked all afternoon. His heart sank when he saw several missed calls and a text message from Brigitte. He knew she would be fuming from the way they had left things. The truth was, he still hadn't found time to process any of the things going on, including the fact that they were expecting his child, the newest Battenberg heir.

Max opened the text, which read, "Call me. We need 2 talk." It was time stamped 4:30 p.m., but the calls had started even earlier. He muted the television and dialed her number. After a few rings, she picked up.

"Hello." Brigitte spat out the word.

"Hi. How are you?"

"Fine. Just trying to figure some things out." She breathed a sigh of frustration into the phone. "I've been afraid to go to my doctor, Max, because I don't want my parents finding out I'm pregnant. At least not until we figure out what we're doing."

"Shit." Max knew he had been holding Brigitte up, but his life as a Rizick initiate had gotten in the way. "I know we haven't had a chance to talk, but I do want to."

"Does any of this even faze you? The fact that I'm carrying your baby?"

"C'mon, Brigitte, that's unfair. I didn't plan for a kid, but if one's on the way I'm ready for it. I mean, if you are...

She paused, digesting his proposition. "You ever wonder if that woman in New Orleans, that psychic — if she's the real deal?"

Brigitte's words slammed into Max like a punch to the guts. Of course she was referring to Indigo. He could still hear her voice echoing in his mind. *Such a friend will cause nothing but grief.* At first, Max had been insulted by the medium's verbal assault. For that reason, he had remained resistant to the message within it. The sad part was, Indigo had been dead on, so far. He had indeed caused Brigitte anguish, along with several others. That weekend of Mardi Gras, he had been terribly touchy about Indigo's divinations, and Brigitte knew this. She had touched a nerve by bringing up the incident. Even now, she had no idea that Max had returned to New Orleans to see the medium. He certainly didn't want to reveal that he now believed in her predictions.

In the end, Indigo had brought to light many life aspects that Max wished to safeguard in the shadows. The true impact of his actions, both past and present, was only now becoming crystallized like a mirror. To his dismay, he didn't like what he saw in himself, particularly in the deceptions of his alter ego Ian. Perhaps he had led Brigitte on. He knew she hoped to be Mrs. Battenberg one day, but he was still unsure what he wanted. In many ways, his sexuality remained undefined, and Max was unsure of his true face. Did the real Max resemble Ian more than the face he presented to the world?

As the single heir to a multi-billion-dollar fortune, Max certainly was the entitled rich kid who rarely encountered boundaries to the things his heart desired. Compared to the average person, he led a life of leisure, working whenever time allowed and traveling to any location at whim. His initiation had of course changed things along with his father's current condition. When he added Brigitte's pregnancy to the list of recent realities, Max felt the true weight of his newly emerging role. All of a sudden, nothing seemed particularly fun. The games of youth, it seemed, had now been replaced with serious ramifications. But given the circumstances, Max was doing his best to cope.

"Max, did you hear me?"

"Yeah, I did. I need to be in DC for now. As soon as I can sneak away I will, so we can talk in person, okay?"

Brigitte's resolve softened a smidgen. "All right. If you're stuck there, I can come to DC, too."

Max knew Brigitte wanted them to work as a couple. "My father's got me and Otto doing full days right now. I don't want you coming if I don't have time. I promise I'll be back soon, maybe even tomorrow, okay?"

Brigitte sighed. "Fine."

"If you want, we can also swing by my doctor. He can give us a referral to make sure everything's okay with you and the baby."

"All right. That's probably not a bad idea."

Max and Brigitte exchanged pleasantries, and for a brief moment, their relationship was as it had been before his initiation. When he hung up, Max somehow felt relieved. At least for now, the fire of Brigitte's discontent had been quelled. But there was so much more he had to be unnerved about. The things he heard during the day's training haunted him. He harbored no delusions about the world and how it was run. Max knew people like his father were making decisions that affected entire countries, but he hadn't fully understood the true scope of control wielded by the world's power brokers. *The Rizick Group*. Besides the graffiti he had seen in Chicago and Mexico City, he doubted many people had even heard of it.

Max ordered room service and quietly ate a gourmet hamburger with asparagus and French fries. In his pre-initiation world, he would have eaten in one of the capitol's finer restaurants before visiting some chic nightclub to explore the DC scene. Tonight, however, he felt drained. It didn't even occur to him to unmute the television, so he ate in silence.

Shortly thereafter, he undressed for bed and slid between

the hotel's five-hundred-thread-count sheets. Physically, he was exhausted. He expected sleep would come swiftly, but it didn't. Instead, the harsh truths of the day marched through his mind. In fleeting moments of clarity, Brigitte and her pregnancy troubled his brain. He contemplated marrying her and raising a family, but he wasn't even twenty-five yet. To further complicate things, he had skillfully avoided the central questions of his personal and professional lives: *Who am I, and what do I want?*

After an hour of tossing and turning, Max sat up in bed. While half beneath the covers, he crossed his legs and tried organizing the zillions of thoughts bouncing around in his skull. With a deep inhale, he closed his eyes and slowed his breathing, affirming the same phrase, *I will sleep. I will sleep. I will sleep...*

Just when he thought he could feel himself relaxing, a tickling sensation echoed in his brain. The solution Aurelia had injected in his skull was further dissolving the calcified shell surrounding his pineal gland. A subsequent pulse of blood engorged the area and caused the tingling. In the same instant, a memory surfaced of him and Otto standing in the elevator at the National Archives Building. In some virtual form of slow motion, Max watched Otto punch in the code. The keypad displayed ten floors, including the ground floor and mezzanine, but the numbers skipped from floor six to floors fifteen through eighteen. Otto had executed the sequence in precise order: *3-16-18 and the "mezzanine" button.* Strangely enough, Max hadn't realized he had even paid attention.

He wondered about the memory. First, how had he recalled it, and why was it resurfacing? He reached over to pick up a pad and pencil and jotted down the numbers. In a sudden moment of clarity, he realized just what it was he had to do.

CHAPTER 5

The following morning Max awoke, having barely slept. He should have been drained, but surprisingly, the opposite was true. To his astonishment, he was energized. He showered, dressed, then glanced around the room. Remembering, he crossed to the nightstand and tore off the top page of the notepad where he had jotted down Otto's elevator code. Before he left the room, Max folded the paper and slid it into his pocket.

Crossing the lobby, he spotted Otto in a huge armchair, chatting on his cell phone. Max approached. "Didn't think I could make it on time, huh?"

Otto held up a hand, motioning for Max to hold until he finished his call. Seconds later, he hung up and smiled. "How are you, my friend? I figured I'd swing by in case you overslept."

Max hugged Otto affectionately. "I told you I was good, Otto."

"Ready for another round?"

Nervous laughter escaped Max. He couldn't be sure if it was natural or due to the strange affliction from the man at the yoga studio. "I'm not sure how to answer that. That was some crazy sh—, I mean knowledge, you guys were laying down yesterday."

"It can be overwhelming the first time you hear it, but you know education never ends."

Max smiled as he contemplated Otto's wisdom. In past months, his father's friend had been a better mentor than Demetrius himself, who most times played absentee parent. Max had discovered inconceivable things. If he hadn't witnessed the grandeur of the underground installations, the bullet train, or the science fiction aspect of his own initiation he would never have believed any of it.

Otto patted Max on the shoulder. "We better get moving."

They headed outside to the waiting Town Car and were shuttled to the National Archives for another day of training. Once they were in the building, they waited patiently for a vacant elevator. Early morning traffic made one hard to come by. Full elevators continued to arrive until Otto lost patience.

"We've gotta commandeer one." An elevator eventually opened to reveal no one inside. "Here we go." Otto hurried

Max on board. Just as the doors were closing, a collegiate-looking gentleman rushed up. Otto quickly held out a hand to dissuade him. "Catch the next one, please."

When the doors closed, Max watched Otto key in the code. It was precisely the numbers he had jotted down the night before. He resisted cracking a smile as he ran his hand over the folded-up paper in his pocket.

Otto and Max returned to the same room as the day before. This time, the pasty redhead was sitting alone at the table, sipping from a cup of coffee.

"Good morning, Mr. Battenberg," he sung as he set down the coffee mug. "You ready to get started?"

Max's smile was sheepish. "I hope I can keep up."

"Don't worry," the Kewpie doll retorted, "you'll have access to everything you need."

While he and the redhead were speaking, Otto crossed to a credenza with snacks and coffee displayed on top of it. He poured himself a cup. "How about you, Max, you want anything?"

"Maybe later."

Otto grabbed a muffin and joined them at the table.

When the redhead saw that Max and Otto were settled, he scooted his seat closer to the table without expression. "So, I have good and bad news. Mostly good for us, though." The redhead took a visual survey of everybody's faces. "Some idiot leaked the actual location of our next Rizick meeting."

Otto did not seem impressed by the news. "That happens all the time."

"Mostly because we're the ones doing it for misinformation. This time it was a true breach." The ginger man raised his eyebrows, holding on to the secret no one else knew. "The Ritz-Carlton, Istanbul."

Otto studied the man with a quizzical expression. "What's the good news then?"

"They believe it's better to wait and select a new venue, which gives us more time to get him prepared. Takes a little pressure off, don't you think?"

Max leaned back in his chair with a sense of relief. "How much extra time are we talking?"

"I'm not exactly sure. Could be a few weeks, or a few months. Either way, we have breathing room to get you up to speed." Not wanting to seem overly pleased, Max stifled a smile and nodded. "Sounds good."

For another five minutes they sat drinking coffee and chatting about nothing in particular. Then, the redhead turned to Max with an air of seriousness. "We better get started. You may wanna grab a cheat sheet and make some notes."

The man jumped up and removed a notepad from the credenza. He handed it to Max and took his seat again at the table. Otto nodded, and they resumed their training. First, Max was shown charts of political leaders across the globe, democratic or otherwise. For more than four hours, they focused primarily on China, but there were also lessons on Russia, India, Central America and Brazil. Otto and the redhead pointed out names Max would need to be aware of during the upcoming meeting. He also learned what power brokers were being removed from authority, and more importantly those who would be replacing them in new regimes. Feeling like a student again, Max jotted down each name.

Otto and the redhead revealed identities of influential people who would support their and the Battenberg point of view. Otto and the ginger tutor also provided names of staunch adversaries to their cause. Max recognized a few but was astonished to learn that these people were also select members of the Rizick Group.

"So, what does that mean?" Max questioned. "Isn't the Rizick Group a unified front?"

"No," Otto laughed, along with the redhead. "That's the whole point of Rizick meetings. Members vote because it's nearly impossible to reach consensus with multiple people, let alone within a group of 300."

Max glanced again at his list of friends and foes. For the most part, none was well known. He was certain the population at large would be astonished to know who the true puppeteers were behind governments and political figureheads.

As world resources dwindled, countries like China, India, Venezuela and Brazil were becoming increasingly relevant in the global scheme. It was also made known to Max that several

African countries had been earmarked by the Rizick Group and would soon rise to prominence. For hours, he was quizzed until Otto and the redhead were satisfied of his clarity. After a brief break, the redhead turned to Otto.

"Should we move on to Clean Slate?"

Otto looked hesitant, but acted as if he was trying not to appear so. "I don't see why not."

"Okay," the redhead continued while pressing a button embedded in the table. A thin pen-like device telescoped up from the center of the console. Once it snapped into place, it began projecting the image of a keyboard on the table and a larger, full screen image against the wall. Max had seen the technology in high-tech magazines, and it didn't surprise him that it was readily available in their hidden underground.

The redhead began typing on the virtual keyboard, and a crisp photographic image snapped into place against the wall. It was a shot of blue skies with billowy white tracks crisscrossing back and forth, as if a skywriter had drawn a game of tick-tack-toe across the heavens.

Max studied the image a moment before he spoke. "Chemtrails?"

The redhead smiled, seemingly impressed. "You're familiar with them then?"

Max was nonplussed. "Actually, not really. A friend of mine rants about them and other conspiracies. It's condensation, right?"

Otto frowned in response. "Close, but no cigar."

The redhead interjected. "Your friend's actually right. It's part of an operation called Stardust, which has been active twenty years or so."

Max jotted down the name but was still unclear. "Okay. What's Stardust?"

Otto and the redhead shared a glance, debating who should answer. Finally, the redhead removed a booklet from the table and began casually reading from it. "It's a cocktail of different metals: aluminum, barium, aluminum oxide, manganese, zinc, various bacteria, a few molds… They tinker quite often with the recipe, otherwise the body develops resistance."

Max wanted to laugh, not from the humor of it but rather

from an uncomfortable ridiculousness. "Fuck! So, my friend was right?" Max watched Otto and the other man nod. "He did say it was a government conspiracy, to make people sick, or sterile, or something like that."

The redhead hit the return key on the virtual keyboard. The projected image advanced to a shot of downtown Los Angeles with chemtrails scarring the skies. The images continued scrolling through shots of various cities, including New York, St. Louis, London and Barcelona.

Otto studied Max's reaction to the pictures before he spoke. "Your father's fairly pleased with Stardust. He'll want you to vote yes on it."

"What's the point of all this?"

Before Otto could reply, the redhead cut in. "The cocktail accomplishes a multitude of things. Sterility. Compromised immunity. In certain communities, docility; in others, aggression."

Max tried to ignore it, but the uneasiness he had felt a day earlier was kicking into gear again. "I thought that was all urban legend."

Otto and the redhead shared a glance before shaking their heads.

Max looked up to see a projected shot of chemtrails painted across the skies of Atlanta. "I don't understand. Docility, infirmity, aggression..." Max couldn't help but ask the obvious question. "Aren't we all breathing the same air?"

Otto observed the redhead's deference before he continued. "Exploding populations, global warming, it all has to be dealt with. Stardust is the early phase of a larger program called Clean Slate. You maybe aren't aware, but the vaccinations we receive, and the vitamins *we* take, all of them contain counter-agents against anything detrimental in Stardust."

Max slid back from the table and stood. "Okay, so that's real? I-I…" He stammered, hunting for the right words. "I didn't know. Wow. It makes me afraid to ask, but… what is Clean Slate?"

Otto and the redhead faltered, exchanging glances again. It became clear each man wanted the other to explain. In the end, Otto took the reins again.

"At each meeting, it's the largest issue of contention. It won't be any different at this next one." Otto hesitated a moment. "Clean Slate is a population control project."

Max heard the words and understood their meaning, yet he still felt lost. *It can't be what I'm thinking.* "I'm sorry," Max relayed, "but I'm missing something, right?"

Frustrated with Otto's manner of tiptoeing, the redhead finally interrupted. "For more than a decade, Rizick has voted on whether or not a program should be instituted to control the population."

Max felt there was definitely more to decipher in their explanation. "You mean like in China?"

"Not exactly," the redhead replied. "Maybe 'control' isn't the right word. China attempted to reduce growth by limiting births. Clean Slate isn't about growth, it's about reducing the population, rather dramatically."

Max, who had always been a moderately sharp student, was finally beginning to take this in. "So, what? Ruin people's immune systems and then what? Wipe them out with some kind of illness or a virus or something?"

Otto knew Max now understood. "You can imagine why such a vote hasn't gone through as of yet."

"Well, yeah," Max answered. A question he felt hesitant to ask popped into mind, but he continued nonetheless. "How does my dad want me to vote on this?"

The redhead looked to Otto, allowing him to answer. "In the last six votes your father voted yes. He expects you to do the same."

"Shit." Max scooted away from the table and crossed to the credenza where the coffee and snacks were. He took a deep breath and ran a hand through his hair.

"Max," Otto continued, "this isn't something to get emotional about. It's a numbers game. Your dad has commissioned a dozen or more reports to study the pros and cons of this project. One way or another, the population has to be reduced. The question is, will it be done deliberately, or do we wait for some kind of a catastrophe? Because nature will do it for us if we don't."

"I know my dad's important, but this... is this something we should even be talking about?"

"I can show you the reports. Oil in the Gulf is probably 30 percent of what it used to be, or less. The polar ice caps are melting. There's extreme weather everywhere, and yet clean water is ever more difficult to come by. Animals across the globe are becoming extinct, and there are more than 800,000 people going hungry as we speak—a number that will only get worse. It's up to responsible parties to act, and that's us, Max."

"So, with no further discussion, I'm to vote yes on this?"

"Discussions are welcome. Demetrius and I have had many. It makes perfect sense that you'll want to do the same. But you need to know that when the time comes, Demetrius will expect a yes vote on Clean Slate."

"Of course." *And he always gets what he wants.*

Finally, the redhead spoke with an urgency he hadn't yet displayed. "I wish I could say to take as much time as you like, but before you know it you're going to be at that meeting. If you have concerns, you need to let us know now."

"I do have a question," Max exclaimed. "How many people are we talking? A few hundred thousand? A few million?"

With each question Otto and the redhead continued sharing glances, which Max hardly found reassuring. Finally, Otto stood and approached Max by the credenza. "Like I said, it's a numbers game, and there are a lot of factors involved."

"All right. So, give me a number."

"Clean Slate is designed to reach somewhere around an eighth of the population. Frankly, that's what we'd like to end up with."

The figure didn't immediately register with Max, until he realized exactly how Otto had phrased it. *That's what we'd like to end up with.* Clean Slate had been devised to eliminate seven-eighths of the world's population. Both the idea and the number were staggering. "But wait, that doesn't make sense. That means you're talking over five billion people." Speechless and dumbfounded, Max returned to the table and plopped in his chair. "I'm sorry, but you guys are fucking with me, right?"

Both Otto and the redhead remained stone-faced, prompting Max to scoot his chair back from the table again.

"I'm sorry, guys, but I need a break."

Without awaiting a response, Max stood and left the conference room. In the hall, he found the nearest bathroom. The facility appeared private and residential, complete with top-of-the-line fixtures and mood lighting. He opened the faucet and splashed cool water on his face. Max stared at his reflection in the mirror, wondering how he had ended up in the precise position Indigo had foretold. Although he hadn't planned or intended it, there were potentially countless lives in his hands.

Suddenly, the atmosphere underground felt stale and oppressive. Feeling dizzy, Max planted himself on the closed toilet seat and shut his eyes. "Fuck!" He found it increasingly difficult to breathe. "This is insane." Visualizing the scope of Clean Slate anguished Max as images of Hitler's holocaust loomed in his head. He envisioned fields of mangled, emaciated corpses piled high and rotting in the wind. *Wiping out 90 percent of the population is insane!* A wave of nausea swept over Max, and he stood to open the toilet seat. He pressed his arms against the wall to lean over the commode. After several deep breaths, the intense urge to vomit retreated.

At one point, standing in for Demetrius had seemed glamorous, but decisions like Clean Slate were not at all what he bargained for. To say Rizick members found the initiative controversial felt like a gross understatement. *How could anyone be asked to put forth such a program?* After what seemed like several minutes, Max regained his sense of calm. Feeling more composed again, he finally exited the bathroom.

When he returned, Otto was alone in the conference room. His father's friend looked up playfully. "Thought I was gonna have to send a search party after you. Where'd you go?"

"Had to use the restroom." Max motioned toward the redhead's empty seat. "He get impatient?"

"He's a busy man, Max. Neither of us thought you'd be gone that long."

"What are you talking about, Otto? I stepped out for five minutes."

Otto glanced at his watch and shook his head. "More like an hour. I know this is a lot, and it's not easy stuff to digest."

Perplexed, Max looked at his phone and realized he was losing time again. *The man at the yoga studio. What did he do?* The redhead never returned, but he and Otto continued talking for another hour. Some of Otto's topics were compelling, but Max's true attention remained on a preposterous population control initiative. *Clean Slate.*

Finally, Otto packed up his things and prepared to leave. Little did he know, Max had no intention of continuing their established routine.

"Otto, if you don't mind, I'd like to use the internet. I can get it with that virtual keyboard thing, right?"

"Of course."

"Believe it or not, I remember the elevator code. If you need to take off I can find my way above ground."

Otto wasn't entirely comfortable with the decision, but Max trumped him in the hierarchy of control. As such, Otto would have to honor Max's wishes regardless of what they were. "I guess I'll see you tomorrow then." Otto smiled affectionately.

"Yeah, I'll be here on time. I promise."

"Sounds good. Try to get some rest, and tomorrow we'll do this all over again. I'll get you those Clean Slate reports too. That way, you can take some time looking them over."

Max forced a smile, but didn't respond. Otto understood why he was displeased, since Demetrius had at one time also been dissatisfied with the Clean Slate "solution." It was for this reason he had continually ordered reports, hoping at least one of them would offer a different recommendation. Otto knew it would take Max time to settle into the idea, just as it had his father. Fortunately, they had been granted extra time before the next meeting. Otto patted Max on the back and then disappeared from the room.

Max felt physically and emotionally drained from the day's

activities. While he appreciated Otto, he wasn't looking forward to another day with him and the redhead. He took a deep breath and began typing on the virtual keyboard. He first looked up the distance between DC and Chicago, which was roughly 700 miles. Max quickly did the math and realized if he used the high-speed underground train, he could be in Chicago in less than an hour. He removed his cell phone and dialed his father's assistant. On the third ring, she picked up.

"This is Rosalee."

"Rosalee, it's Max Battenberg."

"Hello, Mr. Battenberg, what can I do for you?"

"A couple of things, actually. First, are there any updates on my dad?"

"All things considered, he is doing quite well. I mean, you saw his injuries. They're quite extensive. The main factor in his recovery, of course, is time."

"All right, good." Max was happy to hear of his father's improvement. "The other thing: I haven't really been able to sleep here in DC. If I use the train, I could get to Chicago in less than an hour, right?"

"Absolutely, Mr. Battenberg. We're looking at just under fifty minutes, actually. But it was assumed you wouldn't want to commute."

"Actually, I prefer to sleep at home. How do the trains work?"

There was a minor pause before Rosalee spoke. "I'm sending an application to your phone. It will appear like travel agent software, only when you enter your itinerary, it will trigger the first available train."

"Perfect. Do you know when the next one is?"

"One moment, Mr. Battenberg." Max could hear Rosalee typing at her console. After a brief wait she continued. "A train can be there in twelve minutes."

"You're kidding?" Max was stunned and pleasantly surprised.

"The underground network is quite efficient, Mr. Battenberg."

"In that case, I'll just get my things from the hotel in the morning."

"Very well, Mr. Battenberg."

"Thanks, Rosalee. You rock."

Rosalee laughed softly into the phone. "Thank you, sir, that's very kind."

After some cursory pleasantries Max hung up, grabbed his things and headed to the underground platform to catch the next transport. The underground rail network impressed him, and he hardly understood why its existence was being kept secret. Why wasn't such technology being made more widely available above ground?

In less than ten minutes, the train pulled in and Max boarded. In no time, he was rocketing toward Chicago at speeds upwards of 700 miles per hour.

CHAPTER 6

*R*osalee had been correct. In under fifty minutes, Max was riding a stealth elevator, rising out of the depths into a local Chicago office building. He immediately hailed a cab and returned home to shower. After dressing, he entered the hall, where he encountered his house manager, Cora.

"Hey, LC, how are you?" Max had utilized a more familiar moniker for Cora. The abbreviation stood for Lady Cora, as he had typically addressed her as a child.

"Very well, sir. I see you've been traveling again."

"Yeah, just doing stuff for my dad."

"Very nice, sir. Is everything in order here at the house?"

"Now that you mention it, I do have something for you."

Cora, who always sought to be of help, offered Max a warm smile, prompting him to continue.

"Remember, not too long ago, we discussed a journal my mother had?"

"Of course, sir."

"I asked my dad about it, but he didn't remember anything."

"Your father is a busy man."

"It would be a great help if you could remember where she might've left it."

"Well," Cora began as she tried piecing together what some might consider ancient history. "When we spoke before, I mentioned that your mother often misplaced it. It was such a long time ago. If I had to guess, I would say it was in one of the European estates, sir. Probably in France. I mean, in those years, that's where she spent most of her time."

"Okay." While he hadn't intended it, Max's voice grew serious. "I have an assignment for you then. Can you please check any of the estates where you think it might be? There's no rush. And if you want to visit your family in Italy while you're there, you should."

"Oh, very good, sir! That was a long time ago, but I do have a few ideas where to look."

"Great, LC. I'm just trying to piece together some things that her journal might help me work out."

"Of course, sir. I'll make arrangements first thing tomorrow, and I'll let you know the moment I find something."

"Thank you, LC. I gotta run. I'm meeting Brigitte."

"Make sure to say hello for me."

"Will do." Max gave her a peck on the cheek and a smile; it was good to see her again. He had to admit he felt uplifted being back in Chicago. The commute from DC was so quick and easy that he probably covered the huge distance more quickly than it took some of Chicago's suburban commuters to get home.

After a quick drive across town, he arrived at Brigitte's. Max strolled up her driveway and knocked at the door. She answered with a stunned look on her face. "Oh my God, Max. What are you doing?"

He smiled a devilish grin. "I told you I'd be back."

"But I thought you had to be in DC."

Max shrugged, nonchalant. "Filling in for my dad has its perks; I didn't realize I could commute."

Genuinely thrilled, Brigitte grabbed Max and pulled him into the house for a kiss and a tight embrace. After the heartfelt greeting, they agreed to order takeout and open a bottle of wine. The day's topics had been heavy, and Max appreciated the small slice of tranquility that he and Brigitte could share. For a long while, they chatted about nothing, allowing Max to forget such things as the family legacy and his father's dreadful condition. Brigitte helped to steer his mind off of chemtrails and population control. If only for a few fleeting moments, it was like old times. Then, from out of nowhere, Max burst out in laughter. *Not now,* he lamented. *Not again.*

As expected, Brigitte turned to gape at him. "Babe, what's so funny?"

He had no idea how to explain the outburst. *A homeless man performed some form of voodoo on me.* He fought the outlandish desire to laugh and the fresh tremors he felt building in his extremities. *What do I say? How do I cover?* Finally, Max spoke. "I don't know. Just considering how strange life can be." He used every inch of his might to squash down the chuckles, which kept reappearing at the most inopportune moments. Unable to provide what he considered a reasonable explanation, Max lied, "I gotta run home real quick. I just need to grab a few things. Then I'll come back and spend the night, okay? I want some quality time, even if it's just for the night."

It was Brigitte's wish to maintain her resolve, but a huge smile appeared on her face instead. "All right."

He leaned in and kissed her. "I'll be right back."

"When you get back, can we please discuss the important stuff?"

"Ssshh." Max put a finger to her lips to silence her. "I've already arranged everything. Tomorrow morning, at 6:30, we'll head to my doctor for that referral." Max gently rubbed his hand across Brigitte's flat belly. "Is that okay?"

Brigitte smiled. It was difficult to tell in low lighting, but Max thought she might be blushing. "I suppose that'll be fine, Mr. Battenberg."

He hugged and kissed her. "After we're finished, I have to meet Otto back in DC." Max pulled himself away to glance at the time on his phone. "Oh, shit, I gotta run so I can get back." He snatched up his keys before returning to offer Brigitte a good-bye kiss. "I shouldn't be more than an hour or two."

"Okay. Drive carefully then."

Max made his way to the door and blew Brigitte one last kiss before turning to exit. He came down the steps into her drive-way. With each step he felt the weight of his current circumstance. There was a twisted irony in their unexpected pregnancy, especially when a program was being considered to dramatically reduce the population. *Shit.* If voted in, Clean Slate could potentially wipe out billions of innocent people. No matter how he tried, Max could hardly conceive of a scheme with such scope. He shook off the feelings, vowing to focus on the things he could control. At least he had quelled one fire by returning to Chicago to see Brigitte. Now that the evening was growing late, he still had one last thing he needed to do.

§ § §

Max steered his top-of-the-line Range Rover through the streets of Chicago until the Golden Arch Yoga Studio came into view. The building address — 7129 — figured in a prominent display against the studio's outer wall. In a peculiar prophecy, Indigo had provided the same number months before during a trip to New Orleans. Max still found it difficult to determine whether or not this had been a coincidence... *Or had she intended I meet the homeless man?*

Just as he had hoped, the vagrant was seated in lotus position in his usual spot across the street from the studio. His eyes were closed, and a red plaid blanket covered his legs and a portion of his belly. Because the entire block was red-curbed, Max was unable to park, but he pulled up diagonal to the sidewalk anyway. His bright headlights shone on the man, who subsequently lifted a hand to block the glare, squinting to see. Max immediately jumped from the car and approached in an aggressive manner.

"What the hell did you do to me?"

As the vagabond's eyes adjusted, he lowered his hand. His eyes were intense like a predator's and sparkled against Max's headlights. The strange man's gaze reminded Max of lions he had seen in wildlife documentaries just before a kill. It held power even when his face somehow remained calm and serene. After what seemed an eternity, the man answered back. "I awakened something in you. But this is what you needed."

Max trembled as he stood between the car and the curb, his headlights backlighting him as if he were a performer on stage. Despite the situation, the homeless man appeared strangely unaffected. He remained seated, and his face seemed a blank slate as he quietly returned Max's stare.

"Whatever you did, I haven't been able to — I haven't been in control." To his own disbelief, Max chuckled. Just as before, the laughter was uncalled for, but Max couldn't help himself. He laughed again. "You see what I mean?"

The man finally stood, and the dirty blanket fell to his feet. His stature and frame were imposing, not at all diminished by the shell of poverty. He was sinewy with broad shoulders and a square jaw. It was clear he hadn't shaved in weeks, but somehow his beard looked clean and manicured. Nevertheless, he was still a homeless man, while Max was from a powerful clan. But then Max softened, feeling he should be more polite. "What's your name anyway?"

"People call me AJ."

Max reentered his car and closed the door. AJ watched as he switched off his lights and parallel parked beside the red zone. He shut off the engine, and the street became silent. Max stepped from the car and crossed to AJ. He remembered how filthy his hands had been during their last encounter, but it seemed rude to avoid touching him now. Max extended a hand. "I'm Max."

AJ smiled but didn't extend his hand in return. "We shouldn't acquiesce to things we don't wish to do."

Max withdrew his hand, somewhat embarrassed that his repugnance had been so transparent.

"Did you believe you had veiled your distaste? Taking my hand was the last thing you wanted."

"Okay." Max felt even more self-conscious being called out about his actions.

AJ laughed quietly. "It's written all over your face, my friend."

An urge to argue arose in Max. At the worst, he wanted to defend his polite and seasoned upbringing. Deep down, however, he knew such a protest would be pointless. In the depths of his heart, he felt aware that this strange man could see him somehow, not as he wanted to appear but as he was. "So," Max continued, "can you please explain exactly what you did and why you felt you needed to?"

AJ pondered the request, pausing to look up and down the street. Max was certain he was formulating some kind of explanation, but AJ continued otherwise.

"If you were as polite as you believe, you would invite me into the car, so we can speak in private. You aren't parked legally anyway." AJ retrieved the red plaid blanket and wrapped it tightly around his shoulders.

If Max hadn't wanted to shake AJ's hand, he hardly wanted to convene in his car. But he had already been rude and needed to save face. "C'mon, man, hop in."

While AJ crossed to the passenger side, Max secretly hoped he wouldn't bring the blanket. Max typically kept a meticulous car, and AJ didn't exactly seem a modicum of hygiene. When AJ reached for the door handle he caught a glimpse of Max's expression. The pauper hesitated before removing the blanket and tossing it on the sidewalk against the wall. Max didn't fully understand the move, but he was happy AJ had done so. *It's like he's reading my mind.*

Both men closed their doors to a warm and cozy interior. Within seconds, Max smelled the pungent odor of AJ's unbathed body.

"You could've brought your blanket." Max offered.

"Another untruth," AJ decried as he cracked open the window to aerate the car. "Dishonesty is unbecoming, don't you think?"

"Okay," Max said, slowly cracking the driver's side window. He decided to get to the point. "I met a woman in New Orleans — a psychic, in fact. She's the one who suggested I come here. I presume because she wanted me to meet you."

AJ appeared not to follow Max's story. "I'm sorry, but I don't know this person, and I've never been to Louisiana."

"Really?" Max displayed his own confusion, but somehow he knew AJ was being truthful. To his chagrin, the homeless man's stench became unbearable. Max attempted subtlety, but it didn't go unnoticed when he rolled his window further down.

A tinge of disappointment washed over AJ's face, accompanied by a knowing smile. "You have a lot to learn, my friend." AJ briskly rubbed his hands together as if he were using them to start a fire. After several seconds, he cupped his hands in a ball and blew into them. He slowly opened them as a magician would when releasing a tiny bird.

Max immediately smelled it. The pungent smell of several weeks without a bath had transformed into a brilliant perfumed aroma. The odor alternated between jasmine and a summer breeze of magnolia blossoms and honeysuckle. AJ swiped his hands down his arms, legs and torso as if he were drying them on his clothing.

Now, instead of trying delicately not to breathe, Max was freely inhaling the fragrant aromas. He chuckled to himself. "How did you do that?"

"In life, everyone we encounter has a purpose of some sort.

The struggle, for us, is to remain on our paths, in the moment, without becoming a detriment to the experiences of others. I realized I was compromising this encounter, so I chose to express something different."

Max felt speechless and completely perplexed. How had AJ managed to change such a powerful odor to a fragrant perfume? He shook the question from his mind before he continued. There were so many other things he wished to know. "I'm guessing I don't need to explain why I'm here."

AJ smiled, flashing a set of surprisingly perfect teeth. "I wouldn't be so sure. Why not enlighten me?"

"Ever since you did... whatever that thing was, I've been losing time—losing track. I'm also having weird spasms in my arms and legs. And crazy, inappropriate laughter... It's embarrassing." Max chuckled, only this time because he found a sad humor in his predicament.

AJ listened before turning to gaze through the passenger window. "That's not why you came."

"Of course it is. I swear."

Still looking through the window, AJ shook his head in disagreement. "There's a light in all of us, Max, if only we dare let it shine. But you—the first time I saw you it was clear to me—your light is a beacon. Take away the cars and all the other toys, and people will still be drawn to you."

Max leaned forward and, inexplicably, rested his head against the steering wheel. He felt it necessary to pose a question or construct a thought, but he had no idea where to start. "Why do people keep telling me—Honestly, I don't see it."

"It's easy to get bogged down with everything else going on: work, families... material things sometimes make it tough to find the way. We must constantly strive to maintain balance and purpose. Then, even the best distractions or smokescreens become ineffective at derailing us from what it is we're meant to do."

Max took a moment to digest AJ's words. "But how are we supposed to know what that is?"

AJ fixed his gaze on Max. "You must look within for the answer. After all, only you know."

Mired in confusion, Max sat back and looked AJ directly in

the eye. After a short pause, he turned away, mumbling under his breath. "Great, more fucking riddles." The more he thought about things, the less sense any of it made. Something had somehow led him to invite a homeless man into his car who could magically transmute a filthy stench into perfume and instruct him on the intricacies of life.

"It's up to us to decipher our purpose. The answers are all around us. Someone like you will attract others searching for meaning. But, like a magnet, you will also draw powerful negative energies to you. This is why I did what I did. I awakened something in you. Something you'll need to stay on your path and find your way."

"But that's not why I came here. I need to know what you did, or for you to undo it."

"Evolution involves change, my friend. It's the opportunists, driven by selfishness and greed, who work tirelessly to prevent any true growth from happening. There are always forces meandering to engulf us, but you shouldn't worry. There are also positive energies being made manifest. What you are experiencing, what it is that I did, is all part of the positive."

Max stared at AJ, astounded by how completely different he seemed from the image he had previously envisioned. "What the hell are you, some kind of a street monk?"

AJ laughed out loud. "I am just a man. Not more nor less than anyone else. You must listen to the voices, Max. When you feel good, bad or embarrassed about something, it's because there are little voices whispering to you about universal morality. What you feel here," AJ placed a hand over Max's heart, "will not betray you."

"You say you don't know this woman I told you about, but I'm certain she wanted me to meet you."

AJ smiled, flashing his perfect teeth. "Anything's possible. What's good is, you're listening to your instincts. The answers are usually around us, if only we choose to pay attention."

Max glanced at the clock on his dashboard. It seemed he and AJ had been chatting for ten or fifteen minutes, but the clock read 11:30 p.m. "Shit." Max sighed deeply. "How could we have been here that long? I'm sorry, I have to go. Is there anything else you wanted to share?"

AJ smirked with disillusionment. "And the lesson is already lost." He reached over the armrest and motioned toward Max's heart. "The answers are all there." Then he raised his finger and pointed to the space between Max's eyebrows, "and here. The heart and the third eye will reveal everything you need to know. Seek outwardly, and you will easily be deceived."

Feeling entirely out of his league, Max took a deep breath and chuckled. "The third eye, huh? There's a poster at the yoga studio, something about Kundalini chakras."

AJ smiled knowingly. Max took notice, remembering his initiation and the lights he had seen illuminated up and down the spines of everyone in the pyramid chamber.

"Is that what you're talking about? I can't say I know much, if anything, about it."

"If only we could instantaneously learn all there is to know." AJ opened his arms, gesturing at their surroundings. "But then none of this would be necessary, now would it?"

Max hardly knew AJ, but he felt exceptionally comfortable in his presence. At the end of the day, this man was a stranger, though, and Max had to be up early with Brigitte the next morning.

"I sense fear in you, which is curious for someone of your background... humility perhaps? To clearly know the truth, you must release your fears."

Max felt exhaustion settling in, and he knew Brigitte would be waiting. "I have to go. Maybe I'll come again tomorrow."

"May I offer a word of advice?"

"Of course," Max replied.

"Whenever possible, spend a little thoughtful time alone. This is important for you. Actually, it is for all of us."

Max looked intently at AJ. "Are you asking me to meditate?"

AJ sized Max up like an art critic evaluating a painting. "People sometimes don't like that word. But focus is something everyone can use, especially these days." AJ pushed open Max's passenger door and stepped from the car. "There's a simple technique where all you need do is concentrate on the third eye. It's the area between your eyebrows." AJ took his right index finger and pressed it against his own forehead, between his eyebrows. "Right here. Just clear your thoughts, and keep your attention on this area. In time, one day, your third eye will open, and you will be made witness to unmistakable truths."

"Are you kidding?" Max asked, still skeptical despite everything he had experienced since his initiation.

"Hardly, Mr. Battenberg. You should try it."

Max fixed his gaze on AJ, whom he found fascinating. With a polite nod, AJ closed the door and hopped onto the sidewalk. He maintained a friendly smile, still watching Max through the window.

Max hadn't paid much attention to his body, but now that he considered it, he felt relaxed, almost as if he had received a massage. He started the car and pulled from the curb, waving to AJ as he made a U-turn and headed down the street. He glanced in his rearview mirror to see AJ returning to his spot and covering himself with the red plaid blanket.

Max made his way back to Brigitte's and used his key to enter. He found her asleep, and figured she had gone to bed annoyed. It was nearly midnight after all, and he had promised to return sooner. He knew there were only a few hours left to sleep before their doctor's appointment. As he climbed in bed, AJ's advice resonated in his head. *Thoughtful time alone.* He drifted to sleep, repeating the words over and over in his mind.

CHAPTER 7

*M*ax sprung up in bed when the alarm sounded. He was still tired, but it was the kind of fatigue a 24-year-old could easily push aside. Brigitte's spot in the bed beside him was empty, but he could hear the shower running. With a deep stretch of his arms and legs, Max rose and crossed into the bathroom, startling Brigitte when he pulled open the shower door.

"Oh my God, Max. You scared me."

"Sorry," he grinned. Max gazed at her and was instantly struck with her beauty. Brigitte's skin, which had a natural olive complexion, seemed entirely unblemished and smooth from head to toe.

Water glistened on her as it cascaded down her body. Her normally dark, curly hair, now sopping wet, appeared straight as it fell from the back of her head like a trail of wet paint. Max removed his underwear, which he often wore as pajamas, and stepped into the stall. The sting of hot water further awoke him as he crossed behind Brigitte to monopolize the jet stream.

He reached around with both arms and cradled the flatness of her stomach. "I can't believe there's a tiny Battenberg in here," he whispered, kissing the back of her neck.

Brigitte giggled softly. "Max, we're gonna be late." She turned and kissed him passionately. By now, the clear glass shower door was turning opaque with steam.

"I know," he whispered in a deep and throaty voice. He kissed her back before turning to retrieve a tube of shower gel. "And we need to be on time. I pulled strings for this appointment."

Drawing in her breath, Brigitte pushed Max away onto the shower wall. "Had you come back last night, like you said, we maybe would've had time for this."

Max ran a hand through his hair. "I know. I'm sorry. I lost track of time." While honest, he knew the explanation was a poor excuse.

Brigitte tilted her head and smirked — her way of saying *whatever*. "Finish washing up and get ready."

In record time, he and Brigitte dressed and headed out to the car. He pressed his remote to disengage the Range Rover's locks. Without hesitation, Brigitte climbed into the passenger seat. She shut the door, and a startled expression instantly appeared on her face. She sniffed the air as Max shut his door and started the car. Unable to contain herself, Brigitte blurted it out, "If I didn't know any better, I'd say that's a woman's perfume."

Max immediately noticed the fragrance AJ had created hours before. *Oh, shit.* He looked at Brigitte with guilt, but he knew he was innocent. "Trust me, it's not."

Brigitte frowned, her suspicions not fully assuaged. "Well, what is it then? It's a little flowery to be yours."

Max hesitated, but he knew the truth was preferable to anything Brigitte was thinking. "A few days ago, I let a homeless guy sit there, and he stank up the car. I had to get it treated. That's what you're smelling."

"What?" Brigitte looked repulsed by the idea. "Why did you let a homeless person in the car?"

"It's a long story, Bridge."

"Well, thank God you got it cleaned." Brigitte settled into the seat before leaning over to kiss Max's cheek.

He sniffed the flowery scents AJ left behind. He hadn't expected they would still be so robust. Whether or not Brigitte believed him he couldn't be certain, which was ironic. He had sometimes lied on more serious occasions. Now that he had offered the truth, he felt Brigitte might not be entirely convinced.

They turned onto the street where Max's doctor was located. They were cutting it close, but in the end they would be on time. He pulled into the underground parking and expertly maneuvered into a spot. Max rushed Brigitte onto the elevator, turning to her once they were inside.

"Can I ask a favor?"

"I'm not so sure you've earned that just yet."

Max stepped closer and stroked her face. "Hopefully, I can change that perception." He kissed her lightly. "It just occurred to me, I won't have time to drop off my car."

"You want me to take it?"

"Yeah, if you could keep it, or drop it at my place, whichever's easiest."

Brigitte looked up at the elevator's ceiling, contemplative. "You sure you want that? I might figure out where that perfume came from."

"You think so, huh?" Max laughed and poked Brigitte as the elevator doors opened. She squealed as they filed into the hall toward the office. Brigitte paused at the door, growing serious.

"Then you won't mind if I get it detailed again?"

"Just let LC handle that. It's already scheduled for next week." Growing hopeful, Max smiled sheepishly. "So, you'll do it?"

"Of course, Max. What do you think, I'm going to leave your car here?"

He clasped his hands together, as if in prayer, then he bowed before Brigitte. "Thank you."

She chuckled as they entered the office, but all laughter ceased when she spotted Phyllis behind the front desk. Brigitte's stunned expression quickly replaced any perception of levity in the air. As always, Phyllis' face lit up.

"Max, Brigitte, how are ya?"

Max was confused. *Wait, they know each other?* He felt even more perplexed by the shocked look on Brigitte's face. "You guys know each other?"

"Of course," Phyllis chimed before Brigitte could answer. "The Sturdivants are patients at Dr. Bettencourt's satellite office across town."

"Oh," was all Max could answer. There was something about the connection that disturbed him, but he couldn't quite put his finger on it.

Even now, Brigitte still had a deer-in-the-headlights expression plastered across her face. She offered Phyllis a weak smile. "How are you?"

"Fantastic, hon, I can't complain."

Brigitte turned and whispered to Max under her breath. "You never said Bettencourt was your doctor."

"I didn't realize you knew him, Brigitte."

"Maaax," she muttered, "aside from my brother, no one in my family knows I'm pregnant... That's why I didn't want to come to him in the first place."

Before he could respond, Dr. Bettencourt approached the

front desk. "Hey, guys." He stared at Brigitte a moment. "Were we scheduled today?"

"She's actually the one I needed the last-minute appointment for," Max explained.

Bettencourt was very shrewd. In only a few seconds he put the puzzle pieces together, and a look of understanding washed over his face. "Why don't you guys come on back?"

The rest of their visit was typical as doctor's appointments go. A test was performed that confirmed Brigitte's pregnancy. Other blood samples were sent for analysis, and her heart, breathing and blood pressure were checked. In total, the appointment lasted no more than a half hour, at which point Bettencourt wrote his referral. Max made certain of their doctor's plan to respect their privacy. Satisfied, they hustled from his office with only a small margin of time for Max's return to DC. Once they were in the car, he skidded from the parking structure and punched the pedal to the floor. The large Range Rover accelerated as he gunned around corners and blasted through an occasional red light.

Part of him wanted to inquire about Brigitte's affiliation with Dr. Bettencourt, but there wouldn't be time to fully explore this. Only months before, Bettencourt had removed his GPS chip in confidence. Max felt he could also be trusted to keep their pregnancy under wraps. After a dozen minutes of banal discussion, he screeched to a stop before the building that served as a gateway to the secret underground network. Once again, Brigitte adopted a curious look on her face.

"Why are we stopping here? Aren't you leaving from O'Hare?"

"Yeah, um… Otto and I are caravanning. He wanted me to meet him here. I guess he has an appointment." To Max's surprise, the lies were becoming more and more effortless. He kissed her before grabbing his overnight bag and hopping from the car. "Just drive it, if you want. I'll come by in the next few days to get it."

"Are you coming back tonight?"

"Depends how late we go. Either way, I'll call you."

"Sounds good." Brigitte scooted into the driver's seat, then adjusted it and the mirror. "I'll speak to you later then. Love you!"

"Love you, too." Glancing at the time, Max turned and ran into the building. Once inside, he found the same elevator he had ridden the night before. Because it was early morning, a large congregation of people was waiting. He knew there would be no time to waste. Another elevator opened, and the entire group disappeared inside. Several other people arrived just as the doors were closing.

Max repeatedly poked the down button, praying for the desired elevator to arrive. When it did, there were other people already on it. He and a few others stepped on. Max waited patiently while the elevator descended through the parking levels. He glanced again at the time. Only five minutes remained before the train. When the final passenger exited on one of the lowest parking levels, another group of people was patiently waiting to ride up.

Just as Otto had done at the National Archives, Max held up a hand. "Sorry, folks, this one's out of commission." A woman started to protest, but he cut her off. "Another will be here any minute."

As soon as the doors closed, Max entered the same underground access code: *3-16-18 and the "mezzanine" button.* The elevator jerked slightly as it descended beneath its supposed deepest level. After coming to an abrupt stop, it began moving through a horizontal shaft. Seconds later, Max was plunging into the deep underground.

A week earlier, he had found the secret system intriguing. Now, as he descended into the earth's belly, he felt the return of a nagging restlessness. He didn't understand why, but it seemed the feeling mostly reoccurred in Otto's presence. This was strange, of course, because Otto was presumably in DC, 700 miles away.

The elevator finally came to a stop. When its doors opened, Max darted for the platform. A minute later, he could feel a strong gust whipping his hair. He knew this was good news, and he sighed, having made it in time. Wind from the sleek, strangely silent train whished by as the vehicle slowed to a stop. Max still felt a sense of awe seeing the ultra-modern transport. Like some prehistoric dinosaur, it appeared like a giant steely snake. Its magnetic technology allowed it to float silently above some semblance of a train track.

Max carried his overnight bag aboard and made his way to a private cabin. As the train gently nudged forward, he noticed several unavailable cabins, perhaps containing occupants who were nevertheless cleverly obscured by opaque glass. He wondered who might be inside of them: presidents, royals perhaps, or deal makers like his father.

The train's ride was comfortable and smooth, making it hard to believe they were already approaching the speed of sound. To satisfy a potentially morbid curiosity, Max crossed through multiple cars, heading toward the train's rear. Each time he reached the end of a car, he triggered the automatic doors, and they swished open, allowing him to pass. As he approached the tail end of the train, he noticed there were no longer any passengers present.

Three cars away from the caboose, Max thought he stumbled upon the very thing he hoped to find. Until now, all of the dual sliding doors between cars were constructed of wood and contained window panels in them. This allowed passengers to view adjacent cars without actually entering them. Now, Max stood before a single, sliding metal door with no window panel. He pushed the button, triggering it to open. As the rear car revealed itself, Max couldn't help but stare.

The compartment was designed unlike any of the others. Soft incandescent lighting illuminated the passenger cabins, but Max was now gazing into a stark compartment without windows that was lit with harsh fluorescent lights. Near the ceiling on each side, there were six-inch metal louvers that could be opened for ventilation. A single pathway led from the front to the rear, flanked on each side by rows of metallic benches, like church pews. Attached to the feet of every bench were multiple sets of chains and shackles.

Max took a single step inside the compartment, but thought better of fully entering. While the decor was comfortable and modern in the forward parts of the train, this particular car felt like a jail cell. Max worried that he might get trapped inside if he allowed the door to close. He gawked a long while, wondering what such a car might be used for. He had already questioned Otto about this once before, but he was determined to ask again.

Max knew he was standing within the confines of some bizarre mobile prison, but he wondered who might be sequestered there and why. He turned and headed back toward the front of the train. Halfway across the car, he heard the metallic door slide shut, obscuring the detention compartment from view.

Again at the front of the train, Max spotted several empty private cabins. He chose one, slid inside and locked the door, hoping to sleep at least a half hour. He set his phone to alert him to the train's arrival and then took advantage of the remaining time to nap.

CHAPTER 8

Thirty-five minutes later, the buzzing alarm jarred Max awake. He took a deep breath to gather his composure and waited for the DC stop. The original plan had been to return to the hotel to retrieve his affairs. He had also hoped to intercept Otto in the unlikely event that he had stopped by. But Max realized there would be no time for such a detour. He exited the train and made his way to the conference room. Inside, the pale man with grayish blond hair was sitting alone, drinking coffee.

Max greeted him coolly. "Good morning."

He looked up with a deadpan stare. "How are you, Mr. Battenberg?"

"You can call me Max. I never caught your name, though."

The man seemed thrown by Max's inquiry. "Sometimes, anonymity is best down here. But my name's Levi, though." Levi's hand was at rest on top of binders that he slid across the table toward Max. "These are the reports your father commissioned for Clean Slate. Mr. Khrzinsky mentioned you might want to take a look. I believe you'll discover, just like your father, that the numbers don't lie."

Max and Levi shared a glance. Even in silence, an exchange of thoughts was made. Levi knew Max didn't yet comprehend the purpose of Clean Slate, but this was true for anyone who was just learning about the program. At the same time, Max sensed uneasiness in Levi, but he couldn't quite place his finger on what it was.

Max opened the first report and thumbed through it until he landed on page 42. He began to read.

EMISSIONS OF THE INDUSTRIAL WORLD: Many experts believe the environment has already been irreparably damaged by emissions from the industrial world. The largest offenders reside in countries like the U.S., China and India, whose populations exceed 0.3, 1.4 and 1.2 billion respectively.

Max glanced down the page at charts and graphs that mapped out the problem of carbon emissions and its progressive damage to the environment. He skipped 50 pages and found a section on consumption.

> CONSUMPTION AND DWINDLING RESOURCES: For more than
> a decade, the world's population growth rate has been in decline.
> While a rate decrease remains desirable, the long-term incremen-
> tal change remains insignificant. Birth rates, in recent years, have
> dropped to 1.89%, while increasing lifespans have reduced global
> mortality rates to 0.79%, the aggregate of which is a 1.1% growth
> rate. Despite advances in agriculture and animal husbandry, the
> continually increasing population cannot be sustained.

Max flipped a few pages forward, and another headline caught
his eye.

> DEFORESTATION—A CASE STUDY OF HAITI AND BRAZIL: The
> growing consumption of wood has had and continues to have a
> devastating impact on the environment. The particular effects of
> this practice are most evident in countries like Haiti and Brazil. In
> many instances, the forests in these regions have systematically
> been converted into wasteland. The procedure of deforestation is
> a confirmed contributory force to global warming and meteorolog-
> ical change.

Max skimmed further through the report and read how pollu-
tion and global warming had literally choked the air from cities
like New Delhi, Beijing and Mexico City, just to name a few. In
many instances, inhabitants of these locales required oxygen to
breathe. *Is this what happened on Nibiru?* Max wondered. *Was it
their misuse of resources that damaged the atmosphere there?*

He continued flipping through the apocalyptic report, distressed by the overall picture and by the conclusions being drawn.
According to the report, the only "solution" to rectify the situation would be found in massive depopulation. This remedy was
a little-known program called Clean Slate.

Max looked at various statistics with a sense of disbelief before
skipping to the end of the report. One of the final chapters predicted the fall of OPEC and its members. Countries like Saudi
Arabia were experiencing dwindling oil reserves that had sub-
stantially weakened the cartel. Increased mortality rates were
forecasted in poorer nations, since residents were expected to
perish in the absence of currently existing fossil fuels. Clean Slate
was simply considered a method of accelerating the process.

Max flipped back to another section of the report.

HIGH FREQUENCY ACTIVE AURORAL RESEARCH PRO-GRAM (HAARP): It is officially reported that HAARP technology is intended as an ionospheric research program. The HAARP device, however, has other useful applications that could easily be utilized by Clean Slate. Without alteration the combined use of HAARP, i.e., radio waves, sound and microwaves, can be weaponized to alter weather, bring down aircraft or destroy architectural structures. The elegance of HAARP design lies in its undetectable nature. Neither the human eye nor the ear can perceive its operation. Examples of HAARP's efficiency should be noted in the following HAARP-related events:

A. On September 11, 2001 – In the interest of preventing evidence recovery, the HAARP beam is aimed at each of the World Trade Center's already damaged Twin Towers in New York City. Extended exposure to the beam results in their successful demolition.

B. December 26, 2004 - Over a ten-minute period, the HAARP beam is successfully aimed at tectonic plates located on the floor of the Indian Ocean. The end result is a fault shift measuring a moment magnitude of 9.2. The subsequent energy released is estimated to have been more than a 1000 times that of Hiroshima's atomic bomb. In the end, a cataclysmic tsunami devastates an array of countries with the highest casualties in Indonesia, Sri Lanka, India and Thailand. Final population decrease of 250,000.

Max recalled the images of desolation he had seen on news channels. Entire villages had been erased by the giant wave that swept away cars, buildings and inhabitants alike. During his years at Yale, Max had heard multiple conspiracy theories, but it was eerie to read about them in proven reports that he knew were not conjecture. HAARP was sold to the public as an innocuous research device, but the Rizick Group's intentions for it were much more sinister. To those who knew of the device's existence, HAARP seemed futuristic, even out of this world. To Max, it was now no more remarkable than entering Teotihuacán's Pyramid of the Moon and witnessing life on far distant worlds. With a sense of awe he continued to read.

C. August 23, 2005 – HAARP beams are successfully used to augment the strength of Hurricane Katrina (to category 5) and to steer her ashore. Final population decrease: 1,833.

D. May 12, 2008 – After its prior successes, HAARP is utilized in China's Sichuan Province. The resulting earthquake measures a moment magnitude of 8.0. Final population decrease: approximately 70,000; missing or presumed deceased: approximately 18,000.

E. January 12, 2010 – The HAARP beam is aimed at Haiti/ Dominican Republic. The resulting earthquake measures a moment magnitude of 7.0. Final population decrease: approximately 100,000–160,000.

Max looked up from the report, daunted by its dramatic details of population reductions. At the same moment, Otto entered the room.

"Good morning, gentlemen."

Max looked at Otto, still flummoxed by the report. "Hi, Otto."

"Max, how are you?"

"I'm not sure."

Otto and Levi shared a glance, but they did not exchange words. Otto glanced at the binder in front of Max. "Is that one of your father's reports?" With a knowing smile he watched Max nod. "You know he did at least ten of those, and they all indicated the same conclusion."

Max was beginning to understand what that conclusion was: "Wipe the slate clean."

Before Otto could answer, Levi chimed in, directing his words at Max. "You should know Clean Slate is Rizick's single, most controversial issue. It's not that anybody even really wants it, but there are those of us who understand its necessity." Levi stood and leaned forward, pressing his hands down against the table. "Right now, population management is our highest priority. Every single time Clean Slate goes up for vote, it never passes in its entirety. So instead, we have an earthquake here, a tsunami there. We get to trim away the fat without truly addressing the problem. As Otto mentioned the other day, either we do it, or we wait for nature to. It's not like it hasn't already happened, right? They're called extinctions. The question is, do we want to leave it up to nature to rectify the problem? If we do, who stays and who goes will no longer be within our control."

"I'm not so sure it should be." Max felt he should finally weigh in. He noticed a small exchange between Levi and Otto. It was barely a glance, but he knew they were concerned. "Tell me about the shackles on the train."

Otto looked surprised. For a moment, he dipped his head to the side, hardly eager to respond. "If Clean Slate passes, and one day it will, we're going to be left with the task of rebuilding. How do you imagine we'll do that? Using people like you and me. Starting over's going to require doctors, builders, nurses, engineers… teachers. Many won't be allowed to bring their families, so I doubt they'll be venturing down here, not willingly at least."

Max stared at Otto with a sense of incredulity. "This is insane. So the plan is to forcibly bring them here, hoping what—that they'll turn around and work for us?"

Levi plopped back into his seat. "Isn't that already the case? You think your employees at that publishing company are showing up because they love their jobs? Most of them already feel hostage. What difference does it make if we bring them down here?"

For more than an hour, Max, Otto and Levi continued their discussion, throwing out the pros and cons of Clean Slate. At the start, his tutors appeared open to a disparate point of view, but Max could tell they were slowly losing patience. Finally, Levi scooted back from the table and stood in frustration.

"Look, Max, you seem like a good kid, so please don't take this the wrong way. What we're doing here is not really about you or what you want. There are 300 people on the Rizick committee. You being initiated doesn't make it 301. The only reason you're here is to serve as your father's proxy because he's stuck in New Mexico. We need you to be clear about your role. You are an envoy. I'm sorry if I sound blunt, but your opinion doesn't matter here."

Until now, Levi had mostly been pleasant, but Max didn't care much now for his tone. He turned to Otto, who nodded to further validate Levi's point of view.

"He's right, Max. Your father will expect you to cast his vote, not yours. It's not like we don't appreciate your hesitancy. To be truthful, Demetrius was reluctant too, at first. But now he wants Clean Slate, and frankly, it's the right thing to do. Just for clarity's sake, are we on the same page with this?"

Max looked into Otto's eyes. Even though they didn't share DNA, his father's friend had been as much of a paternal figure to Max as Demetrius. "Yeah, Otto, I guess. It's just..." Max gazed at the floor. "It's hard to envision the things you guys are talking about."

"Just get through this first meeting, and the rest will start to make sense afterward."

For another three hours, Max continued his instruction on how to vote in his father's stead. At the day's end, he wandered onto the underground train platform, both physically and emotionally spent. Without hesitation, he quickly hopped the next underground train back to Chicago.

CHAPTER 9

*T*he moment he resurfaced in the Windy City, Max hailed the first cab he could find and traveled across town toward the Golden Arch Studio. During the drive, he wondered about his current predicament. Only months before, his life had been effortless and carefree. On his eighteenth birthday, he had taken control of a sizable trust fund, but he had used it mostly to travel and party across the globe. Now, it appeared there was a steep price to pay for his birthright, and Max was being asked, among other things, to become an unwilling executioner.

During his initiation, he had pledged an oath to keep secret everything he was learning. He didn't dare disclose the Rizick Group's maneuverings to anyone he knew. But a stranger perhaps, someone like AJ, could suffice as a potential sounding board for issues that continued to dog his mind. Max still felt uneasy about making any disclosures, but he was determined to give it a try. For one, AJ had an uncanny sense, seeming to know things even when they were unspoken. While he appeared homeless and thus powerless, there was a wisdom about him that Max certainly felt he could use. The cab finally arrived, and he spotted the 7129 building. Max lost hope when he saw AJ's empty spot against the wall. *Damn.*

He requested the driver circle the block a few times, but the exercise bore no fruit. Resigned that there would be no discussion with AJ, he provided the cabbie with Brigitte's address and returned to her house to retrieve his car. After he disembarked, he spotted his Range Rover in her driveway. He crossed to the SUV, got in and dropped his head against the steering wheel.

"Oh, God, what a day." Max breathed a sigh of relief, grateful to be back in his element. In the months following his initiation, he felt he had developed two distinct and disparate lives. In one, he was a child of privilege who enjoyed life without the encumbrances of the average man. This was the Max who lived in Chicago and played hard across the globe. His family initiation, however, had introduced a new reality that Max was still trying on for size. In many ways, his new existence was both literally and figuratively underground. In the newly emerging life, he had a legacy to uphold, and the lives of many were now being placed in his hands.

Max lifted his head from the steering wheel and powered on his cell phone. He pulled up and dialed a contact listed as "New Orleans" in his address book. He had made a point to store the number after his last visit to Louisiana.

After several rings, the psychic Indigo Blue picked up, "Hello." Her voice was raspy like that of a well-seasoned songstress.

I can't believe I'm doing this. "Indigo, hi. It's Max Battenberg." After a prickly silence, he continued. "Are you still there?"

"Yes, Monsieur, I am here." Her tone was a blend of agitation and concern, and her words were punctuated with deliberateness. "Have you uncovered that of which I spoke?"

Max took an extended pause of his own. "Yeah. I just…"

"You should not have called, Monsieur. Only more treachery awaits you as you journey along your path."

"I'm sorry… I didn't know what else to do. The man you wanted me to meet—"

"I am sorry, Monsieur." There was confusion in the psychic's voice. "Of whom do you speak?"

"The address you gave me, 7129. I met a guy there…"

"I apologize, Monsieur, but I do not understand."

"The number you gave me. 7129. I found a building here in Chicago with that address. I met a guy in front… I thought…"

"You have misunderstood, mon cher. This number appeared to me, and I passed it on to you. I have no knowledge of its significance or of this man."

Shit. "Oh, I thought…" Max rested his head against the steering wheel again.

Indigo could sense the desperation in his voice. "Now, do you still doubt all you have seen? I warned that the truth would be revealed."

"Yes," Max chuckled, "you did indeed."

"Then you understand a choice must be made?"

He nodded first before speaking into the phone. "Yes."

"Whatever you choose, Monsieur, you must do so alone. This burden will be uniquely yours. To invite others will only serve to inflict danger upon them."

"Herein lies my point." Max felt a sense of desolation enveloping him. "I don't know if I can do this by myself."

"Shhhh," Indigo whispered as if to coo an infant. She lowered her voice even more. "The necklace, Monsieur. Already, we have spoken too long."

A mere second later, the airy quality of the call went silent, and Max knew Indigo had hung up. He looked at the phone and confirmed so by the return of his home screen. "Damn." Before he could set the phone down, it rang. He figured it was Indigo calling back and moved to press the talk button. In the instant before his finger touched the phone he saw the name Gary Richards flashing on screen. He did not wish to speak with Gary, but he was too fast for his own good. His finger tapped the answer key. *Shit.* He could hear Gary breathing on the phone. After an awkward moment, Max finally spoke. "Hello."

"Max, hey, it's Gary."

Eight hundred miles above, in the expansiveness of Earth's orbit, Aurelia and Sutekh accessed the chip around Max's neck. By simply reading his vitals, they could see how agitated he had become. Embedded deep within the device, there was also a vibratory chip that enabled them to monitor conversations within a reasonable proximity. Together she and Sutekh listened.

"What's up, man?"

"Well, a couple of things. You probably won't believe it, but I've been keeping my eye on the news to see how your dad's doing. I haven't heard anything recently though, so I figured I'd give you a call to find out if he's okay."

"Dude, I'm sorry if I was rude that night."

"Don't fret, Max. If anybody should be apologizing, it's me."

"I appreciate that, Gary. His injuries are pretty severe, but he's expected to recover."

"That's great news. I'm happy to hear it. I know your dad's out of commission, but I was hoping maybe you and I could meet and talk shop."

Sutekh and Aurelia shared a glance as they continued to monitor the conversation. Gazing through the enormous picture window, they observed Earth with its uncanny resemblance to the eye of a giant cyclops keeping watch across the heavens.

"Look, Gary, I've been in DC a lot, but I can't commit to a time just yet. Once I get a better idea of my schedule, maybe we can meet in the early evening sometime."

"Perfect. That sounds great."

"All right, good. Shoot me a reminder over the next week or so, and we'll set something up."

"Fantastic, man. I have some traveling scheduled, but I'll be back in DC in a few weeks. I'll have my people text yours."

"Sounds good, Gary, I'll speak to you soon." Max hit end call, and the transmission fell silent.

In the interstellar spacecraft hundreds of miles above, Aurelia finally spoke. "Things are moving faster than expected."

"Aurelia," Sutekh pleaded, joining her at the huge window, "we have done everything we can."

The tall blonde gazed through the glass, watching Earth in its obscurity. "I'm not so sure about that. I need time to figure this out."

Sutekh turned away from the window as Aurelia proceeded to the center of the room. With a wave of her hand, the copper piping assembly rose from the floor and snapped into pyramid configuration. Aurelia slid inside of it, sat upon her knees and closed her eyes.

Without a word, Sutekh returned his gaze to the blue planet below. Aurelia opened an eye to briefly observe him. Closing it again, she took a deep breath and prepared to enter deep meditation. Sooner or later, the answer of how to proceed would present itself. For Earth's sake, she hoped it would be sooner.

CHAPTER 10

The underground was like a different universe for Max, where he received his education on the real world and many of its harsher realities. For several weeks more, he commuted between Chicago and DC, studying the ways of the Rizick Group. As it turned out, today's Rizick members had inherited an age-old system of masters and servants. While the masses of the West often didn't realize it, the majority of their lives had been dedicated to servitude every bit as much as the workers of the Third World. The Nibirians' most ingenious accomplishment had been convincing an entire faction of laborers that they were in fact free. Just as children sought to please their parents, workers strove to impress superiors, or anyone more successful, with the hope of climbing higher up the ladder. The "survival of the fittest" mentality had much more to do with Anunnaki design than it did with any truth in Darwinian laws.

Max's first Clean Slate study took more than three days to finish. A series of other reports commissioned by Demetrius was also made available to him. He spot-checked a pile of binders and chose an oversized one with multiple analyses on the problem of overpopulation. Max briefly glanced at Otto and his trainers before flipping to a section to read,

STATISTICAL HYPOTHESES AND ASSERTIONS: To date, only one group has attempted mass population reductions approaching the volumes discussed in Clean Slate. Through both trial and error, the Nazi regime discovered the environmental nightmare of mass depopulation and the difficult logistics required to dispose of human casualties in high volume. Mass graves used for cadaver disposal were proven to be systemically infeasible, giving rise to the use of funerary ovens, an only slightly superior solution. CONCLUSION: A slower, more manageable remedy is preferred.

Otto and the others busied themselves, mostly on their phones, while Max skipped to another section of the report and read.

VIRAL SOLUTIONS:

1977 PILOT PROGRAM #13 – ACUTE RETROVIRAL SYNDROME (aka 9ARS6713): Introduced in 1977, ARS was developed to slowly compromise the human immune system. Because of its slow-acting nature, ARS is considered one of several more manageable solutions in the gradual population erosion of less desirable communities. In the 1980s, ARS received the nomenclature Human Immunodeficiency Virus, or HIV.

2002 PILOT PROGRAM #43 – SEVERE ACUTE RESPIRATORY SYNDROME (aka SARS6943): Coronavirus SARS6943 is considered by many to be a swifter-moving, more virulent agent. Due to its increased efficiency, the most practical target locations exist in various parts of Asia and the Pacific Isles.

PILOT TIME LINE: January – June 2003

CONCLUSIONS: Abandon Project. While the virus spreads quickly, it has been determined that SARS6943 suffers from instability. Within a matter of weeks, the agent mutated into something less potent than intended.

To better manage a circumstance where even more deaths were anticipated, the Rizick Group had invested large sums of research and development money on a series of slower, more methodical solutions. It appeared the HIV program had been designed to gradually chip away at undesirable populations: gays, drug users and carefully selected ethnic groups had all been targeted with the disease. The unpredictable nature of human conduct, however, hadn't fully been taken into consideration. Bisexuality and other crossover behaviors had opened the door for the disease to commute into unintended populations. Further, the rapidity at which HIV worked was also deemed inefficient. After less than a decade, the HIV program was abandoned, but its legacy was converted into a multi-billion dollar industry, and other more expeditious solutions were being sought.

Max read further and discovered that like HIV and SARS, the H1N1 virus, also known as swine flu, had also been cooked up in Rizick Group laboratories. Each viral agent had carefully been developed and introduced into select geographic locations to test for efficacy in the erosion of overpopulated communities.

Max closed the report. In the dark corners of his mind, he questioned why a collection of individuals with enormous resources would expend such significant amounts of time and money on subjects like genocide. Max shook his head.

Like a welcome distraction, his phone chimed with a text message from Gary Richards. It appeared he had been back in town a few days and was following up for the appointment he had requested a few weeks earlier. Gary was hardly at the top of Max's list of people to meet, but today, it would be a pleasant change. After several SMS exchanges, they agreed to meet at a gastropub of Gary's choosing. Max slipped his phone back inside his pocket. He did not wish to reveal details about his meeting with Gary, especially since Gary's name had been found on the blacklist that Rosalee gave him.

After a cursory glance at the report he'd been skimming, he turned to Otto and his trainers and made a request. "Do you guys mind if we wrap up a little early today? I'm pretty wiped out." When no one protested, Max quickly gathered his things and ascended to street level. He exited the National Archives Building and checked his phone for messages. There was a text from Gary with the address of their meeting point. He hopped in a cab, and 30 minutes later was seated across from Gary, who gave him an enormous grin.

"I appreciate you coming, especially on such short notice."

"No worries. My meeting finished early today."

Gary smiled, punctuating the conversation with an awkward pause. "How're things with you and Brigitte? You said she might be pregnant."

"Yeah." Max wasn't exactly certain that he trusted Gary with this news. "It was just a scare."

"Things were pretty tense at that birthday party you invited me to."

"Yeah, she was pissed because my dad kept needing me to do things, even before his accident."

"How is your dad, by the way? They ever find out what caused that whole explosion thing?"

"It's still under investigation." Max sat back, quietly remembering the way he had learned of his father's accident. "That was a trip, finding out in your hotel. He's doing a lot better, though. I have to fill in for him here and there, at least until he's back on his feet."

"The prodigal son, huh?"

Gary locked Max in his gaze, wearing a lascivious grin. Max looked back blankly, curious as to why his old friend had summoned him. Finally, Gary shook the smirk from his face and continued.

"I'm glad he's getting better. Look, the reason I asked to meet is this: you know I've been lobbying for big pharma for more than a few years now. Aren't there a few drug companies under the Battenberg Industries umbrella?"

"Yeah. But I'm not at all involved in that part of the business."

"I figured that, but there still might be some nice synchronicities worth exploring. Maybe when your dad's better I can pitch them to him. The issues I'm advocating will help all of big pharma. Every year, we have to block some initiative that might allow overseas companies to push their cheaper, generic formulas. In past years, my colleagues and I have been pretty successful at shortening trial periods for new products."

While Gary pitched his agenda, Max's mind proceeded to wander. If Project Clean Slate passed the next Rizick vote, none of Gary's spiel would matter to anyone. Max was still unclear if the numbers proposed by Clean Slate, the billions of lives projected to be eradicated, were to be executed in a matter of months or years. Either way, the majority of big pharma's clientele, or of anyone's clientele, for that matter, would soon be vanishing from the globe.

Gary continued through his speech, which he had likely delivered dozens of times before. Max feigned interest, catching glimpses of his agenda. Big pharma didn't want cheaper drug options readily available to its consumers, nor did it want lengthy testing periods for new drugs that could be potentially harmful.

Max found it difficult to focus, and his attention continued to stray. Whenever it was opportune, he nodded and smiled until Gary wrapped things up about how he and Battenberg Industries might be useful to one another.

"Look, Gary, people think because of the family name that all Battenbergs are somehow plugged in to the inner workings of every company. That's not how it works."

"Yeah, I know you're on the publishing side of things."

"To be honest, I don't know a thing about big pharma, but I can make a call to someone who might." *Rosalee.*

"That'd be fantastic, if you could."

"I'll work on it this week. If you haven't heard anything from me by the end of next week, give me a jingle, okay?"

"Sure thing. I appreciate it, Max."

"Listen, I have to get going. I'm heading to Chicago." Max scooted back from the table and offered Gary a friendly hug before excusing himself to catch the next underground train. Even though he had already made the journey several times, he still found it astonishing that the trip could be made so expeditiously.

Less than an hour later, Max emerged onto the streets of Chicago. An evening breeze swept in across the lake, caressing his face. The gust did nothing to soothe his conscience, however, which was growing heavier with every instruction about Rizick's inner workings.

During their last rendezvous at Gary's Chicago hotel, Max had been terribly gauche. He had slipped and mentioned Brigitte's pregnancy before they even confirmed it. Then, immediately afterward, he had spurned Gary's advances. During that awkward moment, they had learned from a newscast about his father's injuries in the Brazil explosion. Thankfully, this visit had gone more smoothly. In theory, Max was not opposed to helping Gary, but he wondered whether any of it would truly matter.

CHAPTER 11

As if on autopilot, Max caught a cab across town. In no time, he was standing before the Golden Arch Yoga Studio. Nearly three weeks had passed since his last interaction with AJ, but the man's previous utterings still reverberated in his head. Deep down, he wished for an intelligent discourse about the atrocities of Clean Slate, but he doubted someone like Otto would be of much help. Nor did he dare speak with Brigitte or his friend Ted, since he had offered a blood oath of secrecy during his initiation. Further, Indigo had spouted warnings to Ted and Brigitte, predicting doom and gloom if they chose to continue their association with him. Max wanted to spare them that possibility.

He glanced down the street for AJ, but the homeless man was nowhere in sight. Max recalled the calm state he had achieved with his first yoga session. *Maybe if I do another, AJ'll be here by the time I finish.*

He approached the studio entrance, where an enormous golden art-deco statue of a woman in the yogic bridge pose served as an archway. He passed through the double doors beneath her, but paid little attention to the Vitruvian Man poster that was affixed to the glass. Upon it, all seven colors of the chakras were illuminated along the figure's spine.

Inside the studio, Max purchased a T-shirt, yoga pants and a drawstring bag to store his things. He attended the next Hatha lesson and, through a series of deep standing postures, was able to release a great deal of tension. When he exited the studio an hour later, Max immediately spotted AJ sitting cross-legged in his usual spot, with the red plaid blanket draped over his legs. He strode over to him enthusiastically. "I didn't see you earlier. I was hoping I'd catch you after my class."

AJ smiled warmly, looking up at Max. "The virtues of spontaneity. Some call it the backbone of life."

"I can't believe I'm back here again." While AJ did not stand, his presence generated a gentle calm that Max found soothing. Unlike his time underground, Max found his residual tensions melting away. "It's a little freaky, right?"

AJ cocked his head to the side, questioning, "How so?"

"If someone had told me I'd be here, talking to some guy on the sidewalk…" Max hunted for the right words, but AJ interrupted before he could find them.

"People pass by me every day and discount that I have anything to offer. We all have gifts to share, even if it's just company or companionship." AJ lifted his hands and motioned around. "In material terms, I have nothing; this is true. And for this," AJ lowered his hands and rested them on top of one another in his lap, "I am more often than not ignored."

A group of patrons, perhaps from another yoga class, exited the building and kindly greeted AJ. Although he was seated, his back was perfectly erect, but his body hardly seemed rigid. On the contrary, AJ seemed perfectly relaxed.

"I need to speak with someone, preferably someone I don't know. I hope you don't mind, but I thought of you." Max looked around nervously, not desiring to be overheard. "Is it okay if we go somewhere?"

AJ stood, and his blanket fell to the ground. He retrieved and carefully folded it, then stowed it in a small opening in the wall. "Let's go for a walk."

Max was pleased by the idea of a promenade. For one, privacy would allow him to converse freely. But he also noticed the return of the sage stranger's pungent body odor. The perfumed aroma he had created weeks earlier was now gone. Instead, the stench of soiled clothes and compromised hygiene had returned. However, as they turned the corner and headed down another block, Max finally began to unload.

"Last week, you said things I didn't quite understand. I was hoping you could explain."

AJ looked at Max with a quiet intensity. "Your name is Max, right?" Max nodded, prompting AJ to continue. "I'm not sure what you think I know. It's not like I've unlocked the secrets to the universe or something. And even if I had, I'm not so sure I'd be able to share them with you."

"Come on," Max had an expression of incredulity written across his face, "What you did that day… you zapped me with some kind of superpower or something." Max fixed AJ in his gaze. "Be honest. You know stuff. You told me last time that the answers would be here." Max lifted a fist and placed it over his heart.

AJ nodded. "Yes, the heart center. But don't forget the third eye." Without hesitation AJ pointed to the space between Max's eyebrows.

"Those are chakras, right?"

AJ smiled as he and Max strolled into a nearby park. "Yes, that's what we call them. There are seven. That's a sacred number, you know."

"I looked them up online." Max thought back to his experience in the Pyramid of the Moon. After he had swallowed the strange drink, he had seen lights appearing up and down the spines of everyone there. On each participant, he recalled differences in color and intensity. On his guide, Elizar, they were stifled and dull, but they were bright and shimmering on the small baby. Max fixed his gaze on AJ again. "I feel like I might've seen them, but I'm not a 100 percent sure what they are."

"Would you describe yourself as spiritual, Max?"

Although hesitant at first, Max grew pensive. "Yeah, I guess. That means different things to different people, though, so…"

AJ tilted his head slightly with a frown, letting Max know he didn't necessarily agree. "A universal truth is universal. One of them being that chakras are portals from the spiritual side into the physical one. In order to manifest love, here, in this plane, it has to come through the heart."

"And they're all different colors, right?"

"They are," AJ nodded. "It's when they're blocked that their color and function vary. But you would need an extremely heightened spiritual sensitivity in order to perceive this."

Max thought of the anxiety he had been feeling when underground, and how completely opposite he felt strolling next to AJ. More than a few people gawked at them, and Max understood what a strange picture the two of them must have made.

"Unless you know something of the esoteric, chakras are not an easy concept. Think about airplanes and how they're made. A metal skeleton. On top of that, an electrical system, hydraulics, pathways for fuel, exhaust, sewage… And all of that is encased in the fuselage, hidden from the eye. The human body, while more complex, is not so different. The way we see the plane, is how most see the human body: just the exterior. But there is so much more to it. There's the causal body, the astral body, the chakras... Similar to an airplane, all of it is enclosed in the physical form, hidden from view."

"You say they can be blocked, but how do you influence something you can't even see?"

AJ lifted his arms and pointed toward the buildings and cars around them. "Just look around. Everything you see is how. There's machinery in place, and we're all cogs in its wheels. When we don't participate in the *system*, we suffer, largely through fear... of poverty, fear of loneliness, fear of homelessness and rejection." AJ wagged a finger at Max. "Fear is the key. Even the strongest cogs in the wheel are made witness to the punishment of others. This is how you nurture fear, isn't it? If I witness someone being fired, or maybe their salary gets reduced, or they lose their home, or their car, there's fear it could happen to me. This keeps us in our place and prevents us from fully manifesting our desires. That's how you block a chakra. You stifle it using fear."

Max gazed at the small park, which contained a fenced-in, triangular section for a dog run. Both areas were plush with trees and grass, one of Chicago's tiny oases. "When people don't conform to the system, then what?"

AJ studied the dog owners throwing Frisbees and tennis balls. Without hesitation, their pets ran and retrieved them. "Many of them look like me," AJ declared, turning to Max with an intense stare. "Others live on the fringe, out in the wilderness, off the grid. More often than not, life is unkind to a nonconformist. Mostly because there's a system in place that's designed to utilize the masses for the goals of a select few. The majority of us go to school, then we get jobs and work," AJ smiled coyly, "usually, to enrich people like you. Don't get me wrong, I have nothing against an honest day's work. But it should also enhance the life of the worker to some equitable degree. And what if our desire is to choose a spiritual or artistic path? How does the saying go, 'you have to suffer for your craft?' I suppose, sometimes, there are beautiful lessons even in that."

Max turned to AJ, unable to figure him out. "Are you suggesting you're living this way deliberately?"

"We all have our path. Whether *you* see it or not, I am on mine."

Max nodded. "Somehow, I feel like I might understand, except for that whole chakra thing, I'm still a little fuzzy on that."

"No one would expect you to grasp it in one conversation. Just know without them," AJ motioned at the city around them, "none of this would exist. Like I said before," he lifted a hand and placed it over his chest, "the heart chakra governs our ability to give and receive love. When it is closed off, we build walls instead of bridges. Rather than compassion, we offer selfishness and insensitivity." AJ raised his hand and placed it over his throat. "Then you have the throat chakra, which empowers us to feel that our voices matter and that our opinions possess validity. When it is stifled, or closed off, the opposite becomes true. We learn to fear the sound of our own voice, which diminishes us, like our beliefs hold little to no value."

Max listened intently, trying to absorb the message in AJ's words. "Didn't you say there were seven? What about the other five?"

AJ smirked. "I wonder if there's a *Chakras for Dummies*."

"Thanks," Max answered with a touch of sarcasm. He wasn't exactly sure when, but AJ's pungent odor had vanished again. During their last encounter he had been hesitant to touch AJ, but now he felt driven to place a hand on his shoulder as a sign of affection.

AJ smirked again before he spoke. "Last time, we discussed meditation. How's that going?"

"Not so great. After that thing you did, I have moments that feel kind of like trances. Other than that, it's too difficult to clear my head."

"Modern science has confirmed that meditation can lower blood pressure, slow the heart rate. It can establish a sense of overall wellbeing, especially if there's turmoil going on. It can be a light in dark times." AJ studied Max, whose face seemed twisted with worry. "Isn't that how you feel now, Max?"

Max cracked a half smile and peered into space, not wishing to betray any specifics of his concerns.

AJ took note of the discord before he continued. "There is

a meditation I know. It's a simple technique that activates the chakras. I can show you if you want. It'll only take a minute."

Max felt leery, recalling how AJ had zapped him before. "I don't know, man, after what happened last time..."

"I understand. We can try another time, if you prefer."

Max considered AJ's offer. On more than a few occasions, a sort of spontaneous meditation had overtaken him. Other than that, he had no idea how meditation was supposed to occur. "It'll only take a minute, right?"

AJ nodded.

Growing bolder, Max caved to the idea. "Okay, I guess. Let's do it."

Together, he and AJ walked to an area at the other end of the park. AJ extended a hand, motioning toward a bench. "You should sit."

Max took a seat and looked to AJ for instruction.

AJ, who was still standing, evaluated Max. "Can you cross your legs?"

Max pulled his legs up onto the bench and fumbled to cross them. Satisfied, AJ continued. "Sit up straight, and imagine your spine as an antenna." AJ observed Max comply. "Elongate your torso even further, stretching high for the best reception your spine can receive."

Max did as instructed and sat up straighter, lifting his head toward the sky.

"Now lower your chin, and close your eyes. If you prefer them only slightly closed, like you're squinting, you can do that too. Then breathe in, and exhale in normal fashion. We're going to start with the root chakra. Visualize it in the tailbone, at the base of your spine. Its color is red, and it's spinning, pulsating..."

Max carefully followed AJ's instructions. He visualized a light similar to the ones he had seen in the Pyramid of Moon — red and swirling.

"Envision that light pulsating and enlarging, glowing brighter and more brilliant. Imagine it illuminating this bench and other areas of the park. Hold this newer, brighter chakra in place as you shift your attention to the chakra just above it in your groin. This next one is orange and swirling, but it is not as bright as you have just made the root chakra. Remember to hold the intensity of the root chakra in place as you visualize this next one also glowing more brightly, like a miniature sun, swirling faster and faster, thousands of times per second."

To Max's amazement, he was envisioning what AJ asked him to. It helped that he had seen chakras during his initiation in Mexico City. He also thought of the Vitruvian Man poster back at the yoga center where chakras were depicted in colorful illustration.

AJ continued guiding Max through the exercise. Together, they visualized the yellow solar plexus chakra in the abdomen; the green heart chakra in the center of chest and the blue throat chakra just below the Adam's apple. Then they reached the third eye chakra between the eyebrows. Max envisioned the area engulfed in the color of indigo, growing larger and more brilliant, twirling with even more intensity.

Until now, Max had imagined the process in his mind's eye. His visualization of the third eye, however, triggered something. His pineal gland, which Aurelia had been working to free from its calcified shell, began excreting a hormone. Max imagined the twirling purple mass of the third-eye, and a sense of his eyes opening to a brilliant white light overtook him. It was disorienting at first since his eyes were still tightly closed. *How can this be? It feels like I can see.*

To his shock, the blinding whiteness slipped into focus the same way the eyes adjust when exiting from a dark space into the bright light of day. What Max saw next astounded him.

CHAPTER 12

The palace in the Abzu, while nowhere near as lavish as the one in Eridu, still had its appeal. Located on the southern horn of the continent, it offered a perfect view of the ocean. Each chamber and terrace held some resemblance to the ones in Eridu, but they were smaller and fewer of them existed atop the seven-level ziggurat of the building.

Enki stood on the terrace balcony, staring across the ocean. A succession of tall waves crashed ashore, battering the cliffs until a residue of foam was left behind to make its retreat. Normally, he would have found this setting relaxing, but that was not the case this day.

Ninmah rushed outside onto the terrace, her face flushed with incredulity. She stammered, "I-I... I can't believe you're upset about this. I thought you would be pleased."

"No, Mah, I am not. I cannot even fathom that you would believe this account from your assistant Sud."

"Why would I not? She is one of my finest. If she proclaims that Enlil took her, then that is what he did."

"Oh, I trust that he had her. It's the *against her will* part I'm not so convinced about."

"For over a decade you've prayed for Enlil's removal from leadership. How is it you can be displeased by such an accusation? I spoke with Enlil moments before the attack, and Sud came to me immediately after. When I confronted him..." Ninmah couldn't help but feel flustered by Enki's reaction, which was exactly the opposite of what she had expected. "Enki, there's no doubt in my mind he is guilty of this. And in some way you and I are also to blame."

"Ha!" Enki spat out the laugh like a wad of phlegm. "What foolishness is this you speak?"

"You know very well how infantile Enlil can be. He was perturbed by your ploy for father's favor. In fact, I might venture to say he was furious. He made advances when I visited his chambers. And I rebuffed him." Ninmah's attention wandered into the distance where hostile ocean waves were crashing ashore.

"In beauty, very few compare to Sud. It was her misfortune that she stumbled upon Enlil in the hall."

"I fully grasp why you believe I should be happy. But I have labored so tirelessly since my arrival here. Then to be forced into the Abzu… You may not comprehend this, but if Enlil falls, I wish it to be from my own devices. Not because of the whims of some silly girl."

"You and Enlil are not so different, you know? Taking what you want no matter the expense. When will this stop, Enki?"

Enki didn't wish for an argument, so he stepped closer to Ninmah and grasped her hands in his own. He placed his face near to hers and spoke softly in her ear. "Your intentions are noble, Mah. Don't think I don't see that. It's just that things have been set in motion that I wish to see to fruition, on my own terms."

"But this is superfluous. Should he be found guilty, what I've done will result in precisely the same end, and quite a bit more expeditiously, I might add." Ninmah pulled her hands free from Enki's and stepped back, creating distance between them. After a brief respite, she stepped forward again, waving a fist in Enki's face. "This is not your battle, Enki! Enlil may be my full-blooded brother, but he shall be removed from Eridu, perhaps even banished from this planet altogether." Ninmah peered into Enki's eyes with determination, but it was clear he was still displeased. "You must promise you will vote to convict him. To do otherwise would be an insult to me and to Sud."

Enki's reluctance was ineffable, but he finally softened in order to clear the air. "Of course, Mah, I will do as you wish. But you must understand why this hardly feels like a victory."

"If a return to Eridu is what you desire, you shall have it. To execute this goal in such a manner should be of little consequence to you." A strong coastal gust swept in from the ocean, caressing Enki's face and whipping Ninmah's hair. In symbolic fashion, it also served to clear the air. She took her tresses and bundled them into a bun. "I have asked Enlil to bring Ninurta here."

For more than a moment, there was nothing but the sound of the waves crashing and the whistling of the wind. Finally, Enki turned away from the ocean to face Ninmah. "I know Ninurta is your son, but you must understand how it impacts me to bring him here."

"I do." Wavering at first, Ninmah remained resolute. "But as you say, he is my son."

Enki's demeanor shifted as he turned his gaze back to the ocean. "So rarely are we afforded our choice of partner; you know this. But you and I, we chose one another. I believed us fortunate for this." A spring of emotion filled Enki's heart, but he remained careful in his selection of words. "But Enlil, as is his way, interfered, and our union was destroyed by the birth of that child."

"Enki," Ninmah's voice was cautious yet insistent. "His name is Ninurta."

"I have every confidence that your pride in him is well placed." A deepening disdain slipped into Enki's voice. "But the sight of him evokes nothing but dark memories for me. We are never to be king and queen. And while I try not to, I will always resent this."

"Enki..." Ninmah's voice was tainted with remorse.

"Ninurta may very well be an ideal son, but he is loyal to his father... to Enlil. To bring him here undermines everything I have set out to achieve. I must send for my own son then." Once again, Enki found himself in defense mode, trying to determine his next move. "Yes. I shall encourage Marduk to come and look after my interests."

"As you wish, Enki. They are cousins. They enjoy each other's company very much. We shall all be one big happy family then," Ninmah affirmed with an effort at conviction. She took Enki by the hand. "We must prepare for our departure. The tribunal awaits us in Eridu."

Without another word, Enki and Ninmah abandoned the veranda and retreated to their chambers. Within the hour they would need to board the transport. Beforehand, Enki made haste and sent word to his son Marduk on Mars. He had to be prepared for Ninurta's arrival. *Their love child*, he thought with disgust. His nephew, Enlil's son.

Back on Nibiru, after his chance to marry Ninmah had been dashed, Enki had agreed to a new arrangement. In order to ease political tension, Damkina, daughter of the deposed despot Alalu, had been suggested as a potential wife for Enki. This union was a peace offering to the fallen monarch, as it afforded Alalu's clan to continue as power brokers in Nibiru's royal hierarchy. Even though he didn't feel he truly had a choice, Enki had agreed. He held no great emotion for Damkina, but the decision seemed sound for both of them and their upward mobility. In the end, happiness had engulfed him when she provided an heir: their son, Marduk, who was also Alalu's grandchild.

To further placate Alalu, Anu had offered a leadership role on the small red planet called Mars. When gold was extracted from Earth, much of it had to be transported there, where a modest enclave had been constructed. Alalu had full ownership of the outpost, and his grandson, Marduk, had been dispatched there to assist with the final leg of transport to their home planet, Nibiru.

Now that Ninurta was expected on Earth, Enki needed to level the playing field. He needed Marduk at his side. *Father and son against father and son.* He was certain Marduk would be pleased. The child was strong with a solid constitution, but he had suffered due to the strained relationship between his parents' families. A paternal grandfather who had come to power by unseating the maternal one was at the heart of a sticky situation, at best.

Marduk, who like his father had strong opinions, often held his tongue for fear of offending one particular side of his family. *Once he arrives, he will finally be able to play a larger role.* Enki smiled, realizing with clarity that a much larger plan might come into play.

Minutes later, he and Ninmah descended to the airstrip on the landward side of the ziggurat. His pilot, Abgal, had readied one of the more comfortable transports. During the short journey, Enki and Ninmah spoke very little, each spending the majority of the trip staring out at Earth's plush landscape.

Fortunately, the tribunal lasted less than an hour. First, Ninmah's assistant, Sud, offered her version of Enlil's attack. He was then allowed to defend himself, which he hardly attempted. Enlil's testimony revealed that he felt Sud was beneath him. He considered her a form of chattel that could be taken for use at his whim. In no time, Enki and the other judges realized that Sud and Ninmah had both spoken the truth. Enlil, who felt entitled to anything he desired, including a woman's body, appeared clueless as the tribunal began its deliberation.

Enki had secretly hoped his half brother would offer a stronger defense. Enlil had knocked him low by stealing Eridu and exiling him to the Abzu. It had ultimately been Enki's wish to return the favor. He gazed across the chamber at Enlil, who was too pitiful to even grasp the punishment that was about to be delivered. Yes, Enlil would finally be leaving Eridu even if it was not according to his plan. *A shame*, he thought, as the guilty vote came down.

"You cannot do this!" Enlil proclaimed. "Our home atmosphere depends on these operations. They were a shambles when I arrived, mismanaged by a pretender, a charlatan, a fraud..." Enlil stared across the room at Enki, who remained seated on the panel of judges.

Enki couldn't be sure if his half sibling was truly upset or just practicing outrage. Ninmah stood to deliver his sentence, but Enki stopped her. "You mustn't, Mah. It will crush Ninurta if you do."

Ninmah considered Enki's assertion and knew it to be true. She also knew Enki's motives were hardly as altruistic as he would have her believe.

"Please," Enki pleaded, "allow me." Ninmah took her seat, and Enki continued with the declaration of Enlil's punishment. "Brother, for the crime of rape, you are hereby exiled." Like a fountain spring, a deep satisfaction arose in Enki, bursting from his pores. "You must vacate the royal quarters at once and leave Eridu by sundown. From this day forward, you are hereby banished, not only from Eridu but also from the Abzu, or any other Nibirian settlement."

"You can't be serious! Where do you expect I will go? I can't return home now."

"Keep in mind, brother, you are banished from any Nibirian settlement." Enki hadn't expected it, but the taste of victory was sweet. Perhaps Ninmah had been right to organize a coup. "I'm afraid this includes our home planet. This is the council's decree. Is it understood?"

Enlil looked desperate. Although a devious schemer, he was ill prepared for a penalty such as this. "And where would the council have me go?"

Enki stood and waved a hand in the air, prompting a cadre of security officers to arrive at Enlil's side. "These men will help you gather your things. I will have my pilot Abgal deliver you somewhere among the beasts of this land. Or if you prefer, arrangements can be made for you on Mars." He approached Enlil and leaned toward him, holding his voice at a whisper. "Perhaps now you understand that coming here was a mistake."

"Ninmah…" Enlil implored, never having felt such desperation. "This cannot be your decision."

Ninmah looked down, unable to face her full-blooded brother. She eventually spoke. "I fear, brother, because of our status, that we must be held to a higher standard. The decision has been made."

"But where am I to go?" Enlil demanded. "Where am I to go?"

Enki turned to the guards surrounding Enlil. "Be forewarned, he will sabotage anything he can before he departs. You must keep an eye on him until he is safely aboard the transport. I will make sure Abgal delivers him somewhere safe."

Unable to believe the chain of events, Enlil lunged at Enki but was instead escorted kicking and screaming from the room. "Unhand me! I am first heir to Nibiru's throne! I must speak to my father at once! Unhand me, I say! This is heresy!"

A sense of fulfillment overcame Enki as he heard Enlil's exit, his animated voice growing fainter with each step. He approached Abgal, who had been his pilot since childhood. "Take him somewhere far from here, where he'll be safely out of view."

"Of course, your Highness."

"He may need prodding, but make sure the two of you are airborne by sundown."

"Very well, your Grace."

As the panel of judges packed up, Ninmah looked Enki's way. She could see that he was pleased, but she hardly shared his glee in the exile of a devious brother who also happened to be the father of her child.

CHAPTER 13

When he considered the day's events, Enlil felt numb. *Exiled.*
How could this be? It seemed only yesterday that he arrived on
Earth and wrought havoc with Enki's gold operation. Seven days
was all he needed to banish Enki to the Abzu for his incompetence.
Now, thirty-four years later, a detail of guards was marching him
to his quarters like a common criminal.

They had barely allowed time for him to gather a few things.
The evil scoundrel Enki! It was humiliating that Nibirian guards
were being used to escort him to the airfield. Just this morning,
he was king of the castle. Now, as the sun sank toward the horizon, it appeared his rule had now come to an end.

The guards marched Enlil into Eridu's interior courtyard. Plush
green grass and perfectly manicured hedges took the shape of
geometrical marvels: cylindrical, square and triangular bushes
held perfect symmetry throughout the grounds. Topiary workers and other more prominent Nibirian artists, who were staffed
in Eridu, gawked and pointed as he and his escorts reached a
large gate exiting into the garden's outer perimeter.

To Enlil's dismay, Enki and his pilot, Abgal, appeared outside the gate. *He has come to gloat.* Off to the side, one of Nibiru's
poshest transports was parked on the runway. The sight of Enki
normally made Enlil's blood boil, but this evening he felt numb.
Scoffing at his escorts, he exited through the gate and approached
his half brother more calmly than he would have guessed. "You
are planning your return here, no doubt," Enlil proclaimed.

"Perhaps. I have not yet decided. It is important that I continue the gold extraction, both here and in the Abzu. I'm sure
you would agree this is a priority."

Enlil narrowed his eyes at Enki. "You know this isn't over. I
am father's true successor, and I mean to see this through."

Enki gazed across Eridu's landscape, as the sun dipped beneath
the horizon. "I left you Nibiru, but that wasn't enough. You should
not have come here, Enlil. But now that you have, you are correct, you shall see this through."

Enki nodded to Enlil's escorts who, in turn, pressed Enlil away.

Although reluctant, the convicted royal proceeded toward the ship. Enki observed briefly before darting to cut his brother off at the onramp.

"I know you won't comprehend it, but you brought this on yourself. It is hardly what I wanted."

Enlil, somewhat intrigued, studied the face of his half-sibling. "I find that rather difficult to believe."

Enki shrugged nonchalantly. "It is the truth nonetheless. It has been my intention to remove you from this planet, but not like this. Then again… whatever works." Enki turned and addressed his pilot. "Take him wherever he wishes, assuming it meets the terms of his exile."

As always, the half brothers had no love to display for each other, even if their exchange did not contain the vitriol of years past.

I will cooperate for now, Enlil thought, electing not to cause a ruckus.

Abgal, who was much shorter and squatter than either Enki or Enlil, motioned for the latter to board the transport. "Your Highness, if you would be so kind as to board, I will shuttle you to a location of your choosing."

Enlil cracked a smile, turning away from Enki to board the cruiser. After he disappeared inside, Enki patted Abgal on the shoulder.

"Make sure you deposit him somewhere safe and distant."

"As you wish, your Highness."

With a small click of his heels, Enki pivoted around and marched through the gate back into Eridu's gardens. Abgal followed Enlil into the ship, accompanied by a small flight crew.

The royal cruiser's main cabin felt more like one of Eridu's chambers and less like a transport. Its interior was plush with a dozen large cushioned armchairs, each like a royal throne. The cabin floor was a spacious mosaic of tiny ornate stones that formed the image of a griffin. The warm orange-yellow tones of sunset shone through oblong portal windows on the side of the ship.

On his way to the flight deck, Abgal approached Enlil. "Sir, would you like anything to eat or drink before we depart?"

"Just get this thing in the air. We can decide the rest later."

"Of course, your Highness." Abgal continued to the flight deck and prepared the ship for take-off.

Seated on his favorite terrace, Enki watched as the royal transport floated silently into the air. After a moment, it rocketed into the fading horizon. Without another thought, he sighed relief, breathing in the deep richness of Earth's atmosphere.

Tomorrow, I will take in the morning sun upon my terrace. Enki considered his earlier dispute with Ninmah. As it turned out, she was a formidable foe. She had set her mind to punish Enlil for his indiscretion, and within days he was exiled. Armed with a deep sense of contentment that her goal had assisted him with his, Enki retreated into the palace. Soon, his chambers would be readied, as workers hurried to eradicate every evidence that Enlil had ever been there.

While Enki was settling in at Eridu, Enlil was already hundreds of miles away at a cruising altitude of 30,000 meters. After placing the ship in the hands of his flight crew, Abgal returned to the main cabin to find Enlil staring into the night.

"Your Highness, it is already late. If you wish, I can bring us to a region of daylight, or we can establish a cruising orbit until you decide your pleasure."

Enlil studied Abgal's face a long moment. He was Enki's pilot, so he didn't feel particularly inspired to trust him. "My head is not clear as of now. There are sleeping chambers on this ship, are there not?"

"Of course, your Highness."

"Have one readied for me. After I've slept, then we will find a solution."

"I know it is not my place to speak, your Highness. But the tribunal's decision is a travesty of justice. You are the heir to our Lord Supreme Anu."

Finally, Abgal was grabbing Enlil's attention. The young monarch sat higher in his seat. "Yes. This is Enki's doing. But the other judges… they have vendettas against me too, including my sister."

Abgal had worked with Enki for many years, since Nibiru's

eldest prince had been a young boy. He even liked his commander, but he didn't envision a future with him. At least not the future he wished to have. Abgal was terribly ambitious and had been tied to Enki for entirely too long. He had even suffered through multiple decades in the Abzu. Now, through several strokes of luck, Nibiru's true heir was seated before him.

Deep down, Abgal knew it would be advantageous to align himself with Enlil. If the younger brother ever took the throne, he would then be in pole position for an infinitely more important role. For this reason, he would cater to Enlil the way a lackey attends to his master. *If only I could win his favor.*

"For how long have you been in my brother's service?"

"Since you two were very young. I realize, your Highness, that you and I have had little interaction. This is why I was pleased when Master Enki asked me to be your escort."

Enlil studied Abgal with the hint of a smile. "I see."

Abgal could see he was making progress with his master's brother. "If I might show you one thing, your Highness. Before we break orbit."

While his mind had not been clear earlier, Enlil found he was maneuvering, sizing Abgal up. *Perhaps this is a trick.* "I admit it is most intriguing that you propose to show me something."

Abgal smirked, revealing a side to him that was as devious as Enlil himself. "I trust you will find this fact even more poignant when you see what it is I have to show you."

"Very well. You shouldn't disappoint me, though. After the events of this day, I am scarcely in the mood."

Abgal flashed a smile that exuded confidence. "All things considered, I guarantee this won't disappoint."

After a moment's reflection, Enlil nodded, and Abgal retreated to the flight deck. From there, the pilot redirected the transport to a tall mountain peak. After a precarious landing, he led Enlil from the ship. Icy winds whipped across their faces as they descended the ship's ramp into snow. The freezing temperatures and rocky terrain annoyed Enlil, but he followed Abgal nonetheless, driven by a deep curiosity. Finally, Enlil stumbled, nearly falling face first into the icy terrain. Just as he recovered himself and readied his protest, Abgal brought him to a great cavernous opening.

Enlil hesitated at the mouth of the cave. *What if he intends to slay me?* Reaching down, he double-checked that a weapon was still on his belt. The dagger was not large, but it was sharp. Prepared to strike, if necessary, Enlil entered the cavern. He trailed Abgal with a hand lightly poised against the dagger's hilt. He had expected darkness to engulf him, but the soft glow of a bluish-green light illuminated the chamber.

When he saw the hidden items, Enlil was stunned and immediately forgot the cold and his suspicions. Alalu's weapons, the Atu-waa and the Ark were all stowed in the corner where Enki had left them, like countless hidden treasures.

Enlil turned to Abgal, whose expression was one of deep satisfaction. There wouldn't be many opportunities to impress someone of Enlil's stature but, this day, Abgal knew he had succeeded.

Enlil relaxed the hand above his dagger and crossed to Abgal's side. "The weapons Alalu seized."

"Yes, your Highness. This is where your brother has hidden them."

There was no doubt Enlil's mind was racing. "And the Atu-waa as well!" After an extended pause, he spoke. "Is this peak stable?"

"It should be, your Grace."

"But these cannot remain here. We must load them on the ship at once."

"Of course, your Grace. As you wish." Abgal headed toward the smallest item, the Atu-waa.

"No," Enlil interjected, "you must leave that for me. One wrong move, and we shall find our end. Help me with this instead."

Enlil crossed to the Ark and took hold of the handles on one side. Abgal lifted from the other side, and together they carted the gold box toward the cave's exit.

CHAPTER 14

Although he was unable to determine exactly why, Enki felt unsettled. Perhaps it was simply his ego. He had wished but failed to bring Enlil down on his own terms. Already a month had passed since Ninmah achieved the outcome he desired. In the end, Enlil was gone, banished, forever forbidden to show his face in the presence of other Nibirians. Enki should have been celebrating the fait accompli. Instead, a profound sense of unrest plagued him.

In need of comfort and reassurance, he left his chamber in search of Ninmah. At the threshold of her doorway, he could hear a woman's sobs. It was her assistant Sud.

"There, there," Ninmah consoled, "a child isn't the end of the world."

"But, Mistress, you are of royal lineage. Even so, you were impacted by such a circumstance, disallowed of your marriage to Master Enki. Certainly, there can be no hope for me."

"It is true, I did not wish for a child, but I have no regrets." Ninmah was quiet a moment before she continued. "Should you bear a man-child, he will be Ninurta's half brother. Have you thought of that?"

Enki hesitated, then pushed through into Ninmah's chamber. "Mah?"

Both Ninmah and Sud were seated on a chaise. Ninmah had an arm around Sud and was gently stroking her hair. Both women turned, surprised to see Enki standing at the apartment's entrance.

"I apologize if I have interrupted something," Enki exclaimed.

Sud immediately stood and composed herself. "No, that's fine, your Highness. Her Grace was simply kind enough to offer me counsel. But I have many things to do."

Ninmah took Sud's hand. "Are you sure?"

"Of course, your Grace. I am certain. All will be fine." Without wasting a moment's time, Sud gathered her things and exited.

Enki smiled at Ninmah with contrived enthusiasm. "I was bored and figured we might dine together."

"I suppose that would be acceptable," Ninmah replied.

"Very well. Should I have the food sent up, or shall we meet in the hall?"

"Why not have it sent up? We can eat here in my chambers," Ninmah quipped with a curt smile.

"Very well. Excuse me…" Enki hurried into the corridor and quickly caught up to Sud. "My lady, might I have a word with you?"

Sud stopped and quickly swiped at each cheek to conceal her tears. The last time a royal brother requested her time, it had ended in disaster. But just as before, there was no way she could refuse. She forced a smile to compose herself, even though her heart was sinking. "Of course, your Highness."

Instead of returning to his chamber, which was near to Ninmah's, he led Sud into a guest apartment off the main hall. Once inside, he closed the door and latched it, exactly as Enlil had done only weeks before.

Enki quickly spotted Sud's concern. "Please don't fret, child. I am not my brother."

Sud immediately blushed. Fortunately, in seeking out Ninmah, his timing could not have been more opportune. Enki urged Sud to sit on one of two adjoining chaises before he took a seat on the other.

"I would be remiss if I didn't reveal that I overheard your conversation with my sister. Would I be mistaken to assume my brother's attack has resulted in conception?"

Sud bowed her head, overcome with shame. "Yes, your Lordship, I am with child."

Enki considered Ninmah's pregnancy and their failed marriage attempt. *But this is different.* "You might recall, when Ninmah discovered she and Enlil were with child, there was no simple solution. Your situation is different, however. I believe there is an end which could benefit you and Enlil alike."

Sud seemed genuinely confused by Enki's proclamation. "What do you mean, your Lordship?"

Enki remained matter-of-fact in his delivery. "You must realize my brother's assault, and now this pregnancy, will obliterate any prospect you have of finding a suitable mate. Let's just say the sensational nature of Enlil's tribunal has rendered your particular circumstance common knowledge. With a bastard child you will be unable to deny your loss of virtue." Enki spotted tears welling in Sud's eyes as he quickly undid all of Ninmah's efforts to restore her calm. "What if I proposed another solution, though... one that might restore your honor and legitimize this child?"

Sud's eyes lit up at Enki's suggestion. "Oh, your Lordship, but how?" Even with the glimmer of hope, Sud's damp eyes quickly descended into tears.

"Enlil has been banished for his crime against you. Now he suffers one of the worst exiles. And you await your firstborn at the expense of your virtue and the legitimacy of your child." Enki studied Sud's face and the desperation etched upon it. "Were you to be in agreement, and assuming Enlil is as well (I expect he will be) — the both of you must marry."

Sud felt genuinely perplexed by Enki's proposition. "But, your Lordship, such a union would never be allowed. I am not of proper lineage for it."

"Under different circumstances I might agree. But consider this: for you and Enlil to join solves everything for you and for him." Growing more excited, Enki accelerated his speech. "Under general convention, a husband cannot assault his spouse. A union between the two of you will expunge Enlil's record, liberating him from exile. This is why he will agree. For you, your virtue will be restored. You will go from a woman with no prospects to a princess, and very possibly to a queen. And your child will be legitimized as one of royal lineage." Enki watched Sud as the machinations of her mind worked out the details of his scheme. "If this child is to be a sibling of Ninurta's, or a cousin to my own child Marduk, it should be of royal lineage, don't you think? At the risk of sounding presumptuous, I believe you see my reasoning."

Sud's mind raced. She found Enlil repulsive on so many levels, and his attack on her had only intensified her aversion to him. But Enki was right. As a member of the ruling class, she would be afforded certain allowances that might render Enlil tolerable. If such an arrangement indeed could be made, it would give her a voice to be heard. She would be empowered to say no, not only to Enlil, but also to a variety of other unpleasant scenarios. A marriage would elevate her to royal status and provide her baby with a name and a title.

"Come, child," Enki coaxed, "This isn't a matter to ponder. Are you in agreement or not?"

"The way you describe things, Master Enki, I should say I'd be mighty foolish not to agree—if you believe it would really come to pass."

Enki's face blossomed with a smile. "Very good then. I will bring the proposal to council and to Enlil. I trust the details shall be put in motion by week's end."

"Oh, thank you, your Lordship! Thank you." Sud fell at Enki's feet and clutched his legs in a powerful embrace.

With a frown, Enki grabbed Sud and lifted her to her feet. "That's enough, child. I suspect you'll be one of us very soon. It won't hurt to begin acting as such."

In the end, Enki's scheme worked seamlessly. Enlil and the council back on Nibiru were more than amenable to a marriage that allowed a "revision" in the rape incident. As Enlil's wife, Nibirian law left no room for a sexual assault to legally occur. When the union was made final, Sud relinquished her common-er's name and accepted the royal title "Ninti."

Enki knew well that his role in Enlil's marriage had probably decreased his favor with Ninmah, but it had to be done. He had reset the playing field so he could witness the fracture of Enlil's greatest plans according to his own stratagem. The simple thought of it elicited a grand smile.

Through gossip and rumor, Enlil had learned of Enki's involvement in the arrangement, but their rivalry was such that neither ever spoke of it. Nor did Enlil reveal, of course, that he had learned the location of Enki's secret stash of weaponry on the mountain.

Before Enlil made his return from exile, Enki took his leave from Eridu and departed to the Abzu. Ninmah's successful persecution of their brother had created a small hiccup in his plan to destroy Enlil's reputation and credibility. But things were back on track now. No matter how he tried, Enlil would never be able to compete with the Abzu's gold production. Enki's secret hybrid workforce had already ensured this by comfortably bolstering the Abzu's output. The moment Enlil's gold program in Eridu was seen as unmistakably inferior, then he would strike again at his half brother's competency as a leader.

Several days after his arrival in the Abzu, Enki still felt invigorated by his plan. It had seemed routine when his best foreman of the mining operations, a man called Ennugi, appeared in the doorway of his office chamber. Both tall and well built, Ennugi's appearance seemed hardened by years of arduous work in the mines. His complexion, which had been a creamy olive tone on Nibiru, had turned a dark caramel color from days underneath Earth's powerful sun. His hands were as large as Enki's, but Ennugi had a menacing appearance, as if he could strangle a man at any moment.

"Your Grace," Ennugi interrupted, "may I have a word?"

"Yes," Enki proclaimed, looking up.

"It's the men, your Grace. They are disgruntled."

Enki did not know the actual complaint, but he was already without patience. "What is it they ask for now that I have not already provided?"

"Their discontent is not so much with you as it is with his Grace Master Enlil."

"Oh?" Enki took a moment of pause, intrigued by his foreman's proclamation.

"Yes, your Grace. The Igigi workforce believes Master Enlil is in charge of operations here in the Abzu and in Eridu. Are your requests not a reflection of Master Enlil's will?"

In typical fashion, Enki avoided answering and instead began maneuvering, trying to use the situation to his advantage. "What is their complaint, Foreman?"

"For one, they wish to break when the sun is high in the sky. They also believe our current goals force many to work seven days without a break. The crew would like rotations that provide at least one or two days rest in seven."

"Inform your men to organize their complaints and present them formally to Master Enlil when he is next in the Abzu. If they make their discontent known, perhaps Master Enlil will be prompted to act."

Ennugi didn't feel hopeful, but he understood his job was to follow orders. "I will inform them of your Grace's instructions."

Enki had mixed feelings about the Igigi's grievances. On one hand, he was proud of the operation he had created in the Abzu, but he also resented that his workers attributed their success to Enlil. Based on Ennugi's words, he saw an opening to further poison Enlil's command. The opportunity simply felt too attractive to pass up. *Very soon they will beg for my lead, and I will see Enlil return to Nibiru in disgrace.*

CHAPTER 15

Before Max could open his eyes, he became aware of himself again in the park with the unlikeliest of strangers. He peered at AJ from his seat on the bench. They hadn't quite finished their meditation, as Max was in the midst of envisioning the second to last chakra: the third eye.

AJ's voice sounded soothing and melodic as he continued the exercise without missing a beat. "Now, at the top of your head, at the crown—"

"Wait a minute," Max interrupted. "What just happened?"

AJ's face seemed tranquil and expressionless. Jumping up from the bench, Max stared at him, incredulous.

"You did it again, didn't you? You zapped me."

AJ laughed playfully. "No, sir." Then he raised his hands to indicate that he hadn't even touched Max. "We activated the third eye. I thought we were about to finish with the crown. Did something happen?"

"I keep seeing things!" Max exclaimed. He studied AJ's face to ensure he had done nothing to spark this latest episode. AJ remained unflinching. "Maybe we should finish this another time."

AJ nodded with a tranquil smile. "Of course. Would you rather we continue walking?"

Max checked the time on his phone. He felt as if they had been in the park for hours, but the current time indicated they had been together only twenty minutes. "I don't know. I have to get going." Max knew he needed to make time for Brigitte.

"Shall I walk you to your car then?"

"I didn't drive. I just need to get a cab. I can grab one on the way back."

"I'll accompany you then."

Max was still topsy-turvy from the meditation and the rancor he seemed to have witnessed between Enki and Enlil. He and AJ strolled together in silence until they exited the park and crossed onto the sidewalk. With no cab in sight, they continued toward the Golden Arch Building.

"You do realize," AJ commented, "that's fear you're experiencing."

Max looked up at him, intrigued. "How so?"

"The question you posed earlier... how to block a chakra? Awakening them always results in some tangible event." AJ's tone slowly morphed, almost becoming accusatory. "The third eye showed you something. That's what triggered your fear, and it's why you chose not to continue." AJ chuckled as if he had just remembered a private joke. "I suppose six out of seven isn't bad, though."

"Maybe." Max paused, contemplative. "Just a few months ago I wouldn't have believed in any of this. Hell, I wouldn't even be talking to you. It's like the minute I try to get my bearings, there's something new to throw me off."

AJ laughed. "This is true for all of us, Max. It's how the universe works. What is life if not continuous lessons and learning? We have to remain focused on the fact that, somehow, everything is as it should be."

Max quickly took his turn and laughed. "You mean chaotic?"

"Maybe. Or not. It's all elegant design, isn't it?"

Max studied AJ, contemplative. "Design in chaos, huh?"

"Maybe it feels like chaos when it's not. AJ gestured to their surroundings. "Look around us. What do you see?"

Max examined their environs: an upper-middle-class area, only blocks from the yoga studio. The street appeared mixed with both commercial and residential real estate, and traffic was moderate. For the most part, the district seemed to be thriving.

"So..." AJ's face remained inquisitive. "What do you see?"

Max continued his observation but didn't notice anything out of the ordinary. Across the street there were a series of storefronts: a high-end eyewear store, a fashion boutique, an athletic shoe store and a specialty electronics store. Max shook his head, still unclear what he should be observing.

"Look more closely," AJ instructed. "Tell me what you see."

Affixed in the window of the eyewear store there was a large black and white poster of a gorgeous blonde model. A beautiful pair of horn-rimmed glasses sat atop her aquiline nose, further accenting high cheekbones and a strong forehead. Nothing else about the ad appeared unusual to Max.

In the window of the fashion boutique there were sleek mannequins, wearing high-end clothes intended only for those with large disposable incomes. A large backdrop behind the life-sized figures ran floor to ceiling and featured slickly dressed supermodels. The window front of the athletic shoe store was similarly dressed, but their models and mannequins were instead outfitted in sportswear.

Max, who had suffered a long day, found his head hurt as he tried to identify what AJ was attempting to show him.

"You still don't see it?" AJ asked.

"No," Max proclaimed, "I don't."

"A moment ago, you activated six chakras. Keep in mind, there are seven." AJ indicated with a sweeping motion from his chest to the top of his head. "Three above," and with a similar gesture he pointed from his stomach to his feet. "And three below the center." AJ raised a closed fist to his heart and pounded it. "The heart is your center. If someone says you have heart, it's because that chakra is open."

"Okay." Max had passed the entire day learning about Rizick. Now AJ was attempting an entirely different type of lesson.

"The bottom three are the lower chakras. Their function keeps us grounded, rooting us to the physical world — creation and procreation. This is where we find our guts and our gonads. Our baser instincts emerge from these: sexuality, our desire for food, our taste buds, arts, architecture... everything to do with the senses. Today's commercial ads for music, sports, fashion; all of it is pushing us into the lower states, or the things we feel visceral about, like food, sex and the desire for material things. All the things religions typically associate with sin."

Max turned to look across the street again. To his amazement, what AJ described was now visible to him as if it had just been unveiled. The beautiful blonde in the sunglasses advertisement had her head cocked upward and her pouty lips were puckered as if she were blowing a sensual kiss. A slender neckline plunged down to reveal ample cleavage.

Max diverted his gaze to the athletic shoe store. Their ads

featured recognizable athletes who were either nude or scantily clad in skintight sportswear. Everywhere Max turned, he saw ads laden with blatant sexuality, alcohol, big pharma.

"Most of us reside in the lower chakras. With all of this around us, it's hard not to."

Max analyzed every poster and billboard in his line of sight. From what he could gather, AJ's assessment was dead on. "I guess I see what you mean."

"Just 'cause they're called the lower chakras doesn't mean you should think of them as bad. They exist for a reason. It's only when they're out of balance that issues like addiction arise, whether it be to food, drugs, sex… alcohol."

"So, the others are the *higher* chakras?"

"Bingo." AJ tilted his head to the side. "The top three are the throat, the third eye, and the crown. These feed in to our higher selves, or what many would call our spiritual side. It's where morality comes from. Of course, these are much harder to develop, especially when we're being bombarded with all this." AJ took his right arm and swept it from one side to the other like a seasoned spokesmodel, indicating all of the ads and billboards around them. "It's all sex, drugs and rock and roll, isn't it?"

Max hadn't noticed the large billboard for high-end lingerie. A voluptuous model, scantily clad in a camisole, was carefully poised along a large bed, staring invitingly at a man in a suit who stood in her doorway.

"If you watch TV," AJ continued, "you see these images over and over. Radio is the same. The same songs repeat, just like the commercials, over and over. At a certain point, it becomes Pavlovian."

Max squeezed his eyes shut, trying to absorb everything AJ was explaining. Instead he could hear chattering voices in his head: Otto and the other men in DC. "I'm sorry, AJ, I'm really burned." Max glanced across the street at the electronics store, which was still open. An idea suddenly took root in his mind. "I don't suppose you have a cell phone, do you?"

AJ cracked a knowing smile. "It's been years since I've owned anything like that. Why?"

Suddenly, Max felt sheepish. "I don't know. I could see myself needing to talk to you. It probably sounds weird, but..." Max tilted his head in the direction of the electronics store. "What if I picked one up for you?"

AJ studied Max, taken aback by the serious nature of his proposal. "I don't think so. If you need to, you know where you can find me."

Max sighed, somehow disappointed by the response he totally expected. "Fair enough."

He and AJ continued chatting during their stroll toward the yoga studio. People like Max tended to overlook men like AJ, refusing to acknowledge their existence. Today, he examined the imposing man whose long, dark, wavy hair was entwined with intermittent grays. His large hazel eyes were intense as if they held many stories behind them. Like lasers, they seemed to penetrate the surface, uncovering the truth of whoever fell beneath their gaze. AJ's complexion was ruddy, making his ethnicity hard to determine. In some ways, he appeared Latino, but he could easily have been East Asian or any variety of mixed background.

"Listen," Max proposed, "if you want I can get you a room tonight. You don't have to sleep out here."

AJ studied Max, recognizing the sincerity of his offer. "Very kind, but unnecessary. We are each on our paths. While it might seem strange to you, I don't need rescuing from mine."

"I just wanted to put that out there. If ever you need a break from whatever it is you're doing out here." After a few more steps, Max stopped and turned to AJ in seriousness. "There's something I need to ask."

AJ nodded, still paying Max his full attention.

"I may have touched on this last time, I just didn't go into detail. A few months ago, I was in Mexico..." Max faltered a moment, unsure if he should complete his thought. "I know this sounds crazy." He looked at AJ, who remained unflinching, empowering him to continue. "I did this meditative ceremony down there, and afterward I felt like I could see these lights on people. I think they might've been chakras."

Although he seemed impressed, AJ nodded without judgment.

"That's not all, though," Max continued. "Immediately after, I started... I feel stupid even saying this, but I started channeling emotions off other people." Losing confidence, Max stopped and looked across the street. "I can't believe I'm telling you this."

AJ seemed excited. "If what you say is true, Max, this is impressive. It means today is not the first time your third eye has been activated."

"What makes you say that?"

AJ raised his middle and index fingers and pointed at his eyes. "Chakras can't be seen with these. Only the third eye can do that."

Max grew pensive as he and AJ continued their stroll toward the yoga studio.

"I haven't seen them since, but there's other stuff — in addition to that thing *you* did. I didn't realize what it was at first but, somehow, I think I've still been experiencing other people's emotions. It's like their feelings are my own." Max studied the blank expression on AJ's face as they continued walking. "Lately, when I'm in DC, I feel all jittery, like I've had a zillion cups of coffee or something. I don't know if it's me, or someone else. But the feeling sometimes doesn't go away, not until I'm on my way out of there."

AJ accelerated his pace, seemingly excited as he studied Max. "You must be incredibly sensitive then. We're all capable of channeling, but so few of us do. Did you know the Egyptians, from ancient times, believed we possess more than 200 senses?"

Max considered the number, which was more than 40 times the five senses he had learned about in school. "How can that be?" Max quickened his step to keep pace with AJ.

"You've already described a few that fall outside of the categories we know about: seeing chakras, perceiving other people's emotions. Those aren't senses people in the West talk about."

Max considered AJ's point. "Fair enough."

"The physical body and what it perceives is one thing, but there's also the energetic body."

"Okay…" Max's head was already throbbing, and then they were standing once again before the Golden Arch Yoga Studio. Max spotted people inside through the glass double doors and glanced once more at the Kundalini poster. He looked across the street and spotted AJ's blanket still neatly folded and tucked in the opening of the wall. Leery of starting a new discussion, Max squashed down any curiosity he may have had about the energetic body.

"There's more to life than meets the eye." AJ raised his hand and pointed to another large ad across the street. "Do you think that's a billboard? Or that you're wearing a shirt?"

Max laughed out loud. "Yes, actually I do. I mean, of course. What else would they be?"

"Science says they're all made up of atoms, electrons, protons. It's energy, slowed down to create the perception of…" AJ pointed to the city blocks around them, "all of this. The emotions you're channeling? That's energy too. With practice, our ability to perceive higher energies can also be fine-tuned."

Max considered AJ's explanation: atoms, electrons, protons. *Energy.* "It's freaky."

"If you're jittery in DC, I suppose it's because of what goes on there. It's the nation's capitol, where deals are done and policies are made. The energy there must be terribly powerful, and I imagine quite negative. I'm not exactly sure how I know this, but you're being prepared for something, Max. That's why I did what I did that day. Like I said, I awakened something in you. Something you're going to need."

Max looked from AJ to the yoga studio entrance. It had been a while since he looked closely at the poster fastened to the inside glass. Near the bottom of it, the title read, "Seven Power Centers of the Kundalini System." Max hadn't paid attention to it before, but the illustration included a yellow band of lightning that was snaking its way upward, zigzagging through each of the seven chakras.

"Is there a way to control what you did? The spasms, inappropriate laughter… It's like I have Tourettes or something."

AJ nodded to acknowledge Max's concern. "On some occasions, when you open the nozzle to a hose, if the water pressure is too forceful, it causes the hose to flop around wildly, some would even say uncontrollably. That's what's going on with you. It's important not to fear it, though. That's how you'll regain control."

Max glanced up and spotted a series of taxicabs in transit. "All of this is doing my head in. Maybe we can talk more about it another time."

A gentle frown imprinted upon AJ's face before he spoke in a calm, soothing voice. "The next time you channel something negative, visualize yourself bathed in a beautiful, bright light; a light made up of love for yourself and others. Imagine that light as a force field."

Whether or not the technique would work, Max had no clue, but the idea of a shield brought a smile to his face.

"Trust me, it works. When you're out here, you encounter negative things: hatred, anger, fear, disdain. Imagine that directed at you everyday."

Only weeks before, Max had been one of the people directing damaging energies toward AJ. At the time, the sage vagrant had seemed like someone to avoid. In some ways, he still felt like someone to steer clear of, with his powerful stench and heavily soiled clothes. But now, Max patted him on the shoulder.

"I'll be back some other time. I hope that's okay."

AJ bowed his head in a silent nod. Feeling exhausted, Max bid his final goodbye and caught the first available taxi to Brigitte's house.

When he arrived at her door, she threw her arms around him. "I didn't think you were coming."

Max hugged her back. "Sorry, it was a crazy day." After he got settled, Max was able to share the innocuous parts of his day.

To her credit, Brigitte appeared to be in a great mood. Following his day in DC and the evening with AJ, she seemed the best company with whom to end the night. But less than a half hour had passed when a DC phone number began flashing on his cell phone. Max picked it up and gazed at the screen.

Brigitte watched him stare, seemingly in a daze. "Aren't you going to answer it?"

Max pressed Talk and spoke into the receiver. "Hello."

"Sir," a prim and proper man's voice replied, "this is the DC Metropolitan Police Department." The baritone voice was laden with seriousness. "May I please speak with Max Battenberg?"

"This is he."

"Good evening, Mr. Battenberg. My name is Detective Sommers with DC MPD. I take it you're familiar with a gentleman named Gary Richards?"

"Yes." Max felt the pangs of panic. *This call can't be good.* "What's this about?"

"I hate to bother you, Mr. Battenberg, but Mr. Richards was killed this evening."

"You're kidding." Max felt genuinely stunned. "I just had drinks with him earlier today."

"Yes, sir. We secured access to his phone and noticed in his calendar that the two of you had an appointment this evening. We're trying to piece together his last hours. I'm afraid we need you to come down and answer a few questions."

"Certainly." Max was confused, in shock even. *Oh shit, he's on my list, and now he is dead.*

"Very good, Mr. Battenberg. Are you in DC now?"

"No, I'm in Chicago. I'll be back in the morning, though."

"I understand, sir. The sooner you can get here the better."

"This is crazy. I was just with him."

"When do you think you'll be able to get here, Mr. Battenberg?"

"Um… probably early tomorrow evening, I guess."

"We appreciate your cooperation. We'll look for you tomorrow then."

"Thank you, detective." Max hung up and stared at Brigitte, incredulous.

She gazed back, questioning. "What on Earth was that about?"

Max was still in a stupor over the news. "That was the DC police department. My friend Gary—they said he was killed tonight."

"Oh my God, Max. What happened?"

"I don't know. They didn't say."

Brigitte studied Max. It was clear he was surprised, even creeped out by the news.

"Did you say you were with him tonight?"

"Yeah," Max remained in deep thought, distracted by the long list of disparate activities he had performed that day. "We met after my meeting. He wanted my dad's help with his job, lobbying for big pharma."

Brigitte remembered his name. *Gary.* He was the man Max had invited to her friend Marilyn's birthday party. She had never heard of him before that day, and now he was dead. In the back of her mind, she thought of Indigo's warnings during Mardi Gras. *Someone is dead now. Shit.*

Max, on the other hand, considered quite a bit more than Indigo's prophecy. After visiting his father in the underground complex of New Mexico, Demetrius' assistant, Rosalee, had provided him with a blacklist. She had instructed him not to associate with anyone on it, but Max had defied the instruction to meet with Gary. Now he was dead.

"I have to go back to DC tomorrow. The police want to talk with me after my meeting."

"They don't think you had anything to do with it, do they?"

"I don't know." Max hadn't even considered the possibility.

"You better let someone know about this, Max. One of your father's attorneys or something. If the police don't have a suspect, and you met with him the day he was murdered, that could be bad."

"Shit." Even in his mind, the implication was clear. "I guess you're right." He hugged Brigitte tightly. Although she tried to appear at ease, he felt her tense up beneath him. He released her and looked directly in her eyes. He didn't want to address anything Indigo had said in New Orleans, but he couldn't remain silent either. "I'm not saying this to freak you out or anything…" He faltered, unsure how to choose the correct words, or whether he should even finish his thought. "You know Ted and I got slashed in New Orleans, and my father's in the hospital. Now someone I had a drink with is dead. It's just creepy. And I know we never talked about this, but that day we got to New Orleans—"

"Yeah, Max, I know. She warned me and Ted."

Max seemed thrown by Brigitte's response, mostly because it was dead on. "I don't know if I ever told you, but my father said there might be some kind of plot against my family. I'm beginning to think I should be worried about it. Maybe we both should."

Brigitte studied Max, troubled by the news. Her good mood was quickly dissolving.

Before Mardi Gras, he had doubted such a thing as mediums even existed, but Indigo and his father had both proven correct in their assertions. Danger did appear to be looming in his midst like a dark cloud, engulfing anyone who grew too close.

Max stepped to Brigitte and took her by each arm. "Can you do me a favor please?" He watched her nodding, full of trepidation. "I need you to lay low. Just keep your eyes open; be aware of your surroundings. I never thought I'd say this, but we have to take my father and that psychic seriously. At this point, I don't want us taking chances. Can you do that?"

Someone is dead, she thought. *Ted was attacked, and now someone is dead.* "You're scaring me, Max."

He hugged her tightly. "I know. But maybe we should be scared." He pondered his current predicament and somehow knew he would need AJ's wisdom in the coming days. For the most part, his training had come to an end. Not because he had learned everything there was to know, but time was simply running out. The upcoming Rizick meeting could occur at any time. In the morning, he would travel once again to DC to continue his preparation and to be questioned by the police about a murder.

He and Brigitte sat in silence, trying to make sense of the events going on around them. Max had become certain of one thing. Gary's death had changed the playing field once again. *What next*, he thought, *what could possibly come next?*

$\mathcal{T}$he next morning Max followed his usual routine, leaving Brigitte's to catch a morning train back to the nation's capitol. During the ride he informed Rosalee of his predicament regarding Gary Richards. He also made it clear he would like an attorney present. In signature fashion, Rosalee listened but mostly remained silent. Whether or not this was in judgment Max did not know. He supposed it did not matter since she had always been efficient at satisfying his requests. When the time came for him to meet with police later that day, an attorney would be present.

While it didn't seem possible, the original end-date for his training had arrived. Fortunately for Max, the earlier security leak had forced a change of venue. Max felt certain he would not learn of the meeting's new time or location before the final moment. Until then, he would need to continue commuting from Chicago to DC.

He entered the underground conference room and found Otto, Levi and the redhead chatting over doughnuts and coffee. They spotted him and proceeded to take seats at the conference room table. Levi cracked a smile before producing an oversized cardboard tube. He removed a large blueprint from the canister and unfolded it on the table. Smiling first at Otto, he addressed Max.

"Getting these would have been impossible without your father's help."

Max read the schematic, which appeared to be a floor plan for a large complex. "What is it?"

"The layout for the meeting's new location. Considering the earlier breach, not even Rizick's high-ranking members have access to it." Levi seemed impressed with himself before he continued. "Your father felt you should see it."

Max studied the large diagram. In many ways, the color document resembled the directories found inside large commercial shopping malls. Max chuckled when he spotted a large arrow with the words "Battenberg here. "What's this?" he asked.

Otto reached down to help Levi secure the diagram in its unfurled position. "That would be the Battenberg booth, reserved for you by your father. That'll be your spot at the meeting. It's private, and it overlooks the lower level, so you'll have a great vantage point to observe other attendees."

As Max examined the blueprint, he noticed there were two levels to the complex. On the ground floor, there was a large open space surrounded by a myriad of rooms and conference rooms. On the second level, a row of small private rooms were situated like skyboxes above the large open area below.

"Most years," Otto continued, "they build out the location to resemble the floor of the New York Stock Exchange."

"Where's this new location?"

"No one has that detail yet," Otto confirmed. "To avoid another breach, it'll be withheld until moments before the meeting. Just know, once you get there, it'll be laid out, more or less, as you see it here. It's a small caveat, but, hopefully, it'll help avoid confusion."

Max reached in his pocket and removed his cell phone. "Can I get a picture of it?"

"No, no, no." Otto shook his head as he spoke. "If anyone found out we had this, heads would roll. It's better you memorize it, and forget you ever saw it."

"Okay." Max shared a brief glance with Levi and the redhead. After a brief silence, the redhead spoke.

"We're aware this is a lot of information, Mr. Battenberg, but we're sure you'll be fine. Once they get this location built out and everything is in order, you'll receive a self-deleting text message on your phone. That'll happen roughly twenty-four hours before you need to be at the venue. Once you see the location, you'll need to read it within five minutes or it'll digitally erase itself from your phone. At that point, you need to make immediate travel arrangements. Do you understand?"

Max nodded in reply.

"Good," the redhead continued, "I'm sure a plane will be readied for you the moment you receive the communication. Every meeting's arranged like this to minimize information leaks like the one we had earlier. When those conspiracy theorists find out in the final hour, they typically don't have time or resources to interfere."

Levi nodded in agreement. "That's the way we like it."

Satisfied, Otto looked up from the schematic. "I meant to ask earlier, but you were still in Chicago this morning. What's this story about you needing an attorney?"

"Yeah," Max felt badly about Gary and embarrassed that he had somehow found his way into the center of a sticky situation. "I honestly don't know what happened, Otto. After we finished yesterday, I met a friend for drinks. He asked for help with something he was doing at work. Then, last night, I got a call that he was killed. I have no idea if I'm a suspect, but they want to talk to me. I might be the last one who saw him, I don't know."

Otto nodded, clearly perturbed by the circumstance. "Okay. I better be the one to go with you then."

"Good." Max considered the potentially compromising predicament. "That makes me feel a little better."

"We can't afford to get you hung up on something like this. Not with Rizick coming up. I've already made some calls."

"I don't know if Rosalee mentioned it, but Gary was on some list she gave me. She said it was suggestions about people I should avoid." Max moved closer to Otto with renewed intensity. "That's not what this is about, is it? I mean, that's not why he was killed."

"I'm sorry, Max, I don't know the details." A look of concern crossed Otto's face. "It sounds unlikely, but anything's possible. I'll look into it. In the meantime, we'll pay the police a visit to make sure everybody sees you're cooperating."

"Okay." Max wanted to keep his cool, but Indigo's prophecy, if she was right, meant Gary's blood might be on his hands. "I'm sorry I got caught up in this. I really don't know what happened to him."

Otto patted Max on the shoulder. "None of us is as sorry as your friend. Let's head down to the station now. I'll try to make sure it doesn't last more than a few minutes."

Max and Otto summoned one of the secret elevators and returned to ground level. Within minutes, they descended the steps of the National Archives, where they hailed a cab to DC's Metropolitan Police Department. They requested to speak with Detective Sommers and were promptly escorted to an interrogation room. After a short wait, Detective Sommers entered.

"Good evening, gentlemen."

The night before, due to his speech pattern, Max had imagined the detective as a rotund Caucasian male. Instead, a well-muscled African American in his mid-thirties entered. The detective's complexion was that of milk chocolate and his hair was closely cropped and shiny black. A handsome, chiseled face was neatly manicured with a moustache and goatee. Sommers was dressed in well-fitted black jeans and a white Polo shirt. The words "DC Metro Police" were embroidered on the chest where the horse and polo player might have been.

"Thanks for coming down." Sommers smiled, flashing a set of perfectly capped teeth. He extended a hand to Max. "I presume you are Mr. Battenberg."

"Yes," Max confirmed as he shook the detective's hand.

"You must be Mr. Battenberg's attorney, then."

"Otto Khrzinsky, a close family friend, but also an esquire. I will be acting as Mr. Battenberg's attorney for the purposes of this interrogation."

"Whoa, Mr. Khrizenisky, this is nothing that formal. We just wanna ask a few questions to help us piece together the victim's—" Detective Sommers paused to read the name on Gary's file, "—Mr. Richards' final steps. Please, have a seat."

Otto, who was accustomed to the mispronunciation of his name, deferred making any correction. The three men then planted themselves in chairs around a rectangular metal table.

"So," Otto chimed in, not opposed to running the show. "We are dealing with a homicide then? Max wasn't 100 percent sure."

"I'm afraid so." Having dealt with crimes day-to-day, Detective Sommers remained matter-of-fact. "Mr. Richards was attempting to board the metro when someone shoved him off the platform onto the tracks."

"You're kidding!" Max could not hide his disbelief. "I can't imagine why anyone would do that."

"That's what we're trying to figure out, Mr. Battenberg. I think I mentioned last night, we were able to access Mr. Richards' phone. We saw you two had an appointment yesterday. Is that why you were in DC?"

"No," Otto interjected, "Max and I have business here."

Detective Sommers studied Max. "But you were in Chicago when I called. You must've hopped a plane immediately after you left Mr. Richards."

Max knew his father would have remained stone-faced after the detective's question, but he had not yet developed that skill. He thought of the Top Secret trains that were swifter than the fastest planes. Max's face betrayed him. *How do I explain getting to Chicago so fast?* He knew he couldn't mention the train, and he wasn't booked on any flight.

Once again, Otto quickly took charge. "I'm not sure if you know this, Detective, but Max is Demetrius Battenberg's son. Of course he has access to company jets. Given that we have business here, we've been shuttling back and forth from Chicago."

Otto and Max had both made an assumption that Detective Sommers knew exactly who they were. But he appeared starstruck at the mention of Demetrius' name. For a brief moment, Sommers gazed at Max before he continued.

"Okay. We can get ahold of those flight records, if need be, correct?" Detective Sommers carried on, looking at Max.

"Certainly," Otto interjected.

"All right, great." Detective Sommers appeared cooperative as he stood. "Before I let you go, I'd like to show you something, if that's okay?"

Max and Otto stole a glance before Max nodded in reply. "Sure."

"We appreciate you coming down, Mr. Battenberg."

"Not a problem. I feel terrible about this. And it's freaky that it happened right after I saw him."

Without another word Detective Sommers led Max and Otto down the hall to a small room outfitted with audio-visual equipment. The facility, which included a VHS deck and an old-fashioned tube television, felt dated even though other more modern machinery was also present. Max and Otto sat as the detective cued up his video.

After a short pause, video of the L'Enfant Center Metro Station appeared on the archaic TV monitor. The on-screen time code revealed it was the tail end of rush hour, less than an hour after Max's departure to Chicago.

The crowded platform forced Max to carefully study the picture before he spotted Gary. "That's him there."

In the footage, a metro station monitor began flashing to alert passengers of a train's approach. Gary and a score of other people spilled onto the platform, waiting to board the train. A moment before its arrival, a small figure in an oversized denim jacket and baseball cap walked up behind Gary. The person, whoever it was, shoved Gary off the platform. Max's friend fell forward, then disappeared out of frame as he plunged onto the track.

"Oh shit," Max blurted out in spite of himself.

On screen, everyone near the scene reacted in shock as the assailant retreated and disappeared out of view.

Using remote control, Detective Sommers paused the image. "I know it's difficult to watch, but we're hoping you might have some idea who that was who shoved him. Most times, it's someone the victim knew."

"Well," Otto explained, "it's clear whoever that was is a much smaller person than Mr. Battenberg."

Detective Sommers smiled. "Mr. Battenberg is not a suspect, but he may be the last acquaintance to see Mr. Richards alive."

Max glanced again at the paused screen, still in shock about the manner of Gary's death. To his astonishment, he spotted a figure he could hardly believe was there. *Oh my God!* "Wait a minute." Max scooted closer to the screen to make sure. *This can't be.* Frozen in place, and just blurred enough to be artistically impressionistic, there was a shot of the tall blonde who had appeared so many times in his dreams. Max pointed, placing his finger on the screen just below the woman. "This woman here, I've seen her before. Most of the time she's with this guy, I guess he's a dwarf or something."

The detective looked amused. "You mean a little person?"

"Yeah, I know it sounds crazy. But I keep seeing the two of them." To Max's surprise, Otto looked even more incredulous than Detective Sommers.

"Otto, don't look at me like that. My father mentioned the whole Poseidon thing and said I needed to be on my guard. I started seeing whoever that *little person* is the same day, down in New Orleans. I think they've been following me."

Otto had hoped to make a quick meeting of their police visit, but Max was prolonging their progress with his story. Max, however, was genuinely worried, so he continued.

"Maybe they followed Gary after I left, I don't know."

"Now, Max," Otto interrupted, "don't go speculating. Whoever that woman is, she's not the one who pushed your friend."

Max remained insistent as he pointed to the blonde on screen. "You need to find out who she is. I have a feeling she might be involved."

"This is why we wanted to talk to you, Mr. Battenberg. We'll look into it and see if we can locate her. Of course, if you see her first, don't hesitate to let us know."

"Absolutely." Max could see Otto growing impatient and suspected that he might be irritated by his strange account of the woman and her small friend.

Otto glanced at his watch. "I'm glad we could be of help, Detective. We're heading back to Chicago shortly, but you can easily reach us if you have any questions."

"Thank you, gentlemen." Detective Sommers stood and shook hands with each of them. "Should I need anything further, I'll be certain to get in touch."

Max and Otto exited the police station. Max felt assured of a reprimand for his story about the blonde, but Otto seemed otherwise occupied. After a quick hug goodbye, he quickly hailed a cab and disappeared into the streets of DC. Max imagined that his father's friend was off to close one or two additional high-profile deals on Capitol Hill, but the truth was entirely a mystery.

A moment later, Max grabbed his own cab and returned to the National Archives Building. From there, he descended into the underground complex and caught the next train to Chicago. He considered his upcoming role, filling in for his father, but his mind kept drifting back to the blonde on the platform where Gary had been killed. The image of his friend's final moment unsettled him more than he wanted to admit. *What if he was killed because of me?* Otto didn't seem willing to discuss it, but Max knew it was a possibility.

CHAPTER 17

*M*ax still felt uneasy about the upcoming meeting. For one, it was the first time he had been asked to fill his father's shoes, and further, he felt continually rattled by the concept of Project Clean Slate. He had studied the reports, and it was clear that the environment was indeed suffering. For decades, the effects of gross overpopulation had remained subtly imperceptible to many in the First World, but the patterns of global warming had swiftly become irrefutable. Drought, torrential flooding downpours, tornadoes, hurricanes and earthquakes: they had all escalated in scale and frequency. Members of Rizick believed if nothing was done that Sweet Mother Earth might do as the dog does to dry its fur. A violent shake, rattle and roll would eventually clear the land of the populous scourge of man. Despite the dangers, a drastic reduction on the scale discussed in Clean Slate hardly seemed a feasible solution.

Still unclear how to reconcile his personal feelings against his father's desires, Max continued his daily commute between DC and Chicago. Whenever possible, he found time to sneak away for short conversations with AJ. Somehow, these mini-visits created some semblance of a balanced life that nevertheless often seemed absurd in its contrasts.

Although his DC trainers had secured architectural schematics for the new venue, three weeks later, there was still no word about the meeting's location or the actual time frame. On one hand, Max felt antsy and wanted to uncover all there was to know about Rizick's voting process. Another part of him, however, still hoped his father might recover in time to relieve him of this familial duty.

As the days passed, he wondered about Gary Richards and whether or not the police would ever recontact him regarding his murder. But he never heard from Detective Sommers again. He toyed with the idea of a follow-up to see if the perpetrator had ever been found, or if anything had been discovered about the mysterious blonde. But Otto had suggested he steer clear of what might prove to be a very messy murder investigation.

Why was she there? Max could not envision why the woman

whom he first suspected existed only in his dreams was present on the platform the day of Gary's murder. The fact that he even knew someone who had been murdered rattled his nerves, especially given the recent slew of misfortunes with Ted and his father.

At the end of yet another day of training, Max shook everyone's hand to thank them for their efforts. DC had, in essence, become his full-time job that he commuted to Monday through Friday. In the absence of spare time, he had delegated the majority of his Badem Publishing duties to his friend and VP, Chandler Paul.

To conclude another day, Max made his way to the underground platform and returned on the train to Chicago. At home, he showered and changed, then took the Range Rover out, hoping to speak with AJ. The commute and yoga studio conversations had become a strange routine. Max felt unusually calm as he cornered onto the block of the Golden Arch Studio. Building 7129 came into view, and shock overcame Max. The block AJ normally sat upon was completely abandoned, but yellow police tape snaked across several orange cones, blocking off AJ's normal spot on the sidewalk. *Not again*, he thought. *Not already.*

He pulled to a stop beside the cordoned off-area and exited his car. With every step apprehension filled his heart, and a hyper-awareness of his surroundings kicked into gear. It did not register how or why this was a crime scene, but Max felt in his gut that something terrible had happened. While it didn't appear to be blood, there were stains on the curb and sidewalk. Max slipped underneath the tape and examined them. His heart sank as he realized what he was seeing. Blood indeed had been present. A cleaning agent, probably some kind of solvent, had also been used to clean it up. He stood inside the police tape while his mind raced wildly with varying scenarios about AJ's demise.

Seconds felt like hours while he stared at the ground, examining the stained concrete. He took a breath, trying to anchor himself in positivity. *Maybe he was injured, but where would they take him?* The most likely possibility occurred to him: *Cook County Hospital.* Max crossed underneath the police tape and returned to his car. Shifting into gear, he skidded off down the street.

In record time, he screeched to a halt before the emergency room and ditched his car with the valet. He rushed inside, but

Max already knew it would be tricky getting information on AJ. For one, he had no idea what the letters A-J stood for, and he also had no clue about his new friend's last name. He approached the front desk to find a portly African American woman with shoulder length braids neatly tucked into a ponytail. Her day appeared to be going better than his, as she was laughing on the phone.

"She told you what?" A pair of half glasses sat neatly perched on the tip of her nose, making it seem she was looking over them even though that was not the case.

Max stood squarely in view of the woman who smiled to acknowledge him, but nevertheless continued on her call.

"See, I don't understand why she even thought you would do that."

"Excuse me," Max interrupted. "I'm trying to get information on a patient who might have been admitted today."

The woman smiled at Max, but spoke into the phone. "Hold on, girl." She removed the phone from her ear then looked over her glasses at Max. "I'm sorry, what was the patient's name?"

"He goes by AJ."

The woman was curt but polite. "Last name?"

"I don't know. He's homeless. He would've been admitted in the last twelve hours. Big guy, in good shape."

The woman remained pleasant, but Max could tell she was put off by his lack of information. She paused a moment before speaking into the phone. "Girl, let me call you back." She replaced the phone in its cradle, then began a search on her computer. Max waited patiently. After a minute or two, the woman was still typing and staring at her screen. "I'm still checking, sir," she chirped.

After a minute more, she peered up at Max. "I can hardly believe I found him. There is an AJ who was brought in, but there isn't any info on him…"

Still a ball of nerves, Max observed quietly while the nurse read from her screen. Finally, a look of understanding came over her.

"Oh, I see. It's a police matter, sir." She looked up at Max, apologetic. "I'm so sorry. When an intake gets flagged by the police we are prevented from providing details. None are even listed, in fact. Do you know any family members you can call?"

Mired in frustration, Max ran a hand through his hair. "No.

Is he okay, at least?"

"I wish I had something to share. There's just no info here. If you know someone who may have come in with him, they would be able to give you the details. I have nothing here. I'm sorry I can't be of more help."

Max thanked the woman and wandered into the hall, where he found a seat and plopped down. He dropped his head in his hands, trying desperately to come up with a plan to locate AJ. When he quieted his thoughts, AJ's voice resonated in his head: *Did you know the Egyptians, from ancient times, believed we possess more than two hundred senses? We are all capable of channeling, but so few of us do.*

He's here, Max thought. *But where?* He took a deep breath and envisioned the chakra activation exercise that AJ had described. He began with the root chakra: brilliant red, shining brightly. From there, he worked his way up. The sacral chakra, orange and glowing; the solar plexus, yellow and swirling; the heart chakra, green and soothing; the throat chakra, vibrant and blue; the third-eye chakra, penetrating, indigo colored; the crown chakra: purple and ethereal.

He had taken his time, but Max opened his eyes and felt nothing. *I'm too agitated.* He stood and walked to the elevators. After a moment's time, he pushed the call button and waited. Seconds later, the arrival of the elevator alerted with a chime. Max stepped on and took a deep breath. He had no idea which floor to go to, but he figured his intuition might help if only he could listen to it. Luckily, no one else stepped on with him. The doors finally closed, but the elevator remained still.

He reached forward, his finger vacillating between the fourth and sixth floors. *No fear.* He closed his eyes and allowed his finger to lead. Pushing forward, he pressed a button. Max opened his eyes to see the fourth floor illuminated. The elevator lurched upward. When the doors opened, he exited into the corridor but was uncertain which way to go. He took a deep breath and began walking. Without really knowing his destination, he strolled to the end of the corridor and stepped into the last room on the right. An elderly woman was there, in bed, with a breathing tube snaking out of a tracheotomy in her throat. Her eyes pleaded with Max, but he quickly exited.

He checked three additional rooms, but didn't find AJ in any of them. As discouragement settled in, he stepped into a fifth room and saw AJ staring back at him. Max's face lit up. "I can't believe I found you."

AJ looked pleased and a little befuddled. "How'd you know I was here?" The left side of his face was bandaged along with a portion of his left arm. Aside from that, he looked solid and intact.

"No offense, but this is where they bring homeless guys. They wouldn't tell me what floor you were on, though. I just started walking around until I found you."

AJ smiled at Max, seemingly satisfied with his performance. "What the hell happened?"

"I was in my usual spot when a car drove by. Someone threw acid on me." AJ seemed disappointed by the story. He gazed at Max, who was sporting a look of incredulity. "Oh, come on. This is not the first time something like this has happened. I've had soft drinks thrown at me. Someone even threw urine on me once. I actually thought that's what it was this time, until it started to burn. Lucky for me, the yoga studio hadn't closed. One of the girls called 9-1-1."

Max recalled the stained sidewalk. "Who do you think did this?" The question hung in the air.

AJ's left eye had bandages partially covering it. He stared at Max through the other. "Does it matter?"

"Kind of, AJ. It does to me."

"The options are, it was random. Or someone did it because they don't like homeless people. Or maybe it was because of you, if that's what you're worried about. Whether it was intentional or meant for a stranger, I don't know. Either way it boils down to things we've talked about: anger, fear, disconnectedness, people operating in the lower chakras." AJ fixed Max in his gaze.

"I'm worried maybe I do have something to do with it."

"Worry solves nothing, my friend. We each have our own karma and a unique path to walk. Today was merely a step in my journey."

Max returned AJ's gaze with a sense of awe. "You may very well be one of the most fascinating people I know. I'm still trying to figure out what you did to me, by the way. And that perfume thing in the car…"

Once again, AJ appeared pleased. "That's great that you found me, since you didn't know where I was. It seems you're beginning to listen to that inner voice."

"I don't get it… Why're you on the streets, I mean?"

AJ spit out a laugh. "Isn't life the most shocking, unbelievable play ever written? Whether you see it or not, the streets have been a blessing to me. The things I've discovered, I could never have learned anywhere else."

"You still believe that, even after today?"

AJ nodded with a cool serenity that Max found difficult to comprehend, given the circumstances.

"I wish I could share in your enthusiasm. Even in my own life, I wish I could trade what it is now for what it was six months ago. It was much simpler then."

AJ smirked with a light chuckle. "The Law of Impermanence always handles that, my friend."

Max studied AJ, trying to recall what he knew about the term. "I remember reading something about that in school."

"It's a simple rule, really. It states that everything in existence will be in a constant state of change. Therefore nothing can remain the same for long. Your life may have been different six months ago, and I guarantee it will be different six months from now. This doesn't make you special. Impermanence applies to us all."

Max understood AJ's point on a theoretical level. At the same time, the premise seemed too obvious to be useful.

"All the enlightened ones understood this: Jesus, the Buddha, Mahatma Gandhi… Suffering is the human condition. It grows out of attachment to things we wish to keep a certain way. The problem is, we can never keep things the way we want them. The Law of Impermanence dictates this. Look where I am now, for Chrissakes."

"Okay, I get it." But Max still felt bemused. "It just seems so basic, though."

"It's a universal law, Max. You can't question those. From the moment the ovum meets the sperm, a state of constant flux begins. One cell becomes two and then four and so on. We've each been undergoing change since conception. Growth and eventually decay, that's what's in store for all of us."

"I get it, but is that the best way to look at life?"

AJ laughed. "Yeah, well, that's the veil talking."

"Excuse me." AJ had mumbled the phrase, but Max caught it nonetheless. Indigo had used the term weeks before. *The veil.*

"Maybe your life seemed simpler six months ago, but it wasn't. It just appeared that way. That's what we call delusion."

Max studied AJ, nonplussed. "The veil, huh'?"

AJ responded with a nod. "An artist uses it to cover a masterpiece before showing it to the world. Covering it doesn't change what it is, though; it only prevents you from seeing it. It masks the truth, but the reality underneath remains. Isn't this how delusion works?"

"I'm glad you're okay, AJ. It just seems you should've used all this wisdom to avoid having acid thrown on you."

Both Max and AJ laughed, and they were each grateful for a lighter mood.

"How long do you think you'll be in here?"

"A short while, I imagine. They don't keep someone like me for long."

"But where will you go? It may not be safe back at the yoga studio."

AJ didn't seem troubled. "That's life's beauty, isn't it? I can go wherever I like. If I decide to go back, I will. What I won't do is allow myself to be governed by fear."

Max felt like urging AJ to do otherwise, but the reality of their circumstances seemed entirely too unreal. In sum total, they had only spent a matter of hours together. Although it didn't feel like it, Max hardly knew AJ at all. "So, if I don't find you here, I'll probably find you there?"

AJ mulled over the idea and nodded. "I suppose so. Like I said, life is unbelievable, unpredictable, sometimes shocking."

"I'm sorry, AJ, but I need to get going. I'll try to come again this week."

AJ gazed at Max with a warm smile. "Thank you, sir."

Max shook AJ's hand then turned and exited the room, taking note of the number on the door. On his way from the hospital, he phoned Brigitte to inform her that he was heading her way.

Due to the late hour, he had anticipated a sour mood, but Brigitte was relaxed and casual on the phone. They carried on exchanging pleasantries until his arrival. Even then, Brigitte remained upbeat. Max found her new approach perplexing, but he was grateful for a peaceful wrap up to his day.

"How much longer are you going to do this DC thing?" She questioned.

Max shrugged. "I wish I knew. My father's improving, but I have to handle some of his affairs until he's back on his feet."

Brigitte surveyed the intensity on Max's face. "I bet he's proud of you."

Max took his turn and studied her. She seemed different somehow, but how could she not be while expecting a child? He stepped closer and wrapped his arms around her in a warm embrace. "Thanks for putting up with me."

Brigitte hugged him back, and the two of them considered the drastic changes that had come to pass. *A baby*, they thought silently, both of them wondering exactly what the future might hold.

"Come on, mama, let's go to bed." Max grinned at Brigitte, and she smiled coyly back, confirming what he had imagined she was thinking. He took her by the hand and tugged her toward the bedroom. His intention was quickly interrupted by his phone's chime, alerting the arrival of a text message. He fumbled for the phone until he saw the screen, which read, *Nafsika Astir Palace Hotel, Vouliagmeni, Greece.* "Oh shit."

"What is it?" she questioned.

Max looked from the phone to Brigitte, his stomach fluttering with nerves and excitement. "I was told I'd receive travel arrangements. I think they just came."

Within seconds, Max's phone rang. He saw Battenberg Industries flashing on the screen. He pressed the talk button. "Hello."

"Mr. Battenberg, it's Rosalee, in your father's office. How are you, sir?"

"Fine. What's up?"

"I have your father on the line. Would you please hold?"

"Of course," Max replied.

After a brief moment, Demetrius came on the line. "Maximilian, it's your father." His voice, while stronger, hadn't yet regained its reverberant authority.

"How're you feeling, pops?"

"Not as well as I'd like. I suppose we both knew that, though." Demetrius sighed into the phone as if every word he spoke was an effort. "I take it you received the meeting's new location?"

"Yeah, I just got it."

Demetrius took a deep breath. "And you've gleaned the importance of a Battenberg presence there, correct?"

Max quickly grew apprehensive. It was just like Demetrius to wait until hours before the meeting to pressure him. "Dad, why do you think I've been preparing all these weeks?"

Demetrius continued as if Max hadn't spoken at all. "There's someone who will be there that you should be wary of. His name is Odeon Rutherford."

Max remembered the name, but could not piece together the details of his background. "Who is that?"

"Most think him an academic, a political science lecturer."

"Yeah, the Harvard-Oxford guy."

"Don't let the professor persona fool you. He is extremely powerful. I could never prove it, but I believe Odeon was behind the accident that killed your mother and brother."

"What?" Max felt dumbfounded by his father's revelation. "What're you talking about?"

"The accident, Max." Demetrius sighed deeply. "There was evidence suggesting they were run off the road. I didn't want to tell you until you were old enough to digest such a thing."

"But it wasn't just Mom and Christian, Dad. Uncle Charles was there too."

"At the time, Odeon and I had both become significant members of Rizick." Demetrius' voice wavered or trembled, Max wasn't sure which. He was either upset or perhaps it was due to trauma from his own accident. "We didn't agree on a lot of things, and he felt that I crossed him." Demetrius cleared his throat. "Rosalee, you still there?"

"Yes, Mr. Battenberg." As usual, Rosalee's voice was calming and serene. Max hadn't realized she was still on the line.

Demetrius sighed again. The conversation was draining him.

"Bring Rutherford's file with you so Max can have a look at it."

"Of course, Mr. Battenberg."

The elder Battenberg pushed on, unrelenting. "My jet is being prepared. Keep in mind, this morning's notification may or may not be the meeting's true location. But you'll head that way unless otherwise instructed."

Demetrius paused, breathing heavily into the phone.

"Pop, you okay?"

There were muffled voices on Demetrius' end until an unidentified male voice spoke into the receiver. "I'm sorry, but Mr. Battenberg has to rest. He has instructed that Rosalee complete your debriefing."

"Thank you," Rosalee chimed in, "I will take it from here." There was a tiny click as Demetrius' connection dropped. After a brief silence, Rosalee continued. "As your father stated, the majority of attendees will arrive tonight. This is a customary practice. Your father's usual protocol, however, is to arrive in the morning, literally minutes before the meeting begins."

"Then that's also how I'd like to arrive," Max replied.

"Very well, Mr. Battenberg. I'll also need your feedback as to how you believe others may think you'll arrive. For safety reasons, we operate with a complex decision matrix. Once all pertinent factors have been considered, some variations may need to occur in our mode of arrival."

Max and Rosalee proceeded through a checklist of details before he was told a car would be sent to shuttle him to his father's private jet. Prior experience had proven that Max would be whisked away, and his level of preparedness was of little consequence. He hung up and turned to Brigitte, feeling hurried and a little agitated.

"What?"

"I can't believe this." Max stared, incredulous, at Brigitte. "I thought I could stay, but it looks like I have a plane to catch."

"But, Max, it's almost midnight."

"I know." He stepped closer and encircled her in a tight embrace. "I'm getting tired of this bullshit. I know you are too."

"Why own planes if you can't schedule them when it's convenient?"

"I couldn't agree more, Sturdivant." He leaned in and kissed her. The lingering embrace deepened, but Max understood there wouldn't be time for more. He peeled himself away. "I really wish I didn't have to go."

Brigitte stole a moment to catch her breath. "I don't want you to either."

Max composed himself, taking a moment to adjust his clothes. "Filling in for my dad has to slow down at some point." He reached across and caressed her face. "I appreciate how understanding you've been through all this."

Brigitte smiled and kissed his open hand. Realizing there would not be time to spare, he looked again at the text message on his phone: *Nafsika Astir Palace Hotel, Vouliagmeni, Greece*. Before his eyes, the message digitized itself into fragments until it became unreadable. Without warning, the phone screen blacked out as if the battery had been removed. Within seconds, the Smartphone rebooted and seamlessly turned itself back on. Max looked up from it, trying to maintain a blank expression. "I know it's late, but my father's sending a car to pick me up. I need to get home and pack."

"Where are you going?"

He kissed her gently. "That's confidential, I'm afraid." Max offered a frivolous smile. "You know Battenberg business is top secret." His attempt to lighten the mood fell flat, as Brigitte studied him, eager for an explanation, but certain she would not get one. Given the circumstances, he could not afford, nor did he want, to prolong the conversation. "You should get some rest. I'll call tomorrow, okay?"

Brigitte felt bowled over again, but the off-kilter sensation was slowly becoming routine in the Battenberg world. "Okay. Just be careful."

He kissed her once more before softly running a hand across her belly. "You do the same, and lock up, okay?"

Brigitte accompanied him to the door, where they hugged and kissed one last time. Without further conversation, he rushed into the night, and Brigitte locked and dead-bolted her door behind him. She knew he would be in good hands, but the secrecy worried her at the same time. Standing at her window, she watched his Range Rover lights illuminating her driveway. He turned the car around, and his taillights quickly disappeared into the night.

CHAPTER 18

$\mathcal{B}$y the time he got home, it was just after midnight. Max rushed to his closet and sorted through the clothing needed for his trip. He assembled a dozen or so garments in a pile, then hurried to the mirrored facade of his panic room. He pressed his open hand against the glass, allowing it to scan his palm imprint. Within seconds, the hidden keypad appeared. He entered the entry code and waited as the vault door unlatched.

Max rushed into the panic room and took down the black leather case containing the Anti-k Device. He unzipped it and quickly noticed a missing piece. *The dial! Where is the dial?* The component he recovered from the Money Pit was crucial to the artifact's operation, but it was missing. The Anti-k Device was useless without it. *Where is it?*

Max rummaged through his shelves until he found the dark leather box from the Money Pit. He opened it, but its plush velvet interior did not include the component. "What the hell?" He returned to the black leather case and completely unzipped it to ensure he hadn't missed anything. The element was nowhere in sight. He double-checked the shelves. There was no doubt in his mind that the piece had been removed.

He thought of the blonde and the midget. He had not been able to confirm their existence until that day at the police station. *They've been here again. I know it. What if they did kill Gary?* According to the detective, the footage was captured seconds before Gary had been pushed onto the tracks.

Max wanted to retrieve his surveillance footage to see who, if anyone, had infiltrated his home. *There isn't time, though. Rosalee is too efficient.* In just a few minutes, a livery vehicle would pull up and whisk him off to the airport to board a Battenberg jet to his first ever Rizick Group meeting. He checked the weather in Greece before making the selections of what to place in his bag. Within minutes his doorbell rang and his phone chimed, alerting that a car was outside waiting for him, as expected.

At the door, the driver took his bags and escorted Max to the car. He was swiftly shuttled across town to a private hangar for

Battenberg Industries. When he boarded Demetrius' private jet, he was surprised to see Otto and Rosalee already sitting and chatting. Even more intriguing to see were the two DC trainers, who were both seated in a separate area of the cabin. Max nodded to acknowledge them before taking a seat next to Otto and Rosalee.

His father's assistant smiled softly before rummaging through her briefcase on the floor. A moment later, she handed Max a manila file with the name "Nickelodeon Rutherford" on it. He opened it and immediately began thumbing through its contents.

SUBJECT: Nickelodeon "Odeon" Rutherford, age 65, is of Scottish and Northern English descent. His family ancestry traces back to the Plantagenet family line in the English royal family tree.

EDUCATION: Ph.D.'s in economics and archeology from Harvard University and a political science degree from Cambridge. Note: Rutherford is considered a premier expert in all three fields.

FINANCIAL POSITION: $10 Million approximate net worth. Note: While Rutherford is not financially in the same bracket as most other Rizick members, his political and economic influence is far-reaching, even global.

CURRICULUM VITAE: Lecturing positions at Oxford, Cambridge, the Sorbonne and many of the U.S. Ivy League schools. Matters of opinion, when espoused by Rutherford, are considered impactful not only in academia but in the private sector as well. EXAMPLE: Rutherford's opinions on the oil market during the Baghdad invasions drove OPEC prices down.

LANGUAGES SPOKEN: In addition to English and German, Rutherford is fluent in all romance languages.

While flipping through the file, Max also found a section on Rutherford's history with the Battenbergs. Twenty years earlier, he had traveled extensively, lecturing on the economic changes he saw occurring throughout the world. Many of his lectures covered socio-political change in regions of the Middle East, including Iraq, Iran and Afghanistan. In addition to his opinions on the Middle East, Rutherford was very outspoken about the dangers of North American free trade. He discouraged cooperation between the U.S., Mexico and Canada, proposing that such a move would weaken the U.S. dollar and erode many auxiliary distribution channels.

Eventually, Demetrius had spoken openly against Rutherford's ideas, many of which were negatively impacting Battenberg Industries and their business ventures. Fortunately for Demetrius, he was and continued to be equally high-profile with strong ties to the media. As the head of Battenberg Industries, he was often quoted on television and radio, which successfully allowed him to launch a campaign of spin-doctoring and damage control against Rutherford's policies.

According to the file, Rutherford had approached Demetrius in a Rizick meeting in Vienna more than two decades before. He had warned Demetrius to cease his public propaganda. His precise words had been, "Stop the political meandering or the price will be costly."

But there was only one problem. Demetrius didn't take kindly to directives, and Rutherford's threats had only served to ensure his father would do the opposite. Of course, Demetrius had continued lobbying for causes that benefited Battenberg Industries. Three months after the exchange, his mother, brother and uncle had died in what Max always thought had been a car accident.

As he read deeper into the file, Max felt anger welling inside of him. He only had memories of his mother as a loving and tender woman. If there was truth in what he read, Odeon Rutherford had deprived him not only of a maternal presence but also of a brother's fraternity. Demetrius, with his gruff exterior, had never been an adequate substitute for the nurturing force his mother had been.

Max carefully shut the file and turned to Rosalee. "Can I hold on to this?"

Rosalee smiled softly before she answered. "Let me confirm whether or not that's the original. If so, I will have a copy made for you."

"Thank you, Rosalee."

The remainder of the flight was uneventful. Demetrius' travel staff had simplified all elements of airport arrivals and departures. There were little to no security checks, which made getting in and out of the airport particularly uncomplicated.

The length of the journey and the difference in time zones made for a 7:30 a.m. touchdown at a private airstrip near the hotel in Vouliagmeni. Two large Mercedes SUVs were waiting, and whisked Max and the rest of the crew down a winding coastal highway. It was a gorgeous morning in Greece with clear skies and blue waters that sparkled like glass.

Twenty minutes later, both SUVs turned onto a wide gravel driveway with large cypress trees standing like soldiers along each side. They headed down the path, and a white villa came into view. The classical-styled château sat in the center of a perfectly symmetrical and finely manicured lawn. Its immaculate gardens were decorated with hedges that had been trimmed into precise geometric shapes. As they drove nearer, Max spotted the sea in the background. The mansion sat poised on a cliff, overlooking the water. It was a breathtaking sight.

The caravan kicked up clouds of dust before screeching to a halt at the villa's front steps. Four youthful men, each looking as if he'd jumped from the pages of Italian *Vogue*, scrambled down the steps in white t-shirts and beige linen pants. They stood at attention, prepped to grab bags and usher everyone inside.

Max and Otto stepped from one SUV while Rosalee and the trainers exited the other. The region's rich Mediterranean heat, both oppressive and comforting at the same time, enveloped Max like a warm blanket. Without skipping a beat, Rosalee barked instructions in Greek, and the handsome porters sprung to action, collecting bags and carrying them inside.

She approached Max. "Can you be ready in an hour, sir?"

"Of course," he replied with a smile. "Is this where we're staying?"

"Security stop, actually. Just time to shower and change. If you'd like to stay after the meeting, you're more than welcome to return. Although I suspect your father'll be awaiting a debrief."

"I suspect you're right," Max sighed as they strolled up the steps into the villa.

The moment they entered, a blast of climate-controlled air slapped the heat away. Max gaped at the villa's ground floor. He was familiar with many of the world's most extravagant and lavish places, but there were few equivalents to this Grecian villa.

Its marble floors sparkled with such clarity that he glimpsed his own reflection. Columns were expertly placed throughout the interior and exterior of the villa, giving it balance and symmetry. Hugging each side of the entry hall, a set of winding staircases curled up to the top of a large landing.

One of the porters motioned toward Max. "This way, sir." He had a slight Greek accent tinged with hints of the Queen's English. Max watched him carrying his bags up the staircase. His skin, a dark sun-kissed brown, was the kind of complexion Max knew could only be obtained in certain corners of the globe. The best-known ones were, of course, in the Mediterranean and Brazil.

As Max trailed the porter to the upper landing, he noticed the villa's exquisite details. Every fixture, molding and piece of furniture had been expertly considered and was further complimented by tapestries and Persian rugs throughout. He presumed, if this house were inspected for cleanliness, not a mite of dust would be found.

The porter cut to the right and entered a room with a view of the sea. Max followed behind and was directed toward the bathroom, which was well equipped with every type of towel and toiletry invented.

"Is this to your liking, sir?"

Max surveyed the accommodations and the attention paid to every detail. "Yes, thank you."

The porter smiled before gesturing toward a tasseled, adorned rope hanging near the expansive bed. "Should you require anything, simply pull that cord, and someone will assist you."

"Actually," Max answered as he unzipped his suitor and removed a black suit, "if someone could have this pressed, I'll need it as soon as I shower."

"Of course, sir. We will have that for you shortly."

Max nodded, and the porter stepped out of the room with his suit. He took in the extravagance of the suite, truly impressed by its exquisiteness. He swung open the French doors and crossed out onto a large stone veranda. He had visited Greece several times before, but its beauty had receded from him since his last excursion. Max breathed in the odor of seawater and felt tropical air caressing his skin. He took it all in until it hit him that there were probably only minutes left for him to prepare.

He hurried to the bathroom and showered. While the villa bathroom had none of the technology found in his Chicago home, all of its fixtures and hardware exceeded his in quality. Each tile was individually crafted from delicate pieces of marble, and some seemed of ancient origin. Because of his seasoned upbringing, Max could easily distinguish the difference between industrially manufactured pieces and artisanal ones. He immediately understood that the villa had been assembled bit-by-bit as a piece of art. This was true not only in the bathroom but also throughout the rest of the mansion.

Following his shower, Max exited into the main suite. His perfectly pressed suit was hanging from a clotheshorse that someone had wheeled into the room. He quickly dressed in the ensemble that was specifically tailored to his frame.

He stepped up to the large Victorian mirror affixed to the wall and gazed at his reflection. He ran his fingers through damp hair and remarked how different he looked in business attire. The suit added maturity Max didn't particularly feel he possessed. More strikingly, he became aware just how much he resembled Demetrius. In a suit, Max's presence was commanding and caused him to stand out, but for entirely different reasons than the ones he was accustomed to.

He crossed to his luggage and removed an ultra-sleek, charcoal gray attaché case. Somehow he had reinvented the meaning of "power suit" by adding a younger, hipper slant to the genre. Ready or not, he was about to attend his first-ever Rizick Group meeting.

Max exited his room and crossed down the corridor toward the large winding staircase. He could hear Rosalee orchestrating the staff and was impressed to hear her doing it in what sounded like fluent Greek. When he reached the steps, he caught a glimpse of her in a smart, burgundy skirt suit. The color was bright enough for her to be noticed, but somber enough for complete professionalism. She had fastened her hair into a ponytail that cascaded down her back.

Max completely understood why Demetrius kept her around. She was the total package: beautiful, sexy and powerful at the same time. No matter what Demetrius asked of her, Rosalee produced results with calm and steely resolve. She spotted Max descending the staircase, and for the first time there were cracks in her demeanor. In truth, she found Max incredibly handsome, and for a brief moment her physical attraction revealed itself. A second later she rebounded from the momentary lapse.

"Are you all set, Mr. Battenberg?"

"I am. Let's do this."

She turned to one of the porters who had helped them to their rooms. "Please gather Mr. Battenberg's things, and have them brought to our hotel with our remaining effects." Turning back to Max, she continued, "Most likely, we won't return here, but we'll see how things go."

Max and Rosalee exited the villa and climbed into their SUV, where Otto was seated, typing on his smartphone. Max realized with a heavy yet rather excited heart that his moment of truth had nearly arrived. In just a few hours he would uncover the inner workings of the infamous Rizick Group, and the true weight and responsibility of the Battenberg name would finally be revealed.

CHAPTER 19

On their way to the Astir Palace Resort, Rosalee sat between Max and Otto, hoping to answer any of Max's last-minute questions. Now, at the peak of his anxiety, Max seemed unable to hold any substantive conversation. Instead they rode in silence while the trainers from DC followed in the second SUV.

The Astir Palace sat on a 75-acre peninsula, and a single access road allowed entry or exit to the resort. As the SUVs pressed forward along the route, the landscape narrowed into a causeway with waves gently splashing against both sides. Max was aware of the beauty surrounding him, but he had difficulty appreciating it due to the circumstances of his visit. The warnings about Odeon Rutherford and what he had learned about operations like Stardust and Clean Slate weighed heavily. In some ways, he felt as if they were caravanning off to war.

The SUVs forged ahead on the peninsula, and Max noticed a commotion already brewing. A collection of cars and vans were haphazardly parked along the central road, and there were crowds of people milling about. Many bystanders were equipped with tripods and video recorders and were filming in the direction of the hotel. Others carried picket signs and snapped quick shots of passing vehicles, trying to catch glimpses of the Rizick Group's most exclusive members.

Max immediately noticed why so many people had assembled in the same spot. A dozen or more armed guards were strategically placed to form a perimeter around the hotel compound. As such, a blockade had formed to scrutinize anyone trying to enter the resort. For the duration of Rizick's meeting, any person who was not a guest of the Astir Palace was disallowed entry beyond the checkpoint. A handful of armed guards in local police uniforms were checking I.D.s. Others, dressed in nondescript, navy blue fatigues, had rifles strapped to their sides and were positioned as a second defense further along the road.

As they pulled closer to the crowd, the driver triggered a switch, and the windows began to darken. Within seconds, they were virtually blacked out, making it impossible to see in from outside. To Max's astonishment, their SUVs were customized with glass similar to the windows of Demetrius' Chicago penthouse.

Otto, who continued to study his phone, looked briefly at the crowd outside before he turned to Max. "Remember what I said: the location is always leaked."

Max and Rosalee both nodded as their SUV slowed to a stop at the checkpoint. Without another thought, Otto looked back to whatever he had been reading on his phone.

Like powerful sentinels, large cypress trees stood saluting their arrival in a row along the peninsular road. The protesters had assembled on each shoulder of the roadblock, where they spilled onto the pavement. Although they appeared tightly wound, the men with guns had full control of the perimeter. Picket signs bounced up and down with slogans on them, "Down With Imperialism" and "No New World Order!" Max even spotted signs with familiar stencils like the ones he had seen in Chicago and Mexico City. The images of Odeon Rutherford and George W. Bush were spray-painted in black, and beneath each likeness, the word "RIZICK" was written.

Based on what he knew, the Rizick Group meeting was an event of gargantuan scope. Three hundred of the world's most powerful and influential people would be in attendance, but there wasn't a single true paparazzo in sight. Max scanned the crowd again, but the established media was strangely absent among the horde. No press badges or TV network trucks. Max had stumbled across paparazzi in Mexico City, but these people were different. *These are protesters.*

Their SUV finally reached the front of the armed checkpoint. Without questioning them, one of the soldiers in blue uniform waved them through. Rosalee seemed particularly calm while their vehicles sliced through the mêlée. Once they cleared the blockade, both SUVs resumed a high rate of speed toward the resort. At the hotel entrance, Max could see a fleet of limousines and luxury cars. Those who were in possession of old money, power, or both were exiting and crossing into the hotel lobby. Back at the blockade, a fleet of telephoto lenses was trained on Rizick Group attendees. Each time someone exited a car, bulbs flashed like a field of fireflies on display.

Rosalee smiled at Max while jotting notes in her organizer.

"This resort has always worked well for the meeting. Some of those people out there think they know its location when, in actuality, there are three hotels on the compound here. None of them really knows which one the meeting is in." Rosalee shrugged. "To tell the truth, we don't even know yet."

Their driver maneuvered into the line of limousines approaching the hotel entrance. With the press of a switch, the SUVs windows lightened again. They crept to a stop at the hotel steps.

Rosalee grabbed her briefcase and smiled. "It's not nearly as intimidating as all of this makes it seem."

A troop of hotel valets opened their doors, and Max and Rosalee exited. Max turned back to the crowd of protesters. Some of them were screaming in Greek while others yelled in English. The one thing Max could make out disturbed him. A woman was yelling, her voice cracking. "Murderers!" she screamed repeatedly. "Murderers!"

The DC trainers made their exit from the other SUV. The yelling continued from the perimeter, and he and Rosalee shared a glance.

"Pretty impressive, isn't it?" she quipped.

Otto motioned to beckon the trainers before turning to Max. "I'm heading up. Have a look around the compound if you like. Most of the people you see here are the ones who keep the world rotating on its axis." Otto turned to Rosalee. "Can you escort him up when he's ready?"

"Of course," she nodded, watching while Otto disappeared into the hotel followed by the trainers. The yelling at the perimeter grew louder until Rosalee appeared to lose patience. "Are you ready, Mr. Battenberg?"

"After you."

Pivoting on her heels, she led Max to the hotel entrance. They entered the automatic doors, and the expletives being hurled from the road faded. In a way, Max felt like the air-conditioned breeze had washed the unpleasant words from his ears.

He studied the hustle and bustle happening around the lobby. Rizick Group meetings only happened once a year, and they were an enormous production each time they occurred. A convergence of the wealthiest people on the planet required an array of safety and logistic concerns. Max scanned the room and noticed several recognizable faces. Some were fat OPEC oil barons. Others were business tycoons, not unlike Demetrius.

An older woman with sandy, gray hair passed smelling of the most wonderful perfume. Her shoes sounded like a horse's hooves as she strode arrogantly across the lobby. Max noticed she had golden, bow-shaped buckles on each shoe, and he instantly knew they were solid 24-karat. Although they had been polished to a higher sheen, they were similar in color to the bars he'd taken into Teotihuacán's Pyramid of the Moon. The woman tightly pursed her lips as she passed. It was more of a smirk than a smile, and Max sensed no warmth from her at all.

As Demetrius Battenberg's son, he had spent plenty of time around wealthy and famous people, but he had never been in the presence of so many in one place. Max knew if he calculated the actual worth of everyone arriving to the hotel that the figure would be astronomical. This group of 300 independently controlled and manipulated funds in excess of 80 trillion dollars. Whenever they opened or closed their purse strings, the world economies shivered.

Rosalee smiled as she surveyed the crowd. Coming out of her own daze, she turned to Max. "As usual, your father has reserved a box. He prefers not to draw this kind of attention." Rosalee mobilized a young bellhop by raising an arm and snapping her fingers at him. The young bellhop approached, and Rosalee spoke Greek in a soft and unassuming tone. Max could see the young man was trembling. To be in the presence of such wealth was intimidating, and the porter's nerves were visibly getting the best of him.

With a nervous chuckle, the young staff member led them toward an adjacent corridor. Rosalee and Max followed, and the three of them disappeared from the lobby. After crossing through several hallways, they were led outside, where they caught a brief view of the sea. The bellhop urged them to climb aboard a golf cart. The moment they were seated, the cart jerked forward, and the porter drove them onto a path that was obscured by large screens resembling oversized, outdoor room dividers. Out of view from anyone who might be watching, they began traversing the grounds.

Max watched the first hotel tower disappearing behind them. "Where are we going?"

"The looky-loos probably think we're convening in the main tower. Just because we checked in there doesn't mean that's where the conference is."

The cart headed beyond the path of screens, and the sea revealed itself. Max gazed across the water, which appeared inviting. If only he could walk by the sea or sit by the pool. After a short distance, they arrived at the Astir Palace's south tower.

Rosalee was the first to hop off. "I presume this is the real location."

The bellhop led them into the building and directed them to Demetrius' private box. Max and Rosalee entered to find Otto sitting inside. He turned to Max.

"Pretty boring down there, isn't it?"

Max smirked. "Not exactly your hang-out-by-the-pool kind of crowd."

There were no aspects of Demetrius' private room that resembled the palace's normal modern decor. Instead the space was decorated like a lawyer's office with lots of dark wood and brass fixtures. Max was certain it had been built specifically for this meeting and to Demetrius' specifications.

On the wall adjacent to the entrance, there was a leather burgundy couch. Opposite to that, a huge one-way window looked down on the floor below. Max crossed to the window. Sitting beneath it, a table had been built with three computer monitors and accompanying headphones. Beside the center computer there was a metal box. It had three buttons on it, top-to-bottom, in the colors of red, yellow and green, like a traffic light.

Max looked down on the floor below. A maze of cubicles and computer screens were set up in varying pods. For the most part, everything was arranged how he remembered it on the schematic he had seen weeks earlier in DC. The set-up, as anticipated, was reminiscent of the New York Stock Exchange floor. Max suspected this entire structure had been built for this meeting. In the corner of Demetrius' box, beside the leather couch, there was a mini-bar fully stocked with beverages and snacks. Rosalee checked that everything was in order, then turned to Max and Otto.

"Is there anything either of you require?"

"You're not abandoning us, are you?" Max questioned.

"Your father has strict guidelines as to who can be in here during these meetings. Generally, my presence is not required."

"So, you are leaving?"

"Yes," Rosalee smiled. "Unless there's something else I can get you?"

Max turned to Otto. "What do you think?"

"I'm sure Rosalee has managed every detail." He turned to her directly, "If we need anything we'll be sure to let you know."

Rosalee then did something Max had never seen her do. She curtsied before stepping from the room.

Otto motioned Max toward the desk of monitors beneath the window. "I'll go over procedure with you. This computer terminal here in the middle is yours. Intel will be transmitted through this monitor, as well as through the headphones. Of course we'll be able to oversee what's going on down on the floor. When actual voting begins, that huge apparatus out there in the center of the floor will light up." Otto directed Max's attention to the tri-colored buttons on the metal box beside the computer console. "This is where you'll be voting. Obviously, green is a yes vote, red, a no and yellow, undecided. For each vote, there will be about ten minutes. Did you bring your cheat sheet?"

"Of course," Max replied as he lifted his sleek attaché case into view.

"Well, my friend, voting begins in about fifteen minutes. We won't finish today, of course, so tomorrow will be the big issues. When we are done, you'll have your very first Rizick meeting under your belt. Keep in mind this is a private room. We can see out, but no one can see in. Whatever you vote will be strictly confidential, although we may have to attend a conference here or there."

"Oh, really?"

"There are several issues where your father prefers to know how others are voting. Literally, they're meetings of two or three minutes in rooms along the outside corridor. Think of it as intel gathering."

"Two or three minutes is a little fast for issues of this magnitude, no?"

Otto shook his head. "Time is money, Max. Getting these people to one location is a huge feat, let alone for two days. Trust me, two or three minutes is all anyone can afford. These meetings have gone on for centuries. By now, they're quite harmoniously designed. For the most part, I'll be right here on the other monitor, trying to help you keep track of it all."

"What's the third computer for?"

"It's back-up. In case there are any technological snafus."

Just as Otto finished his last word, the computer monitors all went live. Max hadn't noticed, but dozens of people were now circulating on the floor below, and more were entering. After nearly twenty-five years of waiting, Max's first Rizick Group meeting was about to begin.

CHAPTER 20

Otto crossed to the mini-bar and made himself a drink. "You want anything, Max?"

Max felt his nerves, and a cocktail somehow seemed in order. "There any brandy in there?"

"Certainly." Otto poured Max a double, then handed him the glass. Both men sat at their monitors, and the voting began.

The large screen on the outside floor lit up, and the issue at hand scrolled across it. As Otto predicted, a ten-minute window was provided to vote. Max opened his briefcase and removed his cheat sheet with everything they had covered during his training. As the issues progressed, he punched the red or green buttons to make Demetrius' desires known. Everything was moving fast, but Max had no problem keeping up.

The first votes involved upcoming elections around the globe. Information on different candidates scrolled across each computer screen, but it wasn't about what they had to offer. More to the point, there were detailed accounts about the candidates, both winner and loser, and what they were intended to do. In almost every instance, a particular objective was desired, and the candidates were utilized to bring whatever goal to fruition. If a candidate who was intended to lose began attracting too much attention, a scandal would surface to reset the playing field. If that didn't suffice, a third-party "divide-and-conquer candidate" would be introduced to further divide the votes. Ultimately, the Rizick Group determined the political fates of countries on every continent, but their deepest controls were in South and North America and in Europe.

Later in the day, voting transitioned to international currencies. Because huge sums of money often accumulated in different parts of the globe, there was always a need to redistribute wealth. Industries in China and India had created stockpiles of euros and dollars alike. Max voted to move or fix exchange rates that would shift funds into more desirable hot spots like Brazil and South Africa. Such votes always resulted in new policies and exchange agreements between nations. While jobs in one place were being eliminated, others would simultaneously be created across the globe.

Max had always known that Demetrius and people like him were the true movers and shakers of virtually every industry. With each vote the facts became even more concrete for him. At midday, Otto had food delivered, and Max took advantage of the easier votes for rest-room breaks and to get fresh air.

The final vote of the day came just before 5:00 p.m. The issue at hand was whether or not China should be admitted as a true competitor to the automotive industry.

Otto immediately perked up when he saw the initiative on screen. "Oh, shit. Last year your father voted yes on this. But we need to know we're not stepping on any toes before we do."

"Okay…" Max had no clue what Otto expected of him.

"A conference." He led Max from the private box into the corridor. He slipped the phone from his pocket and waited. Within seconds, a text message appeared that read, "#10."

Max noticed there were numbers above every door, and they were currently near room #18. Otto nudged him forward and they headed away from their box toward room #10. Small crowds of people were circulating through the halls, coming and going to and from the main floor. Only yards further, Max stopped dead in his tracks. He could hardly believe whom he saw exiting one of the rooms. Dressed in a navy pinstripe suit, Brigitte's brother, Bertrand, seemed very much in a hurry.

"Bertrand?" Max couldn't wipe the astonished look from his face. "What are you doing here?"

Bertrand's face was cool, smug even. "The same thing you are, Max."

Max stood frozen, wanting to respond, but unable to think of anything to say. He immediately recalled the day he and Brigitte visited his private doctor. She had known Doctor Bettencourt and his assistant Phyllis. Now her brother was here in Greece, exiting a Rizick Group conference room. *What the fuck?*

"Max," Otto interrupted. "We should get going."

"Yeah," Bertrand added, "I have to get back to the floor. Let's talk later."

"Wh-wait a minute," Max stammered, "is Brigitte here?"

"No." Bertrand stared at Max and Otto, deadpan. "There's no need for us both to be here. I'll talk to you later, okay?" Without another word Bertrand crossed to a stairwell and disappeared through the doorway, descending to the meeting's ground floor.

"Come on, Max," Otto insisted, "we only have a few minutes." Otto jogged two doors down and entered conference room #10 with Max on his tail. Max didn't recognize anyone inside, but a series of handshakes and document exchanges resulted in the consensus that China should be allowed deeper entry into the automotive industry.

Satisfied with his decision, Otto pulled Max from the meeting to return to their private booth. Max completed the day's final vote by pressing the green button to confirm his father's wishes. Exhausted, he sat back and gazed at the main floor beneath them. As voting closed, there was a commotion of people heading toward the exits. Max scanned faces in the crowd to see if he could spot Bertrand. He had so many questions. At the same time, he was afraid to know the answers.

Otto poured another round of drinks before joining Max at the one-way window. "So, what'd you think of your first day?"

Max took one of Otto's cocktails and sipped it. "It's pretty amazing when you think about it. No wonder people are out there protesting." Max took another gulp of his drink.

"You shouldn't worry about that. Those people are fanatics, radicals even. No one takes them seriously. Every year, they upload footage to the internet for other crazies to see."

Max considered Otto's explanation. "Yeah, I get it. My friend, Ted, looks at all that stuff, and I never take him seriously." Max gazed at the floor below, which was quiet again except for the team of cleaners sweeping through. "Who would ever guess that the welfare of billions would be decided by a handful of 300 people?"

"That's the point." Otto motioned to their surroundings. "That's why it's done like this." He finished up his drink in a final swallow. "Tomorrow we do this again. But let's enjoy Greece a little bit first."

"That's a great idea, Otto. Perhaps the best one you've had all day."

Max and Otto gathered their things and exited into the outer corridor. The exodus of the planet's wealthiest and most influential had nearly reached its end. Max looked around, surprised to see how quickly the crowds had thinned. He supposed the bulk of attendees had either returned to their rooms, or they had taken to the streets to enjoy the last hours of sunlight.

To his chagrin, Max spotted another face he hadn't expected lingering in the small group of remaining Rizick members. Odeon Rutherford stood out like a sore thumb. He was actually dressed quite shabbily compared to the finely tailored clothes on most people around them. Rutherford was in a beige linen outfit that seemed much too casual for the affair. Beneath the crinkled suit was a dingy, white, pinstriped shirt, and Odeon's hair was at best unkempt.

Max remembered he was a lecturer, but the nutty professor appearance seemed cartoonish. Some of Rutherford's biggest fans were in academia, but they had no idea how much power he truly wielded. The public persona he showed was a huge deception. People found Odeon eccentric, but his attire spoke of true privilege. If his aura could speak, it would scream, *There are no rules for me, and my manner of dress is of little consequence.*

Since his arrival in Greece, Max had seen many faces, but none of them was particularly high-profile. In fact, had Demetrius been in attendance, he would have been one of only a few well-known attendees who had crossed his path.

While many Rizick members were considered über-wealthy, their names rarely appeared in the press. This was, of course, because Rizick controlled the media, and they didn't want unnecessary attention drawn to themselves. On rare occasions, there were constituents like Demetrius, who were well known and high profile. But there were also the Odeon Rutherfords of the world, people who were moderately known for seemingly innocuous activities.

Otto spotted Rutherford seconds after Max and immediately tensed. "Perhaps we should head back to the box."

"No," Max answered, sounding as terse as Bertrand had earlier. "I'd like to meet him. I've read his file."

Otto grabbed Max by the arm. "Don't mention a thing about today's voting or your dad's condition. If anyone asks, the story is he's resting quietly and will return to work soon."

Max nodded before crossing to Rutherford. He was just ending a conversation with the older woman Max had seen earlier in the lobby, the one with golden buckles on her shoes. She stomped off, and Max couldn't tell if she was smiling or sneering.

"Professor Rutherford," Max chimed lightheartedly, "I was hoping to meet you."

Rutherford was in his late sixties, but he looked to be seventy-five. His skin was fair and veiny, and age spots covered his hands. He still had a full head of hair, but it was mostly gray and frizzy. Expressionless, he peered over a pair of half glasses that were perched on his nose. After a pause most would consider rude, Odeon spoke.

"Battenberg's kid. Terrible thing what happened to your dad. They ever figure out if that was an accident or not?" Rutherford had lived the majority of the last twenty years around the East Coast of the United States, but he still had a slightly British accent.

"Let's hope it was. If someone tried to kill my dad and failed, well... I wouldn't want to be that guy."

Max knew the comment was biting because Rutherford's face finally registered an emotion. His expression was one of shock mixed with outrage as he peered over his glasses at Max. This only lasted a few seconds before Odeon's poker face returned. "This is why it's crucial to determine with certainty if it was an accident. If it wasn't, the responsible party might try again."

"I suppose they could," Max immediately shot back, "but I doubt the opportunity will ever present itself."

Otto, who was impressed with Max's offense, approached and took a spot directly behind him. Rutherford removed his half glasses and shoved them in his jacket pocket.

"Well, as we know, the world is an endless spring of opportunities. It was a pleasure meeting you, Mr. Battenberg."

"Likewise, I'm sure."

Max stared at Rutherford, but neither he nor Odeon extended a hand. With a grunt Odeon spun around and disappeared down the hall.

"What a bastard," Max exclaimed as he and Otto watched him departing.

Otto smiled and patted Max on the shoulder. "I'm not so sure your father would have handled that any better."

"If there's any truth in his file, that man had my mother, brother and uncle killed. It could've been me too. I'm not gonna fucking play nice."

Appearing as if from out of thin air, Rosalee rounded the corner. "How was your first day, Mr. Battenberg?"

"Draining. Right, Otto?"

Otto patted Max again on the back. "His father would be proud."

Max gawked at the empty spot where his father's nemesis had just stood. "I just had a run in with Odeon Rutherford."

"Really?" Rosalee inquired. "And?"

"I don't like him. And I'm not sure why nothing's been done about him." Max pondered the circumstances before shaking it off. As the finality of the day settled in, he felt overcome with fatigue. "Where are we sleeping tonight, by the way?"

"That's why I've come," Rosalee answered. She handed a hotel envelope to Max and another to Otto. "These are your room keys, and the usual protocol stands. No discussions with anyone about room locations, especially given the circumstances. I've already had your bags sent up. Other than that, I guess, enjoy the rest of your day, gentlemen."

Max smiled, still in a haze from his encounter with Odeon. "Thank you, Rosalee." The more he and Rosalee interacted, the fonder he grew of her. It seemed her only goal was to please, and she did an excellent job of it.

He suspected his tiredness was from a combination of jet lag and the day's adrenalin waning from his system. He needed sleep. Maybe later, he would venture out to find Bertrand and uncover his and therefore Brigitte's family affiliation with the Rizick Group.

CHAPTER 21

After the graceless introduction to Odeon Rutherford, Max found his way to the room Rosalee had arranged. He was surprised to learn it was in the north tower of the Astir Palace, which was the first hotel they entered. The suite overlooked the peninsula and offered a spectacular view of the sea. Depending on where he stood in the large window, Max could even see the protesters in the distance. From what he could gather, they were still in holding position, sequestered by the regiment of armed guards.

Desperate for answers, however, he immediately removed his smartphone and dialed Brigitte. *Why is Bertrand here?* The phone rang several times before Brigitte's outgoing message began. He pressed "#1" to bypass it. "Hey, it's me. I got a surprise today when I ran into your brother. I'm guessing you know I can't speak in detail about this, but you can imagine my shock... I'm sitting here, wondering what the fuck is going on." The question had dogged Max the entire evening, but he was only now finding time to fully process what it meant that Bertrand was also in attendance at the meeting. *Shit. Has she known all this time what I went through in Mexico?* There was no doubt in his mind that Brigitte's family was somehow plugged in. How else could her brother be here? "Do me a favor. Can you call me when you get this? Please. I need to talk to you. I hope you and the baby are okay."

Max hung up and removed a sleek, paper-thin tablet from a piece of luggage in the corner. He hoped Brigitte would call back shortly, but he needed to occupy himself somehow. The moment the tablet booted up, he typed in the search term: "The Rizick Group." He was hardly surprised that only a few hits turned up. He clicked on the site at the top of the list, and a single paragraph appeared:

The Rizick Group is an alleged secret society akin to the Bavarian Illuminati, the Bilderberg Group or the Committee of 300. Little is known about its origins or maneuverings, or whether or not the group has any true power or influence on the world stage.

Max surfed through several other sites and discovered a myriad of similar secretive groups rumored to have influence over world affairs: The Council on Foreign Relations, The Club of Rome, MK Ultra, Rosicrucians and, of course, the Freemasons. *The Rizick Group.*

He was unsure how Rizick had managed to remain off the radar. Still curious about his origins and the meeting for which he was currently in attendance, Max typed in the search word "Enlil." Hundreds of sites popped up, describing Enlil as a deity in Sumerian and later in Akkadian, Hittite and Mesopotamian mythologies. For forty minutes, Max read about the legend of his extra-terrestrial ancestor; everything he found appeared relatively accurate when compared with the things he had already learned, dreamed or witnessed.

Max sighed when he read a familiar headline from Enlil's story. "Banished for rape." *How is it this is considered fiction? It's all here.* Max found it uncanny. A story whose origins were firmly rooted in truth had somehow been transformed into myth? During his initiation he had been sworn to secrecy. Max didn't dare speak of his own off-world origins. If he ever did, most would probably consider him stark raving mad anyway. Part of him longed for the Anti-k Device to fill in the remaining blanks, but the missing component made this impossible.

Max recalled the events about Enlil like his own memories. Not only had he been made witness to them, he had also experienced many of Enlil's emotions. He continued reading, in awe. *So much of this is accurate. Nothing has been forgotten.*

He ran multiple searches until he spotted the link: *Mine Workers Mutiny Against Enlil.* Max clicked on the link and began to read. As he delved further into the site, much of Enlil's story unfolded on screen before him:

During his brief flight to the Abzu, Enlil pondered his predicament. He had every intention of uncovering Enki's secret to accelerated gold production in the southern Nibirian settlement. For one, the timing could not have been more opportune since his half brother and Ninmah were away on some excursion. In their absence, he could carefully examine the Abzu operation, illuminating anything Enki was attempting to hide.

When his ship touched down, his brother's foreman, Ennugi, greeted Enlil. It quickly became apparent why Ennugi had been placed in charge. He was a mountain of a male specimen, easily one and a half times larger than Enlil. Like shag carpet, dark auburn curls covered his head, framing up an angular face and a hard jaw. From what Enlil could tell, Ennugi was soft-spoken, but his hulking frame likely did the talking. Despite all of his royal bravado, even Enlil felt a little intimidated, but he wasted no time questioning Ennugi about the Abzu's gold operation: How did they locate the ore? How many shifts were the Igigi being asked to work? When were they given down time?

They toured through the mines while Ennugi diligently struggled to fill Enlil in. "Master Enki has been quite proficient in his wrangling of the workers here in the South." Ennugi took an awkward pause before he continued. "But I would be remiss if I did not speak of their discontent."

Enlil's frown slowly crept into a smile. "Discontent?"

"Yes, your Highness. The mines here are grueling, even more so than they are in Eridu. His honorable Master Enki has identified a workload that the Igigi find tolerable. They are asked, however, to work slightly above this level. If we don't determine some method of relief, I fear they will lose steam. Perhaps not tomorrow, or the next week, but soon."

While he had hoped to delight in his brother's shortcomings, Enlil could barely contain his irritation. "Surely, the Igigi recognize that it is an honor to work the mines. The result of their labor is the salvation of our birth land. How can this not be clear?"

"Of course, your Highness, but the morale here is fragile. I fear if it collapses, production will fall to nil."

"Yes, but in this circumstance they will each be prosecuted to the highest extent of the council. Not even I am beyond reproach, Master Ennugi. Nor will your men be. As a reward for their hard work, they shall now be tasked with increasing the ore's extraction. This way, their contributions will be even more noble and significant."

Only Enlil could issue a punishment and frame it as reward. Ennugi, however, understood the game as good as anyone and forced a smile.

"First," Enlil continued, "you shall acquaint me with the remainder of your operations, step by step."

Out of respect, Ennugi took a bow before Enlil. "As you wish, my Liege."

Later in the day, when his job with Enlil wrapped up, Ennugi consorted with his top workers. Together, they decided it was best to radio Enki for counsel on how to deal with Enlil's unreasonable manner. Upon hearing news of Enlil's antics, Enki could do nothing but smile in his turn.

"My half brother scrambles, Master Ennugi. He wishes to destroy the work we have done in the Abzu, but you mustn't allow him this luxury. I have no idea when, but his supervision of the Abzu shall soon be lifted. Until then, his wants and desires are beyond reprimand. If your men have demands, you must make them known while Enlil is there. Ninmah and I will be several days more until our new laboratory is operational."

"Very well, your Highness." Ennugi's voice betrayed his reluctance. "In your absence, I shall serve as intermediary between his Honorable Master Enlil and the Igigi."

"For now, this is how you must proceed. But worry not, when I return, our routine shall continue as it did before my departure."

"Very well, your Highness." Ennugi was an excellent foreman, but he was also smart enough to know he had entered a game of wills between two half brothers. "I shall inform the Igigi of the situation."

At the end of the workday, Ennugi cautiously entered Enlil's quarters in the ziggurat's royal apartment. He found Nibiru's first prince enjoying a small feast. "Your Highness, pardon the interruption."

With his mouth full and food in hand, Enlil motioned Ennugi forward, allowing him to continue.

"I have done as requested. The Igigi have been informed that they are to increase production."

Enlil finished chewing and swallowed before he spoke. "Excellent." He took a goblet from the table and sucked down several gulps of its contents. "Master Ennugi, I have other questions if you will."

"Of course, your Highness."

"From what I can gather, everything seems to be in order here."

"Thank you, your Eminence. We work very diligently toward this goal."

"While you may receive your instructions from my half brother, you are aware it is I who is responsible for the Abzu's operations, are you not?"

"Yes," Ennugi bowed to show respect. "The honorable Prince Enki has made it clear that all orders descend from you."

The news caught Enlil off guard. "Really?" Before he could finish his thought, loud chatter echoed in the outer hall. "What on Earth..." Enlil spun around to see one of his own guards rushing through the door.

"Your Highness, the Igigi have stormed the temple. Already, they have overcome the Royal Guard. We must move you to safety immediately."

Enlil turned toward Ennugi. From the foreman's expression he could see there was something amiss. "What is this, Master Ennugi?"

Ennugi's face registered concern. "When I relayed your command, the Igigi were disgruntled. Still, I was determined to make your disposition known."

A dark fury arose in Enlil, causing blood to flush his cheeks. "And they dare storm the temple?! Ennugi, you will squash this at once!"

Outside, in the hall, the sounds of a mob grew louder and closer. Suddenly, the echoes of slamming doors resonated through the maze of corridors. Ennugi's face dropped. He knew the ziggurat well enough to know what was occurring.

"They are sealing us in, Your Highness."

"What?" Enlil stared at Ennugi. "How dare they rise against me!" He turned to his guard. "You will hand me your weapon."

"His Majesty, but how will I defend — "

"Hand me your weapon!" Enlil approached and snatched a long golden staff from his guard's shoulder. The slender cylindrical device measured half the length of Enlil's long frame. Toward the center of its length, a small indentation served as a grip. At the very tip of the weapon, two grooves crossed perpendicular to one another like a plus sign.

Without hesitation, Enlil squeezed his hand around the grip. The implement's two perpendicular grooves snapped open at the tip to reveal a circular tube inside. With the weapon armed, he aimed at the doorway and waited. Finally, a large Igigi worker stepped into Enlil's sights. Before the man could utter a word, Enlil fired. A pulse of bluish light shot from the weapon and enveloped the man upon impact.

"No!" Ennugi screamed as the worker immediately went rigid and toppled over like a tree. Ennugi rushed to the man's side. "But, your Highness, he was one of my best men!"

"That may be," Enlil proclaimed, "but this is how insolence will be rewarded."

A second Igigi worker stepped into view in the doorway. His face, while handsome, was hardened from days underneath Earth's glowing sun. He observed the scene a moment. "What have you done?" Then he rushed to aid his fallen comrade.

Ennugi raised a hand, hoping to stay Enlil's trigger. When Nibiru's prince did not fire, Ennugi addressed his remaining worker. "The question is, why have you stormed the temple?"

The worker kneeled over his colleague's rigid body. "It is too late for questions, Master Ennugi. Too many times we have made our concerns known."

"Your concerns are of little consequence!" Enlil bellowed as he aimed the weapon once more. "You will take your men and exit the temple at once!"

The worker, who was also in need of patience, stood and politely pressed Ennugi from the doorway back into Enlil's chamber. The ruckus in the hall escalated as additional men arrived. Two workers lifted the wounded man, spiriting him away while the other mutineers flanked their now apparent ringleader. The Igigi representative bowed before Enlil, seemingly to offer his submission. "As you wish, Your Highness. When you are prepared to hear our concerns, you will let us know."

Enlil's hand trembled on the weapon's trigger as his fury became even more unhinged. A second bolt of bluish lightning shot from the weapon, barely missing a pair of men near the exit. To Enlil's surprise, the same men grabbed hold of the chamber's two ornately carved metal doors and slammed them shut, barricading the only entrance. Unable to contain himself, Enlil triggered the weapon once more, emitting another blue pulse that exploded across the metal with little effect.

"Unlock this barrier at once!" Ennugi demanded.

Enlil looked on in outrage. "You must wrangle your men at once, or they will pay dearly!"

Ennugi shook his head, hopeless. "I am ashamed, my Liege. But I fear we are the enemy now."

For the first time since his arrival on Earth, Enlil's rage was transforming into alarm. "Have I been taken hostage, Master Ennugi?"

Ennugi looked from Enlil to his guard, unable to provide an answer that anyone would find satisfactory. In his heart, Enlil knew he had been played somehow. He could not say for sure, since in theory, Enki knew nothing of his arrival. But in one way or another, he was certain he had been set up.

"Is there a radio in this chamber?"

Ennugi crossed to a console against the wall and opened a sliding door to reveal radio equipment inside.

"You will see to it that each of these men pays for their insolence."

Enlil fired up the interstellar radio and typed a message to his father, relaying news of his imprisonment. He called for the harshest punishment possible for the organizers of the rebellion. In his heart, he hoped a finger could be pointed at Enki as the responsible party. This would be the ultimate victory over his older brother, witnessing Enki's execution for treason against the home planet.

For several hours, Enlil, his guard and Ennugi waited, but the blockade to his chamber stood firm. Instead, several written messages with Igigi demands were passed to Enlil. Their requests had not changed over the decades since their arrival on Earth. They wished for better equipment, shorter hours and faster rotations for rest and relaxation. Each time demands were passed into the chamber, Enlil seized them and shredded them unread into pieces.

The hours turned to days with Enlil, Ennugi and the guard sequestered inside the ziggurat's royal chamber. Enlil considered contacting Enki for assistance, but he could hardly tolerate the idea of requiring his half brother's help. At the top of the eighth day, a message from Anu arrived. *How dare the Igigi play such games when it is the livelihood of our home planet at stake...*

Enlil continued reading with a smile. "His Lord, Anu, will travel here himself to deal with these mutineers." Enlil glared at Ennugi, revealing his pent-up rage. "If I have my way, I assure you they will be executed."

"But your Highness," Ennugi interjected, "these are our most accomplished men, I promise you. To execute them would defeat any goal of increased production."

"Who is behind this, Ennugi? I demand you uncover the insurrectionists of this affair. Be it my punishment, or Lord Anu's, the price to pay will be dear."

"But your Highness, it is your attention they seek, not your wrath."

"Now they will have both. In less than two days, Lord Anu, along with several members of the council, will arrive to see the condition of this outpost."

Ennugi understood it was unwise to continue the discussion and simply bowed his head before Enlil. "As you wish, your Highness."

Max felt awestruck as he read. *How can it be there is so much detail, and yet no one recognizes the truth in it?* He skimmed different sites and different pages, confirming much of the story he already knew and filling in some of the blanks.

Then Max spotted a new link: *Enki And Ninmah Create Hybrid Worker Race.* Curious to see another puzzle piece, he clicked on the link and read.

CHAPTER 22

*T*en days after the uprising, Enlil heard them removing the barricade to his quarters. Still furious at the audacity of his workforce, he rushed to seize the weapon he had used to kill a man at the mutiny's inception. His finger twitched on the trigger, ready to strike if he was displeased with whoever appeared beyond the blockade. To his astonishment, when the metal doors opened, both Enki and Ninmah were standing in the doorway. Ninmah was the first to speak.

"Good heavens, Enlil. What derisory predicament have you fabricated this time?"

Enlil watched Enki, who remained silent with a prominent smirk upon his face. He turned instead to address Ninmah. "Has father arrived yet?"

"He landed this morning, at dawn."

"Why then have I been left here to languish?" he demanded, turning his fury toward Enki. "For your men to rise against me, the state of your operations must have already been dangling from a thread."

"Oh, Enlil," Enki replied, full of arrogance, "must you grovel so? Under my control, these operations were at their highest productivity. Of course, when you arrive there's mutiny." Enki spat out a sarcastic laugh. "After all this time, how is it you are still so ill-equipped to determine how things are run on this planet?"

"Stop it, you two," Ninmah interjected. "Tensions are high enough as is. We hardly need escalate them. Father is with the council now. I'm certain he wishes not to be trifled with."

"Why then," Enlil demanded, "have I been left to wait here in captivity?"

Enki explained, "Because the better part of the morning father and the council have been touring the Abzu, interviewing workers about the procedures here. We expect a decision any moment now, and we should all be present."

Enlil remained smug despite his earlier captive predicament. "Just so we're clear, the moment my banishment was rescinded, the entirety of this planet's operations reverted to my command.

I pray to God father has arrived with replenishments of Igigi because I will, no doubt, call for the execution of every mutineer—" Enlil turned and spoke to Enki with a soft but accusatory tone, "—and any others who were involved."

Enki barely registered a reaction beside the slight lift of an eyebrow. "Shall we go then? Father and the council await."

Without hesitation, Enlil shot by Enki and Ninmah and rushed into the hall. His confinement had lasted long enough! He journeyed down the corridor and spotted decorative preparations for Anu's arrival. For the most part, the settlement in the Abzu was without frills and lacked the lavishness of Eridu, whose palace was even more extravagant than the royal residence on Nibiru. Shame had prevented Enki from repeating a similar mistake on the Abzu's southern coast.

The ziggurat, however, was of solid construction with the type of craftsmanship expected of Anu's family line. Unlike Eridu, the gardens and surrounding temples had barely been adorned with the hieroglyphs and artwork required by those of royal status. For this reason, an installation of statues and sculptures had been made in the days following Enlil's imprisonment.

At the back of the ziggurat stood a modest outdoor amphitheatre. Its stage and stadium seating were all constructed of finely carved stone. Anu and a handful of council members were seated on stage beside a trio of open seats. All three siblings, Ninmah, Enki and Enlil, saw these spots and knew they had been reserved for them.

Before he took his seat, Enlil approached his father and bowed, but Anu shook his head with a disapproving glare. To avoid exacerbating an already discomfited situation, Enlil bowed a second time then took the empty spot closest to Anu. The Abzu's entire workforce had taken seats throughout the amphitheatre, and silence prevailed as they focused their full attention on the main stage. Enlil scanned the crowd, searching faces for the captain who had ordered his imprisonment. Once the infiltrator was located, Enlil intended to dispatch his own justice, and he would not be kind.

Enki and Ninmah took their places, and Anu finally approached the podium at the top of center stage. His voice echoed across the grounds when he spoke.

"It is with great displeasure that the council and I embarked on this mission to Earth. Only recently has our home atmosphere shown improvement over its failings. This is, of course, owed to the operations here in the Abzu, in Eridu, and in other locations scattered across this tiny globe. Let the reverberation of my voice be your final warning that your actions here, of late, will not be tolerated. Such exploits, even in ordinary times, would be severely punished. But this is not a common period in our history; it is an extraordinary one, which makes these offenses that much more egregious. As ruling council, we reserve the right to judge any and all of you who have organized this... uprising."

Enlil continued his observation of faces in the crowd. One way or another, he would make sure that those he could identify would pay. To his disappointment, Anu's stern demeanor seemed to be softening from its usual harshness.

"As I am sure we are all aware, many of us have allowed ourselves to be governed by fear and frustration. Every one of you here is needed. Not only have we observed your duties on this sojourn, we understand the challenges you face. These operations are vast: extracting the gold, vaporizing it, transporting the white powder to Nibiru. We shall seek solutions to better your work conditions, but the flow of gold must continue, whatever the costs. Should we falter, we risk the loss of a home planet to which we can return."

Enki, who was seated beside Ninmah, turned to her, trembling with excitement. "Mah, we must reveal our work now." He struggled to keep his voice a whisper. "We must not remain silent."

She looked at Enki, briskly shaking her head, trying desperately not to draw their father's attention.

But Enki persisted. "This is our chance."

"No, it is not the right time."

Anu's eldest child knew there was a risk to his plan, but intuition told him no better occasion would present itself. Unable to contain his excitement, Enki stood and interrupted his father with a bow. "His Venerable Lord Anu, if I might be permitted to speak."

A chatter of whispers erupted from the council while his father's eyes shot daggers across the stage at Enki.

"What is it you wish to interject?" Anu bellowed, hardly under-standing the disruption.

"I apologize, father. But I trust you may find this interrup-tion worthy of yours and the council's time." Enki watched his father nod, allowing him to continue. "I believe Ninmah and I have discovered a grand solution to the many impediments we face in production."

Anu narrowed his eyebrows. If a remedy had eluded him or the council, he was curious to hear about it. "Carry on."

"It wasn't until I arrived on this planet that I discovered life forms upon it. As you undoubtedly know, they are primitive beings, beyond the recognition of complex language. But Nin-mah and I, we are geneticists. With our expertise, we can use these beings. We have the capability to advance their evolution. If we do so, those indigenous to this planet could assist in work-ing the mines, lessening our need for additional Igigi."

Unable to contain his objection, Enlil leapt to his feet. "But father, to do this goes against every edict we hold true! We are sworn not to interfere with the evolution of primitive life forms. To execute such a plan would equate to the enslavement of a peo-ple, which I might add is also forbidden under Nibirian law."

Anu's eyes flared with outrage. "Enlil! You must show respect when addressing members of the council."

"I apologize, father." Enlil took a bow before he continued. "His Honorable Lord Anu, I would also ask forgiveness from members of the council. As sole commander of the Earth opera-tion, I must object to Enki's proposal. We all know there are laws against slavery and intergalactic genetic tampering. A plan like the one my brother proposes would be both legally and ethically unacceptable for reasons we all comprehend."

Technically, Enlil was not incorrect. Nibiru had established laws prohibiting everything that Enki spoke of in his scheme. Anu and the council members nodded in support of Enlil's objec-tion, but their faces betrayed their true opinions on the matter. Enki's proposition appeared to be a solution to their problem. After a brief silence, Anu finally spoke.

"All that you state is true, Enlil. But remember, these are not ordinary times. It is the cradle of our civilization that we struggle to save. While such laws and edicts have been established for good cause, there may also be great reason here to set them aside." Anu fixed Enlil in his gaze before turning to face his fellow council members. "Is this untrue? What say you, members of the council?"

While members of the council concurred, Enlil spotted Enki quietly bickering with Ninmah in the seats beside him. He couldn't make out what they were saying, but it was clear they were in disagreement about something.

"You are wrong, Mah," Enki whispered insistently. "Now is as good a time as any."

"Enki, no," Ninmah protested. "You've already been exiled. And that little stunt you played, restoring Enlil to power… he will work to have us imprisoned."

"And he will fail," Enki whispered. He jumped to his feet again and addressed the council. "Our solution is sound. It will provide relief to our workers, while forging on with extraction of the ore."

Enlil charged forward on stage. "But there is no guarantee that my siblings will be able to produce said workers in a timely manner."

Enki spat out a laugh. "With what evidence do you purport such a claim? Perhaps it is due to your own scholarly failings in genetics?"

Anu narrowed his brow with disapproval, but Enki continued, feeling entirely undeterred.

"Due to the crucial nature of our predicament, her Highness Ninmah and I would like to request the council's pardon for what might appear to be an infraction." Enki turned to glare at Enlil a brief moment before addressing the council once more. "The truth is, we have already proven our success in this endeavor."

There was a vague hum of chattering among the audience. With a curious look, Anu tilted his head to the side. "Please continue."

"We hadn't actually planned on presenting this just yet, father, but if I may?"

"This may be a first in Nibirian history, but time is of the essence. Carry on."

Enlil looked on with disdain while Enki pulled a messenger

aside and sent him into the temple. Whispers of gossip broke out among the council members on stage and the Igigi workers in the amphitheatre. During the short recess, Enlil approached Ninmah, unable to shake the feeling of scorn he felt toward his older brother.

"What is it you two have planned?"

Enlil turned to Enki, and his words were tainted with accusation. "I knew, somehow, you had schemed to raise production here. I suppose now the truth will reveal itself."

The timing could not have been better. At that moment, one of Nibiru's smaller transports sailed over the amphitheatre, then hovered a brief moment before it landed in an open area in front of the stage. Seconds later, Enki's pilot, Abgal, opened the transport doors and wheeled out a large cage that included two of Earth's indigenous beings. A series of gasps came from the crowd, as no one in the theatre had seen the hominids in such close proximity.

Enki proudly stepped forward to help Abgal position the cage before the council. "As you can see, earthlings are primitive, but they are of solid stock. Genetically, they are not unlike us, although their evolution lags millions of years behind." He held up a hand to the cage bars, and one of the creatures touched it, showing potential for communication, primitive though it was.

An elderly member of the council stood and stepped forward. His face was weathered with wisdom and age. "It seems you are correct. Their constitution appears quite hearty. But without advanced language, how will they be taught to work the mines?"

Enki's face shone with a broad smile. "If allowed to evolve, these beasts would develop language not unlike our own. Of course, we can't afford to wait thousands of years for this to occur. But Ninmah and I—we can alter their DNA and lend some of our own faculties, creating a hybrid of sorts. This will provide them with the tools they need: language, simple reasoning. The remainder of their brains we can leave as is. This will minimize any infraction inflicted upon the evolution of their race."

"Such a feat could take decades," Enlil protested. "What if we rely on their expertise and they don't deliver? Where, then, will we be?"

To Enlil's dismay, he turned to see Enki laughing and shaking his head.

"Wrong again, brother. In genetics, Ninmah and I were both at the top of our class." Enki turned to Anu and the council. "As I mentioned earlier, this scheme was solely my idea, to take liberties here on Earth. But it has paid off."

Enki nodded to Abgal who immediately reentered the transport. Enlil, Anu and the council shared curious looks until Abgal exited a moment later, escorting Enki's first two hybrids from the craft: Adamu and Tiamat, who were now both 34 years of age, descended the ramp and followed Abgal onto the stage. Both looked timidly about the amphitheatre, as more astonished exclamations escaped from the crowd, creating a concert of sound.

"Order!" Anu commanded, silencing the comments. He approached Adamu and Tiamat, examining them up close before he turned to Enki. "What is it we have here?"

"Hybrid beings, father. Part earthling, part Nibirian, with every advanced faculty to understand language and to learn."

With the exception of being somewhat smaller in stature than Nibirians, Adamu and Tiamat looked no different than ordinary Igigi. With thick, dark curls and strong jaws, they were both handsome specimens, but there was a child-like naïveté about them.

"Father, I would like to present to you and the council the first successful specimens of a hybrid program Ninmah and I have been working on: Adamu and Tiamat."

Adamu took a step forward and curtsied before Anu. "Your Highness. It is an honor."

"Yes, your Grace," Tiamat continued, as she approached and dropped to her knees before Anu.

Once again, the crowd erupted with chatter, and Enlil understood how he had been duped. If he had paid more attention, he would have noticed there were new additions to the Abzu workforce. "But father," Enlil protested, sounding somewhat like a child himself, "this is preposterous."

Enki raised his voice to be heard over the commotion. "As you and the council can see, a hybrid program could be most effective to enlarge our workforce, using local provisions. Is that not why we are here, to utilize this planet's resources?" For more than two decades now Adamu has assisted in the mines."

Staring from his fellow council members to Adamu, Anu finally questioned, "Is this true? You have worked the mines."

"Yes, your Highness," Adamu replied. " I have worked them for nearly two-thirds of my life."

"And our tools you find adequate for such work?"

"Yes, your Highness."

To Enlil's horror, Anu appeared impressed by Enki's gross presentation of what was essentially illegal contraband. His father cracked a smile then turned to face members of the council. "Not all of the council is present to form a decision, but I believe Enki's proposition carries merit." Anu felt assured when he spotted other council members nodding approval. "Upon our return to Nibiru, we shall confer with the remaining council members, then a decision shall be made if a hybrid program is to begin."

Enki turned to Ninmah, who felt terribly relieved. While the chance was remote, it was not impossible that they could have been imprisoned, as Enlil was correct in his assertions. They had violated two edicts with their creations, Adamu, Tiamat and forty-eight others that the council didn't yet know about.

Enlil crossed to Enki as the meeting adjourned. "You think you're so clever. These two hybrids can't be the only ones. There are others, and I will expose them."

"Oh, brother, sometimes you can be so dull. Do you truly believe additional workers will produce some negative aspect to our achievement?"

"Father has acknowledged my position as first heir, and you know this. You should also know I will never support a hybrid program. Never. Once he learns that you have concealed Alalu's weapons stash, we'll see what he thinks of you then."

Enki's eyes grew wide at his brother's revelation. No one but Ninmah and Abgal knew of the weapons, so how had Enlil discovered his secret?

Enlil smirked at his brother's surprise. "Do you honestly believe father would not have wanted to know the Atu-waa's location? We'll see how much he trusts you once he finds out." With this last word, Enlil turned and left the stage, leaving Enki to realize that their feud would never reach a genuine conclusion.

CHAPTER 23

$\mathcal{M}$ax found it hard to comprehend. So much of the Anunnaki story had been preserved intact as some strange myth that people no longer believed, if they knew of it at all. He clicked through other areas of the site until he stumbled on the link, *Enki and Ninmah Genetically Engineer Worker Race*. His continuing interest pressed him to click on it, and he read further.

Ninmah understood if their hybrid program garnered the council's approval, they would be expected immediately to commence production of a new worker race. Enki, in fact, in a self-assured manner, had already requested that she reinstate the birth goddesses to begin building their arsenal of Earth-bred workers. In signature fashion, Ninmah once again protested the resumption of this duty.

"It can't be done, Enki. This is why we halted the program in the first place. We cannot expect Nibirian women to lend their wombs to this avail. It is simple; either we make the hybrids fertile or we must abandon the endeavor altogether."

Enki listened, but he refused to discard an idea whose tenets were based on solid thinking and ingenuity. "We have tinkered so many times with this, but the solution evades us." He sighed, upset that they had still not made a breakthrough in the hybrids' fecundity. "We have come too far to fail now, especially in light of Abgal's betrayal. That infidel enabled Enlil to deliver Alalu's weapons stash to father before I could. I fear he may have endangered both our reputations if we do not deliver the hybrid program successfully."

"But, Enki, this was your secret to keep, not mine."

"Until you saw its location, Mah. You have admitted to this already, which makes you complicit."

Ninmah glared at Enki. "You believe yourself better than Enlil, when in fact, you are no different. Neither of you will hesitate to soil those around you in your pursuit of grandeur."

"Calm yourself, Mah. All we need do is keep our promise of

a sustainable production process for the hybrids. Certainly, that should reset the scales in our favor." Enki appeared pensive while staring into space. "Shall I summon Ningishzidda?"

"You would have another son come here, in addition to Marduk?" Ninmah questioned. "Do you truly believe he can help?"

"He has excelled, as we have, at genetics. Perhaps with three minds, we can identify a solution."

The more she considered it, Ninmah appeared amenable to the idea. "Perhaps."

Enki nodded with a smile, to soften the mood. "We must summon him, then."

In less than a week's time, Enki's youngest son arrived from one of Nibiru's more distant Earth settlements. It was true, Ningishzidda possessed a certain facility in advanced genetics, but this was not his sole distinction. Born from an indiscretion between Enki and his mother, Ereshkigal, Ningishzidda also held the title as the first full-blooded Nibirian to be born on Earth. His very existence served as an experiment, of sorts, due to the enormous discrepancy between the passage of time on Earth and Nibiru. In the thirty-plus years since his birth, Ningishzidda had aged to such an extent that he already appeared to be of comparable age to his own parents. Because he had been raised under Earth's shining sun, his complexion had darkened to the color of deep mocha.

For months, all three geneticists toiled in the new laboratory 1400 miles north of the Abzu. In this most up-to-date installation, they spent entire days pouring through genetic code, seeking a cure for the hybrids' sterility. Ninmah knew if they didn't succeed, Nibirian women might be asked to serve as surrogates, an outcome she wished to avoid. During the process, they awaited a reply from Nibiru to determine whether a hybrid program would even be instituted, but such a response never arrived.

The longer time dragged on, the more Enki worried that his proposal would be denied. Part of him wondered whether Enlil had managed to sully the idea, but he also felt his solution was too brilliant to be overlooked. Under his strategy, there would be no need for Igigi rotations. In fact, the answer to Nibiru's gold extraction program had been right in front of them the whole time. His first day on Earth he had spotted the planet's indigenous beings, but he hadn't truly understood the value of such a resource.

Many months lapsed while they researched without a ruling from the council. As the days ticked away, they worked diligently and painstakingly toward a solution. Utilizing the latest holographic imaging software, Ningishzidda pulled up many samples of genetic code, comparing the DNA of Adamu and Tiamat to samples given by Enki and Ninmah. Nearly identical DNA chains floated midair in the room, twirling like large luminescent chandeliers. He eyeballed the links with a black stylus device in hand, identifying specific markers on each section.

Ninmah stood watching one day from the sidelines until she threw her arms in the air, sighing with aggravation. "I am beginning to doubt we shall ever find what we seek."

Equally frustrated, Enki had also stepped away to pace the room. Their morale was wearing thin when Ningishzidda looked up from the twirling models in the center of the room.

"Wait a minute. I think I found something."

Enki and Ninmah approached, both of them beginning to feel equally inadequate.

"Look," Ningishzidda used his black stylus to point from Ninmah's DNA sample to the adjacent one that belonged to Tiamat. "Right here, on Ninmah's chromosome, there is a recessive XY. See where it has lit up." Ningishzidda touched it with a pen and the marker fluoresced in bright purple. "Now, if we move over to Tiamat's chromosome at that exact location, we can see the XY is absent." Ningishzidda could hardly contain his excitement. Deep down he had hoped to be the one who might break the code. "Father, Ninmah, do you see it?"

"Yes, Mah," Enki proclaimed, growing more animated. "This looks promising, does it not?" Enki stepped to his son and slapped him generously across the back. "I pray you are correct."

Ningishzidda smiled broadly. "This is where the break lies in their fertility chain, I am sure of it."

Ninmah smiled while double-checking her nephew's work. "Oh, if this is it," she laughed, "it will hardly be a problem to fix. You know what has to be done?"

"A graft!" Ningishzidda answered before turning to his father.

"I'll need one from you to transplant into the hybrid."

Unable to contain their collective excitement, the geneticists quickly commenced the procedure to confirm if they had indeed resolved the question of hybrid fertility. Ningishzidda began by sterilizing and anesthetizing his father's flank. At the same time, Ninmah prepared a long syringe.

"This might sting a little," she warned.

Enki sized up the large needle, more impressed by its girth than he would have liked. "Is there not something smaller we can use?"

Ninmah shook her head briskly. "This will give us our best shot at a viable sample."

Ningishzidda softly tapped the area where he had anesthetized his father's ribs. "How's that feel?"

"Just go ahead," Enki pressed. "We need to get this done."

Ninmah took the syringe and pierced Enki's side just a palm's length beneath his armpit. Enki winced without complaint while Ninmah further wriggled the needle until she had successfully punctured his rib. "We're almost done," she assured, carefully withdrawing the plunger to extract marrow. A sharp pinch stung his flank as Ninmah siphoned away the requisite genetic material. "Got it." To Enki's relief, she withdrew the syringe and stepped back with the sample in hand.

"All right," Enki lamented, smarting from the sting in his side. "We must fetch Tiamat to see if this is indeed our solution."

Within hours, they had Tiamat delivered to their laboratory. Ningishzidda anesthetized her before transplanting Enki's tissue into her pelvic bone. Over time, the transplant would populate her blood with the absent markers that all Nibirians naturally possessed. "We must, of course, allow a few days," Ningishzidda explained, "so the genes might proliferate."

Nearly shaking with excitement, Enki rubbed the sore area of his side. "Do you realize, if this is the solution, we can begin the breeding program?"

Ninmah could barely contain her fervor. "And we have already enriched the genes that govern their libidos —"

Bristling with pride, Enki completed Ninmah's thought, "while leaving their brains devoid of higher intellectual notions. On the one hand, they will possess language and the ability to learn…"

"But they will also remain innocent and child-like," Ninmah interjected, "with the sort of naïveté that might preserve our edict against intergalactic genetic tampering."

"We needn't worry your birth goddesses, Mah. When the hybrids reach sexual maturity they will breed, and we will be heroes." Enki grabbed his sister in a warm embrace, then turned to Ningishzidda. "And your contribution, my son, shall furnish all the glory you deserve!"

Max's brain felt like a sponge, but in the weeks since his initiation there was simply too much information to absorb. Having tired of his research, he clicked back to his tablet's home screen and returned the device to his bag. He felt heavy with exhaustion after his endless day. While he had been sedentary during most of the meeting, he still felt unclean. He hopped in the shower, hoping to feel revitalized, but the opposite occurred.

Max checked the time; it was nearly 6:00 p.m. locally. This meant 11:00 a.m. in Chicago. He did not wish to retire just yet, even if, technically, he had been up all night. *Perhaps a nap*, he thought.

Max climbed into bed, hoping for an hour's sleep. He set his phone alarm, then snuggled into the hotel sheets. Moments before he drifted off, he contemplated the day's events — how the wealthiest people on the planet had gathered to think of ways to increase what they already had. *Shit*. Max wished for at least two more hours of daylight before the day was done, but his final gaze through the window saw dusk fast approaching.

Three hours later, after he had slept through his alarm, Max awakened to the night sky peeking through his hotel window. A scattering of buildings illuminated the peninsula like a mosaic of brightly dotted lights. At first, he felt disoriented, as his internal clock made it feel like noon. He glanced at the clock and read half past nine, local time. Jumping up, he threw on a pair of jeans and ventured out for food.

When Max stepped from the elevator, the lobby was strangely empty. As hundreds of people had checked in earlier, he expected a little more hustle and bustle. A limousine pulled up in the hotel's circular driveway. A couple he didn't recognize exited in formal wear, but Max was too hungry to pay them much attention. He turned and wandered to the hotel restaurant, where a commotion was brewing.

A man and two women were at the front desk, arguing with the hostess, who had summoned a gendarme to assist her. The armed guard stood by her side, dressed in solid navy blue fatigues with a Glock strapped to his waist. When Max approached, he immediately recognized the threesome. They were protesters who had been at the perimeter blockade earlier that morning. Somehow, they had bypassed hotel security. Max imagined they were there to infiltrate the Rizick Group meeting and gather intel, but they appeared to be arguing for a table. They claimed they simply wanted a meal.

Max waltzed up in the midst of their altercation. When the hostess spotted him she immediately stepped aside, leaving the guard to deal with the demonstrators. She smiled a wide grin for Max.

"Good evening, sir. Are you staying with us at the hotel?"

"Yes," Max responded.

"May I see your room key, please?"

Max handed over his room key, while the argument beside him seemed to be intensifying. Trying to smooth things over, the hostess quickly swiped Max's card through her computer.

"I apologize for the commotion, sir. If you'd just follow me."

Max smiled as the hostess took a menu and ushered him to a table overlooking the water. She deliberately seated him out of earshot of the rowdy patrons before returning to the front desk to further assist in squashing the disturbance. Despite her efforts, Max could see them through the decorative glass room divider. By the time his first appetizer appeared, the Greek police had arrived to escort the demonstrators from the hotel. Within minutes, he forgot about the upheaval and returned his attention to dinner.

Max had hoped a good meal might energize him, but it didn't. After dessert, he exited the hotel onto their pool deck. The night air was mild and felt good against his skin. Max knew there were quite a few guests checked in, but hardly anyone was circulating through the established common areas. He supposed staying out

of sight was the best way to avoid attracting unwanted attention — or maybe there was something else going on.

Curious, he began a lap around the main tower. When he
reached the front entrance he could still see armed guards forming
a perimeter around the hotel. He found the circumstance eerie,
wondering what might occur had the guards not been there.
Because of the immense wealth involved, he imagined every
Rizick Group member was a target for, among other things, kid-
napping and ransom. Throughout childhood, Max had always
taken Demetrius' security measures for granted. In recent months,
however, he began to understand that people like them did have
something to fear. But then again, the masses also had something
to fear if Clean Slate ever passed.

Max retreated to his room, thinking to watch TV or maybe
call Brigitte. The moment he flipped the television on, his room
phone rang, and he grabbed the receiver. "Hello."

The caller spoke in perfect English but with a strong Greek
accent. "Good evening, Mr. Battenberg."

"Yes." Max didn't recognize the voice.

"How was your dinner this evening?" The caller spoke with a
blended accent that sounded Greek and British at the same time.

"Very good." Max assumed it was hotel staff with some type
of customer satisfaction survey, but there was a tone of hostility
in the voice that didn't quite register. "Who is this?"

"We were downstairs waiting to be seated, but they refused
us service."

The protesters? "How did you get my room number?"

"In the picture frame behind the restaurant's front desk, there
is a glare. In correct light, it reflects the computer screen rather
well."

Realizing what had occurred; Max knew this was another
significant breach in hotel security. "Why are you calling me?"

"We are honest people, Mr. Battenberg. Can the same be said
of your cabal this weekend?"

"Is there something I can do for you? — because I'm about to
hang up."

"We were wondering if you might be willing to speak about
this weekend's meeting?"

"You seem to know who I am. Why don't you tell me who you are?"

"My name is Nikolaos Satrazemis."

Max jotted the name down on a piece of hotel stationary. "You know I have nothing to say."

"How about the way you voted today? Or what's on tomorrow's agenda? Exactly which hotel is the meeting in?"

Max smiled into the phone. "I'm not answering any questions, Mr. Satrazemis."

Nikolaos laughed sarcastically. "Yeah, we figured that much. It's rare to see you people do anything for others."

"I'm hanging up now."

"You have a splendid night."

Max hung up and waited, certain that Mr. Satrazemis would call back. If he did, it was his intention to alert the front desk and have them block his calls. But the phone didn't ring. Max considered the conversation, still wondering exactly why the stranger had called. As if on cue, his cell phone rang. Max grabbed it, suspicious to see a blocked number. *Could they have gotten my cell number too?* He pressed the talk button. "Hello?" To his joy, the voice on the other end was one he recognized.

"Hello, sir, this is Cora."

"Oh, thank God. Hi, Cora, how are you?"

"Very well, sir. I wanted to give you the good news. I found your mother's journal."

"You're kidding?" Max felt a pang of excitement stirring.

"I searched the Italian residences, but I didn't find anything there. I'm in France now, at the villa in Aix-En-Provence. It is in my hand, sir."

"That's fantastic, Cora. You're my savior."

"When you asked earlier, I just didn't remember I had packed some things for your mother. Then the accident occurred, and I never had them shipped. Somehow, that box found its way into storage. But I have it now."

"Great, Cora, there's no need to explain. I'm in Greece right now."

"Oh, I beg your pardon, sir. I hope I'm not calling too late then."

"No, it's fine. I'm still on Chicago time."

"If you desire, sir, I can bring the journal tomorrow."

"That's perfect, LC. I'll text you the address, and you can bring it to my hotel."

"Very well, sir."

"Do me a favor, LC. Please don't mention this to anyone."

"Of course not, sir."

"And one more thing only, I promise."

"Yes, sir."

"Recently, I've been experimenting with meditation. If you could have a little corner prepared for that in one of the upstairs rooms, that'd be fantastic."

"Oh, of course, sir."

"I'm not exactly sure how you do that but—"

"It's no trouble, sir. I will have that done as soon as I return."

"Thank you, Cora. You're a godsend. I'll talk to you soon!" Max hung up with a curt sense of satisfaction. *At least something's going well.* He grabbed the television remote and channel surfed until he landed on a disaster movie about the end of the world. It had been dubbed, and the main characters were rambling frantically in Greek. For a few minutes, Max lost himself in the film, forgetting about Nikolas Satrazemis and their strange conversation. Before the movie reached its first commercial break, Max was soundly asleep. The short respite was timely since in the morning he would have to do it all again.

$\mathcal{A}$t 7:00 a.m., the room phone rang. Max sprang out of bed, feeling every minute of his seven-hour jetlag. If he had known the meeting's location in advance, he would have planned an early arrival to adjust to the new time zone. In Chicago, it was just midnight, which prevented Max from feeling fully recharged. On the fifth ring, he finally grabbed the phone.

"Hello?"

He figured it might be Rosalee, or perhaps Otto. Instead there was an accented female voice on the other end. "This is your 7:00 a.m. wake-up call, Mr. Battenberg, sir. Is there anything you require?"

"No, I'm fine. Thank you." Max quickly replaced the phone in its cradle and plopped onto his pillow. Feeling like he might fall back to sleep, he rose like a zombie and stumbled into the shower. It had been weeks since he had enjoyed a good night's sleep, but he was resilient. By the time he bathed and dressed, he would appear refreshed, even if he didn't feel that way.

Max dressed in a gunmetal gray suit. It was one of his favorites. Standing before the mirror, he realized it may have been more suited to a nightclub than a Rizick Group meeting. *Too late now.*

He squeezed hair gel into his palm and wiped it through his hair. Max stared at his reflection, pleased that he didn't look as tired as he felt. In the trendy suit, he looked to be an executive from the music or film industry. From what he could gather, Rizick Group members were ultra-conservative in both their beliefs and fashion sense. While fabrics and tailoring were of the utmost quality, suit jackets were cut to be square and pants rectangular. In symbolic fashion, their garments revealed little to nothing about the bodies or physiques of the people inside of them.

Max's suit, on the contrary, was tailored to fit an athletic frame and hugged him in all the right places. He admired his reflection, making sure he was "Battenberg presentable." Satisfied, he crossed to the nightstand where he had placed his room key. He reached for it and noticed the hotel stationary. The name "Nikolaos Satrazemis" was scribbled on it. Max gazed briefly at the slip of paper, then shoved it in his pocket. Crossing toward the closet, he grabbed his briefcase and left the room.

When the elevator doors opened onto the lobby, Max was not expecting a commotion, especially because of how quiet it had been the night before. He was wrong. Large crowds of people were mingling. He stepped from the elevator, and a feeling of uneasiness overcame him. Once again, he found himself longing for the simplicity of his life before New Orleans and Indigo.

He looked around and spotted the Mediterranean through a huge panoramic window that stretched across the lobby. It was a gorgeous day out, and the beauty of the trees and the sea surrounding the peninsula was breathtaking. Max observed the Rizick Group attendees and realized how disconnected he felt from the people he knew: his peers at school, his employees at Badem Publishing, Chandler, Ted... There were no parts of his new life that he could share with any of them.

He scanned the lobby. From what he could gather, no one seemed to notice the natural beauty of the surrounding landscape. A sense of relief overcame him when he spotted Cora across the room. He made a beeline for her, but a hand reached out and grabbed him. Max spun around to find Bertrand staring back at him.

"Hey, Max."

"Bertrand. I was wondering if I'd see you today."

Brigitte's brother frowned and appeared agitated when he spoke. "Where are you headed after this is all over?"

"I'm not exactly sure. Why?"

"Fuck, man..." Bertrand had been unfriendly the day before, but now he seemed genuinely distraught. "Brigitte had a wreck last night. She's at Northwestern Memorial."

Max studied Bertrand as if he were speaking a foreign tongue.

Bertrand took note of his confusion and continued. "Did you hear me, Max? I was thinking your father's jet... if you're going home... it'll be faster, and maybe I can hitch a ride."

My dad, Gary, Brigitte... and maybe the baby. "What happened?" Max blurted out.

"Honestly, I don't have the full story. There was a collision. I heard her car is mangled pretty bad."

"What are you saying, Bert?"

"Brigitte's in the hospital, Max. The minute this is over we need to get the fuck back to Chicago."

"Why don't we leave now?"

The look on Bertrand's face was one of complete distress. "I'd like to, but... today's votes are too important."

Max stared at Bertrand, and the uneasy feeling in his gut further intensified. "Is she okay then? I mean, I probably can't break away either. Not until the meeting's over."

Bertrand shrugged at their predicament, wanting better alternatives, but not sure how to find any. "See if we can use your dad's jet. When you find out, let me know."

"Can we at least call her? I mean, is she able to talk?"

Bertrand dropped his head before he spoke. "I don't know. She was in surgery when I tried. I'll try again at break. Can we meet where we ran into each other yesterday, in front of room 12? That way, we can trade updates."

"Sounds good," Max nodded. "I'll see you then." Still stunned, he watched Bertrand turn and disappear into the crowd. He couldn't help but think of the agonizing days after his father's accident, while he tried determining whether or not Demetrius was okay. Now, 6,000 miles across the globe, the same feelings arose about Brigitte. The hotel scene surrounding him, the crowd, the view, all of it was spinning — until Cora's voice anchored him back in reality.

"Mr. Battenberg, sir."

Max turned to find Cora looking up at him with a smile. It did not appear that she had overheard his conversation with Bertrand. "Oh, Cora, hi."

"I phoned upstairs twenty minutes ago, but there was no answer."

"I must've been in the shower," Max replied, still thrown by Bertrand's news.

Cora reached inside her Louis Vuitton satchel and produced a tan 5x7" leather-bound journal. A long leather cord tightly encircled it multiple times, fastening it shut. "Here it is, sir." Cora handed the diary to Max.

"Thanks so much, Cora, I can't believe you found it."

She smiled, full of pride, until she noticed the uncomfortable expression on Max's face. "Is everything okay, sir?"

"I'm sorry, I just got bad news — Brigitte's been in an accident."

"Oh my goodness." Cora furrowed her brow with concern. "I am so sorry, sir. Is she going to be okay?"

"That's the thing… From all the way over here, I don't know.

"Is there anything I can do?"

"I don't know." Max appeared lost in thought. "I'll call if there is." Max held his mother's journal in view. "Getting this was brilliant, by the way."

"Of course, sir. Please don't hesitate to call if you need anything. She reached across with both arms, and he surrendered to a hug. Given the circumstances, it was good timing.

Max broke away and spotted Otto and Rosalee across the room. "I'm sorry, Cora… I need to scoot. Thanks for coming all this way." He placed the diary in his briefcase. Under ordinary circumstances, he would have liked to peek inside, but there wasn't time. As Cora turned to depart, he stopped her. "I hope you took time to visit your family. If you didn't, you should."

"Oh," Cora exclaimed with a nervous giggle, "thank you, sir."

It was clear Max's mind was elsewhere. "I'll see you in Chicago then."

"Very good, sir."

Cora turned and disappeared into the crowd. Max did as he had done weeks earlier after Demetrius' accident. He pulled out his phone and dialed Brigitte. Her voicemail kicked in, but before he could leave a message, Otto tapped him on the shoulder.

"Morning, Max."

He ended the call. "How're you, Otto?"

"Ready for another day?"

"Look, when this is over, where are we headed?"

Otto scanned the crowd before whispering the answer. "I imagine your father'll want to be debriefed."

A sense of desperation washed over Max. "I just found out Brigitte's been in an accident. Her brother said it's pretty bad. If it's okay, I'd like to stop in Chicago first."

"Oookaay." Otto dragged the word out with hesitancy. "You mean after the meeting is over, right?"

"I guess, Otto. I mean I'd like to go now, but I assume that's going to be a problem, right?"

Otto nodded. "These meetings are too infrequent. No one leaves until they're done. And today's votes—"

"Are important, yes I know. If it's all the same, I'd like to take the jet to Chicago as soon as we're done."

"That's fine with me, kid. The question is whether or not it's okay with your dad."

"Don't worry about him. I'll talk to him."

The crowd in the lobby suddenly began to disperse. It was like an imaginary bell had rung, and everyone was running to class.

"C'mon." Otto motioned Max and Rosalee forward. "We'd better get situated."

On the way to his second day of voting, Max pulled Rosalee aside. "My girlfriend was in a car accident last night." He felt an urge to mention the baby, but managed to keep his mouth shut.

Rosalee straightened up with a look of concern that resembled a frown. "I'm sorry to hear that, Mr. Battenberg."

"When we're done here, I'd like to take the jet to Chicago to check on her. It turns out, her brother is here, too. He'd also like a ride, if that's okay."

Without expression, Rosalee opened her electronic organizer and typed into it. She offered a brief smile. "I'll look into it for you, Mr. Battenberg."

"I know how my father can be, but I need this to happen. If he gives you a problem, let me know."

Rosalee returned the organizer to her bag. "I should have an answer by this afternoon."

Minutes later, Max and Otto were seated again in Demetrius' private box. Just as it had started the day before, a huge light illuminated the main floor, indicating the beginning of the day's vote. The first hours dealt with issues surrounding international labor forces. The Rizick Group decided on the best places to move production, and what seeds of necessary legislation would be put into place.

Max found the entire process fascinating. Even though he was seeing the Rizick Group's decision-making machinery from within, he still didn't fully understand how they affected the desired changes without the masses knowing about them.

When the afternoon break arrived, he sent Rosalee a text message, asking for an update about the plane. It took less than a minute for her reply. "Sorry. It's a no-go."

Max surprised himself by how furious he became. He dialed Rosalee's number. When she picked up, he didn't allow her to speak. "Can you get him on the line please?"

"Of course, Mr. Battenberg. Just one moment."

He expected Rosalee to say Demetrius was unavailable, but after a short while she came back on the line. "Mr. Battenberg, I have your son."

"Dad?"

"Yes." Demetrius' voice had rebounded some, but it still lacked its original luster.

"I don't know if Rosalee explained, but Brigitte's been in an accident. According to her brother—who's here, by the way—she's in pretty bad shape. I need the plane to check on her."

There was a pause before Demetrius spoke again. "It hasn't occurred to you yet, has it?"

"What?"

"The circumstances of this girl's accident."

Max could feel the conversation shifting. "What do you know about it?"

"It's my business to know who you spend time with, Max. The accident was not so unlike your mother's. For all I know, it has everything to do with your attendance at this year's meeting. Stepping in for me puts you in the crosshairs. Why is she at Northwestern Memorial? That's not a secure location."

"Wait a minute. How the fuck do you know all this and her own brother doesn't?"

Demetrius didn't respond. Instead he took a deep breath. "If you must, have her brought to New Mexico, and you can meet her here. Rosalee can make the arrangements."

Max felt stunned by the conversation. "So, you knew Bertrand was going to be here?"

"Of course, Max. Every unknown is potentially something dangerous."

Max didn't have it in him to be surprised anymore. "I'll see about New Mexico. I guess later on, you can explain everything."

"Very well," Demetrius replied. "Otto says the voting is going smoothly. That's good news. I'll see you when you get here."

Max ended the call and immediately proceeded to the rendezvous spot to meet Bertrand. When he arrived, Brigitte's brother was nowhere in sight. Max looked around, waiting until the break was almost up. With little time remaining, he removed his cell phone and found Bertrand's number. After several rings, he finally picked up, but his tone was distant and tainted with impatience.

"Hey, Max, sorry I couldn't make it."

"What's going on? I'm a little worked up over here."

"There's a lot going on."

Max could not believe Bertrand's cavalier attitude. "I asked about the jet, and my father seems to think we should have her moved to a more secure location. The place he's at in New Mexico —"

"Not happening," Bertrand quipped. "She's fine where she is."

"Okay… Have you talked to her then?"

"Yeah."

"Well, fuck, Bertrand, how is she?"

"Not great. And not too interested in speaking with you."

"What?!" Max felt caught off guard. Only hours before, Bertrand had sought his help, and now he was treating him like a diseased convict. "What are you talking about?"

"She thinks you're bad luck, dude. That, somehow, you're responsible for this."

Max wanted to say, *That's insane,* but Indigo's prophecy and reality both said otherwise. Instead, he remained silent on the phone.

"Look," Bertrand softened but only slightly. "I have to go." Without another word, he hung the phone up.

Feeling shell-shocked, Max wandered back to his father's private booth. He knew things had been dicey between him and Brigitte, but he felt certain they had smoothed things over. As such, he was stunned by her brother's claim. He pulled up her number and dialed.

Otto looked up, saw Max on the phone, and quickly reminded him, "Max, we're back on."

Max nodded, but continued listening to the ring of Brigitte's phone. Finally, her voicemail picked up. He punched the pound key to bypass her outgoing message. "Brigitte, I just ran into your brother. He said you've been in an accident."

"Max," Otto called out, agitated. "The clock is ticking."

"Call me. I need to know you're okay." He turned off the phone and sat next to Otto at the console. The afternoon session was in full swing, and continued for several hours until they finally came around to Project Clean Slate. *Shit.* Max knew what Demetrius wanted. He had seen the reports. He knew the science. The "solution," in fact, was several years late. Turmoil brewed in him as he looked at his monitor. His father had offered to help Brigitte. He loved and wanted to please Demetrius, but...

Otto watched Max, wondering what he was waiting for. "This is it, kid, the final vote."

Embroiled in conflict, Max watched Otto intently while the clock ticked. He shook his head, unable to move on it. "Fuck, Otto. How can we be expected to do this?"

Otto could see the path Max was taking, but only minutes remained to dissuade him. "Don't shake your head, Max. Please don't shake your head."

"You know how fucked up this is, and asking me to vote on it... You said yourself, at one point, even my father was against it."

"He isn't now, though, Max, that's the point. You know what he wants."

"Then maybe he should be here to push the button."

"You've done great until now. Please don't blow it here."

Max stared through Otto, not fully seeing him. He contemplated all he had learned during his underground training. But there was also the knowledge he had acquired from AJ, from his schooling, and from his own gut. After taking careful inventory of his ideas and feelings, he thought he had arrived at a decision. Max lifted his hand to press the green button, but he disobeyed his father's wishes and instead pressed the red one —a vote against Clean Slate.

Otto's mouth fell open in disbelief. "What the fuck, Max! Do you know what you just did?" Otto rarely displayed displeasure with Demetrius' only surviving child, but in this moment he didn't hold back. He stood up. "I'm not taking the fall for this shit. You're the one who'll answer for it. Not me."

"That's fine, Otto. I will."

His father's friend gazed at the screen, awaiting the final results of Clean Slate. "You better pray it goes the way your father wanted."

Together he and Max studied the monitor. As voting closed, the tallies rolled in. Percentages began scrolling on both options, and within seconds, the final numbers appeared:

YES TO CLEAN SLATE – 53%

NO TO CLEAN SLATE – 47%

Otto stood back from the table with a smug look on his face. "You better be grateful it went this way. If you're as clever as I think, I suggest you never pull a stunt like that again."

Max glared defiantly at Otto. Without another word, his father's confidant left the room. Max peered through the one-way glass onto the floor below. The commotion of Rizick's latest meeting began to subside as group members made their exit. Max closed his eyes and took a deep breath. His conscience felt intact, but he found it impossible to unwind. The knowledge of Clean Slate's passage, his betrayal of Otto and his father, and the crisis with Brigitte did not permit such a luxury.

Within minutes, a fleet of limousines commenced its procession at the front of the hotel, waiting to load and shuttle Rizick members away. In just a few hours, even the demonstrators and armed guards would disperse, and the Astir Palace would return once again to some sense of normalcy.

CHAPTER 25

$\mathcal{A}$t the close of voting, Rosalee collected Max and Otto and placed them in a Mercedes shuttle at a secluded corner of the hotel. Their driver circumvented the bottleneck of limousines at the front of the main tower and merged without incident onto the central road. Max glanced behind and watched the Astir Palace retreating from view. The vibe between him and Otto was icy at best. Rosalee did not fully comprehend what had occurred, but she remained professional in her signature fashion.

The SUV traveled several minutes along the coast until Otto finally turned to Max. "It's a good thing Demetrius is your father because a stunt like that would normally have heads rolling."

"Otto, forgive me for not being freaked out about my dad — Brigitte's in the hospital, for crying out loud. And after that vote back there, I don't know why any of this even matters!"

Otto glared at Max, incredulous. "When your father asks for something, Max, you need to do it. You don't get that yet?"

Max glanced at Rosalee, but her face remained expression-less. As the Grecian coast whizzed by, he took in its beauty, but his appreciation was joyless and uninspired. He did not wish to argue any further, so he fell silent for the duration of their ride.

Despite the long journey ahead, Max was relieved when they reached the airfield and boarded the plane. While there were ele-ments of the Rizick Group that he found intriguing, the meeting overall left a bitter taste in his mouth. The concept of Clean Slate was haunting, and its passage made him even more anxious to return home and check on Brigitte. As the Battenberg jet took off and soared over the horizon, Max sank into his seat. He had been certain that his troubled mind would prevent any chance of napping, but he dozed off nonetheless. This was the sole ben-efit of his exhaustion. While he slept, the plane traveled toward Italy and Africa. Soon they would be crossing the Atlantic on the journey home.

After a short slumber, Max awoke to see Rosalee quietly read-ing a magazine. He glanced to where Otto was sitting and noticed him sleeping beside a window. Max stood and stretched before grabbing a seat next to Rosalee. "How are you?"

She looked up from her magazine. "Somewhat tired, but I find it terribly difficult to sleep on planes. I'm so jealous of people who can."

"I apologize if I sound like a broken record, but you guys don't need me. I'm already in the doghouse anyway. If I don't get back to Chicago right away, I may not have a girlfriend by the time I do."

Rosalee maintained her usual pleasant manner, but Max found it off-putting, given the circumstances. He realized that although he had spent quite a bit of time with her, he had little idea who she truly was. The Rosalee he believed he knew was actually a shiny veneer meant to please anyone she came across. Max wondered if she felt any true sympathy to his cause, but there was really no way to be sure.

"Rosalee, come on. We're talking a delay of one, maybe two hours tops. My presence is not required for my father to be debriefed. Otto was at my side the entire time. He's more than capable of catching him up."

"Mr. Battenberg, I would love to land this plane wherever you like. Unfortunately, that's not how things work. Your father alone requisitions this jet, and he's the only one allowed to change its itinerary. Short of that, maybe you can speak with the pilot about a diversion, although even that is unlikely. This is how people lose their jobs."

Max pondered Rosalee's words. "If I wanted to request a detour, that'd be through you, correct?"

A sarcastic chuckle erupted from Rosalee's mouth. Although he was put off, Max did appreciate a glimpse of the real her.

"Mr. Battenberg, right now I'm in quite good standing with your father. I would respectfully ask to be left out of any disagreements between you and him. I can, however, get the travel office on the phone, if you like."

Max mulled over the situation, brainstorming how to proceed. "You know, I think I'll just leave it. How soon before we get to Las Cruces?"

She glanced at her watch. "At this point, just under ten hours."

"Thanks, Rosalee."

She nodded to acknowledge Max as he stood and returned to his seat. Reaching into the overhead compartment, he took down his briefcase and removed his mother's journal. Plopping into his chair, he clutched the leather-bound book and gazed through the porthole window into the open skies. Outside, the sun was making every attempt to set, but their flight path was chasing daylight, leaving them in what seemed a perpetual state of dusk. Finally, Max summoned the courage to untie the cord from his mother's journal.

Inside, the diary pages were made of high-quality rag, and each beige page had a rough deckle edge. A sense of pride arose in Max when he spotted his mother's elegant calligraphy inside. He flipped through a half dozen pages, nostalgic to hold in his hands a remnant of his mother's past.

Turning toward the back, he confirmed that his mother had only partially filled the book's pages. He read from the last entry:

August 15th

Charles arrives today.☺ I was planning to greet him at the airport with the boys, but Christian is the only one awake. Maxi said he felt fine last night, but he was running a slight fever and is hardly his rambunctious self. I will leave him to sleep, and his uncle can surprise him when we get home. Aix-en-Provence is just the get-away I needed. I am certain spending time with Charles will do me a world of good. Hopefully, he can lift my spirits, so I might be a more proper mom to the boys. Demetrius swore he would join us, but the chance of that truly happening is nil. Will write more tonight, since I am enthusiastic that today will be good.

A tear welled in Max's eye, and he quickly swiped it away. He could hardly remember the events leading up to his mother's last day. He didn't recall being ill, but there it was on the page. He felt a gloomy sentiment in the entry's tone, but his mother seemed optimistic somehow, still hoping for brighter days.

Max flipped to an earlier entry:

June 3rd

I can't say I didn't know what I signed up for when I married D. He is a powerful and busy man whom I rarely see. For a time, I believed he might really love me, but there are always doubts. He is hardly ever home. How could I know how he spends his days? Each time we speak his responses are guarded, mysterious even. He reassures me there is no one else, which makes sense. When could he possibly have the time? But there are still suspicions lurking in my mind. While I adore my boys with all my heart, I sometimes question what I've gotten myself into.

Max closed the journal with a feeling of melancholy. No matter how he tried, recollecting this portion of his childhood seemed like an effort. Even memories of Demetrius from this period were but a small archive, since his father had always been working. What he did recall felt like happy peaceful moments between his mother and father. Such infantile perceptions, it appeared, had become the sad victim of adult realities. It certainly made sense that his mother had been unhappy. Even today, Demetrius furnished frequent examples of his detachment. How could his mother's experiences with such a cold and unemotional man have unfolded in any other way?

Feeling too ill-prepared to deal with his emotions, Max returned the journal to his briefcase and locked it. His new life felt too much like a long list of negatives, and he suspected the journal would do very little to lift his spirits. Demetrius was still in the hospital, and now Brigitte was there too. Even worse, Gary Richards was dead just like his mother. Where would it end?

During the remainder of the flight, Max occupied himself with films, magazines and satellite TV. When he got hungry, the jet's private staff served a four-course gourmet meal, complete with champagne and mochi desserts. There was no resemblance between commercial airline food and the meals on a Battenberg jet. In fact, few people ever enjoyed such delicacies as the ones found on a Battenberg flight.

The sun, while it remained low, never quite dipped beneath the horizon. But their flight speed was ultimately insufficient, and after roughly six hours, they lost their advantage and the sun set, allowing them to complete their journey in the cover of darkness.

Max and Otto had barely spoken since take off. After a lengthy nap, Otto stood and stretched with a hearty accompanying yawn.

On his way to the lavatory, he stopped at Max's seat. "We're about an hour out."

Max knew what Otto was doing. He wanted to break the ice before landing in Las Cruces. If Demetrius detected tension between them, he would certainly question why. Otto would no doubt be the one to explain, which was not something he wished to do.

Shortly thereafter, Otto returned to his seat, and the plane began its descent. Demetrius didn't tolerate losing time for anything. The instant a final destination was in sight, his pilots would practically dive until they were on the tarmac. The sensation of such a plunge was unsettling from a passenger's standpoint, but the time it took to land was easily cut in half.

After a rapid descent, the plane leveled off and touched down effortlessly. Max gathered his things and deplaned with everyone into the dry New Mexico climate. Beside the jet, a black Cadillac Escalade waited. They all climbed in as their remaining personal effects were transferred. In seconds, they were on their way for a face-to-face with Demetrius Battenberg. An element of nervousness surged in Max, but not enough to cancel out his anger. He was fuming at Demetrius' stubborn refusal to allow his return to Chicago. Only adding to his frustration, Max had called Brigitte's phone several times, but his calls were still going to voicemail.

During the entire ride, Otto was feverishly messaging on his Blackberry. To be polite, Rosalee had made several attempts at idle banter, but each assay seemed to fall on deaf ears. Max would smile or sometimes smirk, but he didn't have much to say. He wondered what his father already knew of the proceedings at the meeting.

They arrived in the desert at the large rock formation checkpoint. From there they followed the same protocols as before. After passing two armed guard stations, they entered the huge hangar and descended on the freight elevator into the underground mall. Deep within the earth, the elevator doors opened. Otto and Rosalee stepped out and headed for the hospital. After only a few steps Max stopped as if he were glued to the floor.

Rosalee was the first to notice and put her hand out to make Otto aware. "What is it, Mr. Battenberg?"

"I'm going to grab a train to Chicago. Tell my dad I'll be back after I've checked on Brigitte."

Otto seemed perturbed. "Max, don't be silly. We're already here. A few hours won't kill you, or your girlfriend."

Max shook his head in disagreement. "Tell him I'll be back, okay?"

Rosalee stood by, silently watching the exchange. Max held firm, refusing to negotiate. He turned and began heading for the train platform.

"Max," Otto interjected, trying a last appeal, "you're creating a problem where there doesn't need to be one."

"I'm sorry, Otto. I'll be back." In a display of insolence, Max turned his back on Otto and Rosalee and strolled away.

His father's friend and assistant watched him disappear from view as he turned the corner to the train platform. Dumbfounded, they both sighed in unison before continuing down the hall to the underground hospital. Although they walked in silence, they were both clear about one thing. Max had made his decision to leave, and when Demetrius found out, there would be hell to pay.

CHAPTER 26

*M*inutes later, Max boarded the high-speed, underground train. Even though he was certain of having made the right choice, he also knew his decision might create a snowball effect with Demetrius. How big of a problem he couldn't be sure, but it was a risk he had to take. He tried phoning Brigitte yet again, but her voicemail immediately kicked in.

Amazingly, the travel time to Chicago lasted only two hours. Still unable to reach Brigitte, Max quickly fled the train and made his way to the elevator. He keyed in the appropriate access codes. Within minutes he was above ground. He exited the nondescript building onto Chicago's busy, noisy streets.

Max quickly grabbed a cab and headed for Northwestern Memorial Hospital. Because of its proximity, the journey didn't take long. He rushed to the emergency room front desk to inquire about Brigitte's room. The attending nurse informed him that she had a private suite, but its location was privileged information. Max protested at first, until he recalled the situation with AJ. If only he could focus, he knew he would be able to locate Brigitte. But he was agitated and needed to clear his thoughts. Given the circumstances, he was unsure if that was possible. He paced for several minutes more, breathing deeply to calm himself. In frustration, he removed his cell phone and dialed his old friend Ted. It had been a long time.

"Hello." Ted's voice sounded different, hesitant.

"Ted, it's Max."

"Hey, dude."

"I don't know if you knew, but Brigitte's been in an accident. I'm here at the hospital, but they won't release her room number to me."

"Fuck, dude." Ted's voice was serious in an unsettling way. "I'm actually here now. Where are you?"

"At the front, in the ER. I just got in from a trip, so I'm not even sure what happened."

"It's friggin' crazy, dude. Some jerk-off in a Hummer; who fuckin' still drives those things? He fucked up her car pretty bad.

I'm not even sure how she's still alive. They covered the accident on the news, dude; that's how I found out. I recognized her car."

Max was relieved at least to have reached Ted. "What room is she in?"

"Hold tight. I'll come get you."

After he hung up, Max continued pacing, waiting for Ted to fetch him. It seemed an eternity, but finally, Ted rounded the corner, walking briskly while staring at his Apple Watch. The new gadget's GPS technology had mapped out Max's exact location in the hospital. Ted's shoes squeaked against the sterile linoleum as he came into view. Without thinking, Max grabbed him in a warm embrace.

"Dude," Ted laughed, "it's good to see you too."

Max had never shown Ted such affection, but in some way the occasion seemed to call for it.

"I'm sorry," Max proclaimed, "I just came from one of my dad's meetings. It's nice to see a familiar face, that's all." Max paused, his face turning serious. "So, how's she doing?"

Ted looked down and ran a hand through his hair. "I don't know. If you thought I was fucked up at Mardi Gras..." He gazed down the corridor, seemingly in a trance. "At least she's alive."

Max thought Ted's words were loaded with hidden meaning. "Was she by herself?" The question hung in the air like a child's helium balloon.

"You didn't hear? Marilyn was with her. They pronounced her dead at the scene."

"Oh, shit." Ted's words slammed into Max with finality. *Another person dead.* Unable to digest the news, Max remained silent, taking his turn to stare vacantly down the hall. "That was her best friend."

"I know. She's super upset, dude. And she doesn't even know Marilyn didn't make it." Ted stared at Max, who was completely dumbfounded. "The doctors think it'll slow her recovery, so we told her Marilyn's fighting for her life."

Max leaned against the wall in disbelief. "This is totally fucked up."

"Her brother Bert's up there now. He said their parents have been holding vigil since the day of the accident. They finally took off about an hour ago. I'm sure they'll be back later, though."

"Fuck!" Max gazed at the floor, wondering who else might become ensnared in the dangerous web Indigo had described.

"Another thing, Max…" Ted's voice was hesitant. "She keeps rambling about that day at Mardi Gras, when she dragged us in to see that fortune-teller."

Max's heart sank because he knew what Ted was about to say. "She thinks this is my fault, right? That's why she hasn't answered my calls."

"Look, I can't say I believe in that mumbo jumbo… but that *woman* — if that's what she was, chick with a dick, transgender, whatever we're calling it these days — she did say a lot of shit, and in a way, it does kinda seem like maybe we've had a bad patch since then."

Max pondered the growing list of events that had transpired, but he could only focus on one thing at a time. "I understand she might not want to see me, but I need to see her. I need to know she's okay."

Ted motioned for Max to follow him. "Come on, let's go. I'll take you up. Depending on her vitals, they may kick us out, though."

Ted led Max to the elevator. When they entered, Max stepped aside so Ted could select the floor. Max may have possessed the elevator codes to access the deep underground malls, but now he needed Ted to lead him to Brigitte's room. Ted selected the sixth floor, and the elevator jerked upward. When the doors opened, Ted stepped out.

"Come on, it's this way."

He led Max down an empty corridor until they eventually made a left. Each step felt like an eternity to Max. He and Brigitte had argued on several occasions, but there was never a time when she hadn't wanted to see him. Finally, a door on the right opened, and Bertrand stepped into the hall wearing the same suit he had sported two days before in Greece. Seeing Max did nothing to lighten Bertrand's mood. He headed their way, and while Max could not be sure, he thought Bertrand might have been trying to cut them off.

"Bert!" Max interjected with an attempt at levity, "how did

you get here before me?"

Bertrand's face remained stern, and his tone contained hints of animus. "You're not the only one who had a plane in Greece, Max." Bertrand glanced at Ted, hesitating… "Do you think Max and I could speak privately a moment?"

"Of course," Ted offered, aware of the awkward moment. "I'll just wait inside." Without skipping a beat, Ted walked to the same door Bertrand had exited and passed through into Brigitte's room.

Bertrand watched the door swing shut before he turned again to Max. "How they didn't find out on the day of the accident I'll never know. But my parents were about to hear from her doctors that she's pregnant. Luckily, I got here in time to make sure that didn't happen."

"So, the baby's okay then?" Max asked, hopeful.

"Yeah, it's fine. To be frank, I don't particularly know if that's the best thing for you guys."

Max felt his patience growing thin with Bertrand's unfriendly demeanor. "What do you mean?"

"She told me you guys were debating what to do. Getting rid of a child would weigh heavily on Brigitte. But… if it happened in a way she didn't have to feel guilty about, that might not be the worst thing."

"You know, Bertrand, I really wish I knew what the fuck your problem was."

Bertrand gawked at Max, boiling with anger. "That's pretty fuckin' rich, Battenberg. How about we start with you fuckin' getting my sister pregnant without marrying her first? And it's no small thing that she's busted up in this hospital right now. I know you might be new to this, but if you think this doesn't have something to do with who your fuckin' father is, then the whole point of that Athens meeting must be lost on you."

"The only thing lost on me is wondering what the hell you were doing there. Maybe if you had talked to me—"

"Yeah, well, now's not the time."

"No, it isn't, Bert. Shocking as it may be, I didn't come here to see you."

Bertrand's tone lightened ever so slightly. "You know what

she's been saying since she came to? That she doesn't want to see you, Max. If I really believed that, I wouldn't be letting you in there. But somehow, I suspect your presence might do her some good."

The thought crossed Max's mind that a firm punch might rattle Bertrand's presumptuous manner, but he knew this would accomplish nothing. Instead, he stepped around his girlfriend's brother and headed toward Brigitte's room.

Bertrand turned to watch him approaching his sister's door. "Hey, Battenberg." His tone softened again. "My parents looked exhausted. I convinced them to go home for a few hours. It's probably a good idea if you're not here when they get back."

With a curt nod, Max pushed open the door and passed into Brigitte's private room. Ted had taken a seat before the window and was quietly reading from his iPad. He looked up and smiled as Max made his way inside.

The Brigitte he knew was unrecognizable. Her normally perfect face was smashed, battered and bruised. The swelling had contorted the dimensions of her head, and her eyes were black and blue. One side of her head had been shaven to make room for a small tube through which fluid drained. Max was aghast at the sight of his girlfriend. Once again, someone very close had been badly injured. Memories of Demetrius in similar condition flickered through his mind. Brigitte's left arm and both legs were in splints. She was sleeping quietly, a feat only made possible by painkillers and tranquilizers.

Ted approached to wake her, but Max stopped him and put a finger to his lips. "Sshh. I don't want to disturb her." Seeing Brigitte's condition left Max in a frazzled state. He motioned toward the door, suggesting their departure.

Ted took a step away from the bed, but Brigitte spoke as they turned to leave. "Is this what I have to do to get you here?" Her voice sounded as if her mouth were packed with gauze.

"Brigitte!" Max called out, but he wasn't quite sure what else to say. "You are my funny girl..."

Sensing awkwardness in the moment, Ted spoke to fill the void. "I'm gonna step outside. Either of you want a drink?"

"No, Ted," Brigitte blurted out, "that's not necessary." She couldn't quite turn her head, but Brigitte's eyes followed Ted as he crossed toward the door. "Right, Max?" The utterance of so few words already left her feeling winded. Max looked back at her and shrugged.

"It's whatever you're comfortable with, Bridge. That's—"

"See, Ted? He doesn't care." Brigitte attempted to move and her face contorted. It was hard to tell if she was smiling or grimacing. Her head fell back against the pillow, almost as if she had passed out. Ted and Max crossed to the bed, alarm registering on their faces.

"It's okay," Brigitte proclaimed, "it's just my back. Oh, who am I kidding? Everything fucking hurts. Max, I'm not sure if you—" Brigitte took a breath and began coughing. The fit subsided for a brief respite before she spoke again. "That day at Mardi Gras… that medium warned us… me and Ted. It feels kinda real now, doesn't it?" Another fit of coughing overtook Brigitte until she spit into a napkin she had sitting on her lap. "I had to remind Ted about it. She warned him too, after all." Brigitte's eyes darted back to Ted, "Only he hasn't been around you like I have." A lone tear trickled down the side of her face.

Brigitte's words cut into Max, mainly because he knew there was truth in them. Much, if not all, of her misery had been due to his actions. He had withheld feelings and situations, not to mention his other deceptions. But Brigitte wasn't entirely innocent. Seeing Bertrand at the Rizick meeting meant she was somehow involved in it all. Max was determined to find out precisely how, but he would need to do so some other time.

"You think I'm responsible for this, right? For your accident."

Tears streamed down Brigitte's face, and her head shook. Max couldn't discern if she was nodding or trembling. For the first time, her voice sounded close to normal.

"I think if I'm ever going to find peace I need to get away from you. Wasn't that what she recommended?"

"Brigitte, I came as soon as I could, but if me being here is upsetting you…"

"I have no idea how, but they said I didn't lose the baby." Brigitte coughed to stifle more tears.

Max took her hand and softly squeezed it. "I know. Bertrand

told me in the hall." Max smiled, grateful.

Brigitte took a tissue from a dispenser beside the bed, and dabbed at her cheeks. "They did some scans that said it could be touch and go for the next few days." She glared at Max, full of trepidation. "It's a boy, by the way. I can't believe I found out this way."

"Brigitte, you're still in shock, I'm sure, and they have you drugged up. Now's probably not the right time to discuss this."

"Max —" her voice cracked, but she cleared her throat and continued, "can you honestly say you don't think your father had anything to do with this?" One of the machines monitoring Brigitte's vitals beeped as her blood pressure spiked.

"What are you talking about?" Even though her face was bruised and battered, Max could see in her eyes that she was serious. "Why would my father do something like this?"

"Because I'm pregnant, that's why. Why do you think my room is undisclosed? Please don't tell him where I am, Max, you have to promise." Other monitors measuring Brigitte's vitals began bleeping in a cacophony of sounds, alerting a possible deterioration of her physical state.

But he already knows, Max thought. To avoid further upsetting Brigitte, he decided not to reveal this piece of information.

"Okay, that's it, guys," Ted exclaimed. "When monitors are beeping like that, it's time to go." Upon that note, a nurse bustled in and began adjusting equipment. She motioned to the men to exit, but they dawdled.

Exhausted, Brigitte turned her head toward Ted. "Are you coming back?"

"Of course," he answered, sheepishly avoiding Max's gaze. "If that's what you want."

"Please." Brigitte took a deep breath, then her body seemed to collapse into the sheets.

Max stroked her hand and lightly kissed her forehead. "I'm glad you and the baby are still here."

Brigitte grimaced from the effort to smile. Ted crossed to the armchair to gather his things, some books and an iPad. He placed them in a leather saddlebag and followed Max to the door. The moment he and Max stepped from the room, the nurse crossed to the door and closed it.

Max turned to Ted. "I'm glad you're looking after her."

"Of course, man. I care about Brigitte too. She's a cool chick."

"Thanks, Ted. How're you, by the way?"

"You know, I'm good. Just keeping it one hundred."

In his second display of affection, Max hugged Ted again. "Call me if you need to, okay?"

"Sure thing, dude."

"I have to bounce. My dad arranged a meeting, and I missed it to come here. I need to see what it was about."

Ted could sense that Max was distressed. He warmly placed a hand on his shoulder. "Like I said, I don't believe in all that voodoo crap with the psychic. And for the record, you haven't caused me any misery."

"Thanks, man. Call me later, okay? Or I'll call you."

"No worries. I'll let you know anything I do."

Max nodded goodbye, then disappeared down the corridor toward the elevators. The air and energy inside the hospital were oppressive, and Max wanted out as soon as possible. Once he was on the ground floor, he pressed his way down the hall toward the ER. As he approached the exit, his stride grew quicker. He hadn't realized it, but he was almost at a full jog when the automatic doors opened. Max ran outside onto the concrete sidewalk and sucked in large gulps of air, hyperventilating.

He took a seat on a nearby bench and gently closed his eyes. He thought of AJ and all of the advice he had delivered. His breathing remained rapid, but he didn't let that worry him. He simply paid attention to the sensations in his body. He made note of the tautness and tension in his neck and shoulders. He remarked anxiousness in his respiration. Over time, his breathing normalized, and he could feel his muscles relaxing.

Max knew he needed to return to New Mexico to face Demetrius, but he didn't let the idea unsettle him. His entire focus was on his own body and what was going on inside of him. When he finally opened his eyes, he was surprised to see a young girl sitting beside him chatting on her cell phone. Her voice wasn't loud, but it carried a shrill, annoying tone. Somehow, Max had tuned her out and was unaware of her when she sat down. He stood and made his way to the street. He planned to return home and shower so he could change before catching the next train to Las Cruces. If Demetrius was perturbed with him, he would find out soon enough.

$\mathcal{M}$ax hailed the first available cab. During the ride home, he realized with clarity that the snowball effect he had been awaiting had not actually begun with defiance of his father's wishes. His life had, in fact, started spiraling out of control the day he reached New Orleans and Brigitte dragged him into Indigo's storefront. After that moment, his relationships had begun morphing along with his understanding of the world. Despite great efforts, Max still couldn't grasp the entire puzzle in which he seemed to be a significant piece. Brigitte, one of his biggest fans, it now appeared had secrets of her own. To make things worse, Demetrius was likely furious with him. For the first time in his life, Max felt truly alone.

Seated in the back of the cab, he considered his legacy and felt completely alienated in every sense of the word. His life was so different from the average person to begin with, and he lacked the connectedness he increasingly hungered for. As the cab turned onto his street, his heart sank. A shiny, brand-new black Lincoln MKZ was parked in front of his house. Max instructed the cabbie to park behind it while he fished the fare from his wallet. After settling the payment he stepped from the cab, but stood frozen behind its open door. Before he could make a move, Rosalee exited the MKZ and approached.

"Mr. Battenberg, hello. Your father sent me to fetch you."

"Yeah, that's what I figured." Max slammed the cab door, startling the driver, who in turn pulled out from behind the MKZ and drove away. "Just give me a minute to shower and change, okay?"

"Honestly, Mr. Battenberg, the last thing I want is to get stuck in the crossfire between you and your dad. It would be an understatement to say he's a little upset."

"All right... But me showering isn't going to change that, is it?" Max studied Rosalee's normally steely demeanor, but an uncharacteristic expression betrayed her understanding of his logic.

"Please, Mr. Battenberg, you're placing me in a very compromising position. If you could hurry, I will be most appreciative."

"I promise I will."

Normally, Max would have invited Rosalee in, but he was annoyed by the circumstances of their encounter. He could already perceive a change in his breathing, a sign he was growing more agitated. To move things along, he darted in the house alone to shower and change. Being in his own home relaxed him, and suddenly he could feel the intensity of his fatigue. He thought of all the crazy events of late; it seemed there was no end to the litany of travels and discoveries.

However, wishing to honor his promise to Rosalee, he promptly returned to the waiting MKZ with a sense of dignity Max didn't fully realize he possessed. Rosalee watched him approach and spotted something different about him. It didn't occur to her how tired he might be, mostly because he always appeared handsome and refreshed. But there was also strength in his demeanor that hadn't been present months ago. She had rarely seen anyone stand up to Demetrius, and that included Max. Lately, however, it appeared the younger Battenberg had resolved to stand his ground.

Secretly, Rosalee took pleasure in seeing Demetrius denied. In her esteem, no one should get everything they wanted. That wasn't how life was supposed to work.

Max opened the door, hopped in the back seat, then turned to Rosalee with a smile. "Okay, let's go."

He knew he needed to ask questions, and Rosalee was likely his best resource to uncover his father's state of mind. Of course, the elder Battenberg had ears everywhere. Even if the chauffeur wasn't listening, there were certainly microphones in the car. With that thought, he figured the trains might be safer and perhaps more secure. Max attempted small talk and waited patiently for their descent into the tunnels. To his amazement, the MKZ drove right by the building he had used so many times to access Chicago's hidden underground. Several blocks later he realized why. They seemed to be heading toward Demetrius' penthouse in the Spire.

Trying to appear calm, he turned to Rosalee. "Aren't we going to Las Cruces?"

"No, Mr. Battenberg. Your father and I returned to Chicago together. He is at the penthouse."

A semblance of panic arose in Max, but he took a deep breath, trying to maintain his calm. "So, what exactly am I dealing with? Is he more pissed about my vote, or the fact that I didn't come to see him in New Mexico?"

Rosalee smiled in a silent response. Max didn't really need to ask the question. The fact was, he already knew Demetrius didn't take kindly to refusals of any kind. Max had assumed he would have more time to prepare for their conversation, but the MKZ was already turning onto Demetrius' street. The penthouse building came into view, and Max's mind raced to assemble a strong explanation.

The car pulled into the parking structure and drove several levels down to what appeared to be a service elevator in a vacant field of parking spaces. Max had never used this route, and for a moment, his mind raced with paranoia. Brigitte had outright accused Demetrius of trying to kill her, and now he was being driven to an abandoned floor in a dark parking garage. On the far right, there were two cars and one was covered in dust, indicating it hadn't been moved in months, if not years. Max surveyed the level for anything suspicious, trying to chase whatever fear from his mind.

He and Rosalee exited the car and crossed to the service elevator, where she inserted a key.

"So," Max chimed in, trying to appear patient, "he must be pretty well recovered if he's back already."

"He's much stronger than before."

Right at that moment, the elevator opened. Inside, it was hardly a service elevator at all. In signature Demetrius fashion, its walls were adorned with mirrors and chrome. What looked like brass handrails were tastefully installed, but Max knew they were fashioned of gold. Rosalee punched access codes into the keypad, and the elevator shot skyward toward Demetrius' penthouse.

"Interesting," Max said. "I didn't know this was here."

"Your father had it installed a few years back. He wanted a more personalized way to get in and out unnoticed."

"I see." Max didn't think it possible, but this elevator seemed faster than the one he normally used. It shot skyward for several seconds before the doors opened into his father's private lounge. Max had waited for Demetrius many times in this room, but he had never noticed an elevator. When the doors slid shut, he was astounded to see them connect into the panels of a Chinese painting he had admired many times before. It was a landscape with a man and woman painted into the field. The tableau appeared to be on large dual panels of wood that fit together side by side into a single image. No one would ever have guessed that it served as camouflage to a secret elevator shaft.

"Would you like anything to drink, Mr. Battenberg?"

"No, thank you, Rosalee. I'm fine."

"Very well. I'll let your father know you're here." In another uncharacteristic move, Rosalee smiled warmly. "And good luck."

Max smiled back as Rosalee exited the room. It was normally Demetrius' custom to keep people waiting, and Max was no exception. He took a seat on Demetrius' couch, intending to use the time to mentally prepare. As AJ had taught him, he closed his eyes to a squint and crossed his legs into lotus position. He took one deep breath and exhaled. He could sense agitation in his breathing. Just as it began to normalize into a more relaxed state, Demetrius entered.

"Glad you could make it." A hint of sarcasm reverberated in Demetrius' tone.

Max opened his eyes, caught off guard by the rapidity of his father's appearance. Demetrius was slightly thinner than he'd been before the accident. Other than that, he seemed like his old self. As distorted and bruised as he had been, there was hardly a scar or blemish on his face. Max had no idea what they had done in the underground hospital of Las Cruces, but Demetrius seemed more like a man who had dieted than one who had been injured.

"Hey, pops," Max chimed in, trying to keep things light. "I can't believe how good you look."

Demetrius was hardly amenable to levity, and he gazed sternly upon his son. "I didn't invite you here for pleasantries, Max. I heard about the stunt you pulled with Project Clean Slate. Were my instructions not clear somehow?"

"No, they were, but I didn't want to vote for it. And Otto told me, at one point, you didn't want to either."

Demetrius narrowed his eyes at Max before crossing to the huge panoramic window to gaze upon the sprawling view of

Chicago. "You always were sensitive, Max. Throughout your childhood I tried toughening you up. To see if I could strengthen your resolve." Demetrius turned away from the window and looked Max in the eye. "To get you to grow a pair, as they say. It appears you finally have. I can't say I appreciate the timing, though."

"Part of me was happy when I found out you had your own doubts. Clean Slate's a shitty thing, Dad. As a matter of fact—"

"Any reservations I had were emotional, and that's not how a Battenberg makes decisions. Maybe you still have to learn that."

"You look perfectly healthy now. Why didn't you attend the meeting and vote on it yourself?"

Demetrius turned back to the window. "Things are not always as they appear. Fortunately, the correct outcome cleared the vote."

For more than a while Max stared at the back of his father's head before he ventured, "I'm going to ask a question, and I hope you can be honest." Demetrius turned to face him, and Max studied his father's poker face. "The first time I came to Las Cruces, Rosalee handed me a list. She said it was people I should avoid. There was a name on there, a guy named Gary Richards. He was a friend, but he's dead now; plus there's Brigitte's accident, and now she's in the hospital. According to another friend, she probably shouldn't even be alive. I know somebody else who's been hospitalized because someone threw acid on him...all of this together with what happened to you—I just want to know, is any of this related to Rizick?"

Demetrius remained pensive before he spoke. "How is the girl?"

"Her name's Brigitte, Dad, and she's not great. She thinks you had something to do with her accident, by the way. From where I stand, I can't say it's an unsound theory. Why was her brother at the meeting?"

"Max, I've explained to you since you were small: We aren't like other people. We are and will always be targets. People fucking want our lives, and many would do anything to see us brought down to size. Is it dangerous to let people get close to us? Absolutely. But this is the price we pay to be up here, where we are right now, at the top of the food chain."

"She's pregnant, Dad." Max could hardly believe it, but Demetrius displayed a discernible reaction to the news. "I didn't want to say anything since we weren't sure what we were going to do. Then all this shit happened before we could figure things out."

Demetrius' mind appeared to be racing. "I see. Her parents are foolhardy. She should be relocated to a safer place. I could have a security detail sent to that hospital to look after her."

"I'd appreciate that." Max could not quite read his father, but there was no doubt the wheels were turning in his brain.

"That list Rosalee gave you… no one on there is a target. But you might be if you continue your association with them. That's the reason the list was given to you. To avoid something like that happening."

Max felt a modicum of satisfaction with his father's response, but there were other things he wanted to ask. "The entire time I was in Europe I kept wondering how someone got in my house. Then it occurred to me, it was you. You took the dial, didn't you? The missing piece from the Antikythera Device."

"Of course I did. There was already enough commotion because of it. It's somewhere safe now; that's all you need to know."

Max was perplexed by his father's move. "It was safe at my house, and you know that. My security system's one of the best in the world. Why'd you take it? Unless you're hiding something."

"I don't want you to use it, okay? That thing is voodoo, pure witchcraft. It was tossed in the sea for a reason. You were in way over your head trying to use it."

"You sure about that?"

For a fleeting moment, Demetrius caught a glimpse of something he had never seen in Max: self-assuredness. He motioned for his son to join him at the window. "Come, I'd like to show you something." Max approached and stood at his father's side. Demetrius pointed toward the streets below. "Look at the view down there."

It was less than an hour before sundown, and rush hour was in full swing. Max followed Demetrius' gaze. He could see the streets were jammed with traffic, and pedestrians were running errands or making their way home. From so high up, it appeared they were peering into an ant farm of workers rushing to and fro.

"Look at them," Demetrius grumbled, "crowding the streets, packing the stores. Don't you see it?"

Max observed, but his face remained expressionless. He felt certain Demetrius was pointing out something specific, but he wanted to be sure before commenting.

"Look, Max! Don't you see it?" Demetrius placed a hand on the back of his son's neck and gently squeezed. Even though he had lost weight, there was still force in his grip.

Max further examined the evening commute but remained miffed. "It's rush hour, Pop."

"Yeah, but what else do you see?" After a brief time, Demetrius guided Max forward, directing his gaze. Without warning, he smashed Max's face against the glass, and a sharp pain shot through the younger Battenberg's nose and temples.

"Fuck!" Max screamed, breaking away from Demetrius and leaping back from the window. "What the fuck was that!?" The look on Max's face was one of total shock. Using his right hand, he checked his nose to see if it was broken or bleeding.

"If you opened your goddamn eyes, you'd see that the air we're breathing is polluted. The streets are crowded. Resources are disappearing. And hell, global warming is real. You've read the reports. It's up to us to stop it before it's too late. The way to do that is Clean Slate."

With the sting still aching in his nose, Max shot back, "I have listened to you my entire life. I have always respected you, even when you were abusive or unkind, telling me to man up or grow a pair, just like you did again today. But what you just did..." Max pointed toward the glass, which was smudged with an oily face print. "That was inexcusable." He continued massaging the bridge of his nose, waiting for the pain to subside. "I can't fucking believe you did that."

"No one tells me no, Max, especially not you." Demetrius fixed Max in his gaze the way a predator does its prey. "If you had voted like I asked, we wouldn't be having this conversation."

"It's not the fuckin' conversation, Dad, it's the way we're having it. Perhaps you've forgotten, but we're all we've got right now. Both Christian and Mom are dead and gone."

"Yeah, well, if only we could rewind time."

His father's statement slammed into Max like a punch to the stomach. "What's that supposed to mean?"

"Forget it. I shouldn't have said anything."

"No, go ahead. I want to hear what you meant."

Demetrius remained smug, as his stare burned through Max. "You know exactly what I meant."

Max did know. His older brother, Christian, had always been his father's favorite. On some level, Max always knew that Demetrius would have preferred that he and Christian switch places in the accident that day. The unspoken truth was, Demetrius had resented Max ever since.

Max's resolve to stand his ground had been firm, but he felt rattled by Demetrius' words. "You're a sick man, you know that."

Demetrius took in a breath. In that moment, Max spotted a cocktail of disparate emotions swirling on his father's face: anger, sadness, melancholy, regret.

Feeling depleted, Max turned to make his exit, but Demetrius snatched him by the arm and spun him around. In a knee-jerk reaction, he grappled with his father until he gained the upper hand. He shoved Demetrius into the large panoramic glass and held him there. For an instant, father and son shared in their collective shock, both of them realizing things had escalated too far. Max unhanded Demetrius and took a step back.

"Please, don't do that again."

The glimmer of alarm on Demetrius' face quickly faded only to be replaced by his normal, steely disposition. He straightened his clothes. "What's happened with you, Max? There was a time when you were a much more respectful child."

"That has to be earned."

"What about you, Max, what do you have to earn?" Demetrius' voice turned to a growl. "Your cars, your condo, your job... how do you think you got all of that? If it weren't for me, you would have nothing. Don't believe for one second that I can't take all of it away. I can."

"So, we're back to threats again?"

"Whatever you wish to call it, Max. I choose to call it results. And, yes, that's what I resort to. If I tell you to vote, you ask on what. And when I say Las Cruces, that's where you go." Growing more riled, Demetrius punched the glass, rattling it even more than he had when he shoved Max's face against it. "Don't think for one second because you're my son that I'll accept defiance from you. It's my way, always. And that little stunt you pulled in Athens means nothing." The myriad of emotions Demetrius had been displaying were dissolving away until nothing remained but the residue of anger. "If I fucking choose to, I could use Clean Slate tomorrow." Demetrius pointed at the streets below. "If and when I deem it necessary, every single one of those people can be erased."

"If that's so true, how come you didn't punish Odeon Rutherford? He killed your wife and kid, and yet he's jet-setting around, living what I'd call a rather good life."

Demetrius felt thrown by Max's statement, but he barely let on. "Rutherford'll be dealt with on my terms. Right now, you need only worry about me. With just one call, I can have you barred from your own home. Before you even exit this building, in fact." Demetrius stared into his son's eyes. "Are we clear?"

Max could feel rage boiling inside of him, but he knew Demetrius might make good on his threat. A single call and his life could be shut down. Max nearly choked on the words as they spilled from his mouth. "Yes, sir."

The look on Demetrius' face was smug. "Now might be a good time to take off then. I'll call when I need you."

Max rode a deep turmoil brewing inside of him. Demetrius had, on occasion, made a point of making him feel inadequate. In truth, his father had seemingly perfected the technique of shaming. Although Max had grown infinitely wiser in the past months, he still felt like a child in his father's presence, yearning for Demetrius' approval. The same part of him wanted to apologize for the aggressive shove and also desired Demetrius' assurance that everything would be fine. But there was also a new Max emerging from the ashes of his old self. The new Max yearned to break from Demetrius' cold and impersonal expectations. It was this new Max who could no longer tolerate his father's gruff demeanor. It was also the new Max who turned and proudly exited the suite.

He spotted Rosalee in the lobby. He knew she, and others,

had probably overheard much of the altercation between him and Demetrius. He and Rosalee locked eyes ever so briefly as he crossed to the elevator. He pressed the call button, and the elevator opened immediately. Max stepped in. "Good night, everybody."

The front desk guards and Rosalee smiled and wished Max a good night. The elevator doors closed, and it plunged downward, causing Max's stomach to drop. Soon, he would be joining the masses that he and Demetrius had looked down upon from the window above. As the lobby grew closer, Max realized he had been holding his breath. He exhaled deeply. The meeting with Demetrius hadn't gone well, but at least it was over.

CHAPTER 28

*N*eedless to say, Max felt distressed. His first impulse after leaving his father's had been to phone Brigitte, but given the circumstances that was hardly an option. He considered reaching out to Chandler and Ted, but neither of them would be capable of empathy toward him. It was their belief that Max led a charmed life and had no basis for true problems or complaints. Besides, he could not share details of what was truly going on with either of them.

Then it came to him whom he needed to see. AJ had displayed unparalleled wisdom about a multiplicity of things, and he was entirely approachable and non-judgmental. In the end, it was a strange deck of cards that life had dealt Max. Perhaps AJ could help explain why his life had unraveled into this new and complex realm. In a matter of months, the daily decision matrix he normally used had evolved from nightclubs and destination parties into global-scale life-and-death decision-making.

Max had no clue if AJ was still hospitalized, and frankly, he didn't think he could suffer through another hospital visit. AJ's acid burns had been extreme, but the hospital had likely discharged him anyway since he lacked the resources to pay for his stay.

Max hustled home to retrieve his Range Rover and swing by the yoga studio. If AJ was not around, he could attend a class while he waited. If nothing else, to do so would probably help him relax. Max navigated the tail end of rush hour until he pulled up before the Golden Arch Studio. He glanced at the spot where AJ normally stationed himself, but it was vacant. He parked and stepped from the car. Max pulled his gym bag and mat from the rear hatch, then headed into the studio.

The studio door swung shut behind him, and Max took note of the atmosphere. While Demetrius' penthouse was top-of-the-line and beautifully furnished, the energy there was steeped in a structure of fear. Over the years, Demetrius' insistence on excellence had resulted in dozens of people losing their jobs. In addition to that, efficiency studies had led to rounds of routine layoffs every three years or so. In the end, the ambiance at Battenberg Industries felt heavy with tension and anxiety. The yoga studio, on the other hand, was simple and minimalist with an air of tranquility. The combination of low incandescent lighting and soft, peach-pastel tones made for an appropriately soothing decor. Scents of sage and nag champa tickled Max's nose. He took a deep breath, and the calming effect of aromatherapy washed over him.

He approached the front desk to find a cute blonde behind the counter. Her hair had been coiffed in a precision bob, and she was chatting with a mixed-race patron whose dreadlocks hung in a ponytail between her shoulders. Both women sported looks that were a mixture of shock and disappointment. The mixed-race woman kept shaking her head in disbelief.

"A couple of times I came by, but I didn't see him. That's why I asked."

The blonde took a deep breath. "It's so sad. I still can't believe he did that."

"Me neither," the other woman chimed.

Max did not wish to speculate whom they might be speaking about, but in the end he could not help himself. He hesitated, unsure if he could entertain an answer to the question now lingering on his lips. *Please, no more bad news.*

Silence floated in the air a short while before the blonde turned to Max. "I'm sorry, sir, are you checking in?"

He cleared his throat, but his voice still faltered. "You guys don't mind if I ask who you're talking about?"

The blonde nodded. "Do you know AJ? The guy who sat out front."

"Yeah. He's in the hospital, right?"

"He was," the blonde replied, her face somehow apologetic. "We just found out he OD'd. We don't know the whole story, but they're saying he stole a vial of morphine or something."

"You're kidding," Max exclaimed. "But he didn't do drugs."

"They said they found him with a needle in his arm."

The woman with dreadlocks shook her head in disbelief. "Which I don't believe for one second. I talked with AJ all the time. He may have lived on the streets, but he was no addict. I don't believe it one bit."

"No," Max said, "I don't either. I just visited him in the hospital a few days ago."

The dark complexioned woman's voice grew more agitated. "I tell you what, because he's homeless I bet they won't investigate. I know Chicago PD. In their eyes, he was some bum, working the system to get his hands on drugs. I bet they're even saying he threw acid on himself."

The blonde nodded with an equal look of incredulity. "I wouldn't be surprised if that's the story."

Max couldn't conceal how flummoxed he felt by the news. "I had a few run-ins with him when I first came here. Still, it didn't take long to figure out he was one of the clearest people out there."

The woman with dreadlocks nodded. "I know, right?"

The blonde took a deep breath from behind the counter. "I don't know if you guys knew, but he helped out here and there. The owner here even offered him a job. I really thought he was about to get his life together and get off the street." She turned to Max. "I'm sorry, we've been going on. The seven o'clock's about to start. Did you want to head inside?"

"I don't think so." Max shook his head, forcing back the surge of emotion he felt. *Is this me, or am I channeling?* "I'm not in the mood anymore."

"That's when you need a class, honey," the brown-skinned woman forced a smile. "They always leave me feeling peaceful."

"Thanks, but…" Unaware, Max continued to shake his head. "I think I'll pass this time."

The woman sporting dreadlocks affectionately rubbed his back. "I know how you feel, baby. I feel the same way."

"You guys have a good night." Max wandered outside and returned to his car. He climbed behind the wheel and contemplated what he'd heard. *AJ dead?* Deep down, he knew whatever had occurred probably had something to do with him. Whether he liked it or not, Indigo's prophecy had come to fruition. The body count was rising, and there seemed to be no end in sight.

He started his car and drove in a haze of confusion and sadness. Moments later, he entered his driveway, and his father's threat flashed through his mind. Had Demetrius changed his access codes? When he triggered the remote, the garage door opened. Max breathed a sigh of relief and parked inside. He hit the remote again to shut the door. While it closed, he stepped from the car and looked around. He keyed in the house access code and immediately went to his room. He could hear AJ's voice in his head, telling him to meditate. *Look within for answers.*

He passed into one of his additional rooms and spotted the meditation corner he had requested. A large wooden tableau depicting the Buddha was affixed on the far wall with a single shelf beneath it. Two vases, one holding a lily and the other bamboo, were expertly placed beside a series of tea lights in lotus-flower candleholders. An incense burner sat between the vases, holding a single stick of incense that had already burned to a nub. Max caught the scent of sage in the air, and he noticed a box of incense on the floor beneath the shelf. Like a flattened out beanbag, a rose-colored pillow cushion sat atop his hardwood floors, as if it were praying to the Buddha.

Max smiled and muttered, "You did good, Cora." He lowered the lights, lit a fresh stick of incense and removed his shoes. He sat lotus-style on the cushion and closed his eyes. To the best of his memory, he ran through the steps explained to him by AJ. One at a time, he concentrated on each chakra, activating them from the root to the crown. Max took a few deep breaths. After several minutes, the tension of the day melted away. He pondered his situation and the questions he had meant to ask AJ. *What am I to do with all this?*

Somewhere in the depths of his mind, Max perceived a voice. At first, it seemed distant, its message unclear. He probed his thoughts more deeply until a faint whisper registered: *You know what to do.* The idea resonated, but Max remained unclear of its full implication. For the first time ever, he abandoned himself in meditation. After what seemed a long while, he finally understood.

Max jumped up from the cushion and reentered his bedroom. He spotted the briefcase he had carried in Greece. In his earlier haste, he had tossed it atop his bed. He opened it and removed his mother's journal from inside. He carried the leather-bound diary into his closet and stashed it in a drawer beneath a collection of T-shirts. Satisfied, he returned to the bonus room and slipped his shoes back on. He scurried down the steps on his way to the garage.

At the bottom of the staircase, he switched gears again and doubled back to the living room. He flipped on the TV and turned up the volume. Then he removed his pendant with the microchip from around his neck. He placed the minuscule device on his couch along with his cell phone. Satisfied, Max stepped out onto the upstairs balcony. He closed the door behind him and surveyed the street below. Nothing seemed out of the ordinary, and no one seemed to be watching. He slipped over the railing, then swung down until he was hanging from the ledge. He released his hands and dropped nine feet to the pavement below. Max dusted himself off before heading down the drive. He exited his property and disappeared into the darkness of Chicago's streets.

CHAPTER 29

*I*t took several blocks before he could locate a cab. He told the driver his destination, and the cabbie began weaving in and out of traffic. Minutes later, they crossed into a modest neighborhood. Finally, the cabdriver dropped him before an expansive mid-rise complex. The structure was a huge cubic monstrosity that lacked any form of architectural concept. Devoid of balconies, its facade resembled a prison or some other impersonal public institution. Max stood in front, looking around to see if he had been followed. When the coast seemed clear, he headed to the entrance, where he searched through the directory of tenants. He found the name he sought and dialed the corresponding code. He could hear it ringing through the intercom. Finally, Ted's voice came through.

"Hey, Max, what's up?"

Max looked up and noticed a closed circuit camera pointing in his direction. He nodded toward it. "Hey, Ted, I need to talk to you."

The buzzer blared, cueing Max to enter. He quickly crossed to the elevator and rode to Ted's floor. After making his way to the door, he raised his hand to knock, but Ted pulled it open first.

"Hey, dude, what brings you this way? You slumming it?"

"I just need to talk." Max pushed his way into Ted's apartment.

"Oookay." Ted closed the door behind him.

"Can you lock it, Ted?"

Ted frowned at the request. "All right." Then he latched the door and pursued Max into his living room. The space was a monument to Ted's true passion. Instead of looking like a home, it looked more like an office at Google. There was a modest couch, a couple of chairs and standard beige apartment carpeting. A huge desk sat directly opposite the couch, and a series of computer monitors and equipment was on top of it. Ted was a tech-savvy gamer who built websites and freelanced, debugging various types of information technologies. Some even considered him a hacker, a moniker he fervently rejected.

Max understood that he might be more paranoid than he needed to be, but the news of AJ precluded his taking any chances.

"I am glad you're here."

Ted smiled, still unclear why Max seemed so agitated.

"I'm beginning to think Brigitte might be right."

Ted frowned again. "About what?"

"Maybe I *am* cursed. It's like bad luck's overflowing onto everyone around me. That fucking attack at Mardi Gras, my dad getting injured, and now Marilyn and Brigitte... It can't all be coincidence, right?"

"If it isn't, I should probably be shitting that you decided to come here."

Max, oblivious to Ted's attempt at humor, crossed to the couch, thought about sitting, then decided against it. "Don't worry. I made sure I wasn't followed." Max's mind seemed to be racing. "When I leave I have to get one of those throw-away phones." He approached Ted, his face riddled with tension.

"Dude, you keep this up, I might really get worried."

"Brigitte's right," Max muttered, "it's like Indigo said."

Suddenly, it occurred to Ted whom Max was referring to. "You mean that *woman* in New Orleans."

Max nodded with a smile. "Yeah, her. Remember, like Brigitte said, she warned you guys. We need to be careful from now on, that's all." Max could see Ted getting nervous, but he did not have the luxury of explaining. "Look, I came by to search for something. I didn't want to do it at my house because, more than likely, they'll know."

Ted stared at his friend, worried that he might truly be losing his mind. "I'm sorry, Max... who is they?"

Max gazed intently at Ted. "It's better if you don't know." He gestured at Ted's computer console. "Can you look a number up for me? It's someone in Greece."

Ted studied Max and realized he was serious. "Okay, who is it? Some hot chick, I hope."

"I wish, but no." Max fished the folded-up sheet of paper from his pocket. He unfurled it and read aloud from the Astir Palace stationary. "His name is Nikolaos Satrazemis. Is there any way to get the number without anyone knowing we did a search?"

Ted fixed Max in his gaze, trying more seriously to assess the situation. "I have to admit, you're starting to spook me out with all this psychic-Miss Cleo shit. I mean, fuck, if a Battenberg, a Rothschild, or a Rockefeller says there's shit going down, I'm gonna tend to believe it."

Max's expression didn't falter. "I can't give you any details, Ted. And frankly, I'm more comfortable with you being spooked. It's better if you take this seriously."

"Is this some New World Order shit?" Ted studied Max briefly. "It is, isn't it?"

Max stared at Ted but offered no response. "Look, if there's a way to place this call without it being traced, that'll be ideal. If not, I'll figure out some other way."

"Fuck, Max, you really are spooked, aren't you?"

"I just can't abide anyone else getting hurt."

" Just tell me, does this have anything to do with FEMA coffins?"

"What?" Max didn't immediately recognize the reference.

"You remember, we argued about 'em in college. It's those coffin-sized containers that FEMA's been stockpiling. There's a shitload in Georgia, some in Louisiana, Tennessee... I showed 'em to you on YouTube, and you got all defensive 'cause I said the world's elite was behind 'em."

The conversation had taken place many years before, and Max did recall bits of it. Even before college, Ted had been an avid conspiracy theorist, and Max hardly wished to stir any additional fears or anxiety in him. "I kind of remember. Can we grab the number, though?"

Ted studied Max, not entirely convinced of his sincerity regarding the memory. Preferring not to argue, he acquiesced and took a seat at his desk. His computer monitors were in sleep mode. Ted tapped a key to wake them. "Okay, where exactly in Greece is this guy?"

"I met him near Athens, but I can't say for sure if that's where he lives."

"Okay... " Ted had hoped for more to go on. "I suppose we can start there then. Spell the name for me." Max spelled, and Ted commenced typing with such rapidity that the keys clicked like a symphony of strange insect calls. After little more than a minute, he spoke. "Looks like they have four listings for Nikolaos Satrazemis."

Max hadn't expected it would be that easy. He looked at Ted a long moment before he spoke. "Can we call any of them without being traced?"

"I suppose we can bounce off a few different servers to obscure my IP address."

"It has to be foolproof, Ted. I can't have you in jeopardy again."

"Dude, you know I'm a tech geek. You have to trust that."

"Let's do it then." Max grabbed one of Ted's chairs and dragged it to the desk. They rang the first number, which yielded no answer. "Oh, shit, it's already after midnight there, isn't it?"

Ted looked at Max, still trying to glean the smallest clue of what might be going on. "It'll be morning in a minute if you wanna wait."

He contemplated Ted's suggestion. "If one of these numbers is his, I don't think he'll mind."

"All right." Ted dialed another number. A woman answered with a groggy voice, making it clear she had been asleep. Ted handed Max a headset, and Max slipped it over his head.

"Sorry to wake you, ma'am. I'm trying to reach Nikolaos Satrazemis."

The woman replied in Greek, but her perturbed state resonated through the line.

"I'm sorry, ma'am, do you speak English?"

"Nikolaos is sleeping. It is very late."

"Ma'am, were the two of you at the Astir Palace outside of Athens a few days ago?"

Without hesitation the woman hung up, causing Ted to frown. "Dude, it might be a good idea to wait a few hours and call when they're awake."

"No. Let's try the others." Max watched Ted punch in another number before he quickly interrupted. "You're still doing the no-trace thing, right?"

"Oh, shit. Good call." Ted started over and added the required steps to cloak the call. After a pause, the phone rang twice, and an answering machine kicked in. While they listened to it, Ted whispered, "You wanna leave a message?"

Max nodded and spoke after the beep. "Hello, I'm trying to

reach Nikolaos Satrazemis. We spoke briefly at the Astir Palace a few days ago. If this is your —" Max stopped short when a click on the line grabbed his attention, as if someone had picked up. "Hello? Is someone there?"

No one responded, but Max and Ted could hear breathing on the other end. They stared at one another, intrigued, until a man's accented voice finally spoke.

"Are you the man from the restaurant?"

"Yes." Max glanced at Ted and realized his friend was completely confused. "Was that you who called my room?"

A moment of breathing continued. "Yes."

"Is there a way we can speak?" Max felt certain he could hear the man shifting in bed.

"Where are you now?"

"Back in the states. In Chicago."

A lengthy silence ensued until Nikolaos finally spoke again. "We shouldn't speak on this line. Someone will contact you shortly."

"How?" Max awaited a reply, but the line quickly went dead.

Ted studied his old college friend, still wondering what the hell was taking place in his living room. "Dude, this is all very cloak-and-dagger. I don't know if I should be excited or worried."

Max looked at Ted, but his face remained blank. "I can't believe he hung up."

"You know what time it is over there. It was kind of rude to call at this hour, don't you think?"

"How's he going to call back, though?"

"I doubt it'll be here, unless this guy's better at the tech than I am."

Max and Ted shared a glance, considering the possibilities. Finally, Max shrugged before changing the subject. "How's Brigitte doing?"

"She's recovering, dude. On the mend, but it's gonna take a minute. I'm sure she just needs time, and she'll come around. Being busted up and pregnant can't be a good combination."

"Yeah. I guess."

"What about your dad? How's he?"

Max contemplated the question, but given their most recent

meeting, he was unsure of the appropriate response. "He's lost some weight, but other than that he's good."

"Cool."

He and Ted had been chummy all through college, but the current moment felt awkward, mostly because of the things Max was not saying. Hoping to erase the quiet, he finally chimed in. "I hardly know this guy. I don't have a clue how he plans to contact me."

"I kind of get the feeling he knows." Ted studied Max's face, searching for the slightest hint about his impromptu appearance and the strange blocked call they had just placed. "I wouldn't worry too much about it."

"You're probably right."

"Who is this guy again?"

Max took a breath, afraid to draw Ted any deeper into the intrigue. "I met him at that meeting I went to in Greece. I'm hoping he can... maybe help with some stuff." Max could see Ted's brain working, trying to put the puzzle pieces together. "Ted, I know it's confusing. Please don't mention any of this to anyone, especially Brigitte."

"Dude... you're starting to wig me out."

"I'm serious. If you start running your mouth, we could all end up like my father and Brigitte, or worse."

"Max, what exactly is it you think I can say when you haven't told me anything?"

Max could see Ted's frustration building. "I'm sorry for dragging you into this; I just needed someone's help. And you're right about the timing. It's late over there. Maybe we can try again one day in the afternoon when you're around."

"Sure thing, dude."

"Okay, cool. In the meantime—"

"I get it, dude, I'm not retarded. You were never here."

Satisfied with Ted's allegiance, Max gathered himself to leave. "Is it okay if I don't go through the front?"

Ted took a deep breath, still hoping for answers, but fully aware he would not get them. "Come on, follow me." He stood and led Max to his door. "You can go through the garage."

Ted escorted Max to the underground parking structure and

showed him how to exit. Max didn't notice anyone observing as he found his way to a busy intersection, where he immediately caught a cab. He made one stop at a local pharmacy to purchase a pay-as-you-go cell phone. Max had no clue how Nikolaos intended to contact him, but he hoped he would do so soon. He needed to speak with someone who understood the Rizick Group and the damage they were doing. Maybe there was still a way for him to extricate himself from at least some of the mess he was in.

Feeling both jet-lagged and drained, Max returned home and entered through his front door. He quickly undressed and slid into bed. *Finally, I can sleep*, he thought, as he closed his eyes and slipped into deep slumber.

CHAPTER 30

*M*ax felt disoriented at first. The noises weren't terribly loud, but there was a commotion somewhere in his room. *In the closet,* he thought. *It's coming from my closet.* For the most part, he considered his home impenetrable due to its extensive security system. A network of surveillance cameras and code-controlled power door locks prevented anyone from moving unhindered throughout the property, or at least that had been the intention.

It turned out his fortress was not as secure as originally imagined. At some point, his father had dispatched a minion to retrieve the dial from the Money Pit. *Someone's here again.*

Max fought to open his eyes, but his lids felt heavy and sluggish. He was groggy too. Once, a while back, he had taken sleeping pills without properly following instructions. *This medication should be taken only when you can dedicate a minimum of eight hours to sleep.* Hoping for a restful flight, he had popped one of the pills before boarding a five-hour red-eye. In the end, the flight crew had struggled to wake him. He still recalled how wobbly he had been that day, wanting to wake up, but somehow unable to compel his body to do so. For some reason, he had the same feeling again.

In an act of pure will, Max forced his eyes open. Then a new struggle began for him to turn his head, which he somehow managed to do. *Yes...* Max could see the door to his closet. *It's ajar.* A soft blue light bounced off the mirrors inside of it, illuminating the large chamber as well as a slivered portion of his bedroom.

The more his focus sharpened, he thought he could hear a child's laughter. *Or maybe the soft cries of an adult?* His efforts to climb from bed yielded weak results. His limbs, like his eyelids, felt heavy and unresponsive. But anger arose in Max that his home was being infringed upon once again. He and his father had argued, and Demetrius admitted to taking the dial. *Has he come for something else?*

Focusing every ounce of his intention, Max willed himself from bed. He rose like the Frankenstein monster and dragged his limbs across the room toward the closet. The soft blue light escaped through his closet door, expanding like a thin slice of pie until it spotlighted a tiny portion of the wall across the room. Max approached the source, and the azure glow illuminated his face. He reached the closet door and pushed his way inside. He hadn't fully pondered what he might find: perhaps his father, Otto, or maybe even his father's head of security, Logan. Instead it was the blonde woman, crouching beside his table of sweaters. *Oh my God, she's here.* To Max's shock, she had his mother's journal in hand. *She's reading from it.*

He felt certain she had noticed him shuffling through the doorway, but she didn't look up. *Is she crying?* He tried to speak but quickly realized his mouth was more lethargic than his limbs. It appeared the utterance of a single word would require intense concentration. He inhaled and forced himself to verbalize: "Whah—"

Before he could finish he felt out of breath, but it was enough to attract her attention. The blonde jumped to her feet, clutching the journal. Her eyes were wide and full of surprise. For an instant, Max thought he was in a dream. Part of him still wanted to believe that the woman and the midget were simple figments of his creative mind, but he had seen her in the police video. *And now she's here!*

Like Polaroid snapshots, memories of the strange duo's comings and goings crystallized in his mind. The small man in white face had been lurking in the corners of his life since Mardi Gras. Like phantoms of the night, the blonde and her cohort had also visited his hotel in Mexico City, as well as Brigitte's home, where they had assaulted her. *Now, she's here again. Why? And where is he?*

Slowly, Max's faculties began to return. He urged forth each word with deliberateness: "What... are... you... doing?"

Without thinking, Aurelia dropped the journal on Max's sweater table. With a swipe of her hand she wiped both tears and distraction from her face. In the same instant, a gazelle-like alertness imprinted upon her. Max noticed her quickly surveying the large closet. *An escape route... she's looking for one.*

No sooner than the thought crossed his mind, Aurelia darted around the table. Like a seasoned soccer player, she headed his way. She faked to the left, but recovered and headed to the right instead. Although his reflexes were clumsy, Max anticipated the move. He intercepted Aurelia and tried tackling her to the ground.

His initial assessment of her lithe frame left him believing she might be fragile and willowy. He even feared he might injure her by forcing her to the ground. It turned out the opposite was true. In an effortless move, Aurelia flipped him into the air. With an awareness that felt like slow motion, Max perceived his feet leaving the ground as he rolled around Aurelia's arm in an involuntary somersault. *How did she do that,* he wondered before he hit the carpet on his back. She held a hand to his throat to stabilize him. Seemingly, from out of nowhere, the small man appeared.

"Wait a minute," Max protested.

Before he could utter another word, the squat man placed a red sticker upon Max's forehead. Within seconds, the room went black.

It was light outside when Max awoke. He sprang up in bed and peered through his window, looking out onto the Japanese garden courtyard in the center of his condo. It wasn't huge, but feng shui had created a perfect area of tranquility and positive energy.

Max normally enjoyed the view. Today he leapt from bed and flung open his closet. Not a thing inside appeared out of sorts. Each garment was in its place, perfectly organized. Max crossed to the spot where he thought he had seen Aurelia. *I know she was here.* He examined the area where she had been reading his mother's journal. Panicked, he yanked up a pile of sweaters and rejoiced when he discovered his mother's journal was still there. He surveyed the space, still unclear how they had gotten in. *How did she know it was here?*

Then he spotted it. The table housing his sweaters was constructed of finely polished cherry wood. But there was a blemish on it. The discrepancy was no larger than a tiny speck. *A teardrop.* Max remembered she had been crying, and the evidence had evaporated onto his closet table. He experienced the urge to review his surveillance tape, but he knew nothing would be there. The blonde and her accomplice were like ghosts. If they had bypassed his security systems, Max wondered if they could indeed walk through walls.

Gripping his mother's journal, he returned to bed, trying

to ascertain what had occurred the previous night. *How do the blonde and midget figure into the scheme of things?* No matter how he tried, Max could not see the bigger picture. His initiation had informed him of his true bloodline: a descendant of the Anunnaki. Attending the Rizick Group meeting had clarified even more who truly controlled the globe. As it turned out, the New World Order wasn't so new after all.

Max gazed into his atrium, lost in thought, wondering what the blonde and midget wanted. Outside, two black and yellow orioles flew down and perched atop the branches of his perfectly manicured trees. Their playful chirps felt like music, but Max's fascination quickly turned to sadness when he considered the people who had lost their lives or who had been gravely injured. Of course, such casualties paled in comparison to what was to come with Clean Slate.

Max reached for his mother's journal and opened it to a random page:

> *So often, we believe we know it all when most times, what we think is reality couldn't be further from the truth. My years of extensive education could never have prepared me for the life I now have. There's an expression here that says, "Be careful what you ask for." All these years later it holds new poignancy...*

Max flipped forward several pages and continued:

> *I am filled with mixed emotions right now. I can't believe L had the audacity to show up at tonight's opera performance. What was she thinking? When I got over the shock, I insisted she leave. She wasn't too happy about that. What if Demetrius had seen her? It could have been a disaster.*

Max read the entry several times. "L." *Who is "L?"* He shut the journal and looked outside a long while at his Japanese garden. Snapping out of it, he grabbed the remote control on his nightstand. He activated his flat-screen TV, which deliberately descended from the ceiling. Max surfed through several channels only to be confronted by breaking news. A well-dressed newscaster was at the top of his diatribe:

"A 7.3-magnitude earthquake struck off the coast of Panama City this morning, devastating much of the Panamanian capital..."

Max was aghast at the images of collapsed buildings and injured survivors. Estimates had casualties between one and two hundred thousand with nearly twice as many people injured.

Max couldn't help but wonder about the HAARP device. While he had become extremely savvy with regard to things of this nature, the idea still seemed too far-out to consider. With the memory of his garden and the birds fading from mind, he switched off the TV and climbed from bed. Before day's end, there was a lengthy list of things he needed to prepare.

He phoned Chandler in the office; it had been nearly a week since they had spoken. Demetrius wasn't entirely wrong when he called Max unmotivated. It was true he had been given every opportunity, and perhaps he had grown complacent. He certainly played more than he worked, and he had never really approached life with the seriousness that Demetrius expected. Now it seemed that reality had caught up with him. Whether he liked it or not, the pressure was on for him to grow and evolve, and he needed to do so as quickly as possible.

As Badem Publishing's vice president, Chandler normally didn't answer calls. He picked up, however, when he spotted Max's number on the caller I.D. "Hey, man, you back in town or what?"

"Yeah. I'm not sure for how long, though."

"So, are we seeing you this week?"

"I should be in later this afternoon. That's why I'm calling, actually. I need a favor."

"Anything, boss man. What's up?"

"Can you get our best reporter to check out a story?" Max tried to sound casual but found it difficult to mask his concern. "There was a homeless guy who was pretty much a fixture at this yoga studio I joined. Some yahoos drove by and threw acid on him last week."

"You're kidding. You joined a yoga studio?"

Max appreciated the attempt at humor, although he did not find it funny. "C'mon, Chandler, this is serious."

"Sorry, man. That's an awful story. Did they catch whoever did it?"

"I don't think so. He ended up in the hospital, and now he's dead."

"Fuck." Chandler appeared genuinely stunned. "What happened?"

"They're saying he stole drugs and OD'd. I want some fact-checking, though. He was at Cook County and went by the name AJ. If there's an autopsy, I'd love to know what they found."

Chandler finished scribbling down Max's request. "Okay. I'll put Liz on it. She's thorough and fast. Don't be surprised if she has something for you by the time you get here."

"Thanks, Chandler, that's fantastic."

"Any particular angle you're looking for?"

"Nope. Just let me know what she finds out."

"All right." Chandler finished jotting down his notes. "You up for lunch later?"

Max considered the idea. "Yeah, maybe."

"Cool. We can catch up this afternoon then. Try not to be late. I'm already hungry."

After settling their lunch plan, Max hung up and showered. He dressed in a slick gray two-piece suit for his return to the office. He bounded down the steps toward the garage and noticed an envelope at the front door. Max froze. He knew his mail didn't typically arrive until later in the day. Who had pushed an envelope through his mail slot? Perhaps they had left it while he was sleeping. He crossed to the door and picked it up to discover it wasn't an envelope at all. It was a sheet of paper folded over with "M. Battenberg" scribbled across it.

Max opened it and read a set of instructions in courier font: *At 4:17 p.m., take brown line south at Merchandise Mart station, second from last car.*

The note was not signed. Max assumed it was from Nikolaos Satrazemis, but how had he known so easily how to find him? In theory, the Battenbergs could not be located with ease. Demetrius' security measures were meant to ensure this.

He folded the note and shoved it in his pocket before continuing into the garage, where he climbed into his Range Rover. Throughout the morning he ran errands, none of which held any true urgency. But Max was paranoid and wanted to confirm whether or not he was being followed. To conclude his tasks, he filled the Range Rover with gas and drove to Northwestern Memorial, where Brigitte was convalescing. He stopped in a no-parking zone and pondered whether or not he should go inside. Brigitte had been clear that she feared for her safety around him. But Max was concerned and missed her company. He agreed, or at least hoped, that Ted was correct: she would come around once she healed from the physical wreckage of her accident. With this in mind, he pulled from the curb and left his car with the valet across the street.

Max proceeded to the sixth floor under the assumption that Brigitte would be in the same room. If she had been moved, he would have to play the guessing game again to find her. He passed the nurse's station and headed toward the same wing as on his previous visit.

When he caught wind of Ted's voice, he knew Brigitte was still there. He reached the doorway and spotted Ted sitting beside the bed, clutching Brigitte's hand. At first, it seemed innocent, but Max took a step forward and noticed Ted's thumb softly, tenderly stroking Brigitte's wrist.

He froze in place, unable to process the scene unfolding before him. *Ted and Brigitte?* He understood quite well that he was not an ideal boyfriend, but Ted, it appeared, was overstepping boundaries better left alone. He stood a moment longer in the doorway, observing, but little more was needed to understand that something intimate existed between Brigitte and Ted. He had never witnessed this version of them, but memories suddenly flooded his brain, fleeting moments among the three of them that had seemed innocent at the time. In retrospect, perhaps Max had simply chosen to see things that way. He quickly shook off whatever feelings of jealousy he found stirring inside of him. *It's about Brigitte right now.* Anything else that might be going on would have to wait.

While the swelling in her face had considerably lessened, Brigitte actually seemed more bruised than before. At the very least, there was something recognizable of her former self. Without another thought, Max pressed into the room.

"Hey, guys."

Ted turned and jerked his hand away. "Max. How are ya?"

Max smiled at Brigitte. "I know you may not be ready to see

me. But I wanted to check on you anyway."

Brigitte attempted a smile, but the pain in her body prevented it. "Hi."

"How are you?"

She shrugged, then grimaced from the pain.

"Hey, Ted." Max looked at his friend with a mixture of emotions he did not yet comprehend. "Do you think she and I can speak privately for a sec?"

"Sure." Ted crossed to a chair in the corner and grabbed his jacket. Before exiting, he shot Brigitte a look. "I'll come back another time, okay?"

Brigitte did the best she could to nod, and Max intercepted Ted at the door to address him in a hushed whisper. "Thanks for your help last night, by the way."

"No worries, man."

Max shut the door behind Ted, then took a seat beside Brigitte. "The swelling's gone down."

To the extent possible, Brigitte attempted a smile, but a scowl is all she could muster. "You're not insinuating that I look better, are you?"

He realized the question was more about humor than anything else, but it hardly lightened the mood. "It's difficult to see you like this, Bridge. Especially given what happened to my dad."

"People keep getting hurt around you, Max." Brigitte took a deep breath and sank deeper into her pillow. "I'm sorry the way I acted earlier. It's just this whole thing is scary."

"I know." Max softly squeezed her hand. "I'm having a tough time, too." He paused momentarily before speaking again. "I hate to ask this now — I know it's not the best time…" Max fixed Brigitte in his gaze and dove into it. "Why was Bertrand in Greece?"

"Max," Brigitte breathed a deep sigh, but her reply was just a whisper. "You know exactly why."

His mind raced with possibilities. For an instant, Max was thrilled that he was not alone in his knowledge of the Rizick Group. But he considered Brigitte's silence in the days following his initiation a betrayal. *She knows exactly what I went through.* "Brigitte, do you understand how crazy that is?"

"Yes. But they explained to you, didn't they? The rules, I mean."

"Of course they did. But the night I came back from Mexico, I tried talking to you..." Max felt bulldozed by Brigitte's cavalier attitude. "You're saying you already knew what I'd been through down there."

"I had an idea. I couldn't say anything, though. Not unless you said something first."

"What the fuck, Brigitte. I was going crazy that day."

"Max, think about it. It's not like I have a crystal ball. Unless I knew exactly what you went through, which I didn't, there was no way I could say a word. And yes, you almost told me, but you didn't. Had I said the wrong thing without knowing for sure, I would've breached my oath. Do you know what they'd do if I did that? If I divulged something before you were supposed to hear it? I'm not a Battenberg, Max. You might be able to get away with something like that, but you see where I am right now."

"Do you really think that's what this accident was about?"

"Yes, Max, I do." She watched him look away, and it occurred to her what he was thinking. "You do too, don't you?"

"I don't want to, Bridge. But what that woman in New Orleans said..."

Brigitte appeared confused at first. "I didn't think you believed in that." Then she laughed and winced from the sting of it.

"Careful, Sturdivant." He stroked her arm until her face relaxed. "Why do people keep getting hurt around me?"

"Maybe you should ask your dad."

"I did. That didn't go so well. And you see where all his precautions got him."

Brigitte took a deep breath and exhaled. "He's been at this a lot longer than we have, Max. That has to count for something." She took a moment before continuing. "Since we're talking honestly now, there's something I'd like to know."

"Sure." He took her hand once more.

"Who was Gary Richards?"

Max's face betrayed that the question had thrown him off kilter. "A guy I met in college. Don't you remember? I brought him to Marilyn's birthday party."

A look of anguish dropped like a veil over Brigitte's face, and she sighed. "They still haven't let me see her. Have you gone to check on her?"

Max made every attempt to appear inconspicuous but was only remotely successful. "Not yet."

As if on cue, a Filipina nurse swept into the room and addressed Brigitte. "How're ya, sweetie?"

Brigitte turned her head to the side, pressing it deeper into the pillow. "The same, I guess."

"I noticed your vitals seemed a little spikey. In particular, your blood pressure." The nurse approached the monitors and read them a second time. "Is it because of this handsome gentleman?"

"Probably," Max volunteered, blushing slightly, but also relieved for the rescue. "We've been discussing something we probably shouldn't be."

The nurse shot Max a disapproving glare. "I'm not usually one to kick visitors out, especially the young cute ones. If my patients aren't doing well, though…"

"That's okay, ma'am." Max stood and gently kissed Brigitte's forehead. "Get some rest. I'll come back another time."

Brigitte suppressed her smile, more from the pain than her discontent with Max.

The Filipina nurse checked the wires connecting Brigitte to various monitors. After a moment, she turned to Max and spoke in a soft but firm voice. "Have a good night, sir."

"Make sure you take good care of her, okay?"

"There's no place better than here for that."

Max knew this to be untrue. Months before, his own father had appeared in worse shape than Brigitte. Now, after a relatively short stay in a deep underground facility, he looked like brand new. He wished he could do the same for her. He blew Brigitte a parting kiss, then turned and strode down the hospital corridor.

CHAPTER 31

Max retrieved his car from the hospital parking deck and headed to the offices of Badem Publishing. For many weeks, his DC training had precluded him showing his face at the company he was ostensibly running. He had promised Chandler he would stop by, and the time was ripe for him to make an appearance.

Of course, Max had the best parking spot. He swung his Range Rover into it and went into the building. The workspace was essentially one wide-open bullpen with a few offices built against the outer walls. In typical fashion, Max's office was the largest. He crossed the floor and noticed the usual signature change in the posturing of his employees. People who had been chatting or surfing the internet immediately busied themselves with various tasks. Each time he stepped into work, a small office frenzy occurred.

Chandler was in the art department, signing off on a layout for the upcoming issue of a popular entertainment magazine. He noticed Max and waved him to the table.

"Good to see you, Battenberg. You'll be pleased to know we're almost ready for press."

"Fantastic," Max exclaimed with mediocre enthusiasm. In addition to everything else, Ted and Brigitte were now a distraction. Trying to remain focused, he returned his attention to the layout on the best- and worst-dressed celebrities. "It looks great, Chandler. I knew there was a reason I keep you around."

"Thanks, man." Chandler smiled at Max and realized just how much he missed having him there, both at and outside of work. "That research you asked about—I passed it on to Liz. She's been on it since morning if you want to give her a call."

Max and Chandler left the floor and entered Max's office. Max closed the door behind them, then took a seat at his desk. Chandler pulled up a chair and stared warmly at Max.

"What's up? You seem kinda off."

Something in Max wanted to break out in laughter. "Dude, my life's so crazy right now."

"What's going on?"

"We haven't talked yet, but Brigitte was in a crazy bad car accident, and she's pregnant."

"Oh shit." Chandler's face showed genuine concern. "I'm sorry, Max."

"The baby's okay." It was the first time Max had spoken of these predicaments out loud. "Her best friend, Marilyn, was with her. You know the one whose party we went to? She didn't make it, and Brigitte doesn't even know." The facts of Max's life were impactful, even in his own voice. "It's only been a few weeks since my dad's accident. It's like, he came out of the hospital and Brigitte went in."

"Fuck... That is a lot."

"Sorry to get all Debbie Downer on you. My father threatened me yesterday, too. Said he'd cut me off unless I do everything he says."

Chandler seemed troubled by Max's news. "What happened to make him say that?"

"It's a long story. I had an older brother who was my father's favorite. He passed away a long time ago. Somehow, it seems I'm always trying to make up for that."

Chandler wished to console Max, but he wasn't sure how.

"Look," Max assured, "I'm only venting. I could keep going, but I won't. I'm here for lunch, and to find out what Liz has to say."

Chandler grabbed hold of Max's desk phone and pulled it across the table toward him. "Let's find out." He picked up and punched the intercom button. "Sarah, it's Chandler. I'm here with Mr. Battenberg. Can you connect us to Liz's cell phone, please? She's in the field."

Sarah didn't answer back, but a few seconds later they could hear Liz's phone ringing. Liz was one of Badem's more accomplished reporters with an extremely diverse background. She had worked in a variety of industries and never burned bridges. As such, she was extremely well connected. After three rings, she picked up.

"Hello, this is Liz." She spoke fast and made no effort to mask her bubbly demeanor.

"Liz, it's Chandler. I've got Max Battenberg here with me. Were you able to find anything out on that homeless guy?"

"Oh my God. Hi, Mr. Battenberg. You guys are not going to believe what I found; this hospital story is really fishy. I'm actually here now. AJ, a/k/a Abel Worthington, Jr., the son of Judith and Abel Worthington, who are both still alive by the way — they live in a trailer in Visalia, California. This guy was pretty fascinating. At 17, he joined the Marines, probably to escape the trailer park. Served in Desert Storm, but was never the same when he got back. I spoke to his parents. They said they hadn't seen him in years. Needless to say, they were pretty upset to hear what happened."

"He was in the Army?" Max could not hide his surprise.

"Yeah, seems like Desert Storm messed him up, though. According to his parents, he was sort of lost afterward. I guess he did some soul-searching, which led to some kind of meditation retreat. Parents are convinced they brainwashed him there. When he got out, he gave all his shit away, pretty much ended up on the streets. But people said he was all enlightened, like a Buddha or something. It's a sad story."

Max took a moment to digest Liz's update before he chimed in. "Liz, has an autopsy been done? If not, are they planning one?"

Liz barely took a breath as she recounted all she had learned. "I don't know if you guys knew this, but I used to intern at the morgue. After you called this morning, I made a few calls. One of my coroner buddies is there looking him over right now, but there won't be a full autopsy for at least a couple of days."

Max understood why Chandler had chosen Liz. Her enthusiasm always helped her get to the crux of a story. She took a deep breath and continued.

"Here's the thing, they're saying he stole drugs and OD'd on them. You know, that whole homeless guy, drug-addict thing. A nurse apparently found him with the needle still in his arm, but even she doesn't believe he had any kind of drug habit. He did have tracks on his arm, as if he had been shooting up before. But my coroner friend said none of them were scabbed over. There are no scars. He believes those 'tracks' may have been made just before his death."

Max listened, but he didn't really need to hear more. Intuition convinced him AJ had been murdered, and presumably another death was on his hands. He looked across the table at Chandler, feeling the need to shield him from the dark cloud engulfing those around him. Too many people had been injured, or worse. All of it had to stop.

Liz offered several additional details about AJ's story, then vowed to continue digging. Before they hung up, Max and Chandler thanked her.

Even though he had promised, Max didn't much feel like going to lunch. Instead, they ordered takeout and caught up over sandwiches. Max did miss spending time with Chandler, but doing so had not proven possible in his recent life.

Chandler stared at Max as if he were reading his mind. "So, when are we gonna hang out? It's been a long time, chief."

Max pondered his VP's proposition. In many ways, he longed for the carefree days of "hanging out," but now he had other people's safety to consider. Given the way things had been unfolding, there was no guarantee he could keep anyone safe anymore. "We'll figure something out." Max glanced at the time on his desk phone: 3:35 p.m. "Oh, shit. I gotta boogie. I've got a meeting across town at 4:15."

"I understand you've been traveling, but let's hang out one of these days."

Max stood and hustled to the door. "I'll call you, I promise." He stepped out and crossed the main floor. Max noticed employees busying themselves. Others sighed relief that he was exiting the building.

He returned to his car and quickly drove across town to the Merchandise Mart metro station. The huge structure, located on the Chicago River, was a well-known landmark and an integral part of Chicago's skyline. Max glanced at his phone to see the time: 4:05. He drove to the nearest and priciest parking lot, where he stashed his car. With little time to spare, he hustled across the street and entered the Mart.

Shiny linoleum floors and beige walls comprised a network of design stores with extravagant window displays, each featuring an array of products: fabrics, tile, lighting… Max followed signage pointing toward the metro station. He ascended a stairwell and approached the entrance. In order to confirm he was following the proper instructions, Max removed the note from his pocket and read. He continued to the southbound platform, looking at the time again: 4:10 p.m.

With only minutes to spare, he awaited the 4:17 train. It was the start of rush hour, so a good-sized crowd was already queuing up on the platform. At 4:13, a train arrived, and the platform emptied. Max felt fortunate to have arrived when he did. Seeing the earlier train made it clear he wasn't well positioned to catch the second to last car. More people arrived as he moved down the platform.

Minutes later, the 4:17 arrived. Max boarded the second to last car and took a seat before subtly looking around. He didn't notice anyone of interest. A moment later, the buzzer sounded, and the doors closed. The train jostled its passengers as it began moving southbound into Chicago's loop.

At the next stop, another group of passengers boarded. A large behemoth of a woman took a seat beside him, crowding Max into the corner. On her lap she carried a large handbag, which had knitting paraphernalia and a paperback book stuffed inside of it. She removed the paperback and began reading. Max glanced over to observe her. While she noticed the nosy gesture, she smiled but didn't speak. The woman adjusted the position of her book and slid it closer to her knees. Max spotted a question written in black marker at the top of the page: "Do you have your cell phone? Shake or nod your head."

Max nodded.

Pretending to read further, she turned the page. Max spotted another question scribbled like a title across the top of the page: "Do you know if there's a chip in you?"

Max nodded then casually pulled the pendant from around his neck. He dangled it in front of the woman, so she could see the tiny microchip. The woman chuckled loudly but made it seem as if she was laughing at something amusing in her book. After a brief moment she turned the page again. There was another question: "Do you have any other electronics on you?"

Max shook his head. He was unsure if she might really be reading, but there were extended pauses before she would turn the page. Finally, she flipped the page again. This time, instead of a question there were instructions: "Place your phone and any electronic devices in the bag."

Max surveilled the car to make sure no one was paying attention. Satisfied, he slid his cell phone and the pendant into her bag. The woman turned her page again to reveal a new set of instructions: "Wait here and put on this coat. It will serve as a jamming device." She removed a lightweight, three-quarter length coat from her handbag and tightly wedged it between them. The train arrived at its next stop, and the shuffle of people exiting and boarding began.

"Oh, this is my stop." The large woman took hold of her bag and bolted from her seat. She bulldozed through the crowd and exited the train with Max's cell phone and his tracking microchip.

Almost immediately, a man who had just boarded took her spot. Max looked apprehensively at the thin coat before he slid it on. Wearing the new attire, he eyed the man beside him and thought it curious how much he looked like an eagle. His large nose hooked downward, and balding gray hair was cropped closely to his head. The man hardly paid Max any attention at all, or so it appeared. At the next stop, more travelers boarded, prompting the new neighbor to look up. Without warning he spoke, and Max was surprised to hear a French accent.

"Nikolaos said you are offering help."

Max had convinced himself the passenger was a stranger, but now he was making contact. "I would like to talk about it."

The man nodded. "How far are you willing to go?"

"I don't know. It depends."

"Do you have access to the underground malls?"

Max felt caught off guard by the question, but he nodded nonetheless. "I've been to a few."

"And there are population control programs, no?"

Clean Slate. Max wanted to turn and stare at the man, but he could feel his paranoia stirring. Instead, he scanned the car to make sure they weren't being observed. The Frenchman took note of Max's reaction and cracked a friendly smile. "What about tonight, are you free?"

Max stared casually through the window. "I can be."

"At 8:00 p.m., a cab will come to your home. Leave your phone and any electronics behind. You'll meet several important people who can evaluate how you might help."

As the train slowed, Max felt unsettled, unsure if he had made the correct decision to come. "What about my things? My phone…"

"Continue riding through the loop. They will be returned before you reach the Mart." The train came to a halt, and the man nodded to Max and exited.

Max did as instructed and remained on the train throughout the loop. One station before Merchandise Mart, a woman entered with a young boy at her side. She was younger and thinner than the heavyset lady, but she had the same handbag with knitting paraphernalia sticking out of it. Max watched her, but she hardly acknowledged him. Upon their approach of the Mart, she removed what looked like a sack lunch from her handbag. As the train braked, she stumbled and fell into Max. With no hesitation, she dropped the lunch sack in his lap.

"I am so sorry, sir. I apologize."

"No problem," Max replied, slipping off the coat. "Go ahead and take my seat." Max stood and left the coat sitting on the bench.

"Thank you." The woman sat on the jacket, and her small son wedged himself beside her.

Clutching the lunch bag, Max headed for the exit. He peeked inside and saw his phone and the pendant. When the doors opened, he stepped from the train. Max felt certain he would feel anxious and paranoid, but instead he felt exhilarated. He slipped the pendant back over his head and shoved his phone in his pocket. If nothing else, it was going to be an interesting night.

CHAPTER 32

Subsequent to his meeting, Max left the Merchandise Mart and returned home. He pulled into his garage and sat behind the wheel as the automatic door closed behind him. When it shut, an eerie silence pervaded. Normally, his home served as a refuge or a great escape. His father, however, and the blonde and her cohort had put an end to this comfort by violating his privacy. Unsure how else to proceed, Max removed his cell phone and dialed Indigo's number. On the second ring, a computerized voice kicked in. "The number you have reached has been changed, or is no longer in service. If you feel you have reached this message in error, please try your call again..."

Max listened to the message again as it looped and restarted. He could not say for sure whether he even liked Indigo, but her feedback had proven an invaluable resource. The last few times he had required assistance, she had been there. Now she was gone, too!

Things were happening so quickly now; Max felt time had somehow accelerated. Why on earth had he agreed to meet with complete strangers? Nikolaos Satrazemis and a band of other unknowns. Max knew this was dangerous, not only for him but for everyone involved. He debated whether or not to inform anyone of his plan. What if he was heading into a trap, or a situation he could not control? Perhaps the people Nikolaos had arranged for him to meet were planning his abduction. Since childhood, Max knew he could easily be the target of such schemes. Under more usual circumstances, he would have confided in Brigitte, but now the only ones he could dare alert were Chandler and maybe Ted.

AJ would've said to meditate. Max finally stepped from the car and retreated to his meditation corner upstairs. He removed his shoes and sat in lotus position on the large cushion. For the first few minutes, fear and anxiety bounced around his head, until a slow and deliberate tranquility settled over him. He delved deeper in an effort to clear his head, but a multitude of feelings arose in him instead. *I should at least meet them,* he thought, considering the meeting he had consented to with the strangers on the train. *I can decide later whether or not to move forward with whatever scheme they might have planned.*

As the minutes passed, Max felt his tensions melting away, and a greater sense of calm pervaded. His breathing, pulse and heart rate plateaued, and he felt resident in a peculiar gray zone between mindfulness and slumber. Before he knew it, a series of staccato beeps interrupted the quiet. They sounded miles away, but he could hear them nonetheless, growing closer and louder. With each breath, they grew more pronounced until he realized what the commotion was: honking. *Someone's blowing the horn.*

In that instant, Max was jarred from his trance. The honking assaulted his ears as if earplugs had been yanked from his head. He glanced at a clock on the wall. Nearly 8:10 p.m. *Shit.* He jumped up, slipped his shoes on and reached for his phone and wallet. At that moment, his phone illuminated, flashing the name Chandler across the screen. The timing seemed both inopportune and strange. Before he could give it another thought, he remembered being asked to leave his cell phone and the GPS chip behind. He quickly removed the pendant from his neck and plopped it on the table beside his phone. Satisfied, he snatched his wallet and ran downstairs.

When Max arrived at the curb, a yellow cab was waiting. He hopped inside and mumbled an apology for his delay. With an unsatisfied grunt the cabbie pulled away from the curb. He was hardly chatty to the point of being unfriendly, but Max noticed him repeatedly checking the rearview mirror. Max knew there would be little to no chance of these people being followed, and somehow this was a comfort to him.

Once they were miles from his house, Max finally chimed in. "Where are we headed?"

The driver glanced again in the rearview mirror, but didn't immediately answer. Max was unclear if he had even heard him when he finally replied.

"We aren't far."

Max found the answer peculiar, in particular because they drove around an additional thirty minutes. At times, they drove in circles until the driver eventually entered a fast food drive-thru. Max wanted to question why, but he figured it was their desired protocol. The cabbie placed a sizable order before pulling up to the pay window. Max awaited some kind of coded exchange with the cashier, but there was nothing unusual. The driver paid, grabbed the bags and drinks and placed them in the passenger seat.

They pulled into traffic again, while the driver studied his receipt. To Max's puzzlement, they drove another ten minutes before finally arriving at a nightclub. The escort pulled to the curb at the club entrance. A velvet rope corralled a mob of young adults in their early twenties. Multitudes of clothing styles were on display: piercings, tattoos, multi-colored hair, Mohawks and the occasional elevator platform shoes. The cabdriver opened a Plexiglas panel in the barrier that separated him from the back-seat. He shoved the bags of food and drinks through to Max. Max accepted them with a perplexed look.

"What am I supposed to do with these?"

The man motioned toward the velvet rope. "Take it to the front, and tell 'em it's for Derrick. They'll escort you upstairs. Then we can see what you're made of."

"All right." Max felt demeaned by the task and how it was couched by the cabbie. "I guess I'll deliver their food then." He exited the car, trying to balance the bags of food and a drink holder containing three beverages. He crossed to the entrance and chuckled out loud when several patrons yelled, "Can I get fries with that?" and "Got enough to share?"

At the club door, Max followed instructions and addressed the bouncer. "This is for Derrick."

The doorman raised a hand, gesturing for Max to wait. He held his eyes on the line then yelled out. "Cindy, can you show this guy where Derrick is?"

A young Asian girl, who appeared to be channeling a Japanese anime character, approached with colorful tattered clothing and spiky, red hair. She hustled across to Max and glanced at the food bags. "That smells good. I eat there all the time."

Cindy led Max into the building and up a flight of stairs that flanked one of the club's larger dance floors. She was a little too bubbly for Max's taste, and she didn't stop talking the entire time. "Oh my God, that smells so good. I should ask Derrick if there's extra. Sometimes there is, you know?"

They continued up another flight, and the loud thump of

techno music vibrated the walls. Finally, they arrived at a door at the end of a dark hallway. Cindy banged on it, and a hand-some African American answered. Cindy took her hitchhiking thumb and pointed toward Max. "Hey, Derrick, food's here."

"Thanks, Cin. Come on in, guy."

Max entered and immediately sized Derrick up. In many ways, he was the true embodiment of a Rastafarian. He had beautiful, milk-chocolate skin and jet-black dreadlocks that framed his face like a lion's mane. Max noticed a few gray hairs in a goatee that corralled a set of full lips. Several gray locks were also on his head and provided Derrick with an air of wisdom and sophistication.

Before Cindy stepped away, she volunteered one last thing. "If there's leftovers, definitely throw 'em my way."

Derrick took the bags from Max and pulled a burger out of one. "Knock yourself out." He tossed it to Cindy.

She thanked Derrick, who proceeded to close the door and latch it. The room reminded Max of the booth he and Otto had used for the vote in Greece. It was smaller, but a huge one-way Plexiglas window looked over the dance floor below. The music caused it to vibrate even though the room seemed to be sound-proofed.

In the center of the room, there was a card table with four chairs around it and a bulky metal briefcase on top. A large couch was placed against the wall on the right. A short, plump Chinese woman was seated upon it with a fashionable French hairdo, which seemed to contradict the grunginess of her clothes. She smiled and stood as Max carried their drinks to the table.

Although he wasn't smiling, Derrick's face was pleasant. He followed Max and set the food down beside the drinks. "I can't believe we have a friggin' Battenberg in our midst. Can we call you Max, or do you prefer Maximilian?"

"Max is fine."

Derrick extended his hand. "I'm Derrick."

The Asian woman stood and approached. She offered Max her hand as well. "And my name's Missy." She and Max shook hands before she slid the metal case over and opened it.

Max immediately recognized what was inside. "A lie detector."

Missy smiled apologetically. "I hope you're not offended. It's just protocol."

"I understand."

While she set up the lie detector, Derrick crossed to the window. A sizable crowd had formed on the dance floor below. The club was dark until strobe lights and lasers flashed, allowing fleeting glimpses of the crowd. Derrick turned from the window and retreated to the table. He took the chair facing the door and slid it back. "Max, if you'll take a seat here."

Max did as asked and sat with his back to the window. He felt exhilarated to be in the presence of people who knew about the Rizick Group and wanted to speak openly about it. Because of the oath made during his initiation, he remained uncertain what was safe to disclose. He still wondered if these were people he could trust. Once he took a seat, Missy started attaching wires and electrodes to prepare him for the test.

Max watched her before diverting his attention to Derrick. "I have to say, I was impressed how quickly you guys set up this meeting."

Derrick, while cordial, wasn't friendly. "We'd be foolish not to make it a priority after the quake this morning."

Max studied Derrick and Missy. He remembered everything he had learned about Clean Slate and the HAARP Device. "You think that was manufactured?"

Missy and Derrick forced smiles but didn't respond. Max realized they were not amenable to an open discussion before the lie detector test had been administered. Missy finished rigging Max into the apparatus, then she nodded to Derrick.

He pulled up a chair and ripped open a fast food bag. "You hungry, Max? We have extra."

Max hesitated, "I haven't... I rarely eat fast food. It does smell good, though."

Derrick removed a burger and fries, then slid the remaining ones across the table to Max and Missy.

Max glanced at Missy, who ripped open her sandwich and tore into it. "So, it's okay to eat while we do this?"

"Of course," Derrick replied, biting into his own. "The more relaxed you are, the better. Unless, of course, you're one of those people who can lie when you're relaxed. That wouldn't be so good."

Missy chewed through her burger, quickly scarfing it down. "I guess we're ready then." With a nod from Derrick, she turned to Max, who was eyeing the burger in front of him. "You ready?"

"Yeah." Max pushed the burger and fries back to Derrick's side of the table, and Missy began.

"So, when I ask a question, just give a simple yes or no answer, okay?"

Max nodded, prompting Missy to continue.

"Is your name Maximilian Battenberg?"

"Yes."

"And your father is Demetrius Battenberg?"

"Yes."

Missy read a few other questions to which the answers were known. She jotted down a few notes to establish a baseline, then the true questioning began. "Were you at the last Rizick Group meeting at the Astir Palace near Athens, Greece?"

"Yes."

"Was there a population control initiative discussed there?"

"Yes." Max felt thrown by the detail he had not expected them to know. "It's called Clean Slate."

Missy and Derrick glanced at each other, smirking with satisfaction. Max could feel how giddy they were to have him in their presence.

"Are you here to assist us tonight?"

"Yes."

Missy studied the lie detector before continuing. "If it comes down to it, are you willing to risk your own safety in order to help us?"

Max figured he might be putting himself in danger, but he hadn't spoken the idea out loud. "Reasonably, I am."

Missy jotted down a quick notation and continued. "Are you aware that there are underground installations reserved for the elite?"

"I am now."

"I need you to answer yes or no to the questions, Max."

"Yes, I'm aware."

"Have you been in them?"

"Yes."

"Do you have access to them whenever you want?"

Max looked from Missy to Derrick. "Yes, I think so."

Derrick turned and fixed Missy in his gaze, while she studied the graphs printing out from the machine.

"Is it your plan to set us up or sabotage us?"

Max couldn't help but smile at the question. "No."

Missy examined the graphs again. After some intense scrutiny, she nodded to Derrick. "Either he's a brilliant con artist, or he's telling the truth."

"Great." Derrick was bursting with enthusiasm. "Get those things off him, and let the man eat. Sorry we don't have something better for you, but this is a tight operation we're running. While you eat, I can explain what it is we need."

"Okay, cool," Max exclaimed, biting into the lukewarm burger.

A softer side of Derrick surfaced as he began. "To answer your question from earlier, we do not believe the Panama quake was a natural disaster. There've been quite a few shakers in that region already, which, in theory, means there shouldn't be any build-up of energy that could produce a quake of that magnitude. Instead, we believe it has all the earmarkings of HAARP."

Max was incredulous. Rizick had followed through on yet another manufactured catastrophe that appeared to be the work of Mother Nature. *But these people know about it!* So far, Max had kept his oath to keep everything secret. He hadn't even said a word to Brigitte until he discovered her own family involvement. But Derrick and Missy seemed to know almost everything about the underground malls, HAARP and the population control program. For the first time in months, Max felt he could speak freely. He looked to Derrick, who was staring at him, full of fervor.

"All right, Mr. Battenberg, this is why we asked you here. We believe we know quite a bit about your cabal and this project you call Clean Slate."

"Your guy in Greece also called it the cabal."

Neither Derrick nor Missy seemed impressed by Max's observation. Finally, Derrick continued, "Correct us if we're wrong, but our intel indicates that Clean Slate has two parts to it. The first involves chemtrails, which we see occurring across the country and abroad. This targets immune systems and fertility, which we know are both considerably down on the count. The second part of the program relates to various inoculations, the main ones being flu shots of any kind. Of course, the "World Health Organization" has fervently been pushing those. H1N1 is a fairly recent one, but there've been many others, including HIV, SARS, and swine flu. How am I doing so far?"

Max had the remains of his burger lifted to his mouth. He returned it to its wrapper on the table. "So far, I'd say you're doing pretty well. How do you guys know all this?"

"Rizick isn't the tight ship you all think it is. Our group's been around forty plus years now, and we have pretty good intel. The problem is, our operatives can only climb so high, which is why your presence here is landmark."

Max nodded, then ate the final bite of his hamburger. "So what is it you want from me?"

Derrick picked up a rubber band from the table and tied his locks into a ponytail. "As we speak, there are researchers on standby, waiting to create an antidote to whatever superbug you guys are cooking up. We know it's a virus, and we need you to get it for us."

A look of helplessness crept over Max. "I don't have a clue how to get my hands on something like that."

Derrick pushed his chair back from the table and crossed to the Plexiglas window. The dance floor looked to be twice as crowded as before. Derrick turned from the window to face Max. "We know where it's housed. It's in an underground facility in Washington DC, beneath the Smithsonian. If you have access, you just need to come up with a plan on how to get it. Without being detected, of course."

"Yeah, you make that sound easy. People around me are getting injured or dying lately. No offense, but I don't want you to join their ranks."

Missy slurped down the last of her soda. "You have any idea when this next virus might be released?"

"No."

Both Missy and Derrick shared a glance of trepidation. Derrick

retrieved a backpack from the corner of the room. He removed
a tourist map of the Smithsonian.

"Here's a map of the National Portrait Gallery at the Smithsonian. There are several large laboratories beneath it. One of them
contains toxins and viruses that are way more deadly than anything at the CDC. Some are even rumored to be extra-terrestrial."

There. He said it. Derrick and his team seemed to know everything about the Rizick Group and the initiatives they had voted
on in the last meeting. At the same time, Max couldn't be sure
if they knew about Nibiru and the Anunnaki connection. But it
sounded as if they might.

Derrick glanced at Max and could easily see he was distracted.
"You still with us, Max?"

"Yeah, of course."

"If you have entry codes to that installation, which we assume
you do, you can gain entrance through the museum." Derrick
directed Max's attention to the map. "Access is located here, off
the G-Street entrance in the new arrivals section. Between the
Courtyard Cafe and the Nan Tucker McEvoy Theatre."

"I'm not sure if the codes I have work there, but I guess I might
have access. Although you should probably know my dad threatened to cut me off."

Derrick turned serious in expression and tone. "Max, we need
this sooner than later, especially since we aren't clear when they're
planning to use it. If you can, if you're willing to do this, it'll be
invaluable to our group, not to mention to the millions of lives
it might save."

"Not millions," Max uttered in a grave tone. "We're talking
billions." Derrick and Missy looked at each other. Max scooted
away from the table and approached the Plexiglas window. Staring down upon the dance floor, he thought about the partiers and
how lucky they were to be so oblivious to the atrocities going on
around them. Right now their only concern was having fun. Little
did they know, decisions were being made that would likely wipe
out the majority of them and their families. Max quietly recalled
the days when he was like them, stumbling around unaware and
carefree. Finally, he spoke again. "First let me see if I can get in
there. Then I'll let you know what I can do."

Derrick nodded agreement. Satisfied, he reached into his back-pack and removed a walkie-talkie. He handed it to Max. "Very few telephones are secure. Someone will contact you tomorrow at midnight to see what you've uncovered. Then we'll go from there."

Max spent a few minutes exchanging courteous goodbyes before descending to the ground floor to catch a cab home. During the ride, he watched the night streets whizzing by and realized for the first time that he was not alone. Suddenly, he could see Indigo's face and hear her words, *Your burden is heavy. The weight of the world is upon you, and very soon you will have a decision... a decision that will decide the fate of many...* Sighing deeply, he nestled deeper into the rear of the cab. Part of him wanted to disappear into the vehicle's upholstery, but Max knew well that this was hardly an option.

CHAPTER 33

*T*he cab had just reached the perimeter of Max's neighborhood when he decided to switch gears. He did not have his cell phone or the tracking microchip on him, so he instructed the cabbie to drop him at Ted's building instead. The driver grunted when he heard the request, but he turned the cab around and delivered Max to the front of Ted's building.

Max did the same as he had done the night before, buzzing Ted from the downstairs intercom. While he waited, the urge to confront his friend arose. Why had Ted been in Brigitte's hospital room when he returned from Greece? And why was he stroking her hand so tenderly earlier that day? In his heart, Max knew Brigitte could not be guilty of anything more egregious than his own infractions. On many occasions he had stepped out of their relationship to have indiscretions, oftentimes with women and sometimes with men. None had led to emotional attachments, though. He suspected if Ted and Brigitte were involved, it would be due to some emotional element they were exploring.

Max stood waiting at the front of Ted's building. The idea was beginning to dawn on him that he was not home when the buzzer finally blared to signal that the door had been unlocked. He pulled it open and slipped inside.

For the second night in a row, they convened in Ted's living room. It was unclear exactly how, but Max knew his friend's technical expertise would come in handy. He stared at Ted's smiling face, still happy to have his confidence, but threatened at the same time by his developing relationship with Brigitte. The irony wasn't lost on Max. There was something karmic in the way things were playing out. He and Brigitte had both deceived each other. He had kept his alter ego Ian from her, while she had never informed him about her family's involvement in the Rizick Group.

Ted looked at Max and quickly noticed that there was something off. "You okay, pal? Or should I be worried?"

"I have a lot on my mind, that's all. Including Brigitte."

Ted took a moment before he continued. "Yeah. I know. The

swelling's gone down, but she has a ways to go."

"Her vitals went all screwy after you left today. The nurse actually asked me to leave."

"I realize you guys have a lot to work through... it's probably not the right time, though; that's why they haven't told her about Marilyn." Ted pondered the situation. "It's strange, huh? The last time we were together was in New Orleans, and I ended up in the hospital. Now we're doing sick time for Brigitte. If we're not careful, you'll be next."

Ted and Max sat quietly looking at one another, each trying to figure out what the other was thinking. At the start, it seemed they were two friends, simply enjoying one another's company. But then the silence became awkward. Finally, Ted sighed.

"Still not ready to fill me in on whatever's going on?"

Max figured he could ask the same question of Ted. He decided to focus instead on the ways his friend could help. "I was hoping you could answer a hypothetical question."

"Okay... Shoot."

"If I wanted to videotape a place where cameras are not allowed, how could I do that?"

Ted smiled through his frown. "All this mystery has me intrigued. It's like you're this new and improved spy-Max. I think I prefer him, though." Ted sat and started typing at his console of triple monitors. In no time, he had located a series of high-tech gadgetry websites. He pointed out several surveillance tools that might be helpful. Dozens of sites featured spyglasses and camera pens, or nanny cams hidden in light bulbs and stuffed animals. Max scanned the options, but nothing felt like a match for his needs.

"Wait a minute." Ted jumped up abruptly, startling Max. Without another word, he left the room.

Max took hold of the mouse and continued scrolling through the sites on Ted's screen. After several minutes, Ted returned with a pair of reading glasses and a pen. He placed the items on the desk before Max.

"I bought these last year. The pen is totally cool and works really well. Glasses aren't that great but they do the job. There's a camera here and here." Ted pointed out the lenses on the devices.

"Manufacturers claim they're made of materials that prevent them from being detected by monitoring equipment. Not sure if that's true or not."

"Is there a way to find out?"

Ted looked at the ceiling, pensive. "Let me send a few emails. I'll see what I can find out. You can take those with you, by the way. I should have an answer by morning, if not before."

Max glanced at the time and saw that it was already midnight. This perhaps explained why Ted's energy seemed to be fading. For the first time since he could remember, Max had no interest in returning home. He loved his house and all of the amenities it afforded, but he felt more and more like a prisoner there. Demetrius had given him everything he desired, but the flip side of such luxuries had been the sacrifice of his privacy. The house, cars and toys, all felt like leashes that were becoming more tightly wound.

Part of Max desired to spend the night at Ted's, where he could remain off the radar. The memory of Ted with Brigitte earlier that day, however, left Max feeling awkward. He stood and wished Ted goodnight before he returned downstairs. The moment he stepped into the street, he felt exposed: the son of a billionaire who was out late with no car or cell phone. It wasn't exactly a recipe for success. Battenbergs were typically shuttled or drove in expensive cars. Never in life had Max been in so many cabs. He thought of the paradox occurring. He was nearly twenty-five and, in theory, coming into his own, but Max felt more unsettled than ever. He thought of AJ and all he'd learned about higher and lower chakras. Was such turmoil the result of some chakric imbalance?

Max hailed a cab, arrived home and checked his cell phone for messages. Chandler had phoned twice, but it was too late to return his calls. Instead he slipped the microchip pendant around his neck. Satisfied, he peeled off his clothes, climbed in bed and slept. Perhaps it was exhaustion, or that his decision to help Derrick and Missy had somewhat put his mind at ease, but Max remained soundly asleep throughout the night.

The next morning, he awoke early and gazed upon his Japanese garden. He studied the sunshine on his manicured bonsai tree, pondering the long list of things he had to accomplish. He would journey to the Smithsonian to confirm if he had access to Rizick's underground laboratory there. But access was not the only task. If he did gain entrance, he would have to assess the feasibility of procuring a viral sample while remaining undetected.

Max showered and dressed in one of his better suits. Within minutes, he was en route to Badem Publishing. He removed his burner cell phone and called Ted, but it rolled into voicemail. "Ted, it's Max. Just wondering what you found on those items we talked about. Call me at this number, and if I don't answer, just say yea or nay. Thanks, man."

Minutes after he left the message, the alternate phone rang. Max answered to loud music playing in the background. "Max, it's Ted. I didn't recognize your number. I did get an answer, and it's yea."

"Awesome, man. I'll talk to you soon and let you know what's going on." Max didn't necessarily think the alternate phone was being monitored, but multiple facets of paranoia still held him hostage. For this reason, he hung up, thinking better of conducting any lengthy conversations.

When he arrived at the office there was the usual hubbub going on. Chandler was hustling to-and-fro when he spotted Max from across the room.

"Battenberg, what brings you in at this hour?"

Max forced a smile. "I got your message last night, but it was too late to call. Can I talk to you a sec? In my office."

Chandler frowned at the request. It wasn't typical of Max to arrive so early in the morning, and now he was requesting a private meeting. Chandler suspected some employee or perhaps multiple ones were in trouble. The two of them crossed to Max's office, and Chandler closed the door behind them.

"What's up, man? You didn't call back last night, and now you're here early. Am I being let go?"

"Yeah, right! No such luck, my friend. I need a favor, that's all."

Curious, Chandler nodded his head, both relieved and intrigued.

"If you don't mind, I'd like to borrow your car for a few hours."

Chandler was a little thrown by the request. "Okay. May I ask why? Don't you have like a fleet of your own cars?"

"Yeah, but I need to run an errand, and I don't want my car getting recognized."

Chandler smiled, slightly amused. "What's his or her name?"

Normally, Max would have filled Chandler in on the details, but this time he simply stared. After an awkward pause, he continued. "It's not like that. I wish it were that simple."

Realizing that he wouldn't have the details, Chandler continued. "Okay. How long do you think you'll need it?"

"Till the end of the day, that's all. No more than a few hours."

Acquiescing, Chandler fished his keys from his pants and tossed them at Max.

"Thanks, man. When I get back, I owe you a meal. Wherever you want."

"Sounds good. I don't suppose I'll be going anywhere till then anyway." Chandler looked through Max's office window and noticed employees scrambling about. "So, that's it, you just came for my car?"

"That's all I need."

"I better get back to it then. One of our photogs sent the wrong file. It's always something."

Max seemed fidgety, betraying more edginess than he hoped. "By the way, if anyone calls for me, you should say I'm in a meeting and can't be disturbed. Even if it's my dad."

"Oooh, Battenberg," Chandler grimaced at the idea. "That's a tough one."

"Don't worry, he won't call. That's what I need you to say, though, if he does."

"All this mystery has me enthralled, but your wish is my command."

"Thanks, Chan."

Chandler turned with a smile and left the office. After he closed the door, Max removed the microchip pendant and locked it in his desk along with his regular mobile phone. He slipped the pay-as-you-go telephone in his pocket and exited the office to the parking lot.

Chandler owned a beautiful, eggplant-colored Porsche Cayenne. Max jumped behind the wheel and swung the car out of Chandler's spot. Thus incognito, he exited the parking lot and headed for the Chicago office building with access to the secret underground railway.

A half hour later, he caught the underground train to DC. During the ride, he removed his mother's journal from a small satchel he had with him. Max wished he could recall more memories of the maternal figure who had penned the flowery cursive in the leather-bound diary. She seemed so distant now. He opened it and began to read:

> *Have I deluded myself? I must admit, a part of me thought I could transform water into wine, stone into gold. My husband is, and has always been, a man who fully accepts his role. He is a conqueror, a victor, someone who truly loves the game. But in order to win there must always be a loser. Today, it is me, for I have learned her name. Sandrine. I have not seen her yet, and I'm not so sure I want to. Still, there is curiosity on my part… It's shocking to know how susceptible I've grown in this place. How long can I stay here? If it wasn't for the kids…*

Max couldn't help but wonder what the ellipsis meant. What were the three dots meant to convey? *Sandrine.* It was no surprise that Demetrius had engaged in affairs. Over the last decade, he had learned that Demetrius was indeed a conqueror and a victor. To settle for one woman was not his style, and Demetrius certainly felt entitled to anything he desired. There weren't many Battenbergs, including Max, who didn't feel the same.

Max perused his mother's journal and drew closer to Fiona with the turn of every page. Her fears and triumphs filled the parchment with raw emotion that intrigued and saddened Max at the same time. Even though it was just a journal, it created an affinity for his mother that had been missing. There was a soft gentility in her writing that he knew she must have possessed in person.

Soon, however, the train arrived in DC. Max was unsure how the underground network connected the location of his training to the facility beneath the National Portrait Gallery. For this reason, he surfaced in front of the National Archives in the spot where he had repeatedly met Otto. From there, he took a taxi to the G-street entrance of the Smithsonian's National Portrait Gallery. Max followed Derrick's instructions and headed to the elevators in the new arrivals wing.

It took several minutes for him to find a vacant elevator. He quickly jumped on and entered the access code that had worked everywhere thus far. The elevator descended a brief while before it began moving horizontally. Max knew this meant he was accessing a secret shaft to the underground. He put on the camera glasses but waited to activate them.

The doors to the elevator opened, and Max stepped into an area that was completely unlike the previous underground malls he had visited. This installation seemed as old as the one where he had studied with Otto and the trainers, only it had been refurbished. Many of the light fixtures and moldings appeared antique, and some had several layers of paint. The floors, however, had recently been installed and were sparkling white.

Max switched the camera glasses on and began to walk. In the other installations he had seen groups of people, but there seemed to be no one here at all. He began wandering in search of his reconnaissance. From outward appearances, Max seemed calm, but his heart was racing. The access code had allowed him entrance, but he was unclear if he was even supposed to be in this facility. He glanced at the ceilings to assess if there were any surveillance cameras around.

A door opened, and a man exited wearing white gloves, a white lab coat and protective goggles. When he spotted Max, he stopped and stared, somewhat startled. "Can I help you?"

Initially, Max was at a loss for words. Just as panic was beginning to settle in, he thought of what to say. "I'm Max Battenberg."

The man immediately straightened to attention and observed Max more closely through his goggles. "Oh, I apologize, Mr. Battenberg. I don't think I've seen you down here before."

"This is my first time, that's why. I had my first Rizick meeting, so I'm familiarizing myself with Clean Slate."

The man in the lab coat nodded. Although Max couldn't see his entire face, he perceived a sense of understanding beneath the mask. "Well, this is where it happens." The man gestured toward the door he had just exited. "Don't worry, I know this gear looks scary, but I'm clean. Decontamination protocols are very stringent down here."

"Good to know. So, what happens now since the vote's been cleared?"

"Weaponization's almost done. Once that's complete, we all need to be inoculated. Then it's just a matter of time before we begin bringing people down."

"Isn't it kind of scary working with this stuff?"

"Of course. But the fallout it's going to create is way scarier. Thank God I'm down here is all I can say."

"What else is down here?"

"Mostly laboratories. We're also working on crops, making sure we'll be able to grow them down here without the sun. There are a few private lockers, too, for the ultra important. I'm sure your father has one."

Max perked up at the mention of top secret lockers. "Oh, yeah. Where are those located?"

The man raised his arm and pointed down the corridor with a gloved finger. "Right, left and right. It's a hall of lockers. You can't miss it."

"Thanks." Max watched the man traverse the hall and disappear through a door. He peered into the laboratory, and found he had a good view of what was within. A large containment chamber ran from ceiling to floor. The large octagonal device was constructed of stainless steel and glass. Thick protective gloves were built into its assembly on three sides. The gloves snaked into the device's interior, permitting the user to safely handle potentially deadly agents.

Max surveyed his surroundings to see if anyone was watching. *No one.* He strode through the maze of hallways, following the man's instructions until he arrived at a large metal door. A thick pane of bulletproof glass was embedded in the frame at eye level. He peered through it into another large corridor with a series of numbered doors on each side. Just as at his house, there was a keypad beside the door.

Max fumbled with the pen camera Ted had given him, then switched it on. The night before and earlier that morning, he had experimented with its positioning in his jacket pocket to get the best perspective. He adjusted it exactly as he had practiced, then tried to open the archive door. It was securely locked. He keyed in the access code he had used for the elevator, but it was ineffective. He tried several other codes, but none of them worked. Growing anxious, he keyed in every code he knew, including ones from Demetrius' penthouse. Finally, the lock disengaged, and Max pulled the door open.

He stepped into the hallway of vaults and gazed at the long corridor of doors on each side. It was deeper and housed many more lockers than it appeared from beyond the metallic door. Each vault was numbered. If Demetrius had one, there would be no way to determine which was his. Max could not help but wonder what his father might have chosen to stash here, miles beneath the Smithsonian and normal human life.

He filmed the space and made his way back to the main hall. He wanted to capture as much footage as possible, but he figured there couldn't be more than a few minutes of video memory remaining. He found a chamber with crops growing inside of it. *Just like he said*, Max thought. To substitute for sunlight, there were rows of brightly lit lamps affixed to the ceiling. Amazingly, corn and rice were growing quite well.

Max spent less than twenty minutes in the underground laboratories. Satisfied, he surfaced in the National Portrait Gallery and hailed a cab back to the National Archives Building. Later that night, he hoped to sit with Ted and see if the footage revealed anything of consequence. The idea that he might be asked to return and steal a weaponized virus both frightened and exhilarated him. While he pondered this, his cab turned onto Independence Avenue. He laughed aloud, thinking of the irony. Deep beneath the streets of DC there were laboratories and secret archives, but *none of this*, Max thought, *has anything to do with independence.*

CHAPTER 34

I did *it*, he thought, *just like James Bond*. Max felt good, having made it to DC and back in less than three hours. He parked Chandler's Porsche and strolled into Badem Publishing just before 4:30 p.m. After greeting several employees, he made a beeline for his office, but Chandler intercepted him.

"Hey… you just getting back?"

"Yeah." Max tossed Chandler his keys. "Thanks again for that."

"No worries." Chandler's face betrayed his desire to further question Max, but he didn't dare trouble him. Besides, he had a more compelling curiosity on his mind. "So, who's the funky diva?"

Max turned to Chandler, anxious to get to his office. "What?"

"Are you expecting anyone today?"

Max thought about it, hoping he hadn't lost track of an appointment. "I don't think so."

"There's a couple here for you in the lobby. They've been waiting about an hour. They wouldn't say what about, though." Chandler sported a huge grin. "Wait till you see them." He twisted his lips into a grimace that should have been comical, but Max wasn't so sure he found it funny. Chandler snickered. "I asked if they wanted to come back later, but they were most insistent about waiting; they said you'd want to see them." Chandler shrugged, allowing his body language to pose the question, *what do I know?* "They're in the lobby."

Max felt his curiosity piqued, but his interest in knowing who had come to see him was also accompanied by an unnerving sense of dread.

"You should probably peek and see whether or not you even want to talk to them. If not, I can have them escorted out."

"Thanks, Chandler." Max thought better of delving any deeper. "I'll go check it out." He strode down the corridor toward the front lobby. As he rounded the corner, he caught sight of a woman's legs adorned in black, leather stiletto-heeled boots. *Who is this?* He peered further around an obstructing room divider and spotted the woman's upper torso. She was reclining in her seat with her back against the wall and her legs outstretched before her. When he fully rounded the corner, he saw her face.

Indigo Blue was seated beside her associate Tommy. The medium sported perfectly manicured purple nails and a large mane of black Tina Turner hair. Both her makeup and attire were overdone and certainly more suited to the nightclub than the office. Badem Publishing's staff included creative types who were stylish and trendy, but the setting still didn't encompass Indigo's eccentric style. The boots she had on seemed to go up to her thighs, but the majority of her legs were covered by a dress made from strips of gauzy red and black fabric.

Max called out to her. "Indigo."

The psychic and Tommy rose from their seats. A bulky tan leather saddlebag hung from Indigo's shoulder. Max had no idea what she had inside, but it looked cumbersome.

"What're you doing here?"

Indigo studied Max, trying to discern whatever she could on his face. "I had to close my shop."

"I figured as much. I tried calling, and the number was disconnected."

"It is no longer safe," she whispered. "Still, I had to speak with you again. Have you made up your mind, Monsieur Battenberg?"

Max feigned ignorance, even though he understood the question perfectly. "About what exactly?"

She gazed intently into his eyes. "You know of what I speak, mon cher. You have a choice to make. Have you done so?"

Suddenly, Max became aware of his staff. Several employees, including Chandler, had strategically placed themselves to observe Indigo and her flamboyant, androgynous style.

"Why don't you guys come on back?" Max motioned them forward, shepherding them down the corridor toward his office. The walk, while brief, felt like a runway show, since all eyes were on them. Indigo hardly restrained her colorful flair, sashaying like fashion's highest-paid model. She and Tommy swept into Max's office. He closed the door behind them and motioned to a set of chairs in front of his desk. "Why don't you have a seat?"

Indigo and Tommy dropped into the chairs, and she carefully set her large bag beside her on the floor. Max gazed at them in disbelief, but was glad to see them at the same time. He took his seat across the desk from them before he spoke.

"I don't know where to start. I have to admit I thought you guys were crackpots when we first met. Now, it feels like I'm the one going crazy. Everything's become so complicated. And people all around me are getting hurt. Or worse."

Indigo shared a glance with Tommy, who still hadn't uttered a single word. "Did I not warn you, Monsieur? You chose to dismiss it as folly."

"I know. I didn't believe in any of this stuff back then. Part of me wishes I still didn't."

"But, Monsieur, this will not go away. When the universe beckons we must answer her call." Indigo studied Max intensely. "I will ask you once more, have you made your choice?"

Max returned the medium's steely gaze. "I think so…"

"I will advise you as I do other clients; the suffering on this planet shall always equal the resistance we offer to that which we know to be true."

Max laughed, shaking his head. He had phoned to speak with Indigo several weeks before, but now that she was in front of him he didn't know what to ask.

"If more answers are needed, you must use the tools I provided. Antikythera will reveal much."

Max dropped his head. "I can't use it anymore—my father confiscated the missing piece."

Indigo turned to Tommy. "Tu vois? J'avais raison de venir."

Tommy nodded his head once. "Oui."

The seer turned to Max, her eyes filled with determination. "There are other ways, Monsieur." Without hesitation, she reached into her satchel and removed a small thermos. She placed it on the desk before Max.

Max peered at the container. "What's that?"

"A family recipe. To enhance the sight. I sense this is already strong in you." Indigo raised an eyebrow, as if she were daring Max. "The Shamans in Peru discovered Ayahuasca. Here, a recipe of peyote achieves a similar goal."

Max stared across his desk at Indigo and Tommy. "You brought that for me to drink now?"

Indigo and Tommy both nodded, while Max contemplated the idea. He could use an advantage. Had it still been possible, he would have utilized the Anti-k Device again.

"Okay. Pour it then."

Indigo removed the lid from her thermos and poured the concoction into it. She handed it to Max, who peered into the makeshift cup. The liquid inside was dark yellow like dehydrated urine. There were also tiny flecks and particles floating inside, as one might expect with a ruptured teabag. He raised the cup as if in a toast, then Max downed its contents. The concoction was bittery sweet with an aftertaste of licorice. He had no clue how long it had been in the thermos, but it was still warm. He handed the cup back to Indigo, who quickly refilled it. She sat back with the cup in hand.

"Now, what?" Max inquired.

"Patience, mon cher. In just a moment you will feel its effect." Indigo raised the cup and drank down an equal portion of the elixir. "This time, we will share the sight."

Like a train arriving on schedule, the potion gently nudged Max's consciousness. The room did not spin, but it felt like they were floating on a large magic carpet. "Whoa." He leaned back in his chair, prompting Indigo to scoot forward.

She reached across the desk. "Give me your hands, Monsieur."

Max rolled his head from side to side. "I didn't expect it to work so fast." He wheeled his chair forward, reached across the desk and took Indigo's hands.

She inhaled deeply, also feeling the impact of her family potion. A powerful jolt rocked her body, but she clung tightly to Max's grip. "The sight is stronger in you than I thought." She took in several labored breaths. "Still, I won't be swayed." With her deepest will, the medium focused her attention. "You must surrender, Monsieur. Release yourself."

Max perceived the room beginning to spin. He closed his eyes, and his skin prickled as if a million electrical sparks were parading across it. In an instant, everything grew still and Max opened his eyes. He expected to see Indigo and Tommy sitting across from him. Instead he was made witness, once again, to a distant reality from a past long gone.

CHAPTER 35

It had been months since Enki's presentation, but a festering anger still boiled in his brother Enlil. Enki had been shameless enough to parade hybrids through the amphitheatre before members of the council. It turned out that for decades, both he and Ninmah had been breaching Nibirian law, experimenting with earthling genetics. Secretly, Enlil envied their maneuver. He hadn't thought his sibling capable of such a devious plan. Now he understood Enki was a stronger adversary than he first imagined.

To make things worse, they had been successful in their halfbreed experimentations. They even called the first female Tiamat. Millions of years earlier, Nibirians had used the appellation for the planet they were now on. Back then, Earth, or Tiamat as it was known, was more than twice its current size, but its rotation had placed it in the crosshairs of their own planet, Nibiru. The titanic collision of the two celestial bodies had smashed Tiamat in two. Today, its largest remnant had been renamed Earth, and the other notable surviving fragment was the moon. Smaller lingering debris eventually came to be known as the asteroid belt.

Months had passed since Enki and Ninmah's proposal. In order to secure permission for a hybrid program, their father had beamed a message to the remaining council members back on Nibiru. Following the grand debacle of their presentation, Anu had left the Abzu, journeying to Eridu for its more extravagant accommodations.

The decision must have been made, since their father had finally summoned the important players to Eridu. Enlil had found out that Enki and Ninmah had arrived hours before, and he presumed the remaining council members had cast their votes from Nibiru. The time had ultimately come for everyone to learn whether or not a hybrid program would be instituted as part of Earth's gold operation. The possibility that it might succeed left Enlil feeling sick to his stomach, but he made his way to the assembly nonetheless.

Like everything else in Eridu, its amphitheatre was larger

and more decadent than the one in the Abzu. A huge half-shell structure had been erected over the main stage to better bounce acoustics into the audience. Large columns were artfully placed throughout the space, and the work of several key artisans was etched in stone on the stage walls as well as on the benches in the audience. Flagging each side of the stage, two gargantuan statues of gladiators stood like sentries, facing the crowd.

For more than an hour, the theatre filled with Igigi and high-ranking Nibirians. Both Enlil and Enki had rallied their troops, gathering whatever support they could muster.

When the council members were all in place, their father, Anu, took to the stage and gazed intently across the audience. "First, I must offer thanks to all of you. Your efforts have been indispensable in the extraction of this planet's gold. And your participation remains crucial to the livelihood of our home planet." Anu surveyed the theatre as mild applause erupted. "We understand the work here is difficult, and there has not been as much relief as you would like. But consider our goal. If the gold is not mined, there will be no home awaiting our return. My son Enki and my daughter Ninmah are both skilled geneticists who have offered a solution: hybrid workers." Anu scanned the silent faces of his audience. "As many of you are aware, an endeavor such as this goes against Nibirian law. Still, I have taken it to council. Given the dire nature of our predicament, it is the opinion of myself and the council that a hybrid program should be instituted. Enki and Ninmah shall begin it, effective immediately."

A clamor rang out in the theatre as reactions of both shock and appreciation became apparent. In the section where most of the Igigi workers were seated, applause roared. Finally, they would receive the relief they desired. On stage, Enlil dropped his head in disappointment and disgust.

Unable to contain his excitement, Enki grasped Ninmah's hand and squeezed it. "We did it, Mah! We did it. We are now guaranteed our place in Nibirian history."

"Silence." Anu's voice echoed throughout the theatre. "To save our planet we shall work in tandem with these hybrids, keeping in mind that all remaining edicts stand firm and true. We shall not mix or further tamper with this breed whose express purpose is to work the mines." Anu gestured toward Enki and

Ninmah, beckoning them until they both stood and approached the podium.

Still seated on stage, Enlil forced a smile, but there was no joy in his heart at this victory for his nemesis half brother. Already his mind raced to formulate a strategy. Somehow, he had to find a way to sabotage the hybrid program and destroy his brother's plan.

Moments after the assembly's dissolution, Anu beckoned his children to Eridu's royal quarters. Enki and Ninmah were the first to arrive. They both took seats when they saw that neither Anu nor Enlil were present. During the brief respite, they avoided discussion of the tension between them. Technically, they had broken the law, and Enki had rushed to disclose their actions to the council. Even though things had ended well, she resented his maneuvering. When she thought about it, Ninmah realized the tide of their relationship had turned when Enki had tampered with the tribunal proceedings of Enlil's sexual assault.

Enki flashed a genuine smile, still beaming from their recent triumph. "Did I not tell you, Mah, that things would go our way?"

Ninmah smiled, happy at least that they were considered heroes instead of criminals. But before another word could be spoken, Anu and Enlil's voices reverberated in the outer corridor.

"There they are," Ninmah exclaimed.

An instant later, Anu strode through the door with the power of an ox. Enlil followed, rambling off some complaint about the Earth operations. Without a second thought, Anu interrupted him.

"As I'm sure you're all aware, my work here is done. I will return to Nibiru at once. I beckoned you here, for it is not my intention to return to this place. The throne is on Nibiru. For now, you will remain and manage Operation Gold Dust in addition to your new hybrid program." Anu grinned at his children. "I don't expect that I, or the council, will be troubled with bickering, mutinies or hostage situations. We anticipate nothing but complete cooperation, as the goal of our presence here is universal to us all. Is this understood?"

Like a trio of singers, all three siblings replied in kind, "Yes, father."

Anu nodded with satisfaction, then turned to Enki. "You have done well, my son. Effective immediately, your exile to the Abzu is lifted. Before my departure, a ceremony will take place, and a new title will be bestowed upon you here on Earth. From this point on, you shall be known as 'Lord of the Seas.'"

"But, father—" Enlil protested.

"Do not speak, Enlil. Were my instructions not clear?" Anu glared at his younger son, but his face quickly softened. "You shall have your title as well. 'Lord of the Skies' shall be bestowed upon you."

Enlil bowed to show Anu respect. "This is very generous of you, your Highness. But I fear such an arrangement may create confusion. To be clear, I must invoke my hierarchical right. As the son of your first wife, am I not the true heir to your throne?"

Anu stared, indignant, at his youngest son. "What is your point, Enlil?"

"If there is bickering, father, it is because some don't know their station. And while I might comprehend the reasons quite well, we have already chosen to set aside our edicts on genetic tampering and slavery. Will we also abandon the hierarchical traditions of generations past?"

Anu appeared deep in thought for a moment, then he turned to Enki and Ninmah. "He is correct. As Ki's son, he is my truest heir and the next in line to the throne. We must not abandon this tradition. All of you must afford him every authority as my successor."

Enlil's face shone at his father's acceptance of his viewpoint. He was certain Enki wished to protest, but his half brother was too well versed in Nibiru's customs. Enki knew quite well there would be no basis for argument. More than likely, any objection would simply anger Anu, so Enki simply bowed to demonstrate compliance.

"Very well," Anu offered as he clasped his hands with pleasure. "We will repair our atmosphere yet." With a booming voice, Anu called out to his servants, "Bring our best elixir. Tonight we celebrate!"

§ § §

Within a month's time, the hybrid program was instituted. Ninmah and Enki, serving as Earth's chief medical officers, along with Enki's son Ningishzidda, insured that the hybrids were equipped with the previously missing gene that enabled fertility. Ninmah had been absolutely correct in her assertion that the hybrids would breed. In the following decades, the breeding program resulted in immense success. In small but deliberate increments, the emerging hybrid species took precedence over Nibiru's Igigi workforce. Over time, many Nibirian laborers became the overseers of a hybrid mining operation.

In the end, both Anu and the council were satisfied as the production of gold expanded. While years of work on Earth seemed long and arduous, the related passage of time on Nibiru seemed at a virtual standstill. This circumstance allowed Enki's breeding program ample time to ship the desperately needed ore.

Finally, things are turning around, Anu thought as he watched Nibiru's atmosphere improve. He didn't imagine it possible that his two sons could work in cooperation to manage the tiny planet and its rich gold reserves. Fortunately, success had become a reality. The ore was extracted, converted into white powder and shipped off to their home planet. Because of the extreme distance, its first stop was an outpost on Mars, where Enki's son Marduk was second in command. Out of respect, Anu had entrusted the Mars operation to Marduk's grandfather, Alalu, who just happened to be the leader he had deposed.

During the breeding program's first decade, one thing became glaringly apparent: the emerging hybrid female species often possessed unparalleled beauty. In fact, their appearances were often so exquisite that hybrid and Nibirian males alike found them utterly irresistible. At the program's start, Nibirians on Earth had heeded Anu's edict to hold the hybrids separate and to use them solely as laborers in the gold mines. Everyone understood that it was strictly forbidden to mingle or breed with hybrid progeny.

Two decades into the program, however, as the female hybrid population grew, Nibirians found it exponentially harder to resist temptation. Even Enki, who should have been there to set an example, found he was succumbing to his personal desires. One day he took a leisurely stroll, along the Pison, one of Eridu's four rivers. A cobblestone walkway snaked parallel to the riverbank. Igigi gardeners peppered the path, tending to and transforming the landscape. Well-manicured lawns and intricately shaped plants and trees created a sight to behold. Adding to its beauty, Enki spotted a multitude of hybrid women bathing. In his esteem, each appeared more superb than the previous.

Why should I not partake in my own creations? he thought. Enki knew hybrid women found him appealing both physically and also because of his royal status. *No one need know what I do.*

In a lapse of judgment, Enki spied two splendid hybrid females and invited them both to a secluded garden just a stone's throw from the river bank. During several hours of carnal delight, he enjoyed the women in every way he found pleasurable. Much to his dismay, after a month's time, he discovered that both indiscretions had resulted in pregnancy. To avoid any formal retribution, Enki ordered his paternity concealed.

As chief geneticist, he understood quite well why Anu had forbidden such actions. He and Ninmah had specifically designed the hybrid gene pool so the new species could better comprehend instructions. At the same time, the knowledge of evolution, which earthlings had not yet attained, was intentionally withheld. Choice portions of their brains had been left inactive as a meager attempt to honor Nibiru's edict against genetic tampering.

Eight months later, each of Enki's concubines gave birth. A male child named Adapa was born days before a female called Titi. Because he had infused the hybrid gene pool with pure Nibirian blood, the resulting offspring were genetically superior to the other hybrids. He and Ninmah had carefully deactivated select chromosomes, but many of these were, in fact, fully active in Adapa and Titi.

Very few Nibirians interacted with Adapa without taking note of his higher functioning faculties. Although he tried to disguise his inner pride, Enki could not resist educating Adapa as he would a rightfully born Nibirian child. In no time, news of Adapa's excellence spread throughout the settlements. Adapa, who had remained unaware of Enki's paternity, grew overly fond of his master and teacher. At a particular point in his development, the exceptional hybrid became aware of the intrinsic differences between the Nibirian born and the genetically engineered workers on Earth. As he had done throughout his education, Adapa turned to Enki with questions.

"Your Highness, is it true that life spans on Nibiru are so dramatically different from ours here on Earth? And if so, why is there such disparity?"

Enki smiled, unable to mask his ego regarding Adapa's natural curiosity. "The key to this disproportion lies in the length of Nibiru's rotation around the sun and the disparity in the two planets' gravitational forces. In this plane, the vibrational frequency is rapid and leads to accelerated deterioration."

Adapa's face betrayed a hopeful naïveté. "Might I be permitted to visit Nibiru one day where my life span could be extended?"

While Enki was terribly impressed by the scope of Adapa's learning, he could never send him to Nibiru. To do so would risk his father learning of the hybrid's true lineage. "No, Adapa. No hybrid has ever departed this planet, nor will this start with you."

Adapa lowered his head in disappointment. "Yes, Master."

Because of his intellect, Adapa was kept from working the mines and taught as a scholar. Instead of a worker, he was groomed to serve a function similar to the Igigi, instructing the other hybrids in their tasks of building and mining. Decades later, when he and Titi reached breeding age, they did as all hybrids were expected, and procreated with each other. The act of inbreeding, while not desirable, was tolerated to increase the workforce. At the height of her fertility, less than a week was needed before Titi discovered she was with child. Deeper into her pregnancy, a second child was identified, and fraternal twin boys were confirmed. On the day of their birth, they were promptly named Ka-in and Ab-el.

CHAPTER 36

While it all played out as if he were there in person, Max knew, on some level, that he was seeing what Indigo wished to show him. She had fed him her family's secret elixir, and his own ancestral stories were being revealed in vivid detail. Now, in a flash, he found himself in an enormous palace chamber, watching Enki at a large stone desk. To his surprise, he spotted Indigo across the room. She was observing with the same intensity he exercised each time he was shown a piece of the intricate puzzle.

In a flash of inhuman speed, Indigo whizzed across the space and was standing at his side. Without uttering a word, she took hold of his hand, and Ninmah's voice reverberated through the door. They spotted her standing at the massive arched entrance, smiling.

"Enki, look who's here."

Enki turned and saw Ninurta, the bastard progeny of Ninmah and Enlil's affair. "Ninurta, your mother shared news of your imminent arrival."

Ninurta crossed into the chamber and embraced Enki. "How are you, uncle?"

"Wonderful," Enki rejoiced with false but convincing enthusiasm. "I trust your journey was swift."

"It was."

Ninmah observed her brother and son exchanging pleasantries. In superficial ways, they respected one another, but the rivalry between Enki and Ninurta's father Enlil was too prominent for Enki to completely overcome. There would be no way for him to fully embrace Ninurta, who surely held an allegiance to his own patrimony. Of course, there was little doubt in anyone's mind that Enki would now make good on summoning his own son Marduk, who was currently assisting with the Mars operation 44 million miles away.

The rivalry suffered by Enki and Enlil had also been passed to the cousins, although Marduk and Ninurta were certainly more playful and lighthearted about it. On Nibiru, they had served as frisky companions who were both prideful and desirous of status and glory. Until now, their competitive play had seemingly been healthy. Enki, however, could see a growing conflict that likely related to an upbringing by two contentious fathers.

"Well," Ninmah concluded, "Ninurta is no doubt weary from his journey. I still felt he should say hello."

Enki offered a genuine smile. "Thank you for doing so."

Without another word, Ninmah and Ninurta passed through the doorway into the hall. Enki made haste and did as everyone expected, beaming a message to Mars to request that his eldest son, Marduk, take the next transport to Earth. Without a support system to back him up, Enki felt exposed, and he would never be able to maintain his advantage from a place of insecurity.

In a flash, the view of Enki's chamber faltered the way a TV screen flickers from a power surge. Max turned to face Indigo, but she was no longer at his side. Somehow, he was being drawn away, and the scene of Enki's chamber was dissolving from view.

"Monsieur, you must stay with me." Indigo's voice was audible, but she sounded far off.

The vision of Enki crumbled like thousands of tiny puzzle pieces tumbling away until Max could see through into his office. *There she is.* Indigo was seated across the desk, next to Tommy.

In another flash, the Indigo who had appeared and sounded distant was instantaneously at his side. "Stay with me, mon cher." She grabbed hold of his hands. "We have not experienced all there is to see. You must cling tightly to me."

Max clenched his fists tighter around Indigo's hands, causing her to flinch. Then, as if some mysterious switch had been flipped, new puzzle pieces began snapping back into place. In an instant, the view of a gorgeous river emerged: the Pison again. Not a single cloud marred the azure sky, and more than a dozen hybrids were either bathing, washing or landscaping along the cobblestone path.

On many levels, Ninurta could not have been happier. He had finally been summoned to Earth to participate in Operation Gold Dust. Over the years, he had grown envious of his parents and cousins who had abandoned him back on Nibiru. It seemed with every passing year, someone he held dear had been recruited to Earth or Mars. His parents and uncle had been among the first, and now his favorite cousin, Marduk, had just arrived from the tiny red planet where he had been assisting his grandfather. Together, he and Marduk began their stroll along the cobblestone walkway. A gleeful Ninurta grabbed Marduk in a warm embrace.

"I am so pleased you are here, cousin."

Marduk reciprocated the affection by placing an arm around Ninurta as they walked. "Earth is small, but quite beautiful. And the atmosphere here is so much richer than the one on Mars."

"I figured your father might send for you once he learned of my arrival. Does he not recognize it is only because of my mother that I am here?"

"We are fortunate for this opportunity, are we not? With both our fathers on Earth, this may very well serve as Nibiru's secondary throne."

"You are so dramatic, cousin," Ninurta quipped. "You speak as if you've been imprisoned on Mars."

"Think about it. Why was Alalu stationed there? Grandfather Anu wanted him as far from Nibiru as possible. He also wants him far from here to avoid any potential interference with the gold operation. Mars is most definitely his prison. As his grandson, I was persuaded to go there only to placate him. So, don't pretend my presence there is some kind of reward."

"Will you shut up and look around?" Ninurta motioned toward the unparalleled beauty of the Pison and its environs. "You're here now. That's what matters. Besides, I'd rather not argue as our fathers do."

Ninurta removed his arm from Marduk and shoved him off the cobblestone pathway. Marduk stumbled toward the riverbank, but recovered in time to avoid falling in.

Ninurta guffawed while pointing to a band of hybrid women bathing in the water. "Look over there. Are they not magnificent?" Without awaiting a response, Ninurta took off in the direction of the women.

"Get back here!" Marduk screamed, running to catch his cousin. Seconds before a tackle, he glanced aside and spotted her. A fiery redheaded hybrid female with flawless olive skin captured his attention. He abandoned his chase, ambling to a stop to observe her. She was submerged waist-deep at the river's edge, exuding perfect femininity. Her attempt at bathing made her appear to frolic as she splashed water on already glistening skin. An ample bosom stood aptly at attention on one of the most voluptuous bodies Marduk had ever seen.

Ninurta noticed he was no longer being pursued and turned to see his cousin spellbound. Pivoting again toward the water, he took in the object of Marduk's enthrallment and slowly began to applaud. Finally, Marduk recovered enough wit to speak.

"It is true then what they say of the hybrid females and their beauty. How is it possible to resist such wonderful creatures?"

Ninurta sported a smug look. "Who told you we do? We are far from home, after all, and there are not enough Nibirian women to entertain us."

"But the edicts, cousin—they come with punishments, you know this."

"As I said, we are far from home." Ninurta offered a playful wink.

Marduk stared at the redhead, pondering his cousin's words. Even now, the woman remained oblivious to his attention and exited the water. From what he could see, not a single blemish marred her skin. "This one with the red hair…"

"Would you like to meet her?" Ninurta awaited a response, but Marduk was too focused on the hybrid to reply. Ninurta bellowed a hearty laugh, grabbing Marduk by the arm to drag him toward the riverbank. "She can be yours tonight, if you wish it."

"I, well…"

"Oh, cousin, the hybrids were created by and for us. Why should we not enjoy them?" Ninurta approached the water's edge, and his voice boomed, "Tell us, hybrid, what is your name?"

The woman, who had at first seemed completely uninhibited, noticed their attention and rushed to cover herself. "Your Grace, begging your pardon."

"Your name, child, tell us your name."

She lowered her gaze to the water as if wishing she could hide beneath the surface to cover herself. "Sarpanit, your Grace. My name is Sarpanit."

Ninurta smiled while admiring her exceptional physique.

"Very impressive, Sarpanit. You must welcome my cousin Marduk. He is Lord Enki's first-born and should be treated with the utmost dignity and respect."

"Of course, your Grace." Sarpanit turned to Marduk and blushed. "You are very welcome, your Grace."

Although he was hardly proud of it, Marduk found he was also blushing. "You must cover yourself, Sarpanit. Then you can show me what it is you know about Eridu."

"Yes, your Grace." Sarpanit rushed away and gathered a mound of clothing from the base of a nearby tree.

While she dressed, Ninurta turned to Marduk. "You are quite taken with this one, I see. Don't be hasty, though. There are others, and you just got here."

"Never before have I witnessed a beauty like this. I must learn all there is to know about this hybrid race."

Now draped in a simple peasant's gown, Sarpanit approached. Marduk could hardly hide the glint in his eye. The fabric of her garment hugged her body as if an artist had painted it there. Even if the most expert sculptor had fashioned her, she could not have been more exquisite.

She looked down when she addressed Marduk. "When you are ready, I am at your service, your Grace."

A smile twisted onto Marduk's face as he turned to Ninurta. "I suppose I will join you later then."

Ninurta's face collapsed into a frown. "Yes, I suppose you will."

Sarpanit, who had seemed sheepish while naked, appeared to have regained confidence in clothing. Ninurta watched as they made their way down the cobblestoned path. Satisfied, he turned away and strode back toward the palace.

For several months more, Operation Gold Dust proceeded without incident. There were no flare-ups between Enki and Enlil, and complaints from the Igigi were held to a minimum. Given the unusually harmonious state, Enki feared some form of upheaval would occur. He had not, however, expected it would come from his own son Marduk, who had just entered his chambers with a startling pronouncement.

"Her name is Sarpanit, and I am in love with her."

While he didn't wish to belittle Marduk's proclamation, Enki couldn't help but chuckle. "Love her all you want, child, but a union between you and a hybrid simply cannot be made."

"Why not?"

"Consider your future, Marduk. To make such a request is political suicide. Venturing to spawn these creatures was risky enough, and while the council may have waived the edict, it remains in defiance of Nibirian law. Consorting with them is a punishable infraction. You must know such a request will prevent you from ever sitting on Nibiru's throne. A marriage, I'm afraid, will never be allowed."

"Father, if Enlil has his way, which I suspect he will, neither one of us will ever see Nibiru's throne. Is it not unfair then to deny us so many of the other things we desire?"

While he didn't wish to consider Marduk's position on their future, Enki realized it was probably a reality. Neither he nor Marduk would ever sit upon Nibiru's throne. Enlil would make certain of that. Marduk crossed to a large picture window and peered out across the landscape.

"To place me on Mars with Alalu is a laughable injustice. If he is in exile there, how am I not to feel a prisoner too?" Marduk turned from the window, full of intensity. "You realize the Mars outpost will not endure much longer."

While he did not fully comprehend the statement, Enki found his curiosity piqued. "What do you mean?"

"The future on Nibiru may be in jeopardy, but the small red planet has none. It is doomed."

Enki could not be sure why, but he felt alarmed. "What is this you speak?"

When Marduk answered, his face was serious and his words well-punctuated. "I did not know whether or not to say anything, but I have seen its demise. All who remain there are certain to perish."

Though he did not want to believe in a potential glitch in his gold operation, Enki was now fully attentive to his son's words. "And how exactly do you know this?"

"Perhaps it is better if I show you. If you would join me in my quarters, I will explain everything there."

Enki peered into his son's eyes, taking note of his conviction. "Very well then. Give me a moment, and I will meet you there."

Marduk took a deep breath to recover his composure, then turned to exit Enki's quarters. Left alone, Anu's eldest son crossed to the large picture window and gazed across Eridu's gardens. Enlil had made every attempt to transform the compound by altering the landscape and erecting a collection of statues in his likeness. But the stamp of Enki's original design for Eridu was still apparent.

He had no idea what news Marduk intended to share, but a feeling of doom was brewing. He waited a short while before heading into the corridor and strolling to one of the lesser apartments where Marduk was currently housed. After Enki entered, Marduk quickly closed and bolted the door. Many of his Mars effects had yet to be unpacked, and stacks of crates and cases were piled in multiple corners of the chamber. In a nervous haste, Marduk crossed to the window to make sure there was no one observing from afar. Satisfied, he reached outside and pulled the shutters closed, obstructing the view from prying eyes.

"I think you will be pleased, father." Marduk lifted a medium-sized crate from a stack of personal things beneath the window. He removed the lid and brushed aside a pile of loose straw to reveal a rectangular stone tablet inside.

Enki's eyes grew wide, in disbelief of what he was beholding. "The Table of Destiny! Where did you get this?"

"He wouldn't explain why, but Alalu relinquished it when he found out you had summoned me."

Already, Enki's mind was racing. "But I don't understand. This would have been his last hope to regain the throne. He must've seen something."

"As I stated, father, the tiny red planet called Mars will perish. If Alalu remains there, he too will meet his demise. I have seen this. I have also seen that nothing I wish for on Nibiru will come to me. This is why I have requested Sarpanit. There must be some small thing I desire that can be mine."

Enki stared into the crate. The Table of Destiny appeared gray at first, but its surface was uniformly speckled with tiny crystalline chips. Depending on the vantage point, the tablet could appear translucent, as if it were possible to stare right through it. From other angles, it looked gray, beige or blue. Upon its surface were a series of carved symbols and geometric shapes. Although the Table of Destiny was made of solid material, the symbols on it were known to play tricks with the observer's eyes. Nibirian artisans had produced a series of replicas, but they were static and uninteresting. The true Table of Destiny changed its symbols accordingly, allowing its viewers to see exactly what it wished to show them. Each variation depended on its position in the universe, the time of day and the mood of the viewer.

Enki narrowed his eyes as he turned from the tablet to Marduk. "This union you seek with the hybrid you have also seen it, I presume." Enki watched his son nod affirmation. "What else have you seen?"

"I know what you ask, father. Not everything was made clear to me. Still, the Mars outpost must be evacuated."

Enki studied his son's face, full of intrigue. "When should this occur?"

"I cannot say for certain. But time grows short."

"This is monumental, you understand. The Table of Destiny is the final artifact Alalu had in his possession. To surrender it means he has relinquished all ties to the throne. You were right to keep it secret. We will continue to do so while I decide the right place and time to present it to your grandfather Anu."

"Yes, father."

"I will not change my mind about the hybrid either. To marry one is political suicide. If you choose to do so, you may very well live out the rest of your years on Earth." Enki gazed out upon Eridu's gardens, pondering the newest development with the Table of Destiny. "Then again, who are we to argue with fate? If you have seen it, there will be no one who can prevent it." Enki beamed at the sight of Marduk's face, which was glowing with excitement. "I would still ask that you contemplate this decision. If your desire endures, I will provide you with one of the most lavish weddings any Nibirian has ever seen."

"Thank you, father!"

Now armed with an unstoppable smile, Marduk helped his

father reseal the crate containing the Table of Destiny. Both of them knew quite well that its possession could easily mean the difference between failure and success for Nibiru's leader. No doubt, Enlil would insist on becoming its guardian. Enki, however, would do everything in his power to make sure that never happened.

CHAPTER 37

$\mathcal{A}$s promised, Enki made arrangements for one of Nibiru's most lavish weddings. For more than a few days, transports had alighted on Earth with dignitaries from Nibiru and Mars. Together, choice inhabitants of all three planets would celebrate the unorthodox union between his son Marduk and the hybrid Sarpanit.

Because of his surplus deliveries of gold, Enki found a wealth of favor in the council back on Nibiru. They had granted him the right to construct an additional temple for Marduk's nuptials. The newest structure, a medium-sized step pyramid, was a short walk from Eridu's central palace and faced an expansive, grassy field. The grounds surrounding it sat enclosed by a great wall of stacked asymmetrical stones that stood three meters tall and were comprised of sixteen layers of limestone blocks.

For several weeks, Igigi and hybrid workers had scrambled to design, build and landscape the grounds to ensure that they met royal standards. A variety of indigenous trees and bushes were tastefully planted throughout the grounds. Through topiary artistry, each had been transformed into a perfect geometric shape, some of which included circular forms, pyramids, funnels, corkscrews, cubes and rectangular boxes.

Designers from Nibiru had shipped more than a half dozen gowns for Sarpanit to choose from. Because the affair was intended to dazzle even the most discriminating eye, Enki had made a point to personally oversee every approval necessary. In micro-managing each detail, he had also assured his ability to invite whomever he desired, from the lowest Igigi on Mars to the most distinguished council members of Nibiru. Anyone of importance would be attending Marduk's nuptials, and everything had to be perfect.

Enki and Ninmah crossed into Sarpanit's chamber, where they found Ninti (who had formerly gone by the name Sud). All of them observed the bride's fitting of potential dresses. Like a factory of automated robots, three artisan seamstresses folded, tucked and pinned different aspects of Sarpanit's current gown.

The lower portion of the elaborate garment was crisp white with accordion pleats. The torso, however, was a bustier of golden thread that fit tightly like a plate of armor. Hundreds of rubies ran in four vertical rows at the front of it, and dozens of golden chains draped down from an ornate collar to form a neck piece that also created the impression of willowy sleeves spilling off of each arm.

Ninti approached Enki and Ninmah with tears welling in her eyes. "Isn't it breathtaking?"

Ninti's observation was impossible to dispute. Sarpanit could not have been more stunning. Enki gazed upon her and finally understood how she had enchanted Marduk. Struggling to do so, he finally tore his eyes away.

Ninti gawked at Sarpanit's gown, full of longing. "If things had been different, I might've had a wedding so lavish."

There was no way Ninmah would ever admit to it, but on many levels she felt like Ninti. Her attempt to marry Enki should have resulted in a ceremony as extravagant as the one about to occur. Instead, her indiscretion with Enlil had obliterated that proposition. Unable to hide her feelings, Ninmah now unleashed years of pent-up acrimony on Enki. "Lovely or not, the spectacle of this event is at best irresponsible; no one should know this better than you."

Enki stared back at Ninmah, dumbfounded.

"Don't feign ignorance, Enki. You know very well of what I speak. We worked tirelessly to create the hybrid program. Finding the correct genetic pattern for the half-breed brain took decades; uncovering the faculties needed to work the mines and those requiring deactivation to preserve their species' natural evolution. You will undo years of work, allowing a Nibirian to breed with one of them. Such is the recklessness of fools, and each infraction reanimates every aspect of dormancy we toiled to preserve. Why can no one see this?"

It was difficult to impugn Ninmah's position, but Enki still felt a need to assert a defense. "No one knows better than you and I how tradition can sometimes force unfavorable circumstances upon unwilling victims. It is because of my relationship with Enlil that Marduk has been and will continue to be denied a great many things. To indulge his desire for the hybrid is the one thing I can provide."

Sarpanit held still for her fitting, listening to the royal siblings debate the merits of her marriage as if she were not there.

"Please, Enki," Ninmah continued, refusing to back down. "If Marduk's violation of the edict was unique, I might imagine overlooking it. But you, in addition to Enlil and many others, have engaged in multiple indiscretions. Do you presume anyone is so stupid not to grasp the source of Adapa's facility when his resemblance to you is so uncanny?" Ninmah turned to her former assistant Ninti for confirmation.

After wavering a moment, Ninti finally spoke in a bashful manner. "Whether it be hybrids or Nibirian women, there are many men who claim what they desire without fear of repercussion."

Without skipping a beat, Ninmah continued her tirade. "Brother, if you continue along this path, it will not be Enlil but your cravings that jeopardize your claim to the throne. The incredible hunger Adapa demonstrates for knowledge and longevity will pale in comparison to the upcoming generation of bastard offspring."

Enki sensed rage in Ninmah's passion, but he did not wish to argue any further. "Your point is well taken, Mah."

"I shouldn't wish to report this nonsense to father, but the council will need to know if circumstances continue in such an objectionable fashion."

Because they had not been born into royalty, neither Sarpanit nor Ninti felt qualified or entitled to weigh in on the matter. Both women stood by, observing while an uncomfortable silence ensued. Enki and Ninmah forced smiles, watching as Ninti and Sarpanit wiped tears from their faces.

Less than a week later, Marduk and Sarpanit wed in a ceremony dignified of Anu himself. Guests from Earth, Nibiru and Mars filled Eridu and all the surrounding settlements. On the day of the ceremony, Earth had seemingly transformed into a veritable extension of Nibiru, complete with hundreds of familiar Nibirian faces and resemblant terrain.

Approximately 1,200 guests took seats inside of a walled in enclosure surrounding the newly-built step pyramid. The audience formed a horseshoe configuration with multiple rows that stretched from one end of the pyramid, paralleling the courtyard walls all the way to the other end. Seated as such, every invitee had a clear view of the pyramid's inner quad and face. For nearly an hour, a battalion of musicians performed, center stage, dazzling the crowd with orchestral feats.

During several routines, dancers spilled onto the field to engage in unparalleled displays of athleticism, flipping, jumping and contorting. Enki and other important figures sat near the pyramid at the front of the crowd, enjoying the festivities in all of their glamour. Minutes before sunset, the music stopped, and every performer vanished from the scene. The enormous wedding party remained in their seats with their eyes trained on the empty courtyard.

As with every Nibirian structure, the step pyramid followed the guideline that it align directly with the sunrise and sunset of each equinox. Little by little, the sun disappeared behind the pyramid until it was completely backlit.

While the guests awaited their next spectacle, Sarpanit had climbed to the top on the pyramid's opposite side. Handmaidens trailed behind, carrying the bright white extension of her gown's enormous train. It spread out like a giant peacock's tail, nearly covering the top portion of the structure. The final rays of sunlight set the dress and pyramid aglow in shades of red and burnt orange. With careful strides Sarpanit crossed the top of the structure until she came into full view of her audience. The roar of cheering and applause exploded as she stood atop the pyramid's apex, overlooking the crowd. She had rehearsed her entrance many times throughout the week. After counting to sixty, she took her first step to descend toward the inner courtyard.

Every alteration had been made to her gown to ensure it fit her voluptuous frame precisely and beautifully. The white fabric of her train and the gold and jewels of her bustier all reflected the evening sun in a way that should have been impossible. Due to the sun's position, she should have been backlit and descending in shadow. But the pyramid's complex construction actually bent the light around the building, illuminating Sarpanit like a starlet. By the time she had descended a fourth of the pyramid's face, her handmaidens arrived at the top with her train and took to their own descent behind her.

At the bottom of the steps, a luxurious, hand-woven rug created a stage similar in color to red wine. A border of gold thread surrounded it, and Marduk stood upon its edge, watching as Sarpanit made her way down the stair. Even though she had not been born a royal, she had all the necessary poise, beauty and dignity. When she reached the pyramid's base, the women released her train, and it contracted into a narrow wake of fabric. Sarpanit stepped onto the burgundy-colored rug and took her spot beside Marduk.

Like clockwork, a Nibirian priestess approached and began the traditional ceremony to join Marduk and Sarpanit in the brief but official bond. Months of preparation had included new construction, landscaping, tailoring and rehearsals for pre- and post-ceremonial entertainment. In the end, the intense production had taken place for a ceremony that lasted less than two hours.

Visitors were more than impressed by Eridu itself and all of its staging. Tours had also been planned for council members who had never been to Earth to familiarize them with the gold and hybrid operations. During the week of festivities, all of Earth's officers, including Enki and Enlil, were on their best behavior. Those who had committed infractions by consorting with hybrid concubines made sure to hide any evidence of existing offspring.

When the week came to a close, a mass exodus began as the majority of invited guests departed. While it wasn't obvious at first, Ninmah noticed a peculiar circumstance that she felt required attention. The population of female hybrids had significantly diminished as scores of women had seemingly evaporated into thin air. Very little detective work was needed, however, to locate the vanished females.

Armed with her newfound knowledge, Ninmah called a meeting among Earth's Nibirian officers. Enlil, Ninurta and Ninti were the first to arrive, followed by Enki, Marduk and Ningishzidda. Satisfied that everyone was accounted for, Ninmah crossed to close her chamber door before she began.

"I have already made Enki aware of this problem, but it has now become exacerbated. Without our prompt attention it may become insurmountable." Ninurta studied his mother, seemingly perplexed by her position, but she paid him no mind and continued. "There are no secrets in this palace, so I doubt any of you are confused as to why I've summoned you here. The hybrid bloodline has been sullied. As if this were not damaging enough, the species we created, the one we were meant to leave unfettered, has now been whisked off planet."

"What are you talking about, Mah?" Enki's question floated in silence and was plastered across the faces of the other men.

Ninmah shared a glance with Ninti before she continued. "I'm sure none of you has the slightest clue what damage you've done. Word of the hybrids' beauty has spread to Nibiru and Mars alike." Ninmah fixed Enki and Marduk in her gaze. "Dozens, if not scores, have been spirited away by the guests of Marduk's nuptials. There are rumors that some have even been taken home to Nibiru. Lucky for us, those latter claims are unsubstantiated, at least for now."

Enki and Enlil both cringed upon hearing the news. *Hybrids on Nibiru!* Neither brother had been successful at hiding his indiscretions, but they were in positions of power. As members of the ruling class, they had resources to rectify their personal infractions. This was less true for the working-class Igigi on Mars. Hybrids on other planets would be trickier to conceal and would also be considered contraband by the ruling council. Ultimately, Enki and Enlil would be blamed for any defiance of Nibiru's edicts.

Enlil, who had been strangely silent, finally interjected. "I cautioned all of you from the start against this hybrid solution."

Ninmah spun around, unleashing all of her displeasure upon Enlil. "Surely, you don't deny that you yourself are an offender. All of you have set poor examples." She turned to face the other men, but no one dissented. "Even my own child—" she shifted her attention to Ninurta. "Are you not guilty in kind?" Ninmah studied her son closely, but he remained silent. "I suspect you are. Certainly, you are aware, in the eyes of the council, none of us is above reproach. As leaders, you will no doubt wish to punish others for crimes you yourselves have committed."

"The solution is simple," Enlil retorted. "When our work here is done, we must purge this planet of the hybrid population."

"What foolishness is this you speak?!" Enki decried.

"In the grand scheme, is their life span not inferior to ours? It is but a raindrop in the storm of our lives. We have bred them, educated them, fed them and clothed them. If left to their own devices, they will surely perish in our absence."

"This is hardly a solution, Enlil," Enki rebuffed. "Without their help, the flow of gold will cease, even under the particulars of your command. Don't we owe more to their species than to relegate them to a slow and cruel demise?"

Until now, Marduk had refrained from speaking, but he finally interjected, "You can't expect I'd include Sarpanit in such a solution. While her blood is hybrid, we have joined, and she must be afforded the same consideration we Nibirians enjoy."

Enlil smirked at the protests of his brother and nephew. "What would either of you have us do? At the very least, I say we slaughter those we have sired. Certainly, no one here will disagree with us disposing of evidence."

In his heart, Enki understood the sound logic of Enlil's plan. The creation of hybrids was the council's exception, but their disobedience in breeding with them would never be tolerated. If found guilty, he and Enlil could both be stripped of their titles and imprisoned. Enki's pride, however, for his precious hybrid creations, was unfaltering. "We would, no doubt, be breaching some other Nibirian law with such a solution."

"Under Nibirian law," Enlil sneered, "hybrids should never have been created in the first place. To remove them shall hardly interfere, in particular since our atmosphere, it appears, has regained its strength. The eradication of the hybrids will restore this planet to its original state, as it was before our arrival. Is this not a goal we should strive to achieve?"

Enki wished for support to save his creations, but he knew each offender risked exile or imprisonment for their hybrid progeny. Neither he, nor Enlil, nor their sons were exempt from this possibility. Through everyone's silence, Enki understood that tacit consent had been reached. One day soon, the hybrids would be purged from Earth's population.

CHAPTER 38

$\mathcal{M}$ax opened his eyes and spotted Indigo sitting across from him. A brief moment passed before he became aware of the sweatiness of his palms. He looked down and realized he was still clenching Indigo's hands tightly in his own. "Sorry." He unhanded the medium and scooted back from his desk.

Indigo wiped her hands across her dress to dry them. She looked at Max, gingerly massaging each hand. "You are very powerful, Monsieur Battenberg."

"This time was different," Max explained, trying to ascertain how Indigo had inserted herself into his vision. "I assume you saw everything I did."

She glanced briefly at Tommy before returning her gaze to Max. "The Akasha offers many opportunities to learn."

"All of this feels like the stories of the Old Testament: Adamu, Adam; Ka-in, Ab-el; the sons of God taking women as wives... why is this frickin' considered mythology then?"

"The truth needed to be hidden, Monsieur, until now. I'm sure you can tell, the time for liberation has arrived. The Bible, even in its alterations, has more accuracies than not."

Max glanced at his wall clock, full of wonder. "Has an hour passed? How is that possible?"

Indigo stood, swept her thermos off Max's desk and stowed it in her satchel. "My family recipe is not like the Antikythera Device. Sometimes, the sight is warm and smooth, to be consumed delicately like a multi-course meal. Had you consumed enough of the potion, there would have been no need to anchor you." Indigo motioned to Tommy. Without uttering a word, he stood and crossed to the window. He gazed outside upon a perfect view of the street. "Since our last rendezvous you have grown quite powerful. I have every confidence, when the time comes, you will know what to do. This is the last time we shall meet." With no further explanation, Indigo and Tommy gathered themselves and crossed to the door.

Max headed them off before they could open it. "What if I need to get ahold of you?"

Indigo smiled warmly, but her demeanor remained resolute. "This shall not be possible, I'm afraid. You are quite aware it is no longer safe. Tommy and I have taken enormous risks by coming here. From this point, we shall bid you Adieu." Indigo swung open the office door and watched Tommy exit. "You must promise you will be careful, mon cher. Until now, danger has circled about you, but its noose grows tighter. If you are not cautious, you shall soon find yourself in harm's way."

Max stood in the doorway and watched Indigo join Tommy in the outer corridor. They offered no further goodbyes and hustled down the hall until they passed around the corner out of sight. Max observed his employees tracking Indigo and Tommy as they exited the building. A low level of bickering and gossip seemed to permeate the main floor, but Max closed his office door and returned to his desk. He removed the microchip pendant from his drawer and rehung it around his neck. He considered his latest activities, meeting with Derrick and Missy, and infiltrating the underground bunkers. Indigo had warned that harm would come his way, but Max no longer needed a medium to discern the dangers lurking around him. In the months following his initiation, he had grown attuned to the same energies Indigo was reading.

He checked his cell phone for messages, but didn't find any. Only months before, his phone had constantly been ringing, but Max had begun shutting people out, even when that was not his intention. He slipped the phone in his pocket beside the camera glasses. In the same instant, there was a knock at the door. Max looked up. "Come in."

The door swung open to reveal Chandler sporting a look of incredulity. "I know I'm being nosy, but who was that? Everyone in the office is talking."

"Yeah, I figured that much." Max racked his brain, trying to decide where to start. "That woman's a medium who Brigitte and I met in New Orleans during Mardi Gras."

"A woman, Max? Really? I mean, that's what has everyone talking. I'm pretty sure that was a tranny. I mean you realize that, right?"

"Yeah... that's what I thought, at first. Does it really matter?"

"I guess not. But a psychic? I mean, come on... a psychic

tranny? You don't really believe in that kind of hocus-pocus, do you?"

"I'm sorry, Chandler, can we talk about this later? My mind's wandering."

"You still up for hanging out tonight?"

"I don't know. Maybe."

"I won't ask why you needed my car, but were you able to accomplish what you needed?"

"More or less."

Chandler was hoping for more, but he could see that Max was somewhere distant. "Good."

"I appreciate you letting me use it. That really helped. How busy are things right now? I'm starving."

"You want dinner now?" Chandler knew there was enough work to keep him busy the entire week, but there was no telling when Max would next make himself available. To guarantee some quality face time, Chandler quickly agreed. "All right."

Minutes later, they were headed to one of Chicago's posher restaurants where they enjoyed an extravagant meal. Throughout the courses, Chandler could see that Max was distracted. By the time dessert was served, he could no longer hold his tongue.

"So, what happened today? First, you need my car for some mysterious reason, then you receive a visit from some strange New Orleans psychic. I'm sorry, but I would love to know what's going on."

"It's not worth talking about, Chandler. It's just crazy stuff that goes along with being Demetrius Battenberg's son."

Chandler nodded, now fully aware that Max would remain unbudging. "Fair enough. I do have a few things to wrap up at the office, but I'm probably headed to the club later. You feel like joining? Maybe it'll help get your mind off things."

Max enjoyed Chandler's company, but he still needed to meet with Ted about the video footage. Plus, Derrick and Missy had promised to contact him at midnight. "To be honest, it's probably the kind of distraction I need. I'm not sure I can, though. How about I check in later and see where you're at?"

"Sure, okay."

After he paid the bill, Max didn't waste time driving to an

office building a few blocks from Ted's house. He parked underground and secured his phone and microchip pendant in the glove box. Armed with the alternate cell phone, he sent Ted an SMS message: "u home?" Ted did not respond until Max was a block away. When he reached the door, Ted buzzed him in. Max stumbled through the door and handed over the borrowed surveillance devices. Ted promptly plugged them in and uploaded the video. At first, it was just footage of hallways and the man in the lab coat.

"Where is this place?" Ted questioned.

"About an hour from here." Max wasn't lying. He knew, however, that Ted would have no concept of DC being an hour's journey from Chicago.

Ted examined the footage and noticed there were no windows in the building. When shots of underground crops flashed on screen, Ted became more intrigued than he expected. He turned to Max more insistently. "Where's this again?"

Max withheld his reply. Once all the footage had been viewed, Ted restarted it. During the second viewing, he examined the video more closely. "I don't see much when it comes to surveillance, but I'm no expert." Ted pointed out a couple of fixtures in the hallways that looked like cameras. Satisfied, he continued, "Can I share this with anyone? I have a contact who'll know more about this stuff than me. If I'm lucky I can probably get an answer by morning."

Max felt hesitant, but his safety was at stake. In order to accomplish his task of retrieving the viral agent he would need to do so without being detected. "Yeah, maybe you should send it. Don't tell your contact what it's for, though, or who gave it to you."

"I don't know what it's for," Ted mumbled, while staring at the monitor. "So, it's okay to make a copy to send?"

"Yeah, but do me a favor and delete everything once you get an answer. It'll be better that way."

Ted shook his head, still mired in confusion. He re-saved the files and handed the small USB drive to Max, who thanked him profusely. Without hesitation, Max exited Ted's apartment and darted into the streets of Chicago. He strolled several blocks to his car, on the lookout for anyone who might be watching. Max climbed behind the wheel of his Range Rover, removed the items from his glove compartment and skidded off toward home. He glanced in the rearview mirror, relieved to see no one in pursuit.

Finally settling down, Max considered the long list of escapades he had accomplished in a single day. Then his cell phone came jarringly to life. He picked it up and saw "Battenberg Industries" flashing on screen. Max gazed at the phone, wondering whether or not the excursion to Ted's place had raised any red flags. Taking a deep breath, he finally answered. "Hello."

"Mr. Battenberg, it's Rosalee. How are you?"

"Hi, Rosalee, what's up?"

"I have Mr. Battenberg on the line for you."

Max immediately felt the incursion of tension in his neck and shoulders. The reaction saddened him, to know that his relationship with Demetrius had deteriorated so. "Okay. Put him through." Max pulled to the side of road and parked; his hands gripped the steering wheel tightly. Hold music played a short moment, then Demetrius came on the line.

"Max, it's your father. I need you to swing by the office."

The childhood anger Max harbored had begun a hibernation of sorts, but it started to reawaken. Demetrius had never respected his or anyone's time. The younger Battenberg cleared his throat in an attempt to sound casual. "Okay, Pops. What's up?"

"I noticed the last few days you've been spending time at Badem Publishing."

"Okay…" Max failed to understand the proclamation. "That's where I work."

"But you've been initiated, Max. It's time you take a larger role with me here, at Battenberg Industries."

Max was taken aback by his father's declaration. "You want me to leave the publishing division."

"Of course. Now that you understand your role, I need you here."

A desire to argue stirred in Max, but he suppressed it. "When should I come by?"

"Tell Rosalee you want the first available, and I'll see you then."

"All right." Max took a breath before he continued. "Listen, dad, I need to ask something while I have you on the phone."

"Okay."

"Does the name Sandrine mean anything to you?"

Demetrius took a moment before he responded. "I don't think so. Why?"

"I saw the name in one of mom's journals. I am trying to figure out who she is."

"Yeah, that doesn't ring a bell."

Part of Max did not trust his father's response. If he had been in Demetrius' presence, perhaps he could have discerned the truthfulness in his poker face, but that was of course not possible. "All right."

"I'll see you soon then."

Demetrius placed Max on hold before he could respond, and Rosalee immediately came back on the line. Max knew Demetrius always had a heavy schedule, and his "first available" was in four days. Even that required Rosalee to shuffle appointments. Max jotted the time down before he realized he had a question.

"Rosalee, before I let you go, I wanted to ask something."

"Of course, Mr. Battenberg."

"I'm sure you know — my father wants me to assume a larger role in B.I. I need the locker number for the DC vault, if you have it."

There was a brief pause before Rosalee spoke. "Yes, Mr. Battenberg. I will send that information to your phone... You should have it now."

Max saw the text message appear at the top of his screen. He thanked Rosalee, hung up and opened the SMS. Demetrius' Smithsonian locker was number 36. Max did not just wonder what Demetrius had stored there; he was determined to find out.

CHAPTER 39

By the time he arrived home, it was nearly 8:00 p.m. Max quickly tore off his suit and changed into a comfortable pair of sweats. The walkie-talkie he'd been given was on a table in the corner. He picked it up and turned it over in his hands. He knew Derrick and Missy were supposed to contact him around midnight, but he hoped to speak with them sooner about the video footage.

Max debated the pros and cons of trying to reach them when suddenly the walkie-talkie came to life. A man whose voice he didn't recognize spoke. "Are you there?"

Before now, Max hadn't paid much attention to the particulars of the device. It took a moment to locate the correct switch, then he clicked it on and spoke. "Yes, I'm here."

"Have you made your decision?"

"I have. The answer's yes. But I need to speak with someone later tonight."

For nearly two minutes, there was radio silence, then a voice crackled through the handset again. "Come outside in twenty minutes. Like before, no cell phones, no electronics."

Max wanted to bring the USB drive, but wondered if it would create a problem. He spoke again into the walkie-talkie. "No, I can't in twenty. How about in two hours?"

Nearly five minutes passed before the voice replied. "Two hours it is. Remember, no cell phones, no electronics."

"Okay."

Max slipped out and drove across town to Northwestern Memorial. He rushed to Brigitte's room and found her resting peacefully. Not wishing to disturb her, he tiptoed to the chair beside her bed and quietly sat. The swelling in her head seemed to have subsided. For the first time since the accident, the dimensions of her face were approaching normal. Her drainage tubes had also been removed. Even through her bruising, Brigitte's beauty was still evident.

Max double-checked the time on a wall clock. Perhaps she would wake before he needed to return home. He closed his eyes for a short and achingly needed respite. It hadn't been his intention to nap, but he awoke nearly forty minutes later, disoriented. He sighed, crossed to the bed and for a minute watched Brigitte, who seemed too peaceful to disturb. With a sad smile on his face, Max made his way to the door and departed.

As soon as the door swung shut, Brigitte opened her eyes. While Max had been asleep, he hadn't noticed her stirring. She had caught sight of him dozing in the corner, but like him had chosen not to awaken the other for a multitude of reasons.

For one, Brigitte had been initiated into the Rizick Group an entire year before Max. She was certain he did not fully comprehend the ramifications of their involvement in the group. For thousands of years, Rizick Group families had ruled over the masses, and their methods of control had been absolutely fine-tuned. The Sturdivants, who had nowhere near as much influence as the Battenbergs, understood the futility of trying to reinvent what their ancestors had built. It made no sense tinkering with ancient tradition, and their compliance with the rules only stood to benefit them in the end.

Brigitte's family also knew that Max belonged to an entirely different echelon of Rizick. As established as their rules and traditions were, Demetrius was one of very few who had the power to change or circumvent them. Too much variation from the old ways, however, was dangerous, even for Demetrius. This fact had aptly been demonstrated with his "accident" in Brazil. Very powerful people had sent a message that he too could be touched.

Brigitte hated to admit it, but the paranoia she felt may have been affecting her reason. Months earlier, in New Orleans, they encountered Indigo, who, admittedly, was a strange case. Whether or not Max and Ted believed in extra-sensory perception had nothing to do with Brigitte's personal beliefs. In the past, she had been to several mediums, and on each occasion, too many details of her life had been revealed, things no one could possibly have known. Experience had made her a confirmed believer. On that day, Indigo had warned them in no uncertain terms: she and Ted were to stay away from Max, or danger would befall them. *How could they not believe when we were attacked less than ten minutes later?*

Immediately following the encounter, Max and Ted had both landed in the hospital with more than minor injuries. Of course, it had been Ted who had suffered the brunt of the attack. Only pure luck had prevented Brigitte and Max from being more gravely injured. But she could not ignore the fact that she was now in a hospital, broken and bruised.

Ironically, she and her family had spent years jockeying her into position. She had attended all the right schools and the appropriate social functions. If ever a daughter could capture a Battenberg's attention, Brigitte was that girl. With her stunning good looks, she could easily have been a model, but she possessed the smarts to do more.

Her family knew if she and Max married, the Sturdivants stood to gain exponentially in wealth, power and influence. On the surface, it had seemed everything was progressing splendidly, until the day of Indigo's prophecy at Mardi Gras. The prediction that Max would cause her anguish had scared her. Even before their encounter with Indigo, Brigitte had harbored a particular phobia about Max. *I am unsafe with him.*

Now, Brigitte was carrying his child, and the truth was, she had absolutely no idea what to do. Should she run away or seek shelter in Max's arms? In her heart, she still loved him—about this there was no doubt. But she could not spend a lifetime living in fear. *Yes, the Battenbergs are powerful, but none of that influence saved Max's mom.* Filled with an angst that verged on terror, Brigitte rolled onto her side and immediately smarted from the aches and pains in her body. *This can't end well,* she thought. *There's no way it can.* Finally, the tears unleashed and Brigitte sobbed for a long while into her hospital pillow.

Max returned home and did as instructed: he stashed his phones and the microchip in a drawer. When the appointed time arrived, he ran downstairs and found a cab waiting for him. The drill this night was similar to what had happened previously. For nearly twenty minutes, the driver circled through different blocks until they finally arrived at a building in the Arts District. Max chuckled when he saw the location. They could not have been more than six blocks from Badem Publishing.

The driver pointed to a concrete building with a sleek sign that read, *Gallery Genet* above it. "That's where you're headed," he instructed.

Max spotted a life-sized sculpture of a woman in one of the display windows. The voluptuous nude figure was in warrior pose and clung tightly to a sword. Most of her was anatomically correct with the exception of one arm and both legs below the knees. These sections of her limbs were comprised of industrial parts and created a strange fusion of biology and metallurgy.

Max exited the cab and crossed to the gallery entrance. Once inside, he discovered a grand photography exhibition on children's sweatshops across the globe. Huge photographs captured the images of young children working on farms and in factories on every continent. There were stunning shots of poor Asian, Mexican and African children. Some were smiling, but an unfortunate desperation resided in many of their faces.

Max circulated through the space only to find more arresting shots of Australian Aboriginal and Eastern European kids. The children in each portrait were in varying states of physical health: clean, dirty, well fed or malnourished. Almost universally, their small hands were soiled and calloused. The photographer had captured an eerie juxtaposition of harsh conditions coupled with the innocent hopefulness of youth.

Max was poignantly moved by the photographs. Only after he had seen the entire exhibit did a stunning Black beauty approach. The woman was impeccably dressed like a high-fashion model, and her upright posture exuded authority. She stood erect as if the weight of the world was upon her, but she felt determined to carry it. Her long, jet-black tresses were tightly pulled into a bun that revealed the exotic angles of her face. As striking as she was, there was a glimpse of something feral in her eyes. Max imagined that her demeanor prevented most from the mere consideration of crossing her.

"Good evening," she offered, smiling warmly at Max. "Are you enjoying the exhibit?"

"I love it. These photos are amazing. Are you one of the artists?"

"Oh, no, darling. My name is Genet." The tinge of a foreign accent infused her speech. "I own the gallery here."

"Fantastic. What a great space."

Genet nodded to acknowledge the compliment, then shook Max's hand. "Very pleased to meet you. And you are?"

"Max."

Genet released his hand before continuing. "Welcome, Max. This exhibit is the work of one artist, a woman who goes by the name Sasha." Genet's accent, while slight, remained just prominent enough to be sexy.

"You have a lovely accent; where are you from?"

"Ethiopia, darling." Without changing gears, she turned back to observe the photograph on display before them. "What I love about Sasha's series is how she has represented every continent. It's quite shocking to know children exist in such conditions across the world."

The more he listened, Max felt certain Genet was somehow involved with Derrick and Missy.

"Please, allow me to show you the rest of the gallery."

Genet took Max by the arm and led him further into the building. He had no idea what perfume she had on, but the scent was intoxicating somehow. He inhaled it, only to be reminded of the fragrance AJ had created in his car.

In the gallery's rear, she led him up a set of metal stairs. At the top, they entered a loft space where they found Derrick seated alone behind a desk. Genet closed and locked the door behind them. The space was tastefully furnished with modern pieces of glass and chrome. More importantly, Max noticed concrete brick walls covered by thick padding. The room had been soundproofed, which is why they were there. Max withdrew the USB flash drive from his pocket.

Before he could speak, Derrick jumped to his feet behind the desk. "You were told not to bring electronics."

Max waved it before Derrick's eyes. "I know, but I thought you'd want to see this. It's the footage I shot underground."

Derrick and Genet shared a glance. Genet took the drive from Max and crossed to her desk. She unlocked a drawer and removed a wand similar to the ones used by the TSA at airports. She switched it on and waved it over the drive. It didn't make a sound, failing to alert. Genet looked up, relieved. "It's clean."

Derrick's frown quickly morphed into a smile. "Let's have

a look at it then. But, Max, you have to promise not to do that again."

Genet plugged the drive into her computer and opened the video file with Max's footage. They watched together, and both Derrick and Genet's faces lit up like they had just won a huge Las Vegas jackpot. When the underground crops appeared on screen, Derrick's face was incredulous.

"Will you look at that? They're planning bountiful lives down there, while we live in havoc and chaos up here."

Genet shook her head in disbelief. "It's inconceivable." She turned to Max with a tinge of venom infecting her voice. "It's like the seed vault in Svalbard. Genetically modified food for us with a stockade of natural seeds in a Norwegian mountain for them. We have to put an end to this bullshit."

Max turned to Derrick, switching gears. "I thought you might be interested in this, but that's not why I'm showing it to you. In case you hadn't noticed, I was never trained as a spy. I need you, or whomever, to evaluate this, so you can let me know what kind of precautions I need to take before I go down there again."

"Of course," Derrick answered.

"How soon can that be done?"

Derrick and Genet shared a silent exchange before she offered a reply. "Probably by noon tomorrow."

"That fast?" Max was impressed and a little surprised.

"Darling, we don't have time to waste. Everyone understands the urgency of what it is we're doing. The question is, how quickly can you grab a sample of what they're cooking up down there?"

"The minute I know it's safe. Remember, this thing is lethal, and I'm not experienced with deadly viruses and toxins."

Derrick came around the desk and stood beside Genet. Max watched them standing side-by-side and realized how beautiful they were together. On their own, Genet and Derrick had powerful personas with fit physiques, but somehow they were more stunning as a pair. They observed Max sizing them up until Derrick finally spoke.

"The sooner we get this thing, the better. There's no telling how long it'll take to make a vaccine for it. We'll make sure you have the necessary equipment to transport it and the protocol to do so safely."

"Darling," Genet continued, speaking to Max in regal fashion, "if you can get this, our network will open up drastically to you. I can hardly describe how excited we are to have someone like you on board."

Derrick's face was hopeful as he nodded in agreement. "If you're comfortable, let's plan for the day after tomorrow. We'll make sure you have everything you need in addition to a transport protocol."

Max nodded, filled with a mix of excitement and apprehension. He felt uncertain of his ability to outsmart the shrewd horde of people to which he technically belonged. But it was too late to turn back now — too many things had already been set in motion.

When their meeting adjourned, Derrick made a call. Minutes later, a cab arrived to retrieve Max. He hopped inside, then reached for his phone. *Shit. It's at home.* He wondered if Chandler was still at work. Without his phone, Max requested the cabbie to detour by Badem Publishing, where he spotted Chandler's car in the parking lot. He tipped the driver and entered the building.

He found Chandler sitting with three layout artists. Max cleared his throat to make his presence known. "Working late tonight?"

Chandler and the others spun around. "Hey, Max. How'd you know we were still here?"

"I didn't. Went to an art show a few blocks away and figured I'd swing by."

"We had a snafu earlier," Chandler revealed. "Long story… But we have to go to press come morning."

"Don't let me interfere, unless there's something I can do to help." He looked over the table at the work.

Chandler smiled. "We're almost done, actually. Can you give us a half hour?"

"Sure. I like the way you've juxtaposed those scenes. And thank you guys for staying late."

Max retreated to his office to review and answer emails while he waited for Chandler. He would miss this office, he thought, once he began with Battenberg Industries. Forty-five minutes later, Chandler appeared at his office door.

"So, what's up? Why're you still here?"

"I don't have my car. When I saw you here, I got dropped off. Figured I'd see if you still wanted to hang out."

Chandler looked tempted, but then he released a deep sigh. "Yeah. That was before I realized I'd be here this late."

"We don't have to stay long. An hour, tops."

Max felt he could see the machinations of Chandler's mind as he calculated the current time and how long it would take to arrive, party and get home, and how much sleep that would allow before morning. Ten minutes later, they were in Chandler's car, heading toward the Library nightclub. Chandler stopped a block away, near the same alleyway where Max had been abducted by his father's men. He turned to Max. "Wait for me at the back door, and I'll open it once I'm in."

Max made no move to disembark. Instead, he shook his head. "Just park and we'll go together."

Chandler's eyes grew wide at Max's atypical proposition. "Are you forgetting what happened last time when your dad showed up?"

Max peered into the alley, and a familiar tag on the wall caught his eye. He had first spotted it months before on the night of his return from the Money Pit. The graffiti depicted a likeness of George W. Bush with a large crown on top of his head. A single word in black paint was prominently written within the head-piece: RIZICK.

Max recalled that fateful night. At the time, he had known nothing of his family's true legacy and its connection to the Rizick Group. *How the times have changed*, he thought, looking back at his friend and VP. "Will you just park already? I need a drink."

Chandler shrugged, then drove forward to leave his car with the valet. He studied Max with a deepening curiosity as they got out to enter the Library. He and Max had frequented gay clubs a half dozen times or so, but Max had never entered through the front door. Chandler turned to him while they paid the cover charge.

"You don't have to answer, but I have to ask." Chandler stared at Max, who finally nodded for him to continue. "Am I hanging with Ian or Max tonight?"

The question caught Max off guard, and his face flushed with embarrassment. "I don't know. Could be Max, or maybe Ian."

"Really?" Chandler feigned surprise, but the face of true sarcasm quickly took over. "I hate to break this to you, Max, but there never really was an Ian." Chandler playfully elbowed Max in the side.

A few months had passed since Max's last excursion at the Library, and the bar looked as if it had recently been remodeled. A water wall at the entrance immediately let Max know feng shui had been applied to the new design. The lights were tastefully dimmed, and there was a dance floor off to the side.

Returning to the club environment felt strange to Max. Since his initiation, he had hardly attempted any kind of social enjoyment. Both he and Chandler had always been comfortable together, but their relationship outside of work was different. On most occasions, they wasted no time reverting to collegiate behaviors. But Chandler realized that Max was somehow different now. In days past, he and Max would have instantly been on the prowl. Tonight, however, Chandler held Max's full attention, and he was surprised to find he liked it that way.

Max ordered their first round of cocktails, officially beginning their night out. Two drinks later, the friends were getting tipsy. Chandler used the opportunity to his advantage, taking a moment to explore whether or not Max might now answer questions about his mysterious comings and goings.

"So what's going on with you? We haven't talked in a while."

Their third round of drinks arrived, and Max took a sip of his. "I wish I could tell you, man, but you wouldn't believe me if I did."

"Try me. You can start with why you needed my car this morning."

Chandler's attempt to get answers garnered a small chuckle

from Max. The two locked eyes, and Chandler noticed a demeanor in his boss that he had never seen before. The new altered state somehow scared and exhilarated him.

Max longed to confide his darkest secrets, but he was fearful of the repercussions. At least Derrick, Genet and Missy knew what they were dealing with, and their decision to become involved in a makeshift resistance movement had nothing to do with Max. The last thing he wanted was to pull another friend into his own dark web. Max's eyes lit up when a familiar song blared through the dance floor speakers.

"Come on, let's dance." He grabbed Chandler by the hand and dragged him toward the dance floor. As they crossed before the bar, Chandler could not help but be perplexed by the new and emboldened Max. When they reached the dance floor, Max cut through the crowd like a knife, pulling Chandler along until they reached a spot where there was room to move. Max began to dance and Chandler followed suit.

The outing that was meant to last an hour ultimately turned into three, and Max enjoyed every minute of it. As the music thumped, he danced with full abandon and forgot, for a short time, about the tremendous burden ahead of him. The DJ spun one cut into another and transitioned to a high-energy, fast-paced song. Max threw his arms in the air and hollered, swaying to the beat. Chandler stared at him with bemused awe.

Although he didn't believe he knew the Max standing before him, he actually thought he might like him better.

CHAPTER 40

*T*he next morning Max awoke, struggling with a slight hangover. He rolled to his left until something obstructed his path. Startled, he turned to see Chandler sleeping next to him. Max ran a hand through his hair, giving thought to the previous night. He knew they had overindulged with alcohol, but seeing Chandler at his side made him realize the tail end of their nightly excursion was a blur. He lifted the sheets, took an intimate gander and felt relief that he and Chandler were still clothed.

Max was no stranger to the aftermath of overdrinking, so he knew what he needed to do. He slipped from bed and descended to the kitchen for a glass of water, two aspirins and a multivitamin. He tossed the pills back and gulped the water down behind them. Max nearly dropped the glass when a loud squelch rang out and startled him. He spun around to the walkie-talkie on his counter, and a man's voice reverberated through it.

"Hello. Are you there?"

In his waking haze, Max had forgotten about the radio device. He hadn't expected to hear back from Derrick or Genet so soon, nor when he had a guest present. He grabbed it and clicked on the talk button. "Yes, I am."

As usual there was a pause. The device was probably changing channels. Suddenly, the man's voice crackled through the receiver. "We need to see you, as soon as possible."

Before Max could reply, he spotted Chandler at the bottom of the stairs. Chandler pointed at the walkie-talkie with curiosity etched upon his face. "What is that thing? I didn't know those still existed."

Max had no clue how to explain why he had the antiquated device, so he didn't bother. "Man, what happened last night? I don't even remember coming home."

"Why do you think I'm here? You'd probably still be at the club if I hadn't brought you back."

Max hoped no one would speak from the walkie-talkie until he could leave the room, but it didn't quite work out that way. The same male voice sounded through the receiver. "You still there?"

Max knew that Chandler would have questions no matter what he said, so he answered back into the device. "When?"

"How about in fifteen?" the voice responded. "We'll send a car." Then the radio fell silent.

"What, are you in the military now?" Chandler looked perplexed. "When did you get a walkie-talkie?"

Think fast. "My dad's got me on every kind of leash you can imagine. In real emergencies, these will probably be the only things that work." Max glanced at his stove clock. "Damn, is it already ten?"

"Shit! I gotta get to work. The boss man might fire me."

Max chuckled as Chandler turned and skipped up the steps. The pounding in his head made him anxious for the cocktail of aspirin and vitamins to kick in. With little time to spare, he bounded up the steps behind Chandler to prepare for the car that would be coming in just a few minutes.

Max entered his room and could hear Chandler in the shower across the hall. He retreated to his own bath for a quick shower, then crossed into his closet to dress. Moments later, Chandler peeked in with only a towel wrapped around him.

"You wouldn't happen to have a shirt I can borrow?"

"I don't know..." Max turned and glanced at a shelf filled with stacks of perfectly folded dress shirts, each arranged by color. "What do you think?"

Chandler smirked. Without speaking a word, he pulled a shirt from the white pile and returned to the guest bathroom to dress. When he and Max were finished, they descended to the front of the house, ready to greet the world. Chandler hopped in his Porsche Cayenne and fired it up, lowering the window.

"You coming in later?"

Max honestly didn't know what was in store for him. "Not sure yet. I have a few errands to do."

"All right then. Gotta scoot."

Chandler shrugged and reversed out of Max's driveway. Before he could fully get his car turned around, a black Lincoln SUV pulled up. Chandler spotted the MKC in his rearview mirror. On the surface, there was nothing unusual about a livery vehicle being sent for his employer, but Max had been acting so strange of late. Chandler suspected there was more going on than Max wanted to reveal.

The MKC parked adjacent to the driveway, and Max felt an overwhelming sense of dread. Until now, Derrick had sent only taxis to retrieve him, so who had dispatched the MKC? It could only be Demetrius. Max opened the transport vehicle's rear door and leaned in. "Who're you here for?"

The driver wore a black suit and dark sunglasses. He turned his head robotically, like a real-life cyborg. "They would like to see you, sir."

The plural "they" was all Max needed to understand. Demetrius had not commissioned the car after all. He hopped in the back, wondering why an MKC had been sent instead of a cab. Perhaps he had graduated in his importance to the resistance group. The chauffeur drove Max toward Lincoln Park, one of Chicago's more affluent areas. Only blocks from the water, the car slowed to a stop before a low-rise brick building. According to the sign in front, it was a homeless shelter.

Max knew the neighborhood well but never realized a homeless shelter existed there. Traditionally, people with Lincoln Park money did not permit such elements to be established in their neighborhoods. The driver, who seemed to believe he was the embodiment of liquid metal from the *Terminator* movies, turned to Max and instructed him to enter the shelter.

Max exited the car and strode through the front door. The first person he spotted was Missy. She was standing over a young African American male who happened to be vigorously typing at a desk computer. Missy noticed Max and offered a warm smile. "Hey, Max, I'll be with you in a sec." When she felt sure the young typist was okay, she led Max toward the rear of the shelter.

In the back, a dormitory consisted of one large room with numerous bunk beds squeezed into a series of different configurations. They crossed through the quarters, and Max smelled cleanser and disinfectant in the air. While the area looked tidy, there was still something depressing about it. Max could hardly visualize a good night's sleep in such a space with so many people tightly packed inside. Although all the beds were neatly made up, the bed sheets appeared a dingy gray.

Missy led him to the dormitory's back wall, and they crossed through a large metal door into a conference room. Max was relieved to see Derrick and Genet seated at a large, rectangular conference table. Until now, Genet's hair had always been tied in a bun, giving her a sophistication that demanded respect. Now, she was wearing it down. Its length impressed Max, as cascades of long, black tresses trailed across her shoulders. With the new coif, Genet exuded a raw sexuality that Max had not anticipated.

A metallic case resembling a professional makeup kit had been placed in the center of the table, and a large flat screen monitor was mounted on the wall. The room looked strangely corporate in contrast to the adjacent dormitory.

Max took a seat at the conference table. "How is everyone?"

Derrick seemed hurried in his answer. "Things are going quickly, Max, maybe a little too quickly. We're hoping all of us will be able to keep up."

All eyes were on Max, and despite his now fading headache, he forced a smile. "I'll try my best."

"Wonderful, darling." Genet reached across the table and opened the metallic briefcase. Surrounded by a cushion of foam, a set of smaller, rectangular leather containers was encased inside. If Max didn't know better, he would have presumed they were compact humidors, each large enough to house three full-sized cigars. "This, my dear, is what you'll use to transport the viral agent." Genet removed one of the containers and showcased it before Max. "As you can see, it is slender and discrete. It'll prevent you, or anyone else, from getting contaminated."

Max chuckled nervously. "I suppose that's a good idea."

Genet directed Max's attention to three buttons on the side of the container. "To make this easy, we've set the code to one-two-three. What this means is, from left to right you push each button once. Then a second time, from left to right you push each button twice, and the final and third time, you push them three times each." Genet demonstrated the process for Max. After the third step, the case hissed with the sound of escaping air. Genet pulled it open to reveal two small Petri dishes that were snapped together in one assembly. She lifted one from the case and showed Max how to open it. "Once you secure the sample, which you will need to do very carefully, you can place it back in the case. The Petri dishes will make sure the specimen stays viable.

You can connect it back together like this." Genet took the two interlocking pieces of the Petri dish and snapped them together again before returning the assembly to the leather case. "Then all you need to do is snap this shut." Genet closed the case, and it hissed again, confirming its hermetic seal. "It will create a vacuum. That way, no one gets hurt."

Derrick glanced matter-of-factly at Max. "Once you've completed those steps, you get out of there."

Genet removed the matching leather containment device from the larger metal case. "Here, darling." She handed them both to Max. "They are identical. The second one's only there in case you have a problem with the first."

Max took the cases, and Missy chimed in. "Now, for the footage you shot." Using a remote, Missy launched Max's footage on the flat-screen monitor. "We had our experts go through it, practically frame-by-frame." Missy advanced the film a few seconds at a time and pointed out many safeguards of the underground installation. Sensors and cameras were carefully placed throughout the corridors.

Genet flipped her hair away from her face. "Keep in mind, darling, you may not have caught every security measure on tape. We just need you to be as careful as you can down there."

Barely two minutes into the footage, Max found himself growing weary with all there was to do and avoid. "Look, guys, I'm allowed to be down there, but how do I get this thing without anyone realizing it's me?"

"Max," Derrick replied in an assertive voice, "we're gonna need you to figure that out. This footage is great to look at, but you're the one who's been down there, and it's you going back. As far as we're concerned, the underground is your domain, and we have every confidence that you can handle this."

Max scooted back from the table and stood, betraying the cracks forming in his polished Battenberg veneer. "I don't know. I have this feeling…"

Derrick and Genet spotted his weakening resolve. They nodded to Missy, who in turn paused the video footage. Max paced the floor for some time before returning to his seat.

"Just give me a moment." He closed his eyes and took a series of deep breaths, trying to practice a meditation similar to the one AJ had taught him. Derrick, Missy and Genet watched, waiting patiently for what seemed a long while until Max finally opened his eyes. "Okay. Let's look at the rest."

Missy continued the footage. When they arrived at the segment that Max had filmed of the actual viral containment center, Genet took over.

"Obviously, we were unable to get our hands on one of these machines. The cost and the red flags it would have sent up made it clear that would hardly be worth it. We do have a safety video, though."

Genet stood and placed a DVD in the player. A company instruction video commenced on screen, and she took to explaining how to handle the device. A simple sequence of actions would be required to safely secure the sample. Genet ran through the procedure several times, but her thoroughness only served to make Max's head spin. He also worried that his access code might implicate him in any thefts from the facility. That aspect of the operation he still had to figure out. He turned to Derrick and Genet.

"I realize I agreed to help, but to be honest, this feels like a lot. Now that you've run through what's required… it's like you need James Bond, and that's not me."

Genet shared a look of concern with Derrick and Missy. "You guys, he's right. We can't send him down there without support." Genet's mind appeared to be racing. "Is there a way we could establish radio contact to help talk him through this?"

Missy shook her head. "Most of these bases are more than a mile underground. At that depth I doubt we'll get any reliable communication."

Derrick considered the situation. "What if we placed transmitters throughout the museum? Maybe we could create a coverage area?"

Missy didn't seem hopeful. "We could try, but it might not do anything."

Max listened patiently. Despite their attempts to reassure him, he couldn't help but feel overwhelmed. Suddenly, he found himself wondering just what he had gotten himself into.

CHAPTER 41

When he stepped into Ted's apartment, Max was still shell-shocked from his meeting with Derrick, Missy and Genet.

"Dude, you should see your face," Ted exclaimed, full of levity. "What is it this time?"

Max shook his head. "I need to go back in that building, the one I took the video of. But I'm not sure I can pull it off. What about you? Did you find anything on that footage?"

"Dude, do you ever think you might reveal what all of this is about?"

Max observed Ted, pondering his question. "I doubt it."

"Okay…" Ted examined Max, as if the answers he sought might reveal themselves on Max's forehead like digital ticker tape. "There are a few things I noticed on your film." Ted sat at his console and began once again walking Max through the footage. While he didn't catch every detail that the others had revealed, he did a thorough job.

"Listen, Ted, I totally appreciate this. I wouldn't involve you unless I had to." Max rewound the footage to a point where Ted could see the underground laboratory. "You see this area here? There's some high-tech stuff going on that I want to investigate."

Ted stared quizzically at Max, wondering if he had developed some form of schizoid paranoia. "Max, I'm gonna be honest, I'm not sure what to make of all this 007 shit. It's like you've gone all CIA on us or something. If you want help, you need to give me a little somethin' to work with here."

Max understood Ted's point, but he still felt reluctant. "Remember all those whacky conspiracy theories you used to talk about in school?"

"Oh, shit," Ted leapt to his feet, shaking with excitement. "I knew it! The FEMA coffins are real, aren't they?

Max put on his best poker face. "You know there's a big pharmaceutical division of Battenberg, right?" Max watched Ted's face light up like an Edison light bulb.

"Oh, shit, dude. Is all that crap real about population control?"

Max looked intently at Ted before he spoke. "There's something in that installation. I need to find out what it is, preferably without anyone knowing it was me."

"Dude, you gotta tell me where this spot is. You guys are fuckin' resurrecting the real H1N1, aren't you?"

Max glanced at Ted, and nightmarish scenes ran through his mind: he imagined a Hummer smashing into Brigitte's car, acid being thrown on AJ and a needle being forced into his arm. The memory of Ted being slashed by a scalpel also gave him pause. "Forget it, dude, I shouldn't be talking about this."

"Will you calm down?… When are you planning to do this?"

Max studied Ted, full of trepidation. "In the next couple of days."

Ted looked at Max. Even though he didn't have the details, he somehow felt like a kindred spirit. "Give me a day or two, and I'll see what I can find out."

"Thanks, man, I appreciate it."

The ring of Ted's cell phone blared throughout the room. Ted looked at the screen, and tiny cracks of contrition surfaced in his composure. He quickly stood. "I'll be right back. I gotta take this." He answered the call and spoke softly as he hurried into the hall and disappeared inside his bedroom.

Max felt certain it was Brigitte on the phone. He could hear Ted's hushed whispers echoing from the hall. Ted eventually returned, and Max stared back, questioning his own suspicious mind. "Everything okay?"

"Dude, I ask myself that every day."

Ted was someone whose friendship Max never questioned. Many times, people sought Max's companionship because of who he was on the exterior: a man with resources and influence, the playboy son of a billionaire. Now, Max wondered if Ted had been coveting something of his: Brigitte. Before he thought it through, the question came forth. "How's my girl?"

Ted's eyes betrayed certain guilt as he returned Max's stare. "She's still banged up pretty bad."

"I stopped by the hospital, but she was asleep, and I didn't want to wake her. You two seem a little chummier than usual."

Ted turned away at first before turning to face Max. "Dude,

any friend of mine ends up in the hospital, I'm gonna be there to support them. You aren't suggesting I'm trying to move in on your girl, are you?"

"No. I mean, I don't know... I'm not suggesting anything, I was just pointing out that you two seem chummier than usual."

"If you get banged up like that, I'll be the same way with you."

Max studied Ted, only slightly comforted by his explanation.

Ted took notice that the mood still needed to be lightened. "Once she gets stronger I'm sure she'll come around. Plus, she's pregnant and emotional, you get that."

"Shit, Ted, she believes the accident was my fault! And who knows? Maybe it was."

"Dude, why're you still talking like this? Brigitte banged her head really bad. If anything, that's why she believes that. What's your excuse?"

Max's tone turned morose. "Because people keep getting hurt around me, or worse. That includes you. Why do you think I've been so cautious about telling you anything? I don't need anyone else ending up in the hospital."

"Max, I'm fine, okay? I can help without anything crazy happening to me."

"I don't know. Have you ever considered what happened that day in New Orleans? You took my mask. What if whoever attacked you thought you were me?"

Ted tried digesting Max's theory, but he still seemed miffed by the idea. "That doesn't make sense, though. You believe someone targeting you would actually attack someone in a mask, while you stood by in plain view right beside them? That's not a very smart assassin, don't you think?"

"It's a possibility, Ted, that's all. It could've been meant for me. Then a few months later they get my dad, and now Brigitte? And they're others you don't even know about."

Ted peered into Max's eyes, and what he saw unnerved him. There was clarity in Max's expression that somehow made his strange ramblings seem believable. There was also fear. "But, Max, why would somebody have a vendetta against you?"

"It's possible, Ted. Trust me, that's all you need to know."

Ted glanced from Max to his computer screen. "I want to

show you something." He plopped in the chair and scooted closer to his console before pulling up an image on his screen. It looked to be a webcam in a relatively unkempt bedroom. Books and magazines were spilling over from a nightstand beside an unmade bed. A small lamp was the only illumination in the otherwise dark room.

Max was perplexed. "What is it?"

"You're gonna love this, dude." Ted reached across his desk and picked up a gaming joystick. "Watch." As Ted maneuvered the joystick, the image on screen began to move. At first, it seemed he was pivoting the camera, but the entire field of view changed as the camera rose higher and higher toward the ceiling.

Max felt a new sense of intrigue. "What is that?"

They watched as the webcam traveled out of the room into a hallway. Max could see cupboards, carpeting and a front door. To his amazement, the image of him and Ted slowly came into view. The real Max turned toward Ted's hallway and heard it before he saw it; the buzzing was similar to the sound of bumblebees in flight. Then Max caught sight of it, and his eyes popped open when he realized what it was.

"What the hell?"

What looked like a dragonfly was hovering in Ted's living room. As Ted maneuvered the joystick, the dragonfly responded, flying right and left. It hovered, swooped toward Max and ascended.

"What is that thing?"

Ted smiled from ear to ear. "A drone, dude. It's the latest in surveillance technology — well, sort of. They can do even smaller than this now." Ted maneuvered the mechanical dragonfly until it landed in Max's lap.

Max picked it up and scrutinized it. The device was sandy beige in color with clear, plastic wings that were identical in shape and size to the wings of a true dragonfly. When Max peered more closely, he could see tiny metal bits and the aperture of a miniature webcam. "How come I've never seen one of these?"

"Because you haven't been paying attention. This is military stuff we're talking. I just got it today. I have a friend in Venezuela; he's the one I showed your video to. He gets all kinds of prototype shit. He laughed when I told him about the pen and glasses." Ted reached under his desk and brought out a small UPS box. He passed it to Max who peered inside and found two other prototypes, one in black and the other in white. "They come in different colors, depending on the camouflage you need. Nowadays, you can even get them as small as flies."

Max removed the white drone from its box to examine it more closely. "Damn, this is brilliant! Do you think I can use one?"

"Who do you think I got 'em for, dude? I'm not the one doing espionage shit. They're a little tricky to pilot, though. But I'm sure you'll figure it out."

For more than an hour, Max and Ted experimented with the tiny devices until Max narrowed down how to fly them. He felt enthused that Ted had provided something that might come in handy. In fact, the miniaturized drones could easily make the difference between his mission's failure or success.

CHAPTER 42

The day had finally come. Max stood patiently outside of the National Portrait Gallery while Genet and Derrick completed preparations inside. As discussed, they were armed with a series of miniature transmitters, which had to be strategically placed throughout the museum. The rest of the team hoped a communications link could be established with Max while he was deep underground.

During the early part of the operation, Max remained in front of the building, trying to quiet his nerves. He glanced at his watch to double-check the time. The museum closed at 7:00 p.m., so everyone had agreed that Max should descend into the underbelly of the Rizick Group installation at 4:30 p.m. sharp. Max glanced at the time and saw that it was 4:25. He patted his jacket to confirm that he had the two containment devices. Properly equipped, he strolled casually into the gallery.

Inside, he noticed the crowd was much thinner than it had been during his first visit. He glanced in the new arrivals section and spotted Genet and Derrick. To avoid any associations that would connect them with Max, they had entered through the G-Street entrance on the other side of the building.

Max knew, because they were in new arrivals, that their task of placing transmitters had been completed. He fidgeted with the tiny receiver inside of his ear. Genet's voice startled him when it came through with crisp clarity. "Darling, you should move now, the way is free and clear."

Max glanced in the direction of the elevators and saw no one. He hustled across and pressed the call button. To his surprise, the doors opened to a vacant car. He quickly boarded, waited for the doors to close and punched in the private code. The elevator car descended well beneath the museum's bottom floor before it began its horizontal move through a secret shaft. For the second time that week, Max found himself plunging more than a mile beneath the earth.

Genet's voice became more and more garbled, but he could still hear her. "What about this?" They had discussed different code words, and this was Genet's way of asking if Max was still in receipt of the transmission. To the outside observer, though, it appeared she was questioning Derrick about a portrait or a piece of artwork.

Max replied into a microphone, which was hard-wired into his collar. "Still okay." A moment later, the elevator jerked to a stop. When its doors opened, Max stepped into the corridor. Although everyone figured there would be ample time to secure the viral agent, Max still worried he would not accomplish the task. He was no spy, but he knew enough to realize every project harbored unknown obstacles. He simply hoped none of them involved his being found out or getting contaminated by the viral agent. He spoke into his collar again. "I'm in. Can you still hear me?"

After a brief pause he heard Genet's distorted voice feigning admiration for a painting. "Yeah, I like it."

Their communication system, as high-powered as it was, still experienced difficulty penetrating the underground facility. Max studied the hallway, taking it all in. *I'm a Battenberg, dammit. I have every right to be down here.* Satisfied that the time was ripe, Max stood erect and exhaled. He quickly evaluated a narrow ledge near the ceiling and removed the black dragonfly drone from his pocket. He reached up and positioned it facing the elevator. On the surface, he appeared calm, but Max could feel his heart beating. He waited a moment, watching for any signs of movement. There were none.

He strode down the hall to the containment room. As before, the white corridor was unoccupied. He removed the white dragonfly drone. There was no ledge on which to place it, so Max turned it upside-down in his palm and tossed it up toward the ceiling. The device instantly adhered there, nearly invisible to the eye.

He peeked into the containment room and saw two men in Hazmat gear. Not wanting to draw their attention, he immediately stepped aside and pulled the third mechanical dragonfly from his bag. Above ground, Genet and Derrick were pretending to peruse portraits as, to their dismay, the signal seemed to grow weaker with every step. While Max could hear Genet, he found it problematic understanding her.

With the first two drones in place, he preceded toward the

archival vaults. When he reached the end of the hall, he strategically placed the last beige surveillance drone for a bird's eye view of the corridor. Satisfied, he continued to the vault door and keyed in the same entry code he had previously used. It snapped open, allowing him access, and he quickly found Demetrius' locker. He wasn't sure why, but he felt drawn to it, as if something inside was calling to him.

Max had dozens of codes buzzing through his head. There were access codes for his garage and his house, and the secret panic room inside of his closet. There were more access codes for Demetrius' home and office, in addition to Badem Publishing. He knew he would need to select the right one to gain access to his father's vault, and intuition told him he might only have one shot.

The receiver crackled in his ear, but he couldn't make out what Genet was saying. To avoid any further distraction, he pulled out the headset and shoved it in his pocket. Max knew he would need complete concentration. He leaned forward against the door and placed his right hand over the keypad. He focused on the codes in his head. There was one that continued repeating, but Max felt certain it could not be correct. It was too coincidental.

He stepped to the side and pressed his back against the wall, allowing himself to slide down until he was kneeling on the floor. He shut his eyes. After a long moment, a memory flashed through his brain. It had taken place eighteen years earlier, before the death of his mother. Max recalled himself and a much younger Demetrius standing in the exact same spot, staring at the metal door to the locker. He remembered the young Max had been crying, although he couldn't recall why. In a strange sense-memory, Max felt the wetness of tears on his face. In his mind's eye, he watched Demetrius punching in the code as if it were in slow motion: 7-1-2-9. *How is that possible?* It was the same number Indigo had provided him months before. Without another thought, Max stood and faced the keypad to enter the code. To his astonishment, the vault made a snapping noise as it unlocked.

For some unknown reason, Max felt more uneasy about his father's secret vault than he did about the deadly viral agent he was there to retrieve. He pulled open the metallic door, and an incandescent light immediately illuminated the space. The room was smaller than he imagined. In fact, his closet at home was larger. The area couldn't have been bigger than a six-by-six cell. Max left the door ajar to take full inventory of Demetrius' secret stash.

The first thing that caught his eye was a huge stone plaque affixed to the wall opposite the entrance. At first glance, the object appeared to be a single piece when, in reality, it was an assembly of three stone tablets that fit together.

Upon closer inspection, Max realized what he was seeing. Two vertical, sculpted bas-relief figures comprised the larger, top portion. Equal in size, each depicted full-bodied representations of stunning men. Max gazed into their life-like faces and wondered who they were. The longer he stared, he realized the figures seemed to be smiling back. An uncanny feeling slowly overcame him, and the words effortlessly slipped from his lips: "Enki and Enlil."

Toward the bottom of the tableau, the third and final tablet was inlaid horizontally. Max recognized the smaller element; he had seen it once before: "The Table of Destiny." He felt giddy. *How and why does my father have this?* From what he could gather, the art piece appeared Sumerian, but Max knew it was much older and had origins from beyond Earth. Flowery hieroglyphs covered the lower segment from border to border, but Max had no clue what they meant. Individually, each piece was stunning, but their assembly into one only made them more beautiful. He questioned why Demetrius had chosen to secret away such a beautiful art piece.

Aware that his window of time was shrinking, Max removed and booted up the tablet that Ted had set up for him. When the screen came alive, he clicked through several menus until the fiber-optic application came online. Each of the dragonfly drones began transmitting images to his screen. Max connected the joystick and used it to reposition two of the devices for the exact perspective he needed. Thankfully, the halls were still unoccupied. Max struggled to concentrate. *Get the virus. I'm here for the virus.*

To his chagrin, the plaques on the wall kept drawing his attention as if they were calling to him. Succumbing to curiosity, he removed his cell phone and took several photographs of the artifact. For good measure, he switched the camera to video and recorded several seconds of footage of the entire vault. Satisfied that he had adequately documented the space, he began taking further inventory of his father's secret chamber. On one wall, there were at least five stacks of boxes piled four and five high. Another wall was lined with metal file cabinets.

Max opened a box and quickly scanned its contents. There was nothing of particular interest, so he closed it and stepped away. In a semi-haze, he turned and crept closer to the stone carving. If it truly was the Table of Destiny, why did Demetrius have it? Max took a step closer, hesitantly extending his hand toward the stone tablets. His fingers tingled with the sensation of tiny, cool sparks dancing across them. For the first time, Max experienced a moment of clarity he had never before known. He withdrew his hand, and the tingling sensation immediately ceased.

With a sense of wonderment, he reached forward again. Even before he made contact, the subtle tickling sensations in his fingers resumed and crept into the palm of his hand. Feeling further emboldened, Max moved his hand forward until a finger gently brushed against the stone. Without warning, a thousand pounds of force seemed to rock his body, and the room began to spin. Like billions of strobe lights, images rushed through his head, and Max felt high-voltage electricity coursing through his veins. He didn't so much see his chakras, but he perceived them igniting like colorful bonfires.

Max remembered his experience outside of the yoga studio when AJ zapped him. White lightning had migrated through his body, obliterating his senses. The current episode felt similar, only multiplied a million times. Bright flashes continually bombarded him, but they were each filled with lifetimes of information. Knowledge of the universe engulfed him faster than his mind could process. Finally overcome, Max collapsed on the concrete floor of his father's locker.

CHAPTER 43

*I*n the months following their marriage, Marduk and Sarpanit had ventured multiple times to their honeymoon location on one of Earth's more enchanting tropical isles. During his latest excursion, however, Marduk was alone. His interest in the area had deepened after he noticed a significant erosion of his most preferred beach. From everything he could gather, the idyllic paradise appeared to be sinking along with a cluster of neighboring islands. Little by little, the shorelines in question were being swallowed by the ocean. During his most recent inspection, the tides had encroached another foot upon the beaches.

Back on Nibiru, his father and aunt had become skilled geneticists. Marduk, on the other hand, possessed particular expertise in mathematics. He also believed such skills could be used to explain the phenomenon enveloping the islands. To accomplish this task, he had spent recent months compiling data and inputting it into a mathematical model. The program, while complex, was conceptually sound. Marduk had spent some time studying the results, incredulous as to what they seemed to reveal. He had checked and double-checked: the necessary algorithms had been completed and repeated, and his hypotheses and assumptions now seemed conclusive.

He could wait no more. Clinging to a stone cylinder seal that had his results etched upon it in cuneiform, he ran from his chambers at top speed. Stumbling in the hall, he nearly slipped and crashed into the corridor wall. He quickly regained his balance and sprinted past Enlil's chambers in a beeline toward his father's quarters.

Made curious by the commotion, Enlil and Ninurta abandoned their meal and stepped into the hall to watch Marduk disappear around the bend.

"What has him so agitated?" Ninurta inquired, thinking out loud.

"Perhaps we should find out," Enlil offered as they penetrated deeper into the corridor to pursue Marduk and investigate.

"Father!" Marduk screamed, as he approached Enki's chambers. "Father!" He skidded through the doorway into his father's quarters to find Enki and Ninmah dining.

"What is it?" Enki demanded, nonplussed by the ruckus.

"Why didn't I see it sooner?" Marduk gasped, nearly out of breath. "My model… I have completed it." Marduk waved the cylinder seal in the air. "I have the data, and more importantly, what it means."

"Well, speak then, child," Ninmah interjected.

"It's better perhaps if I show you," Marduk replied. "A parchment, please. Do you have a parchment?"

Growing irritated, Enki pressed further. "Marduk, why not just tell us the results?"

"Because we should have seen it. The cause of the disappearing shorelines… It is Nibiru, father. It is our homeland's approach."

Growing impatient, Ninmah rose from the table and rummaged through Enki's bureau for parchment and ink. When she located the elements, she handed them to Marduk. He lightly brushed the cylinder with ink, then rolled it across the parchment. Within seconds, Marduk's results stood out in the most undeniable way. Flowery Nibirian text displayed a diagram of Earth's solar system and Nibiru's approach. In the margins, numbers and figures described the occurrence of an atmospheric phenomenon.

"It's our history," Ninmah decried, "repeating billions of years later."

Enki continued his examination of the data. It took him only a moment longer to see the full picture. "A near collision —"

"Between us and Nibiru," Ninmah whispered, completing his sentence.

"It won't be so close," Marduk explained, "but Nibiru has already demonstrated the effect of her gravitational pull. The islands here are not sinking; it is the sea level rising."

Ninmah's eyes grew wider as she further examined the report. "The icecaps are melting."

"Yes," Marduk replied. "I can't say exactly when, but very soon, the ice shelf will break away. If the data is correct, the chain reaction of that collapse will result in a deluge. There will be a wave so large, it will engulf the entirety of our settlements, including Eridu and the Abzu. Every hybrid post must be evacuated sooner than not."

Enki immediately grew perturbed at the suggestion. "Surely there is another explanation! I will not stand by and allow everything we've built to be destroyed."

No one had noticed, but Enlil and Ninurta had positioned themselves in the archway of Enki's chamber. Enlil maneuvered into his half brother's quarters. When he spoke, it was with a sense of assuredness. "If such a catastrophe is to occur, we shall do as discussed and allow the hybrids to perish in it."

Everybody turned to offer Enlil an audience. He approached Enki's table and quietly perused Marduk's report. "If this is indeed correct, it provides a rather poetic solution to our hybrid predicament. They have served their purpose, have they not? A natural calamity such as this will end them, while sparing them the cruelty of my earlier proposition. Certainly, in the north, there will be indigenous beings who survive." Enlil shifted his gaze upon Enki and Ninmah. "And your genetic tampering shall artfully be erased. Do you not esteem this manner acceptable for this planet to resume its intended evolution?" Everyone present exchanged glances in a strange and uncomfortable impasse. Enlil, however, read the silence as an opportunity to continue. "We all know what father and the council expressed when they were last here. It is precisely the opposite that has occurred. The hybrid gene pool has been sullied." Enlil turned to Enki. "No one knows this better than you."

Enki wished to protest, but there was no point. They all understood the truth of Enlil's words. For years, hushed rumors whispered concerns of Nibirian men succumbing to their desires for hybrid women. If ever the council confirmed the multitude of indiscretions, they all understood that repercussions would be eminent and harsh.

"Before this most recent development," Enlil continued, staring down at Marduk's report, "I had already made up my mind about the hybrids. But a flood such as this provides a much swifter solution than the one I originally conceived. Each indiscretion, every offense, shall literally be washed away." Enlil stared, smug, at his brother and sister. "Think of the poetry in it. It'll be like we were never here."

Enki could hardly believe the response about to escape his lips, but he spoke it nonetheless. "He is right. In our distance from Nibiru, we have strayed from tradition. For father or the council to witness what we have done shall bring shame upon the operations here. This is not the legacy I wish to pass on."

Enlil turned to Enki and spoke more calmly than he ever remembered doing. "You must vow, brother, never to rescue them, even the hybrids you have sired. I know you, more than Ninmah, have an affinity for them. But your genetic alterations have polluted their race."

Until now, Ninmah had remained silent, but she finally spoke. "For once, we are in agreement. The creatures we discovered are vastly different from the ones we created. We have altered them in faculties, appearance and disposition. In their original state, they are more tender and caring. It is not uncommon to find the purebreds freeing our traps of prey. Such is not the way of the hybrid, who is much more self-centered and often conniving."

"Precisely," Enlil affirmed. "If we do not act now, the hybrid species shall outmaneuver this planet's indigenous population until they are completely overtaken. The beings we first utilized shall cease to exist. We must not allow this to occur. To remove the hybrids shall instead restore this planet's natural evolution, as it was intended."

Marduk also nodded in affirmation of their new hybrid eradication plan. "While these creations are ones of beauty, like my beloved Sarpanit, I fear this is the most correct solution."

Deep down, Enki had no desire to rid Earth of his hybrids, but he had already pushed the council to its limits. To gain approval for a hybrid program had already been a stroke of genius. Then his son, Marduk, had further pressed boundaries by requesting a marital union with Sarpanit. His reluctance remained tangible, but Enki finally succumbed. "All right. I suppose our work, for the most part, is done. Nibiru's atmosphere has nearly been restored. We shall thus allow the hybrids' demise."

In a gloomy synchronicity, cousins and siblings alike, who had never quite seen eye-to-eye, finally found common ground on a topic that would end in the death of thousands.

For a long while, there was silence, until Enlil finally turned to his nephew Marduk and spoke. "Very well then. Will your calculations predict the timing of this event? Such a detail might be handy."

"Yes, uncle. I will need to track the data further. But based on my current numbers, I should expect it shall occur within six months, perhaps a year."

Enlil's grin expanded into a full-blown smile. "This timing is advantageous, I'm sure we can all agree. We must inform father and the council immediately of this gravitational phenomenon. To do so will preempt any pending excursions here. This way, our escapades here on Earth shall remain accessible only to us, as a distant memory." Satisfied with his plan, Enlil turned to Ninurta, in the doorway of Enki's chamber. "Come, Ninurta, let us finish our meal."

Ninurta accompanied his father, and they disappeared into the corridor, leaving Marduk, Ninmah and Enki behind.

Enki looked at Marduk, his face awash with a mixture of pride and disappointment. "Good work, son. Should there be a change in timing, you will be certain to let us know."

"Of course, father." Marduk bowed in subservience. "I will leave you to finish your meal." Then he gathered his papers and the cylinder seal and left the chamber.

The following day, Enki beamed a message to Anu and the council, describing the calamity about to befall the Earth settlements. He included much of Marduk's data and recommended postponement of the council's pending visit. After several weeks without a response, one of Nibiru's swiftest transports broke through Earth's atmosphere. Within minutes, the brothers and sister, Enki, Enlil and Ninmah, assembled on the terrace that afforded them the best view of the transport's approach. Each of them gazed skyward. Because the day was clear, the medium-sized ship was visible as a tiny orange speck. Red flames engulfed it, making it soon appear as a fiery dagger in the sky. As the craft descended, its flames extinguished, and the ship's hull became visible.

Of the three siblings, Enlil appeared the most confident, but there was still a shadow of disquiet haunting the corners of his face. "If the council has sent an envoy, their response must be rather delicate."

The ship continued its vertical descent, growing ever larger in the eyes of its observers. Just when its impact with Earth seemed imminent, the craft slowed dramatically. Metallic wings, shaped like those of an eagle, unfolded at its sides and the craft swept in across the landscape. Within a minute, it touched down outside of Eridu's palace gates.

Before she spoke, Ninmah and Enki shared a glance in a strange, unspoken conversation. "I suppose we should greet our guest. It may be father, after all."

Enki and Enlil's expressions betrayed their apprehension, but the siblings reentered the palace anyway and descended into the garden through the nearest stairwell. Standing directly outside of Eridu's front gate, all three of them perceived intense heat emanating from the ship's hull. The craft's hatch finally opened, and thousands of metallic oval tiles began snapping silently into place to form a ramp, which descended to the ground.

A moment later, a youthful, bearded man with thick, curly red locks stepped into view and came down the ramp. Neither of Anu's children recognized the envoy stepping upon Eridu soil.

"Greetings, Earth council," the stranger proclaimed, walking forward. "I am Galzu. I come bearing news from His Lord Master Anu."

"Why has father not beamed us his response?" Enlil inquired, with more bravado in his voice than intended.

"It is superb you all are here, as this was my task, to gather all three of you."

"Are you so certain we are the three you seek?" Ninmah questioned.

Galzu smelled of perfume, and his beard and locks were expertly coiffed. Garments fit for those of royal status hugged him in all the right places. "You don't remember me, do you?" he responded to Ninmah with a smile.

Ninmah studied Galzu's face, trying to determine why he had posed the question. The stranger appeared younger than her own child. Could he be one of Ninurta's peers? Finally, Ninmah shook her head, unable to answer.

Galzu seemed poised to offer an explanation, but he suddenly changed his mind. "We'll get back to that. Am I not in the presence of your Royal Highnesses Enlil, Enki and Ninmah?"

"Yes, of course," Enlil proclaimed, growing impatient. "What news is it you wish to share?"

Galzu reached into his pocket and removed a rectangular, golden chain-mail purse. He approached Ninmah and extended it to her. "The three of you are meant to open and read this together. Each of you is to examine the seal. If you are in agreement with its authenticity, only then should you open it and peruse its contents."

Ninmah took the pocketbook and scrutinized it. A golden flap on one side had a large gob of red melted wax on it, sealing it shut. Their father's royal crest was imprinted upon it. Galzu studied the siblings. Satisfied that it was their father's seal, Ninmah handed the purse to her brothers. They both examined it and nodded in agreement.

"Go on then," Galzu continued. "Open it."

Impatient, Enlil broke the seal and pulled the flap open. He slid out a piece of parchment and unfolded it. After briefly reviewing the etchings in his father's script, he began to read aloud: "Due to the details of your latest transmission, the council will no longer be conducting its inspection of Operation Gold Dust and the related hybrid program. Fruits of the aforementioned projects have resulted in the desired outcome, as our atmosphere has rebounded here on Nibiru. As such, it is the council's decree that the Earth programs, including the hybrid project and Operation Gold Dust, be discontinued. You will maintain the transport of gold until the final hour of operation, at which point you will execute a complete evacuation. Please beam back your acceptance of the council's decree."

Armed with a smile, Galzu watched Enki, Enlil and Ninmah, expecting a brighter reaction than the one he saw. Instead, the siblings seemed solemn. Never on Nibiru had they been able to build and accomplish the things they found possible on Earth. Yet each of them bristled with pride that they had achieved what they set out to do. Their home, their glorious Nibiru, was no longer in jeopardy, even if those goals had come at a price.

On some level, Enki rejoiced at the idea of a return home. This sentiment, however, was also laced with sadness. On Earth, he had tasted autonomy and freedom from Enlil, if only for a short while. Even after Enlil's arrival in Eridu, he had still enjoyed a level of independence in the Abzu. It did not matter who Enlil thought himself to be in Nibiru's hierarchy. Enki had ruled over Earth and his hybrid creations. *Lord of the Seas.*

In the end, their sentiments were of little consequence. Enki knew their time on Earth had nearly reached its conclusion, and his darling hybrid race would soon be destroyed. When they reached Nibiru at last, he would resign himself to a simple fact: he would always be a prince, but never a king.

"All right then," Galzu proclaimed, "I will inform the council that you are in receipt of their message, and you will respond to them at your leisure." Satisfied with his task's completion, Galzu turned to Ninmah with a bright and shiny smile. He sucked in a deep breath of Earth's atmosphere. "I'm sure very few recall when our home's air was as silky and rich as this."

Ninmah's eyes narrowed, as she took a moment to scrutinize Galzu. He appeared close in age to Ninurta, but she did not remember ever seeing him. Still, there was something familiar in his mannerisms and the cadence of his voice. "It is Galzu you are called, correct?"

Galzu noticed something register on Ninmah's face. "Yes, your Highness. Have you no recollection of me?"

"Should I?" Ninmah inquired, still confused by her father's messenger.

Galzu studied the faces of all three siblings before he continued. "It has been a long time. Have you forgotten our studies about the passage of time here versus its unfolding at home? To learn about it in theory is one thing..." Galzu stared, in awe, at Ninmah. "It is another thing entirely to see it played out, in practice, before your very eyes."

"What are you suggesting, messenger?" Until now, Enlil had exercised patience with Galzu, but his tolerance was growing thin.

"I thought by now, her Lady Ninmah might have recognized me."

"Somehow," Ninmah explained, "there is something familiar in you."

"We didn't know each other well, but you and I studied together."

Ninmah spat out a nervous laugh. "How could this be? You

are closer in age to my son than you are to me."

"Not even Nibiru's wisest fully understand it. Somehow, time here is accelerated. Dramatically so, in fact." Galzu looked from Ninmah to Enlil and Enki. "All who have passed a great deal of time here will discover they have aged." Galzu looked directly at Ninmah. "You and I were classmates, only I studied physics while you did genetics."

Enki and Enlil looked as stunned as Ninmah. It was true; he did appear younger than all of their children.

Enki, staring in disbelief, asked, "You and Ninmah are the same age?"

"No one can explain when the process truly begins. Perhaps it's upon entry into the atmosphere here. Or when we exit the transport." Galzu shrugged, indicating that he had no idea. "One thing is certain, though. The life force we enjoy on Nibiru is cut short in this place."

Staring at Galzu, Ninmah suddenly gasped at the realization.

"Now you remember, don't you?"

"When I first saw you, it hardly occurred to me that we could be peers." Ninmah was aghast, realizing for the first time how dramatic the aging process on Earth had been.

Enlil took both hands and ran them over his cheeks. He had noticed the fine lines in his face, but the increments of change had been small ones, or so he thought.

Enki watched his brother and sister trying to digest the news. "What does this mean?"

"No one knows for sure. It's very possible that you will resume aging in normal fashion once you return. Or not. Perhaps this should be explored before you depart."

Having reached the edge of his tolerance, Enlil interrupted. "Are we done here?"

"Of course." Galzu smiled, despite Enlil's salty demeanor. "I will be here a short time. Keep in mind, the council prefers that you send your acceptance of their terms together."

"Very well," Enlil answered before pivoting on his heels and marching back into the palace gate.

With a meager smile, Ninmah turned to Galzu. "Thank you." She wished their meeting could have ended on a positive note, but the evidence of their aging stuck in her mind like a dark storm. "Enki, why don't we have Galzu shown to his quarters?"

In an effort to oblige, Enki extended a hand toward the palace gate, pointing out the way. "Of course. We will show you the gardens of Eridu along the way."

Galzu understood his hosts' displeasure about his two announcements. It was understandable, but he had no intention of letting it ruin his upbeat mood. For years, he had been curious about Earth and Operation Gold Dust. He also wanted to confirm whether or not the hybrids were as beautiful as rumored. The main purpose of his trip had now been fulfilled, but he was still eager to discover what more Earth had to offer. Like perfect hosts, Ninmah and Enki led Galzu through the gates into the perfectly manicured gardens of Eridu.

The council back on Nibiru had put forth their edict: as much gold as possible was to be extracted from Earth before their imminent departure. For six additional months, the hybrids were pushed to extreme limits. During that time, Marduk continued his collection of data to determine their most efficient exit strategy. To avoid tipping off the hybrids, a gradual withdrawal of the Nibirian population was executed in phases. Each time a gold shipment was scheduled, a small group of Nibirians would depart along with it.

The entire time, Enki had fully intended to keep his word not to interfere with the hybrids' unfortunate destiny. One night, however, he suffered a powerful and moving dream. In it, the envoy, Galzu, appeared in his quarters and instructed that he save a handful of hybrids. He would need to choose the ones he trusted and provide them with the building schematics for a submarine. To do so would enable a small community of hybrids to endure.

During the vision, which was vivid enough to seem real, Galzu led Enki to the window and pointed robot-like across the horizon. To Enki's horror, an enormous wall of water was crossing toward them, obliterating everything in its path. He watched it crash through the outer barrier wall of the palace, sweeping Eridu's manicured gardens away. He turned to Galzu and realized he was once again alone in the room. In a last ditch effort to save himself, Enki sprinted toward his chamber door. When he pulled it open, a wave of water swept him back inside. No matter how he tried, a whirlpool effect prevented his exit. To his horror, more water smashed through the windows, and Enki found he was completely submerged, swirling around in his chambers. Unable to draw a breath, the sad reality quickly settled in. He would drown in his own palace.

Unable to breathe, Enki sprang awake, covered in sweat. He sat up, still reeling from the prophetic vision that had quickly turned to a nightmare. Rising to his feet, he crossed toward the window and stumbled upon a golden cylinder seal on the floor. *That wasn't there.* Enki was meticulous about his space. There was nothing on the floor when he retired hours earlier. He lifted the cylinder seal and examined it. Hundreds if not thousands of cuneiform symbols were embedded in it. Unable to clearly decipher them, he rushed to retrieve a tub of black pigment from his cabinet. Enki quickly brushed the cylinder seal with dye, then rolled it over a papyrus scroll. The symbols, unfolding neatly, revealed something of which Enki could hardly conceive. He studied the papyrus intently. Inked upon its surface were the plans to build one of Nibiru's sturdiest submersible vessels. *But how?*

He ran into the outer corridor, but all was still and no one was in sight. He re-entered his chambers and crossed to the window. The night sky was clear, and a three-quarters moon was high above the palace. *Was this not a dream? Galzu is on the floor below. There's no reason he should even know the location of my quarters.*

For days, Enki mulled over the dream and the appearance of the cylinder seal. He had promised to abide by Enlil's edict not to interfere, but somehow it seemed that larger forces were at work. Enki knew the Table of Destiny was capable of triggering visions, and Marduk had returned with it. *But how could the golden seal have been placed there? What should I do now?*

In the end, he secreted the cylinder seal away, bent upon following its suggestion. For several weeks, he considered how best to proceed with this blueprint that could preserve his precious hybrid race. A decision to reveal news of the coming flood had to be done with caution. If ever he provided the submersible blueprint to the wrong hybrid, Enlil was certain to learn of the transgression. If that occurred, his younger sibling would no doubt call for his head, and Enki could not allow that.

There must be a way, he thought. *There has to be a way,* and Enki was determined to find it.

CHAPTER 44

*E*very time new data arrived, Marduk included it in his calculations. According to his latest model, they had approximately five months before the floods arrived. With so little time remaining, Enki finally made his decision. He would reveal the submarine schematics to one of his own hybrid progeny. Whomever he tasked with the ship's assembly would need to build it quietly, without drawing attention to the project. After days of introspection, he made a definitive decision.

His adult illegitimate son, Ziusudra, was the most likely one to succeed. Of his various bastard children, only Ziusudra could be trusted to correctly build the submersible without leaking news of its construction. Ziu, as many called him, was currently in a newer settlement north of Eridu. The moment Enki felt confident he would not be missed, he took a transport and paid Ziu a visit. Once they were alone and their privacy assured, Enki began.

"I have urgent news, but you must promise not to divulge a word of it, even with your family."

Ziusudra gazed at his father in awe. "Of course, your Highness. Anything you say I shall guard in confidence."

"When confronted with inquiries you must keep news of this to yourself. Your true purpose must, at all costs, remain concealed." Enki studied Ziusudra, who simply nodded with bated breath. "A calamity is imminent. In just a few months time, a great flood shall fully engulf each of our settlements. The council, or the *Anunnaki*, as you call us, has decided to abandon the hybrid race to this force of nature."

In his innocence, Ziusudra found it difficult to grasp the severity of Enki's revelation. "But, your Highness, is a calamity of such magnitude even possible?"

Enki nodded. "Yes, of course. It has already begun, in fact. Any who remain are certain to perish." With this, Enki removed the golden cylinder seal from a large bag draped across his shoulder. He placed it on the table. "Embedded in this are the plans for a vessel. You must build it and save yourselves. You will carry your family along with the seeds of agriculture and animal husbandry."

Ziusudra, who had been well educated as a mason, was a skilled builder, but he was also a simple man. His eyes remained wide at his father's news. "Am I only to save my family, Your Grace?"

Enki nodded. "It is the only risk worth taking."

A look of sadness overcame his son. "So, the others shall be left to perish?"

Enki nodded before speaking with a sense of urgency. "This is why you must build. When asked what you are doing, you must hide your true goal. Mark my words, Ziusudra, should any Nibirian learn of this, it will be yours and your family's undoing. Do you understand?"

"Yes, my Lord." Ziusudra bowed in deference, grateful for his opportunity to survive.

"Since you are a mason, I will leave you to procure your own building materials. You may not contact me, or anyone in Eridu for that matter. If need be, I will come to you, but I am not likely to do so. Are you up to this task?"

"Yes, my Lord," Ziusudra picked up the cylinder seal and held it tightly. "I will build, your Grace."

"Do so swiftly. Only precious time remains." Satisfied that his beloved hybrid species might weather the coming storm, Enki smiled softly. Without uttering another word, he left Ziusudra's chamber and quickly returned to Eridu.

In the months that followed, Enki spent the bulk of his days in his original laboratory where the first hybrids, Adamu and Tiamat, were conceived. While there, he toiled to create an animal husbandry database with male and female embryos of every known animal species in the region. He began with cattle, goats and lambs. He also created embryos for working animals: horses, camels and mules. Dogs, cats and chickens were included along with large predator animals. Little by little, as the cryogenic database grew, he quietly transferred the progeny to a safe storage space for Ziusudra. That way, his confidant could properly retrieve the offspring once his craft was complete.

When the submersible approached completion, hybrids from surrounding settlements grew more curious about it and why it had been constructed. Nibirian airships were commonplace, but such a sea craft had never before been seen. Fortunately for Ziusudra, he had easily convinced the multitude of onlookers that he was building a new and improved housing structure.

At the end of four months, the Nibirian vessel was a spectacle to behold. With three complete levels and twelve-foot ceilings, the craft stood higher than many ancient buildings. Constructed mostly from a specially treated wood, the floor and walls of the top level were inlaid with stone. As such, the ship's sleeping quarters resembled the apartments found in Eridu or the Abzu.

On the lowest level, a huge climate-controlled chamber served as a library with hundreds of individual drawers. Contained in each were the seeds of agriculture and the embryos of animal husbandry. At some point, the deluge would subside, and the waters would eventually recede. At that point, Ziusudra had his instructions to repopulate the region with plants, animals and hybrids alike.

The rain began ten days after the submersible's completion. At that point, Ziusudra packed up his family and transported their effects into the ship. From there, on a high point of land, they waited.

In the extreme north, beyond the point where anyone dared travel, an enormous mountain of ice continued its slow detachment from the polar ice shelf. Just as Marduk predicted, its gargantuan weight eventually gave way, and a major part of the icecap plunged a thousand meters into the ocean. Upon impact, a gigantic tsunami formed, packing the punch of a powerful atomic blast. The resulting wave swept outward, rushing in multiple directions, shearing away everything in its path.

Back in Eridu, Enki had made a decision to remain until the final moment. This was, of course, in defiance of Enlil's wishes. It was Enki's hope that Enlil would depart, so he could confirm whether or not Ziusudra had successfully completed the submersible. Based on what he could gather from trusted sources, Ziusudra had accomplished his goal. His family, along with the embryos and seeds were safely secured inside the vessel.

Much to Enki's dismay, however, Enlil had also chosen to

remain behind until the very end. Now, in the final hour, he could hear his nephew Ninurta running down the palace corridor, screaming for Enlil.

"Father, it has begun! The wave is expected to reach within the hour."

Enki stepped into the hall to find Ninurta running from door to door in search of his father. When he spotted Enki, he was frantic.

"Uncle, it has started! If you wish to stay, you do so at your peril."

"I am having my ship prepared as we speak." Enki's calm was in stark contrast to his nephew's panicked demeanor.

"Very good then. Have you seen my father?"

"Right now, I would trust he's on his terrace."

Ninurta appeared to be catching his breath. "Thank you. I guess we shall see you on the other side then."

Without another word, Ninurta ran into his father's chambers and crossed outside onto the veranda. He found Enlil standing at the railing, gazing across Eridu's landscape. Even now, the meticulously maintained gardens were stunning in their beauty. Like any other day, bees, butterflies and fireflies were buzzing about the array of flowers and orchids. When Enlil spotted his son, he looked up calmly.

"It is truly a shame. The beauty here is unparalleled."

"Father, we must go! Our things have already been stowed in the ship. The only thing left to collect is you."

"Very well then." Enlil gazed one last time at the gardens before turning back toward his chambers. "Say your goodbyes."

Enlil and Ninurta passed back into the palace before making their way to the airstrip. They arrived in time to see Enki standing at the hatch of his circular craft. A peculiar expression crossed Enlil's face.

"Why do you wait, brother? Our time to depart has come."

For the first time perhaps since childhood, Enki did not perceive animosity in Enlil's tone. "My pilot, Abgal, has gone to my chamber to fetch an item I left behind. We shall depart the moment he returns."

"Very well," Enlil proclaimed before he and Ninurta disappeared into their ship. Within a matter of seconds, the hatch sealed itself, and the craft floated slowly into the air. A series of panels began deliberately unfolding beneath the ship until they expanded wide enough to form what resembled an eagle's wings. With this, the craft shot off across the horizon and veered upward until it ascended out of view.

Without hesitation, Enki boarded his own ship and took a seat in the cockpit. He engaged the ship's engines and sealed its hatches. Just as Enlil had done, he guided the ship upward and hovered an instant. A moment later, Abgal appeared on the landing strip, but Enki's ship was already meters above the ziggurat's highest point. Looking up, Abgal immediately understood that the supreme punishment was in order for his earlier betrayal of Enki's weapons stash. Enki nodded with a blank expression before fully engaging the ship's engines.

Instantaneously, his ship shot across the landscape before ascending into the air. Gazing down through the cockpit window, Enki spotted the mammoth wave sweeping the terrain. With surgical precision it chopped down forests and sheered away all structures in its path. In the distance, Enki thought he spotted Abgal scrambling into the ziggurat, but in a moment, the entire structure was engulfed.

From even higher, Enlil and Ninurta observed the same desolation. "This is Nibiru's doing," Enlil whispered. "She has tired of our mission. To the best of her abilities she is calling us home."

As they gained altitude, Enlil and Ninurta watched Earth's landscape dissolve into indistinct shapes and colors. Their cruiser eventually broke through orbit, and darkness enveloped them. As expected, they spotted a small fleet of Nibirian transports. A moment later, Enki's ship maneuvered to join them and disengaged the engines. Together, the Nibirian elite viewed the deluge from afar like some giant expressionist painting.

Back on Earth, persistent rains had already caused extensive flooding throughout Ziusudra's settlement. Rivers of water and mud were pooling while they slowly enveloped houses and roads. The hybrid community was already knee-deep in water, while they hustled to salvage whatever they could.

Ziusudra stood outside the enormous ark, staring into the

skies. One after another, he spotted Nibirian ships cutting across the dark horizon until they disappeared into the clouds. In the absence of the Anunnaki, Ziusudra knew it was now safe to disclose Enki's warnings. He ran deeper into the settlement, screaming at the top of his lungs to anyone who would listen. "A flood is coming, you must seek higher ground! Please, while there is still time, get to higher ground!" To his dismay, the majority of those in earshot either laughed or mocked him. "They aren't listening," he mumbled. "They have to get to higher ground." Growing impatient, Ziusudra bellowed, "Please, save yourselves! I have room for only a few in my ship!"

The settlement was abuzz with hybrids rushing to escape the rapid inundation. Some constructed levees to divert the water away from their homes. Ziusudra watched the commotion, but almost no one listened to his warnings. Out of the mêlée, a family of four approached, stumbling through the mud with giant packs on their backs. Ziusudra immediately recognized them.

"Adapa! Thank Heavens you're here."

Enki's other bastard child had his wife Titi and their sons Ka-in and Ab-el at his side. All four of them were winded from wading through the mud, lugging everything they could carry on their backs. After catching his breath, Adapa spoke.

"We had heard rumor of your project. Yesterday, after yet another day of rain, I recognized that you must've been building this for cause. I told everyone to gather their things, and here we are. I pray you will allow us passage."

Without thinking, Ziusudra motioned Adapa and his family toward the craft. "Come. There is more than enough space."

One after another, Adapa and his family boarded the great submersible. In their final moment, Ziusudra made every attempt to gather as many others as his ship could carry. While he scurried through the streets to seek and rescue, a low roar growled in the distance, growing louder until it became thunder in his ears. He looked to the horizon where trees began falling like domino chips. He could also hear the snapping and popping of wood as an immense wave sheered down buildings, people and foliage. Unable to venture any further, he spun toward the vessel he had built.

"Run!" Ziusudra yelled, galloping through the mud toward

the ship. He spotted Adapa and his wife by the ship's ramp. "It's coming!" he screamed, "Get inside!"

Ziusudra reached the ship, hustled Adapa and his wife inside, and began pulling up the ramp. Other inhabitants spotted the arriving deluge. In a final moment of understanding, they also made their way toward the ship.

"It's too late!" Ziusudra shouted, as he shut the door and sealed it. He leaned against the portal, hoping he had adequately followed the building schematics. "We'll sink if this doesn't hold."

Ziusudra had everyone on board sit upon the benches he had fashioned and tie themselves onto the seats. The ship rocked onto its side as the wave of water impacted its hull. Ziusudra, who was the last man standing, fell to the floor and began sliding across it. Water engulfed the craft, and the vessel tore away from its moorings.

"Hold on!" Ziusudra screamed, clutching for something to steady himself. Somehow, he managed to pull his body up beside the porthole to look out. To his horror, the ark was completely submerged, and he spotted the faces of former neighbors and friends as they swept by swirling about in the current. Herds of sheep, goats and cows were also fighting the torrent as the wall of water buried them. In seconds, the three-story vessel was completely bolstered and moving with the flow.

"Come on," Ziusudra ordered, untying his son Shem from the bench. "We have to get upstairs!"

The ship rocked and bounced, while it raced through the remains of their settlement. Ziusudra grabbed Shem's hand and pulled him to a circular stairwell. Adapa, who had also untied himself, followed and together, they stumbled up the steps until they reached the ship's control room on the top level. Ziusudra made it to his control panel and stared through a large nautical window. Debris from broken trees and crushed houses drifted with them. He carefully steered into the current, and the vessel eventually steadied. Adapa smiled as Titi and their sons mounted the stairs, each of them grateful for the opportunity to be safely inside.

With a smile, Ziusudra fired up the ship's engines, and the submersible jerked forward. From what he could gather, the craft appeared to be nautically sound. He guided them in the torrent toward what should be deeper water. In the silence of his mind, he uttered a prayer, thanking Enki for the chance he had provided for all of them to survive.

CHAPTER 45

$\mathcal{M}$ax bolted up from the floor of his father's secret chamber, staring about the room in confusion. The Table of Destiny appeared to be a simple sculpture of Anu's sons, Enlil and Enki, but the objet d'art had somehow triggered a vision. As the room steadied, Max considered what had happened.

The stone tableau had called to him, even from across the locked door. Max had barely touched it, but the onslaught of knowledge rushing through him was still ricocheting in the far corners of his mind and providing brief flashes of information: obscure images of Demetrius, his mother and brother, Brigitte, Ted, even Chandler. But Max could hardly sort through it. *Are these memories, or the future?* Max felt his head pounding from the overload.

He scooted across the floor and sat cross-legged against the wall opposite the plaque. Still in a state of bewilderment, he had no clue how long he had even been in the room. *Genet and Derrick'll be wondering what happened.* Max rushed to check the time on his phone and was relieved that barely a minute had passed. He waited for some semblance of calm so he could concentrate. *What else does my father have in here?*

In a flash, the best explanation for the vault occurred to him. The secret chamber contained the rawest elements of Demetrius' true identity. All that he really was, all that he hoped to conceal, was hidden here. Max quickly stood and looked around with fresh eyes. Dozens of boxes were labeled with logos from Demetrius' different companies. Max spotted several from the banking and pharmaceutical subsidiaries. He even noticed one from Badem Publishing. He pulled it out and opened it. Inside were stacks of financial statements. Max flipped through them until something caught his attention. His eyes sprang wide when he spotted the name in capital letters: CHANDLER PAUL.

At first glance, the document looked innocuous, but there was something off about it. It took Max a moment. A dollar amount was listed under salary that didn't correspond to what Max knew Chandler's earnings to be. The sum was larger, and it wasn't being charged to the correct overhead account. *This is one of Demetrius' personal accounts.*

A sinking feeling overcame Max. Chandler was one of very few people he trusted. *Why is my father paying him?* While the statement on his father's letterhead didn't define any details, Max had a good idea why Chandler might be on his father's payroll. He glanced at the iPad to be sure the corridors were still clear, but they weren't. One of the lab technicians stepped from the containment center and crossed the hall into another door. Max understood time was being wasted. He needed to secure the virus, but he knew his father's vault contained more to be discovered.

In haste, he opened more boxes and began reading whatever he could. Every 60 seconds he would glance at the tablet screen to monitor the hallways. He knew the longer he took, the more concerned Genet and Derrick would become. But the opportunity to visit Demetrius' vault and unearth the things that he had hidden away might not present itself again.

Max returned his attention to the electronic tablet and noticed the other lab technician exiting the containment room. He leapt to the joystick, preparing to activate the drone he had placed on the ceiling. The lab worker crossed the hallway and also entered the other door. Max crossed his fingers as both doors slowly closed. He released the drone, whose wings fluttered into action. The small device flew erratically at first, but he eventually gained control. Max piloted the drone into the path of the closing containment center door. Without a second to lose, the door swung closed and crushed the drone in the jamb. Max prayed the maneuver had done as expected. Finally, he had a chance to secure the virus.

He immediately gathered his effects, but hesitated. Max turned to observe a file cabinet against the far wall. Unable to stifle the urge, he opened several drawers. After rifling through a multitude of paperwork, he spotted a file with his mother's name on it: "FIONA BATTENBERG ACCIDENT."

Max clung to it, his hand trembling. He opened the file and caught sight of a document resembling a police report. The folder described intimate details of his mother's accident. Max had never been given particulars of the crash that killed her, and now, all these years later, he was not so sure he wanted them. He flipped through the folder until two 5x7" photographs caught his eye. Facing each other on the page spread, there was one portrait of his mother, Fiona. She was just as he remembered: porcelain skin with refined, delicate features and jet black hair. She was smiling in the photo, and her presence exuded quiet tranquility.

But time froze when Max averted his eyes to the adjacent photo. *What the fuck?* He could hardly believe it: the tall, willowy blonde who had been haunting his dreams, the same woman captured in the video footage on the day of Gary Richards' death, was in the other 5x7".

The woman from my closet. "What the fuck is her picture doing here?"

The photo of Fiona looked like a studio shot. The picture of the blonde, however, appeared to have been blown up from a candid shot that she probably didn't even know had been taken. Beneath his mother's photograph, a small sticker had been affixed that read, "SUBJECT: Fiona Battenberg."

A similar label was pasted beneath the blonde's snapshot that read, "SUBJECT: Sister, Aurelia."

Sister! Max did a double take and read the label again. He would never have connected the dots otherwise. With their pictures side-by-side, however, the mysterious blonde did hold an uncanny resemblance to his mother. *What the fuck?*

He remembered the "L" in his mother's journal. Could it have been a code name for "Lia," just as he had used "Ian" to conceal his own identity? Max caught a chill before turning the page to read further. Whoever had written the report had been unable to determine Aurelia's last name or where she had come from. She was still believed to be his mother's sister. Max was flabbergasted. Fiona had been rigidly vetted before her marriage to Demetrius. Even so, it had somehow been determined that her true identity was unknown.

Max found he wanted to laugh at the assertions made in the file. They seemed utterly absurd. He skimmed several pages more, but could hardly comprehend what he was reading: "UNDERCOVER OPERATIVE"; "DNA ALTERATION"; "NIBIRIAN GENE MARKER INSERTION..." Max read the words again, then flipped the page in disbelief. "THREAT LEVEL: High"; "RECOMMENDATION: Elimination."

Max poured over the details of his mother's accident. Suddenly, he dropped the file and watched it fall to the ground, seemingly in slow motion. He was unsure how long he stood staring at it, but it took nearly a minute before he even realized he was hyperventilating. It took another moment for him to catch his breath.

He reached down to retrieve the file along with a dozen other papers. He gathered the rest of his things and shoved them in his satchel. He checked the tablet screen again to see if the hallway was clear. The moment had finally come to accomplish what he came to do. He glanced one last time at the Table of Destiny. Using the tablet, he snapped one last photograph of it, then he hurried from the room.

Focus, Max, focus. He didn't know if he could clear his mind, but he would need to in order to accomplish his mission. *But he killed my mom, brother and uncle!* Max shook it off and double-checked the tablet monitor as he exited the vault. The coast was clear.

He slipped into the corridor and headed to the containment center. Crossing his fingers, he pulled on the door, and it opened. *Yes!* The tiny remote-controlled drone was in pieces where it had been crushed in the door frame. He gathered the debris and shoved it also into his bag. Looking across the hall, he didn't see anyone as he entered the containment room. His heart hadn't stopped racing, and Max couldn't determine if this was due more to fear or to the emotion he felt about the things he had just learned. *He killed them!*

Still flustered, he forgot to replace the receiver in his ear. If Genet or Derrick had tried to reach him, he would have had no idea. He withdrew one of the vacuum-sealed cases from his pocket and pushed in the code to unlock it. It hissed as the case snapped open. Max slipped on a surgical mask and a pair of latex gloves. He then removed the Petri dish as he'd been instructed and loaded it into the appropriate chamber where the virus was contained.

He slowly began executing the steps that Missy had described. His concentration, however, kept breaking as images of his mother and Aurelia invaded his thoughts. Still determined, gritting his teeth, he pushed through the procedures he had been given. Max slipped his hands into the larger protective mitts that reached into the hermetically sealed box. He could see his hands trembling in the thick rubberized gloves. He took a deep breath and opened the tube containing the virus.

Max removed a sample and placed it in the Petri dish. As instructed, he quickly sealed the two parts into one before moving it to the access chamber. He turned and glanced through the window to be sure the corridor was clear. With all steps complete, he opened the chamber, removed his sample and placed it in the leather case. He closed it and heard the hissing sound, confirming the hermetic seal. He slipped it in his jacket, tore away his mask and gloves and tossed them in a biohazard canister in the corner of the room.

Max could hardly believe he had the virus. He quickly gathered himself and hustled from the containment room to the elevator. He pressed the call button and the doors opened. Max stepped inside and then remembered the dragonfly surveillance devices. "Damn."

He returned and grabbed the black one from the ledge. Max put it in his bag and retreated to the elevator. He clumsily removed the tablet and its joystick to pilot the remaining device down the hall. The last dragonfly took flight and buzzed down the corridor until it dropped to the ground before him. Max shoved it in his bag, then quickly entered his elevator access code. He sighed relief as the elevator doors closed and it sprang into action, rushing him back toward ground level.

A moment later, he stepped into the National Portrait Gallery. Max spotted Derrick looking worried and impatient. He and Genet had positioned themselves in front of a stylized portrait of Nina Simone. The caricature, part sketch and part painting, clutched a cat-o-nine-tails. Its eyes were intense, as if there were truly life in them. Neither Derrick nor Genet acknowledged Max in the least. With a subtle nod, Max strode casually from the building with more in his possession than he ever bargained for.

$\mathcal{M}$ax strolled briskly down F Street until he hit Seventh, then he turned and headed toward the metro station. His long legs carried him swiftly until he reached the Place-Chinatown Station. He stopped to observe the crowds of pedestrians hurrying in and out. In the back of his mind, a nagging feeling kept dogging him: Max had a potentially catastrophic virus in his jacket pocket that could be used for the worst biological terror attack in world history.

At the same time, he could not ignore what he had seen in Demetrius' vault. The Table of Destiny, along with a long list of other things he hardly understood, was tumbling around in his brain: *Chandler's on my dad's payroll, and the blonde might be my aunt?* Max felt flummoxed. He had always been told that his mother was from a small Australian family. Her parents were deceased when she and Demetrius met, and her brother had died along with her in the accident. Max didn't know anything about a sister, *a maternal aunt.* The file had not simply suggested the woman was a relation, it had stated it. *Recommendation: Elimination.*

He kept mulling over his father's secrets. After years of thinking that his mother had died in an accident, he had recently been told her death was engineered by Odeon Rutherford. So, why then did his father have a file with "Recommendation: Elimination" on it?

Max felt dizzy. Most people carried wallets or their cell phones inside of their jackets. The leather containment device felt hot next to his chest, like it could burn a hole there. He prayed he had executed the proper steps in securing the deadly virus. He had intended to have Genet on a comlink to assist with the procedure, but this had not gone as planned. The visit to Demetrius' vault, while fruitful, had proven terribly disquieting.

For several minutes, Max waited at the DC metro station entrance, striving to compose himself. All the while, tremors of nervousness afflicted his hands and legs. If he had not followed the proper steps, entering the station could potentially launch

Clean Slate and infect hundreds or thousands of people, including him. He took a deep breath and removed the tiny cigar case from his pocket. It seemed to be properly sealed, and its indicators were appropriately lit.

Max returned the case to his breast pocket and entered the metro station. He already had a Metro pass, so he hustled through the turnstile and quickly made his way to the platform.

The procedure to hand over the virus resembled the steps he had taken in Chicago when he first made contact through Nikolaos Satrazemis. He boarded a train and took a seat. Several stops later, a large woman carrying a satchel took a seat beside him and began reading a paperback from the current best-seller list. Each time Max glanced at her book, he noticed a new message scribbled at the top of the page. They requested he place the containment canister in a satchel that she had placed on the bench between them. Once he had done so, he was instructed to return home and wait for a cab later that night.

After the hand off, Max returned to Chicago and collapsed on the couch in his den. He thought he would feel more relaxed, but a sense of disharmony remained pervasive. He had accomplished his task and more, but the world he thought he knew now felt utterly unfamiliar. In only a few months, his entire understanding of life had been stripped down and replaced with a new paradigm. In a strange paradox, both reality and truth felt elusive at best.

Max sat up and gazed at the shoulder bag from his underground mission. The documents from Demetrius' vault were luring him from inside. He pulled out the stack of papers and spotted his father's financial statements with Chandler's name on them. It was clear Demetrius was paying him for something. Max felt certain he wouldn't like what that thing was when he finally got to the bottom of it. He examined the documents more closely. Nothing in particular jumped off the page until he spotted Chandler's birth certificate. The paper listed Sandrine Paul as Chandler's mother.

Max paused a moment. *Sandrine?* He rushed to his panic room to retrieve his mother's journal. He remembered seeing the name there before. He located several entries where his mother expressed suspicions that Demetrius was cheating with a woman named Sandrine. *No.* Max felt numb when he considered the ramifications. Could Demetrius be Chandler's father? He tossed the file and journal on the table, unable to digest the mere inkling of such a prospect. Max removed the electronic tablet and pulled up an internet photo of Chandler. He had never paid it any notice before, but Chandler could easily have been a family relation.

Max couldn't help but wonder what other skeletons he had failed to retrieve from his father's vault. Thus far, everything he had procured appeared to be a bombshell. He reopened the file labeled "Fiona Battenberg Accident." This time, he read in detail without skimming as he had done before. In an incredible revelation, Max discovered his father's own suspicions that his mother had been some kind of mole who was sent to infiltrate the Battenberg clan. Demetrius' intelligence gatherers even suspected her of somehow altering her DNA to pass through a strenuous vetting process. On the surface, she appeared to be of Nibirian descent, but the report determined this to be untrue. The claims made in the file were completely outrageous and totally in line with everything else going on in his life. As far-fetched as it all seemed, it would explain why he had found the blonde in his closet, crying over Fiona's journal. If he were to believe the intel in Demetrius' secret file, it meant that his father was the rightful engineer of his mother's murder. It also meant that the illusive blonde they called Aurelia was his aunt.

Max threw the file on the table beside his mother's journal. *The blonde and her midget friend!* For many weeks, he had suffered confusion, wondering whether or not they indeed existed, or if they were instead figments of his dreams. If they bore no connection to his father, it meant their technology and skill had allowed them to override his advanced security systems. In addition, they had also been able to make him forget the details of their visits. With such evolved capabilities, Max knew they could be observing him even now. He reached down and looked at the tiny chip in the vial around his neck.

Max leaped off his couch and stormed up the steps providing access to his roof. He exited onto his terrace and strolled into the lounge area. A collection of pricey gray wicker furniture was tastefully arranged beside a covered Jacuzzi. Max approached the railing and peered across his neighborhood, wondering if Aurelia might be watching. The day was completely clear, but evening was fast approaching. The sun had dipped so low that he could barely see it through obstructing city structures. He grabbed the tiny vial around his neck and spoke into it like a microphone.

"Can you hear me? I need to speak with you, Aurelia, if that's your name. Or maybe your little companion is listening. I don't have a clue what you two are up to, but I need—no, I fucking deserve answers! Do you hear me? I know you're listening." Max took a breath then hollered even louder into the microchip. "Do you hear me?"

In what seemed the blink of an eye, Max became aware of being shrouded in shadow. He had not seen its approach, but a large craft suddenly appeared as if out of thin air. The oblong ship hovered silently less than 20 feet above him, dwarfing his outdoor patio like an enormous umbrella.

Max stared overhead, in awe, as a circular portal opened in the center of the ship's underbelly. A soft white light shot down from it, spotlighting an area on the roof. Max watched in amazement. Suddenly, Aurelia appeared and softly drifted down in the light until she was standing beside him. Max stared at her, searching for words.

She took a step closer, and her eyes welled with tears. On many levels, she was as full of wonder as Max. He squeezed his eyes shut, unable to fully process what was occurring. The woman he had feared was a figment of his imagination was standing before him.

He shifted his gaze from the ship to Aurelia. "You look like her."

Aurelia reached out and caressed his face. "So do you."

"I know you've been watching, or studying me, or whatever. How come you didn't just talk to me?"

"It's always been too dangerous, Max. We are not meant to interfere." Her foreign accent, while slight, sounded melodic. "I believe you're beginning to understand this."

"What happened in DC that day? You were on the platform when my friend was killed." Max studied Aurelia and noticed that she could scarcely hide her concern. "The police showed me a video, and you were on it."

Before she could answer, Sutekh appeared in the light emanating from the ship's underbelly. Within seconds, he touched down on the roof and rushed to her side. "Aurelia, have you misplaced your judgment? We cannot be here right now."

"Please, Sutekh, give me a moment."

Due to their history, Max had only now begun to grasp that the small man was somehow not an adversary, and had only been looking out for his welfare.

"But, Aurelia, " Sutekh implored, "the ship… we aren't even cloaked."

"She asked for a moment!" Max insisted, desiring time with the woman who evoked distant memories of his own mother.

Finally, she continued, "Your friend's demise was not our doing, Max. We were surveilling him, to ascertain his intentions. We were just as shocked at the outcome."

Max struggled, trying to digest everything Aurelia was saying. "Okay… so, it's true you're my mom's sister. Is that why you were reading her journal?"

She stepped forward and firmly embraced Max. "You should know it was incredibly brave of her to be here." Aurelia took a step back, still clinging tightly to Max's hands. "Sutekh is right. We have to go. This manner of interference is strictly forbidden." She swiped a tear from her cheek. "I promise, one day soon, I can explain everything about me and your mother." Aurelia and Sutekh turned toward the spotlight emanating from their ship.

"Wait. Can you at least tell me where you're from? Where my mother is from."

"It was never our intention to involve you in the struggle. But oftentimes the chips fall where they will. You are of solid stock, Max, but your heart is filled with duality. We have been watching. It would seem you've made a choice, one your mother would be proud of." Aurelia returned to offer Max a final hug. During the embrace, she quietly whispered in his ear, "Whenever we can, we will be there to assist you." She released him and searched for her bearings before pointing toward the sky. "There," she indicated. "The Seven Sisters is where you'll find our home."

Max followed her gaze, but shared very little of her astronomical savvy. With that, Aurelia and Sutekh crossed into the soft shining spotlight. They leaped upward and continued floating in the light until they disappeared inside the craft. In the blink of an eye, the circular portal snapped shut. Max examined the hull, which appeared reptilian, as if it had been constructed with millions of tiny metallic sequins. The craft hovered overhead two or three seconds more before it vanished from view in a pulse of light.

"Damn," Max thought. He had not intended to speak the swear word aloud, but it had slipped out nonetheless. Months before, he had been bowled over by the awe-inspiring events of his initiation. He did not believe anything could ever recreate the sense of wonderment he had experienced that night in Teotihuacán. He was wrong.

A fucking spaceship! A frickin' close encounter! Only in this case, the extra-terrestrial was a relative. *My mother's sister.*

Max felt dazed when a low rumble pulled his senses back to reality. The thundering growl grew to a roar in his ears, and he turned his gaze to the skies. He spotted two fighter jets, flying in formation. Within seconds, they shot by overhead. Max did not doubt they had been scrambled by the Air Force in response to Aurelia's ship. He watched the jets disappear from view as the deafening howl of their engines faded into the background. He took the small microchip pendant in hand and spoke softly into it. "Thank you."

After a short while, the sun set, and Max retreated to the interior of his home. He plopped on the couch in his den. The files from Demetrius' vault were still spread across the table. Max gawked at the pictures of his mother and Aurelia. *Secret agents. Extra-terrestrials.* He had been sworn to secrecy during his initiation. But who would believe him anyway if he ever chose to tell anyone?

He pulled the tablet from his bag and performed a search of the term "Seven Sisters." Wikipedia popped up, and its explanation consisted of a single sentence: *The popular term for Pleiades, a star cluster named for mythological characters.* Max reread the sentence. *Pleiades.*

He tried resetting the tablet to its home page, but he inadvertently pulled up a photo of the Table of Destiny instead. The memory of his recent caper came rushing back. The theft of a

deadly virus and the retrieval of Demetrius' personal documents should have been the excitement of the day, but this was
ultimately not the case. His life had just gone up a notch on the
unbelievable scale. The ever-elusive blonde had emerged from
a spaceship to confirm she was indeed his maternal aunt.

He glanced at the jacket strewn across the arm of his couch,
and an uncomfortable paranoia stirred in him. Only hours before,
one of the world's deadliest viruses had laid dormant in a Petri
dish in the inner pocket. Max shook off a chill, feeling soiled
somehow. He slipped into his shower and made the water as
hot as he could stand. Then he scrubbed at his skin. Max visualized water rinsing away any contamination or impurities and
carrying them down the drain.

After the shower, he dressed. Max had hoped a sense of relief
would engulf him at the mission's completion, but the sentiment
was fleeting. Yes, he had stolen the virus, but he wasn't scot-free
just yet. It would be hours, maybe days before he could truly
relax. There was a possibility that he tripped some silent security measure, or that he had stolen the wrong sample. Those
were only two of many scenarios that he could not yet rule out.

Later that night, Chandler called. Max looked at his phone,
contemplating whether or not to answer. Relenting, he tapped
the talk button. "Hey, Chandler." Max's voice was matter-of-fact.

"What's going on, buddy?" Unlike Max, Chandler's voice
was chipper.

"Just heading out. What's up?"

"I don't know. Thought I'd give you a buzz, see what you're
up to. Have any plans tonight?"

Max gazed at the files on his table. *Why are you on my father's
payroll?* Given the growing list of things going on, the possibility
that he and Chandler might be related was too much to contemplate. "Look, I have to be somewhere later, but maybe we can
talk afterward."

Chandler could hear an icy tone in Max's voice. "Everything
okay, Battenberg?"

"I'm not a 100 percent sure, actually. But we should talk about
it later." Max's walkie-talkie squelched, pulling his attention from
the call. "I'm sorry, I have to go. But I'll call you later, okay?"

"All right. I might end up at the Library tonight. If you want, give me a call."

Max hung up, and a voice from the walkie-talkie instructed him to go outside. He knew to leave behind any devices that could be traced, but he gathered his wallet and keys. Outside, he found a cab waiting. This time, the driver took him directly to the club where he first met Derrick and Missy. There was no line, but Max could hear music thumping inside. He entered and made his way upstairs just as he had done before. Max knocked at the door, but there was no immediate answer.

After a short wait, Genet opened, smiling from ear to ear. "Come in, darling." She pulled Max inside and closed the door.

Derrick and Missy were seated at the table where Max had previously been given the lie detector exam. This night, they had pushed it up against the window overlooking the dance floor. Upon spotting Max, Derrick scooted back and quickly approached with his hand outstretched. "Good work, brother. We were starting to worry about you earlier."

Max smiled and shook Derrick's hand. "I know, the comlink didn't quite work the way we hoped." Max spotted the containment device sitting on the table. He reached inside his bag, removed the extra one and placed it on the table next to it. "Didn't end up needing that one."

Derrick observed the devices as if afraid to pick them up. Then he turned and flashed a killer smile. "The important thing is you made it, and now we've got it!" He pulled Missy from her seat and hugged her, laughing. "Can you believe it? All our hard work..." Derrick released Missy, then grabbed Genet in a warm embrace. The two of them kissed briefly.

"It's finally in our hands, baby!" Genet beamed. "I can't believe we got it."

Derrick looked at Max so filled with joy that he pulled him into a heartfelt embrace. "Thank you, man. What you did today is amazing."

Missy and Genet joined in to complete the group hug. A moment later, Genet crossed to the corner of the room to retrieve an ice bucket with a bottle of Moet & Chandon chilling inside of it. "Today, we celebrate! To a significant victory against the cabal." Genet peeled away the foil from the cork and popped open the bottle. She pulled four plastic cups from a cupboard and filled each one. "Sorry about the cups, guys. We don't have crystal flutes here." Once everyone had a drink, Genet raised hers in the air. "May our future successes be even bigger and better."

Derrick winked at her. "Here, here!"

Missy raised her glass. "To Max. Without his help, none of this would've been possible. We are blessed to have him on board."

Everyone raised their glasses in unison and drank. Max knew from the flavor that the champagne had not been properly stored, but it slid down easily. He gulped it faster than he should have, hoping that it might relax him.

The attitude in the room was happy and upbeat, but Max felt there was something amiss or not quite right in the air. In less than twenty-four hours, he and the rest of the world would know exactly what that thing was.

CHAPTER 47

$\mathcal{A}$ second cab fetched Max to deliver him home from the champagne celebration. During the ride he thought of his earlier conversation with Chandler. *He might be at the Library.* Without his phone this could be difficult to confirm, but Max knew Chandler well enough to expect he would be there.

Several minutes later, the driver dropped him at the nightclub entrance. Max entered near the techno dance space. Three different rooms played other musical genres, but he presumed Chandler would be on the '80s dance floor. He wandered through the crowd until he felt someone grab hold of him. Max turned to see Chandler holding a drink with a handsome man at his side.

"Hey, I thought that was you. Why didn't you text me?"

"I forgot my phone. I was hoping I'd find you, though." To humor Chandler's friend, Max cracked a semi-genuine smile. "Can we talk a sec? Alone would be best."

The moment turned awkward, but Chandler was a pro at such games. He removed a 20-dollar bill and turned to his companion. "Do you mind grabbing another round?" The gentleman took the money with a smile and gladly stepped away to allow Chandler the appearance of privacy. Chandler then diverted his attention back to Max. "What's up?"

In a lounge area off to the side, Max spotted a couple of vacant armchairs. "Let's sit over there." They headed to the section and sat before Max continued. "I wasn't sure when to bring this up, but then I decided, why not now?"

Chandler nodded, offering Max his almost-full attention, all the while bobbing his head to the music.

"There's a whole lot going on right now, and honestly, I'm not sure who to trust. Brigitte and I are only semi-talking... My father and I fell out; and there's you, and maybe a couple of other people..." While Max spoke, Chandler continued nodding in quiet agreement. "I need to ask a question, and I want you—I hope you can be totally honest with me."

Chandler nodded again with a smile. "Ask away."

"Why is my father paying you?"

The question immediately threw Chandler off kilter. He sat back and looked away toward the bar. "What makes you think —" He started but couldn't finish his sentence.

Like a hawk, Max fixed Chandler in his gaze. "I can see your mind racing; you're trying to think of something, but that's not what I need from you. I want the truth, Chandler."

Chandler squirmed a moment longer. "I figured this would happen. The minute we started hanging out, I knew it would get in the way."

"You still haven't answered my question. Why are you on my dad's payroll?"

Chandler finally raised his gaze and looked directly at Max. "He asked me to keep an eye on you."

Max pondered his response. Demetrius had already implanted a chip in him. More than likely, all of his cars, cell phones and his house had been outfitted with tracking and surveillance devices. Now, his father had also employed Chandler toward the same goal. *Incredible.* "How long ago did he ask you this?"

"From the beginning, Max. You and I hadn't even met when he offered me the gig."

"Whoa." Max could not help feeling betrayed, but he was unsure who was more disappointing, Chandler or his father. "So, working together, that was a job, I get it. What about our friendship, though? Was that a gig?"

Chandler scooted closer to Max and placed a hand on his knee. "That's not how it is, I swear." He looked off again, at a group of club-goers near the bar. "I always wanted to meet you, even before your father reached out. Especially after you started running Badem, which is right up my alley professionally. When I saw a position opening there, I was still assistant editor at the Chicago Reader. Working with you was a step up for me, and the idea that I'd be working with someone I always wanted to meet was appealing."

"Fuck." Max ran a hand through his hair in exasperation. He had hoped Chandler might produce some other explanation.

"I thought if I could at least set up an interview I'd get a chance to meet you, but your father showed up instead. With an entourage of guards, of course. It was pretty intimidating, actually. He had me sign a nondisclosure agreement before we even spoke. Then he offered a lot of money to keep tabs on you…" Chandler's words trailed off. "I don't think he realized it was a dream of mine to work with you."

"How about a woman named Sandrine? Who is she to you?"

Chandler looked even more perplexed than he had before. "You mean my mom?"

Max studied Chandler's expression. His VP and friend appeared truly miffed.

"Why are you asking about my mom? She doesn't have anything to do with this."

"It's nothing. I just saw her name in a file, that's all. Probably some paperwork my father had you do." Max stood and motioned toward the bar. "Looks like your friend got those refills."

Chandler looked up and spotted his companion turning away from the bar, heading toward them. He had a drink in each hand.

"I'm glad we talked, though. I'm going to head out."

"Wait, Max. Don't leave like this. You just got here."

Max turned to Chandler, still sour from the bitter taste of betrayal. "What you just told me was a mouthful, Chandler. I'm going to need time to digest it." Max forced a smile before making his way toward the exit. After a moment's hesitation, he doubled back for a final word. "Look, I should probably leave you with a piece of advice, and I hope you'll take it seriously. You said when you first met my father it was kind of scary or intimidating. If you ever get that vibe again, promise me you'll pay attention to it. Just like you've been watching me all this time, there are probably people watching you. It's something to think about." With that simple word of counsel, Max turned and made his exit.

Chandler stared after him until his companion arrived with their drinks. The man appeared puzzled by Chandler's expression. "Everything okay?"

While Max stood outside of the Library awaiting a cab, a horrific event was occurring across town. Miles beneath the National Portrait Gallery, a secret elevator was rocketing upward from the underground installation. It clicked into place, then began its horizontal move to access the public elevator shaft. Seconds later, it would open into the new arrivals wing of the museum. Only hours before, Max had been in the same elevator.

The lift began its vertical ascent again, shooting toward ground level. When the doors opened, two scientists in white Hazmat suits stumbled out into the new arrivals wing. One of them had spoken to Max only two days before. Both were dressed in protective clothing but had torn away their masks. Neither could stop their fits of coughing as they spat blood onto the floor. In a panic, they watched the elevator doors close behind them.

The men wandered, disoriented, into the wing, searching desperately for an exit. Hours before, both had been completely healthy. Now, they were each suffering from fever and delirium. They made their way to the exit and pushed against the doors, but they refused to open. It was after hours, and the museum was on lock-down.

The man Max had spoken with desperately banged against the glass. "Someone help! Please!"

In the middle of his rounds, a museum security guard heard their cries and ran toward the commotion. By the time he rounded the corner, one of them had already collapsed before the front door. The last man standing appeared to be growing weaker by the moment. He attempted to cover his mouth, but projectile vomit sprayed the guard with a mixture of gunk and blood. Cringing in disgust, the museum employee pulled out his walkie-talkie and radioed for help.

Max was safely in a cab on his way home. He felt melancholic about the state of his close connections, which all seemed to be in flux. His relationships with Brigitte and his father were severely strained, and now his friendship with Chandler was uncertain at best. The idea that Chandler might be his half brother was unfathomable, so Max pushed the concept to the furthest corners of his mind. He reminded himself what AJ had told him about impermanence: *all things, without exception, will change.* In recent months, this principle had crashed down hard upon him, and Max was certain there would be more to come.

Minutes later, the cab dropped him at home. Max punched in

his access codes and ascended his stairwell. He quickly checked his cell phone for missed calls. Both Chandler and Ted had called, and there was a missed call from Battenberg Industries. Max believed his relationship with Demetrius was at an all-time low, to the point that he dreaded seeing Battenberg Industries on his caller I.D. He scanned his visual voicemail menu and retrieved the message. He hoped it was a cancellation of the meeting his father had requested, but he was not so fortunate. A message by Rosalee began to play.

"Hello, Mr. Battenberg. Unfortunately, I've had to shuffle a few of your father's appointments. If you could please be here at 9:00 a.m. tomorrow instead of ten, that'll be perfect. I apologize for any confusion, but as you know, your father's schedule is constantly changing. Please confirm your receipt of this message."

Max confirmed, deleted the message and considered the inconvenient change. Even so, he would report at the time of his father's choosing. Everyone always did. Resigned, he spent the next few hours getting organized. If Demetrius wanted to meet sooner, he needed to be ready. He gathered the documents from his father's vault and carefully read them, making sure to segregate them by topic. He could not be sure how much time Demetrius would allow, but there was no shortage of things to cover.

Back at the Smithsonian, two ambulances pulled up in front of the National Portrait Gallery. Two paramedic teams rushed up the steps with gurneys in hand. When they reached the top of the stairs, they spotted the men in white Hazmat suits, collapsed in a heap in front of the building. Two lead EMTs, one, a portly Korean and the other, a muscular African American, appeared stunned by the amount of blood on their white protective gear. The Smithsonian guard, who had retreated to the interior foyer, spotted the rescue team and exited, still cleaning blood and vomit from his uniform.

After a quick survey of the scene, the Korean medic immediately understood there was something dire occurring. "What happened here?!"

Before he could reply, one of the scientists vomited again, coughing and wheezing to catch his breath. He finally expelled the words, "They're all dead. Everyone down there is dead."

"Down where?" the Korean demanded, as he slipped a digital thermometer in the man's ear.

Bloodshot eyes bulged in the man's head, and sweat poured from his brow. He stared at the medic, delirious with fever. A moment later, the thermometer chirped, and the medic checked it.

"Shit, he's spiking at 106. What the fuck happened here? If we're going to help, we need to know what happened."

The man responded in a stream of projectile vomit that spewed across the medic's legs and belly.

"Fuck!" the Korean medic screamed, jumping back. He turned to his colleague, who was frantically checking the other unconscious man's vitals. After a brief exam, the African American paramedic finally stood and shook his head.

"This one's gone."

A junior medic at the building entrance waved to get everyone's attention. "Guys, I think you need to see this."

Both lead EMTs looked up and spotted the Smithsonian guard bowled over in pain at the gallery's front door. A layer of sweat soaked his brow, and blood began streaming from his nose. He swiped it away, fighting against his own growing panic. The EMTs shared a moment of understanding that, somehow, they had arrived on the scene of something more horrific than first imagined.

CHAPTER 48

The following morning, the sun peeked its head over the horizon. Max had barely slept and was rushing around. He hurried to his computer and logged in to several of his bank accounts. After making a few online transactions, he wrote half a dozen emails. By the time he completed his task list, it was nearly 8:15 a.m. Max quickly rushed to his bathroom to prepare for the day. He peered into his mirror, surprised to see the haggard, exhausted face staring back at him.

With no time to waste, he showered and dressed, donning jeans and a white button-down shirt. Before heading out, Max slathered his face with expensive cream and placed drops in each eye. In his rush to get downstairs, he heard the walkie-talkie squelch to life.

"You there? We have a problem."

Max picked up the radio, but put it back down when he spotted the time: 8:50 a.m. *Shit!* An instant later, he placed the device in his bag and hurried downstairs to the garage. He threw the shoulder bag in his passenger seat and gunned the car into traffic.

The walkie-talkie squelched again. "You there? We need to talk."

Max flipped the bag open to reveal Demetrius' secret files. He removed the walkie-talkie from on top and clicked transmit. "I can't right now. How about this afternoon? I'll be in touch as soon as I can."

Thirty seconds later, the walkie-talkie crackled to life with a woman's voice on the other end. "Okay."

Max suspected it might be Genet since the voice was accented. He steered onto his father's street and spoke into the walkie-talkie again. "Over and out." He parked in the Spire's underground structure and caught the elevator to Demetrius' floor.

Within minutes, Rosalee arrived to fetch him. "How are you, Mr. Battenberg?"

"I'd be lying if I said I wasn't tired."

"Sorry about last night's scheduling change. I'm sure that didn't help."

"It's fine, Rosalee. I get it."

She offered a curt smile and led Max down a corridor toward a Battenberg Industry conference room. "Is everything else okay, aside from being tired?"

"Yeah, a bit more crazed than usual, but good."

She glanced in his direction but kept pep in her step. "It seems that's the way of the world nowadays." She stopped short in front of a small conference room. "You'll be meeting in here. If you'd please just have a seat. Can I bring you anything? Coffee? Water?"

"No, thank you, Rosalee. I'm fine."

Max passed into the room and crossed to a window overlooking the lake. The morning was overcast and gray, and a foggy mist lay haphazardly across the water. He turned and observed the large glass conference table in the center of the room. Taking note of it, he immediately suspected he had lost his father's favor. When Demetrius was unsure of someone, he insisted on glass tables to observe if they were fidgeting or attempting to hide something.

He took a seat and placed his bag in the chair beside him. Chances were, Demetrius would keep him waiting, so he grabbed a remote from the table and activated the flat screen television on the wall. He flipped to a satellite news station only to be stunned by the story being covered. The on-screen anchor, a Hispanic man, stood beside a police blockade that barred entrance to the road. He appeared anxious, even though he spoke in the usual assured tone of a news anchor.

"A strange and deadly illness has already claimed the lives of seven people this morning. According to reports, late last night, a Smithsonian guard dialed 9-1-1 after stumbling upon two unidentified men in the National Portrait Gallery. Somehow, and the details of this are still unclear, both men had become trapped in the museum. The CDC is now reporting that these two have been pronounced dead from a mystery illness."

"Fuck." Max glared at the TV, fully comprehending the implications of the report. He turned the volume louder as the newscaster continued his account.

"Sources report, the emergency medical team who arrived on scene last night has also succumbed to a litany of mysterious and troubling symptoms. This has authorities alarmed, and the CDC has now instituted a quarantine not only for the National Portrait Gallery but also for the dozens of healthcare workers who might have been exposed."

Before he could fully digest what he was hearing, Max heard Demetrius' voice in the hallway. Judging from his tone, he was hardly in a good mood. In fact, he was incensed and yelling.

"I don't care if there's a quarantine! One of you better get down there and goddamn find out what the hell happened."

Max snapped off the monitor just as Demetrius entered the room. The elder Battenberg's face was still red with outrage as he slammed the door behind him.

"Hello, Max."

"Hello." Max thought about the file on his mother and the documents on Chandler. His gaze remained steely and atypically unsympathetic.

"I know I asked you to swing by, but it turns out now's not a good time. Have you fuckin' heard about this goddamn virus? Somebody fucked up big time." Demetrius lowered his voice to a whisper. "You realize this is Clean Slate."

Max felt time come to a grinding halt as sensory overload took hold of him. He did not respond but rather closed his eyes to search for some semblance of composure.

"Max, did you hear me? What the hell's the matter with you? If you think I have time for this, I don't."

Max took in a breath and slowly opened his eyes. Once again, the look in them unsettled Demetrius. After a brief pause, Max spoke in a casual but thoughtful voice. "All these years I've looked up to you, looking for approval…" Max shook his head in despair. "Now, all I want to do is laugh. To think that I ever sought your validation."

His son's words would normally have stirred Demetrius to a frenzy, but he was somehow intrigued by the look in Max's eye. "Do you mind telling me what the hell you're talking about?"

"Let's just say I took a little peek in Pandora's Box." Max opened his bag and removed the file on his mother." He slapped it on the table before Demetrius.

His father spotted the label, *Fiona Battenberg Accident*. He picked up the file and opened it. Demetrius read a few lines, then immediately tossed it back on the table. "Where did you get that?"

"Does it matter? The bigger question is, why does it exist? Because it kind of reads like a death warrant for my mother, brother and uncle. That'd be your wife and son. And the whole Odeon Rutherford thing… What was that about? Some wild goose chase, maybe, to see how angry I could get. Or how far I might go. Is that what you were hoping?"

Demetrius was seething now and spoke with deliberate emphasis, enunciating each word. "Where did you get that?"

The look in his father's eyes was predatory, but Max was unfazed, blinded by his own indignation. "You were an idol to me." Max laughed. "Maybe because you were all I had — one of the richest men in the world. In reality, you're just a selfish and uncaring… bastard. No one should look up to you."

Demetrius hardly listened as the machinations of his mind placed the puzzle pieces together. "This virus. Clean Slate…" It was beginning to dawn on him. "This was you." Even though he hardly seemed amused, Demetrius was smiling, still doing the math. "That's where you got the file. You had no business down there. Do you realize what you've done?" Demetrius rocketed around the table and yanked Max from his chair. Like wrestlers, they grappled a moment longer before Max knocked his father's hands away. With improved leverage, he maneuvered Demetrius from his spot and slammed him against the window, causing it to vibrate into the adjoining room. Max spoke clearly while he held Demetrius pinned against the glass.

"Just tell me, is there anything you're not capable of? Murdering your own wife and child. Who else have you made attempts on? Brigitte. It's incredible she didn't lose the baby. So far, your grandson's okay, though."

Demetrius appeared stunned as he broke away from Max's hold. "What are you talking about? The girl's having a boy."

"Her name's Brigitte, and yeah, she is. Where's your file on her?" Max stepped away, seeking distance from his father's acrimony. "I didn't mention it because she's terrified of you."

"What the hell does that mean?"

Max studied his father's confused reaction. "I know others

who've been injured, or worse... just like you were in Brazil."

"You have no idea what you've done, Maximilian. Preparations had to be made before the virus was unleashed. Don't you realize that once the casualties begin, no one will be able to survive up here? It'll be years before we can return. The underground crops and the staff we need, all of that has to be readied before we can occupy the facilities below. You have jeopardized everything."

Max stared at his father, riddled with contempt. "Isn't this what you always wanted? A fire in my belly." He chuckled, but the laugh did not come from a happy place. "All this time, you've wanted help running this company. Well, now you've got it, because I'm going to help fucking run everything you've built into the ground. When I'm finished, everyone will know exactly who you are. A liar, a cheat... a man who murdered his own wife and son." Suddenly, Max felt a semblance of calm overtaking him, and his voice softened. "How's that for fire in the belly?"

Demetrius smoothed his clothes and offered his son an icy stare. "You were always foolish, Max. Do you honestly believe that little stunt will affect Clean Slate? Because it won't!" Full of adrenalin, Demetrius pointed to the streets below. "Like I said before, if I want to wipe out every single one of those people, I can do so at my whim. That means anyone's slate can be cleaned, including yours, Maximilian. Do you understand me? Be careful thinking there aren't others who can assume your role."

"Like who? Chandler."

Recognition bled into Demetrius' expression as he took note of the true scope of Max's discoveries.

"Yeah, I saw your file on him, too. I have to give it to you, hiding another son may be some of your best work. Why would you keep that from me?"

Demetrius cracked an icy smile while fixing Max in his gaze. "It's too late to ask questions now. The damage is already done. Keep in mind, this meeting here will likely be the last time we see one another."

Max chuckled at the notion. "You consider that a threat?" He gathered the file on his mother's death and shoved it in his bag. "Knowing I had a half brother, that you had a son, maybe that could've filled a void, somehow. But then again, you're responsible for that void, aren't you?

Before Max could reach the door, Demetrius spoke again in a softer tone. "I hadn't planned on either of you being in that car. And certainly not Christian."

Max spun around and, suddenly, the rage in him was gone. "You know what? Nothing you plan should ever be allowed to happen." He paused briefly before pulling open the conference room door.

Refusing to acknowledge his son any further, Demetrius turned away to gaze once again across the gray Chicago sky. Facing the window, he delivered a final edict. "I'm giving you a week. After that, I want you gone from the job and the home. You can hold on to the cars, if you wish."

Clutching the door, Max turned to find Demetrius staring across the lake. For a short time, he studied the back of his father's head. "You're right about one thing. This will be the last time we see one another."

Demetrius stood rigid, overlooking his expansive view. When he turned from the window, the conference room door was swinging shut, and Max was gone. He sighed deeply and pondered what had just occurred. The Maximilian who had just exited was the son he had been searching for all these years. But with a sense of finality, he realized things were not to be as he hoped.

He grabbed the remote and switched on the wall monitor. A blonde newscaster appeared on screen with a surgical mask covering her face. She was in the street, standing a distance away from the quarantined hospital, which was visible in the background.

"Cara Steadman here, reporting in front of Hamilton Hospital, which you can see down the street behind me. The CDC has officially labeled this latest outbreak an epidemic as the death toll continues to rise. Twenty-five people have now succumbed to the mysterious virus in less than twenty-four hours, a circumstance that continues to baffle doctors."

Demetrius' spirits sank even further when he heard the panic beginning. He raised the volume as the newscaster continued.

"If you, or anyone you know, has visited the National Portrait Gallery within the last twenty-four hours, the CDC wants to

speak with you. Just to recap, reports say, late last night, a security guard discovered two unknown men in the National Portrait
Gallery. It appears that everyone who came in contact with these
men has now contracted the disease, which is troubling because
eighteen hours later, there appear to be no survivors—"

Demetrius shut the TV off and pushed a few buttons on the
speakerphone in the center of the table. Seconds later, Rosalee's
voice came on.

"Yes, Mr. Battenberg?"

"Get me the CEO of our pharmaceutical branch. I'm looking
at these news clips and realizing there's an opportunity here. We
need a treatment for this outbreak ASAP."

"Yes, Mr. Battenberg."

"And, Rosalee?"

"Yes, sir?"

"In five days I'd like you to wipe Maximilian's access codes,
globally, across the board."

"Very well, Mr. Battenberg. Should I include his home?"

"Yes. I want everything expunged." Demetrius' normal full
schedule only felt more exacerbated by the epidemic burning its
way through DC. Switching gears, he pushed "end call" on the
speakerphone and hurried from the room.

CHAPTER 49

After fleeing his father's office, Max jumped behind the wheel of his Range Rover and drove straight to Badem Publishing. The office was abuzz with activity, and he spotted Chandler across the room working with a team of layout artists. Max ignored his VP and continued to his office, but the snub did not go unnoticed.

On impulse, Chandler excused himself and made his way to Max's door. He rapped gently but did not wait before entering. "Hey, good morning."

Max barely looked up to acknowledge the greeting. "Hi."

Chandler appeared remorseful as he closed the door. "I was hoping we could talk."

Max paid Chandler little mind. Instead, he yanked open a drawer and began emptying his effects into a box. "I'm listening."

"I know you don't trust me, and I'd be foolish to say I don't understand. It's just…"

Max sat still and turned his full attention to Chandler, who then became even more uncomfortable.

"This is awkward. I swear I feel like a kid around you sometimes." To the best extent possible, Chandler swallowed his embarrassment and continued. "I'm never exactly sure how it works with Battenbergs, but I'm afraid I won't get the chance to say this if I don't do it now."

Before Chandler could continue, the receptionist buzzed Max's intercom with a call. Max requested that she hold all calls, but the receptionist made it clear that the caller was very insistent. Acquiescing, Max picked up to find Genet on the line in a state of agitation.

"I apologize for calling you here, but we've been trying to get ahold of you all morning. Something went wrong."

Max understood Genet's reference. People were dead, and others were dying. Somehow, the virus had been unleashed. He mulled over the steps he had taken less than a day before, but he did not recall any lapse in protocol. At the same time, his father had made it clear that Rizick was not behind the release, at least not yet. An awkward silence ensued while a plethora of possibilities ran through Max's mind.

Genet waited a moment longer before she spoke. "Max, you still there?"

"Yeah. Now's not really a good time, though. Can we maybe discuss this later?"

Growing impatient, Genet exhaled into the phone. "Yes. We will contact you."

Before he could utter another word, the phone went dead. Max replaced the receiver in its cradle and returned his attention to Chandler again. "I'm listening."

Chandler took a moment to formulate his thoughts. "I realize you have every reason to distrust me, but this is me leveling with you, for what it's worth."

Max stared at Chandler, his attention piqued. "Okay."

"Last night, I don't think I really explained myself... but you need to understand, I wanted this job before your father offered it to me..." Chandler stumbled, losing confidence in his explanation. "This isn't easy to articulate."

Max watched Chandler squirm, but he found no pleasure in doing so. He softened his tone but only slightly. "Why don't you try then?"

"Imagine wanting to meet someone more than anything, and the opportunity arises. Shit happens sometimes, even if it's not the way you want it to."

Max nodded, while the thought *if you only knew* traversed his mind.

"By the time your dad reached out, I had already made up my mind, somehow, that I was going to meet you. What would you have done?"

Max sported a bemused look. "I don't understand. Why is it you wanted to meet me?"

"I don't know. I suppose I envied you. A good-looking guy, running a publishing company... his father's a billionaire. Most guys in my shoes would be intrigued, I think. I wanted to know you. I admit that."

Max studied Chandler, trying to digest his admission. "Are you saying you had feelings for me?"

"No. I mean, not exactly. I'm saying this wasn't how I imagined we would meet, but the opportunity popped up. Even though it was strange, I took it. But my friendship, my loyalty to you has always been genuine. That has nothing to do with your father. And maybe that makes me a stalker, but I need you to understand that I've always felt some weird type of bond with you, even if it's only been in my head." Chandler watched Max nodding plainly to the details of his account.

Max's indifference had very little to do with his story, but was instead about a deadly virus sweeping across the city, the loss of his father and the forthcoming loss of his job and home. Even so, Max's unemotional expression rendered Chandler incapable of discerning whether acceptance or sarcasm was resident behind his gaze.

"Chandler, if I had to guess, I'd say you're in way over your head. And the saddest part is, you have no idea."

"About what, Max?" Chandler felt more in the dark than ever.

Max could sense his VP's exasperation. "You might do well to never find out. Let's just say, that bond you describe, I've felt it too. It may be deeper than either of us imagined."

"Okay, so where does that leave us?"

Brothers. Half brothers. Like Enki and Enlil. "You should know my father has cut me off, which means I no longer work here. I can't say for sure what that means for you. Certainly, I think he would do well to keep you on." Max smiled at Chandler. "In fact, I predict bigger and greater things for you."

"What do you mean, cut you off?" Chandler couldn't hide his shock. "Why?"

"I'm sure you'll understand if I don't explain." Max put the things he wished to keep in his box. "My father's a slippery man, Chandler." Max pushed the box aside and surprised Chandler with a warm embrace. "Please be careful with him." In a peculiar fashion, Max still felt an affinity for Chandler that was deepened by the newfound knowledge of their true kinship. *But can I trust him?* It was a question Max could not adequately answer. Chandler had duped him, after all, in order to spy on him for Demetrius. Unable to fully process his current sentiment, Max grabbed his effects and left through the door without a word.

Chandler stood, dumbfounded, and watched through the window as Max quickly left the building.

Max drove away from Badem Publishing, glancing at the building one last time in his rearview mirror. He steered the Range Rover onto a large thoroughfare and exited the city limits until he arrived at the first car dealership he could find. It was a small, nondescript used-car lot with an array of various makes and models. Max stepped from his Range Rover and perused the small fleet. None of the vehicles compared in any way to his top-of-the-line luxury SUV.

Finally, a salesman approached, stopping to admire Max's car. "That's a real beaut you got there." The man walked closer to Max. "What can I do for you today?"

"I'd like to barter my car for one of yours."

The salesman chortled until he noticed the no-nonsense expression on Max's face. "Okay…" He faltered, glancing from Max to the Range Rover. "That's what you're bartering?"

"Yes. You sign over one of your titles, and I'll sign over mine."

The salesman pondered Max's offer with a nervous laugh. "You having a bad day today?"

"Not necessarily."

Brimming with skepticism, the auto salesman looked again at Max's car. "Is that thing stolen or something?"

"No, I'm just looking to downsize."

The salesman studied Max, trying to determine his angle. "The Rover's yours, free and clear?"

"Yeah."

The salesman was a shark in his everyday dealings. He searched for a crack in Max's demeanor, but he did not find one. "What year is it?"

"It's a year old."

"All right, pal. If you're not bullshitting, why don't you take your pick?" The salesman turned, opening his arms to present his display of used vehicles. With a wide smile, he watched Max pace up and down the lot, appraising his options.

Max knew his father used equipment in ways people didn't even know existed. For this reason, he wanted an older car that lacked the technology needed for tracking or geo-location. He stopped before an old Pontiac.

"What's this thing here?"

"That, my friend, is a 2001 Aztek. Runs good for an older car."

"Does it have OnStar or GPS?"

The salesman nearly choked on his laugh. "No, not in that one. If you want GPS, I can get it for you, though."

The previous owner had tinted the windows so dark, Max doubted it was even legal. *Perfect. It'll be that much harder to spot me inside.*

Max had the man open up the car so they could drive around the block, and it seemed to run adequately enough. To the salesman's befuddlement, Max signed over the title to his Range Rover. Completing the rest of the barter took less than 15 minutes. Max made sure to empty the Range Rover of his personal effects before he hopped behind the wheel of the Aztek. He drove from the lot, terribly aware of the difference in maneuverability between the cars. The Range Rover was hulking, but offered a smooth ride, while the Aztek, also an SUV, was squatter in stature and handled more like a truck. Max struggled to acclimate to the pre-owned car's handling. When he pressed the gas pedal the car lurched forward, and Max merged into traffic.

He spent the remainder of his morning visiting each of the four banks where he held accounts. He emptied all four and each time, made his way back to the car, ending up with three cashier's checks and a case full of cash.

With his list of tasks accomplished, Max swung by Northwestern Memorial to see Brigitte. For the first time in a long while, his entrance garnered a smile. He felt relief to see her once again in good spirits and realized how much he missed her. He pulled a chair close to her bed and sat down. "How are you?"

Brigitte's swelling had nearly vanished, but she was still black and blue. She grimaced through a smile. "I feel a little better, but not great. At least we're still here, though—me and the baby, I mean."

Max nodded and smiled back. "Thank God for that."

"You believe in God now?" Brigitte studied Max but found she was unable to read him the way she had in the past. "Are you all right?"

"No, not really. How could I be? Everything's shit right now. You — well, us I mean — my dad, even Chandler… Nothing's the way it should be, and I doubt it ever will be again."

"Max… you of all people have the resources to do something about that. The rest of us can't say as much."

Max smiled, to think that Brigitte somehow imagined he was in control. "I need to go away for a while; that's why I came by. I didn't want to leave without saying anything."

Even though it caused a strain, Brigitte scooted up in bed. "What are you talking about?"

Max could not have been more resolute, but speaking the words aloud felt alien somehow. "My dad and I had this crazy fight, and he fired me. He also asked me to leave the house."

"Max, you can't think he was serious. I'm sure he said that in anger."

"It's more than that, Brigitte. Trust me." A deep sense of shame arose in Max with regard to his father and the Battenberg name. "There are things I found out about him that are indefensible. Things to do with my mom and other stuff… I don't want to get into all that. Let's just say, you might be right that he's why you're here."

Brigitte released an audible gasp. "Oh my God." With a sense of dread, she sank back into the hospital bed. Now riddled with anxiety, she stared out the window. "Am I safe here, Max?"

He glanced at the floor a moment before answering. "I can't say for sure. Hell, I don't even know if I am. That's why I need to stay away a while, at least until after the baby's born. I'm hoping we'll both be safer that way."

Brigitte's mind raced, and a floodgate of tears unleashed. "They finally told me about Marilyn this morning."

"Oh, shit." Max rose from his seat and hugged Brigitte tightly. "I'm so sorry…"

She swiped at her tears and spoke in hushed whispers. "I know it's difficult for us to speak openly, but the idea that she might be dead because of us… I feel sick about it." In a cathartic release, Brigitte's tears turned into sobs, and Max kept hugging her to provide all the comfort he could muster. After a long while, she raised her head and looked him in the eye. "You have to tell me where you're going. I don't think I can have this baby by myself."

Max grabbed her hand and squeezed it. "Will you stop already? I'm not going far. My dad said I have the house till the end of the week. I have to work a few things out before then. We can figure out our plan afterward."

"Fuck, Max. All this time I've been questioning this pregnancy and whether I should…" Tears interrupted her thoughts, and Brigitte resigned herself not to speak her concerns aloud. "None of this is encouraging."

Max strengthened his efforts to comfort her. "I'll keep checking in until I get settled. Hopefully, by then you'll be out of here, and we can take it from there."

Regaining a level of composure, Brigitte continued. "They said I could probably go home in the next couple of days."

"Good." Max felt his mind racing. "If you feel up to it, you should go somewhere. A place no one'll find you. I can help with that."

"No, Max. Not while I'm pregnant. I need to be around the people I love, my family…"

"Okay." Max rubbed her hand. "I don't think I should hang around, though. Not until I know it's safe."

Brigitte eased back against her pillow, distressed by Max's every word.

"Look, I don't want you worrying about my dad. I literally just told him about the pregnancy. Strangely enough, he seemed pleased. I wouldn't be surprised if he sent some kind of security detail."

Brigitte became alarmed at the mention of a Battenberg security force. "No, Max. I don't want that. You can't actually think I would trust your father."

"That's why I'd like you to go somewhere, Brigitte. I can't control what he's going to do."

"But how am I supposed to reach you?"

Max picked up a pen and ripped a sheet from a small pad of paper beside the bed. He scribbled down the number for his burner phone and wrote the name "Emerson" above it. "Text me here if you need to. But you can't tell anyone about this number, Brigitte. Right now, Ted's the only one who knows it."

"Okay." She studied Max intently, finally fully aware of the legitimacy of his concerns.

"Emerson stands for emergency, okay? As soon as you need me I'll be here."

"All right then." She wished her words sounded more convincing, but she did not feel assured enough to back it up.

"I'll be in touch again before I leave, okay?"

Brigitte forced a smile, but it did not dissuade a tear from rolling down her face. "This is all shit, Max. How did we get here?"

"We just have to be patient, Brigitte. It won't be like this forever. We'll figure something out, I promise." He leaned in and kissed her lightly. "That didn't hurt, did it?"

She shook her head. "No, it's fine."

"Is there anything I can do before I head out?"

Brigitte studied Max, trying to glean some idea of his mysterious plan. "No, I'm fine."

"Try not to worry, and I'll be back as soon as it's safe. You can also text me at that number if you need to."

Brigitte forced a smile but held onto his hand as her true affection for Max bubbled to the surface. He released her hand, and with a wink he slipped from the room. Without skipping a beat, he retrieved the Aztek and returned home. Either caution or paranoia pushed him to park a few blocks away. He walked the remaining distance and entered the appropriate entry code to gain access to his house. He knew the possibility existed that Demetrius had already locked him out. To his relief, the door disarmed and he ran upstairs to begin packing.

He knew he wouldn't be able to take much, so he made his choices carefully. Two hours later, Max placed two large pieces of luggage at the top of his steps. He had been awake and on the move for nearly 24 hours, and the need for sleep felt more urgent than ever. Since he had still not heard from Genet, he picked up the walkie-talkie and pressed the transmit key. "Anyone? Just checking if we're still meeting." Max released the transmit key and awaited a response, but there was none. He crossed into his bedroom and collapsed on the bed with the walkie-talkie at his side. He knew someone would get back to him shortly. Seconds later, Max was fast asleep.

CHAPTER 50

While he did not consciously realize it, the rupture with Demetrius had resulted in a rather unexpected benefit. A deep sense of relief had overtaken Max, allowing him a solid and deep slumber. Even though his high-tech security system had been armed, the alarm did not sound when the front door slowly opened. Two figures in silhouette slipped inside and deliberately made their way up Max's stairwell. Had he been seated in his secret control room, Max would have seen on his CCTV monitor that intruders were creeping up his steps. Instead, beneath his silken covers, he was sound asleep in bed.

His panic-room video feeds simultaneously displayed four different sections of the house in black and white. Camera one revealed the intruders mounting the stairs. Both men were dressed entirely in black and had their faces obscured by black ninja-inspired masks. They disappeared from the first feed, then reappeared on another as they made their way into the hall outside of Max's bedroom. One of the assailants removed a small bottle and a piece of cloth. He saturated the fabric with contents from the bottle: chloroform. His accomplice, in kind, removed a compact syringe from an inner jacket pocket.

Inside the control room, Max's surveillance system blinked once, and every surveillance camera ceased transmission. Each picture went from clear reception to grainy snow. Without skipping a step, the men crossed over the threshold into Max's bedroom. They paused and took note of the extreme quiet. No expense had been spared in soundproofing the walls and glass. Both men were assured that no one outside would hear what they were about to do.

They approached Max's bed and observed him in unsuspecting slumber. His diaphragm quietly rose and fell with each breath. The man with chloroform stooped beside his victim, but a sudden shift in Max's position gave him pause. He and his accomplice remained frozen, staring at one another until a resounding thud reverberated on the roof, followed by the quick succession of steps running across it. The intruders shared a moment of apprehension, but the commotion failed to wake Max. The assailants had been certain he was home alone, so who was on the roof?

In the past, similar unexpected scenarios had arisen, and they had always been prepared. Each man felt confident tonight would be no different. Together, they crossed into the center of Max's bedroom, turning back-to-back to assume defensive postures. One of them held Max in his sights while the other watched the door. They stood listening a while, but an enduring quiet pervaded. After a time, they felt satisfied that the roof disturbance might have been some strange anomaly. *An animal perhaps?*

Ultimately, the assailants broke rank and turned to one another, nodding the okay to continue. They took a step toward Max's bed and found Aurelia standing there. *Where the fuck did she come from?* To their astonishment, she had somehow infiltrated the room. Attired in a black suit, Aurelia appeared to be a harmless business executive who had returned home at the wrong time. The man nearest to her, clutching the syringe, tilted his head toward Max, signaling that his accomplice should take care of him while he dispatched her. In a flash, Aurelia kicked out his legs, and he crumpled to the floor, carefully holding the syringe away from his body.

Max sprang up from the ruckus, still in a haze. *Aurelia?* For some unknown reason, his aunt was standing among others in his room. In a knee-jerk reaction, the other attacker lunged, attempting to overpower her with chloroform. Aurelia deflected the rag instead, and delivered a martial arts blow to his hand. He relinquished the cloth, and she snatched it from the air as if they had rehearsed the move a dozen times.

"Max, get up!"

Clearing from his haze, Max leapt from bed and planted his feet firmly on the floor.

Aurelia pressed the cloth against the man's face, but he grappled with her, holding his breath.

"Hey!" Max yelled, still trying to make sense of the struggle going on in his room.

Possessing moves of his own, the assassin disarmed Aurelia of the chloroform-soaked cloth. In another flash, she delivered a knee to his groin, bowling him over in pain. The other attacker, while still on the ground, grabbed for Aurelia's leg, attempting to inject her with the syringe. She, however, began her own offensive. Without hesitation, she dropped to the floor and punched out with an open palm, knocking his head to the ground. Extending the fingers of her right hand like a knife, she jabbed with surgical precision, striking at precise points. In a matter of seconds, she delivered lightning blows to his neck, first on the right then on the left; to both armpits and along several points on his torso and groin.

A panicked look overcame him as the reality dawned on him: *I can't move.* To his utter shock, Aurelia had delivered a series of paralyzing blows to crucial nerve centers, rendering him completely immobile.

The remaining assailant began to understand his emerging predicament. They had no clue who Aurelia was or why she was in Max's room, but she had quickly tilted the scales in his favor. These assassins may have been skilled in deadly arts, but Aurelia had counter-moves, and she was too fast for them.

Desperate to regain an advantage, the remaining attacker fumbled in his belt for a semi-automatic handgun. Max did not hesitate, and roundhouse kicked it from his grip. Leaping to her feet, Aurelia made haste, delivering another set of paralyzing blows. She struck many of the same meridians along the man's neck, torso and groin. Unable to react, he stood frozen before falling face down on the floor. Aurelia wasted no time rolling him over, then Sutekh appeared as if he had always been there.

"Who the fuck are these guys?" Max demanded, but Aurelia shushed him to avoid any compromise in her and Sutekh's cover.

The intruders made attempts to move but found they were unable. Their eyes darted back and forth in panic as they struggled to determine how Aurelia had disabled them. Then Sutekh stepped forth and stood directly over them. Once again, his face was covered in a mask of shocking white mime makeup. Their moment to be startled by his appearance lasted only an instant. Sutekh pressed red circular stickers to each of their foreheads, affixing them between the eyebrows. Instantaneously, both men fell unconscious.

Max took several deep breaths as he looked from Sutekh to

Aurelia. "What the hell's going on?"

She shared a reluctant look with her stocky companion, who retrieved the syringe and held it up in plain view. Aurelia turned to Max, matter of fact. "I'm sorry, Max... But I think you know what just went on." She stared with a telling expression. "I saw that you readied some things. You should probably get them and go. There may be others coming to finish the job."

Max observed the men lying unconscious on his floor. Wasting no time, Sutekh removed a set of square, gunmetal-colored stickers from a pouch. He placed a series of them along the legs of one of the men.

Max persisted. "Do you know who they are?"

Aurelia fixed Max in her gaze, and he instantly understood that his father had been the one to send them. She rubbed a gentle hand along his shoulder. "We'll handle them. You should gather your things and leave." She gazed at Max, cupping his cheeks in her hands. "Coming here was a huge risk, but I didn't see any other way. When they bypassed your security system..."

Reason told Max he should be in shock, but a resounding numbness was all he could muster. "I don't know what to say."

"It's time you left this behind." Aurelia reached across and took hold of Max's chain necklace with the microchip pendant on it. She lifted it in view before slipping it over his head and tossing it on the bed. "From here on out, you must be hyper-vigilant. If this happens again, we may not be able to assist." She glanced at Sutekh, who shrugged with a gaze that said, *I told you so*. She turned back to Max. "Find a place where your father can't get to you."

Max gazed at the men on his floor. "Yeah. I was planning to do that."

"Well, as you can see, he was two steps ahead. You can't let that happen again."

"Aurelia..." Sutekh implored. He appeared once again to be losing patience.

"You should go, Max."

Although hesitant at first, Max crossed to his nightstand and picked up the walkie-talkie. He pressed the transmit button. "Is anyone there? I need to meet now. It's an emergency." He pulled his shoes on and took a jacket from his closet. Max put the walk-ie-talkie in his jacket and turned to Aurelia and Sutekh. "Thank you, guys."

Sutekh finished placing metallic stickers along the torsos and extremities of both intruders. He paused and turned to Max with a reluctant smile. "You are welcome." With that, he removed a sleek, metallic silver device from his pocket. The implement emit-ted a soft light, and one of the men floated effortlessly into the air as if upon an invisible gurney. Sutekh shared a silent exchange with Aurelia, and they both nodded. He then pushed the first man and floated him out of the room.

The walkie-talkie squelched and Derrick's voice came through. "We can meet within the hour. Copy?"

Aurelia looked pleased. "If you require, Sutekh can assist with your things."

"That's fine. I just need to bring the car around." Max lifted the walkie-talkie and answered back. "Sounds good. See you then."

Aurelia gazed briefly at the remaining attacker, then she smiled. "Good." She removed a similar implement to the one Sutekh had. She switched it on, and the same soft light shone upon the remaining man. Similarly, he levitated into the air. "When your mother agreed to come here, it was explained she'd be lost to us. I couldn't accept it, though. I made contact, and she prob-ably paid the price for it."

Max studied Aurelia. A moment earlier she had been a glad-iator in the throes of battle. Now, she exuded a cotton-candy softness that made her seem like a different person.

"She was proud of you and your brother. As I'm sure she would be today... Okay, I need you to go for real." Without another word, she floated the would-be killer into the hall and up the steps toward the roof.

Max took a moment to exhale. While Aurelia and Sutekh removed the intruders, he jogged a few blocks to retrieve his car. He quickly loaded his bags inside and glanced one last time at his house. The modernistic building gleamed against the night sky. Max could not see Aurelia's ship, but he knew it must be there. As if on cue, a spotlight appeared, seemingly from nowhere, shining upon the roof of his building. He spotted Aurelia and

Sutekh floating upward until they disappeared into the craft. The light extinguished, and in a sudden flash, Max caught a glimpse of the ship before it vanished in the blink of an eye. He stared a long while at his house, and the realization settled in that he would never return to it as home. Sadness bit into him, but he had no time left to ponder. He climbed into the used SUV and drove away.

At a rendezvous point less than five miles away, Missy climbed into the front seat of Max's car while Derrick and Genet slipped into the back. They were all anxious to hear why he had summoned them at such a late hour, in particular since he had been radio silent all day. He recounted his latest ordeal but conveniently omitted Aurelia and Sutekh from the narrative. When he finished his story, Missy was the first to speak.

"I'm really sorry, Max."

"I suppose I'd be stupid to say I'm surprised." Max's voice cracked, betraying his true emotion. "It's just waking up to those guys... I knew my dad could be gangster, but..."

Missy reached across and gently touched his arm. "You really think they planned to make it look like an overdose?"

"Yeah." Max considered AJ's alleged demise. "I think they already did it once. Or many times, for all I know."

Genet nodded. "It makes sense. They avoid suspicion, prevent an investigation."

Max was unsure whether or not he should be feeling devastated, but his anger was palpable and rising. "We have to finish this, you guys."

Derrick studied Max with a sense of fraternal concern. "Are you sure you're okay? Something like this has gotta fuck with you."

Max spit out an incredulous laugh even though he saw no humor whatsoever in his predicament. "After what just went down, I'm fucking angry. I want this finished. Now."

"All right, man, I understand. I'm assuming you know why we called this morning. Quite a few people died today. We're worried it might've been because of yesterday's operation."

"I know, I saw that, and I keep mulling it over if I did something wrong. I just can't think what it could be. I followed protocol, just like you told me." Max pondered everything he could remember about the mission. "But I can't say it wasn't me either. I told you, I'm no secret agent. I'm just a guy who went to Yale to study cognitive science."

"I hate to break this to you, darling," Genet corrected, "but one thing you are not is just some guy."

Max smiled at Genet's assessment. "Fair enough. But I don't recall anything I could've done to screw things up."

Missy lowered her head to glance at the floorboards. "The fucking Rizick Group... there's no telling how long it'll take to contain this."

"I know." Max ran a hand through his hair in frustration. "I've been thinking about it all day. If it was me, what do we do?"

After an uncomfortable silence, Genet replied. "At this point, all we can do is wait. We've handed the virus off to the people who can figure this out."

Derrick shook his head with worry. "So, your dad knows you were the one who went down there?"

"Yeah. And he was pissed enough to send those guys to my house." Max observed everyone staring back at him blankly. "You should know I found documents down there too. Inflammatory ones. They might have gotten me flustered."

Derrick paused a moment. "What were you getting documents for?"

"It's a long story."

"Not every task comes off without a hitch, but you have to understand working distracted is not cool, especially on an assignment like this."

"I do understand that, Derrick. Believe it or not, I get that this is a big deal. I wouldn't be helping if I didn't think so. I didn't tell you about the files yesterday because I wanted to know what I had first. If it helps, I think we definitely have leverage against my dad."

"Okay..." Derrick shared a thoughtful look with everyone. "That's good. If you think you're up for it, there are a few people who'd like to meet you tonight. We understand if you're not, though."

Max nodded, somehow grasping the infinite possibilities of his emerging circumstances. In some strange way, the world had just opened up to him. "All right."

"Great. Let's head to the shelter then. You can fill us in about the documents over there."

Genet and Derrick promptly exited and hopped into their own car. Max put his signal on, steered into traffic and drove with Missy across town to the shelter. Derrick and Genet arrived minutes later, and the four of them slipped in through the back entrance. Because it was after hours, the facility was completely booked with men and women who needed a bed. Not a single cot or bunk bed was unoccupied. A cacophony of snores erased any possibility of silence. They tiptoed through the men's dormitory, trying not to create a disturbance. Max could not discern exactly who it was, but he sensed eyes on them. *Someone is watching.*

They made their way to an office in the rear. To his surprise, Max spotted a familiar face through a window whose vertical blinds were askew. Nikolaos Satrazemis, the man who had phoned his hotel during the Rizick Group meeting in Greece, was speaking to someone Max could not see. Derrick got to the metal office door and unlocked it. Nikolaos and whomever he was speaking to both fell silent.

Derrick held the door while everyone entered. He then locked it and properly closed the blinds. Max could not believe his eyes. The other man in the room, the one Nikolaos had been addressing, also had a face he recognized. Max had encountered him twice before while he was in Mexico for his initiation. They had first met on the plane from Chicago, but they had crossed paths again. The second occasion was late at night, following his indoctrination ceremony. Max had tried using alcohol to numb the effects of the bizarre elixir he'd been given. Until now, he had thought it pure chance that someone stumbled onto him making an unwanted spectacle in one of Mexico City's more popular nightclubs. In a strange twist, the same man who had rescued him that night was now standing in front of him with a crew of Rizick Group resistance fighters.

Nikolaos and his new guest sported warm smiles when they spotted Max. Refusing to waste time, the man, whose name Max could not remember, stepped forward and extended his hand.

"Hola, Senor Battenberg. How are you?"

Max shook the gentleman's hand with a look of incredulity.

"We met in Mexico, right?"

"Yes, a few months back. I didn't think you'd remember. You have a good memory then. Jorge Salazar."

Max felt relief to see faces he knew, but he had trouble connecting the dots. "I don't understand. What... what're you doing here?"

"The same thing you are, I suppose."

"Okay..."

Nikolaos grabbed Max's hand in a firm handshake. "We spoke briefly in Greece. It's good to officially meet." He released Max's hand, then turned to Derrick and laughed. "It is very strange having him here."

Derrick smiled at Max. "I thought so too, at first. We're lucky to have him."

"It's nice to finally meet, Mr. Satrazemis."

"Please, call me Niko."

Max remained cordial, but he kept his eyes trained on Jorge. "So, Mexico City, was that coincidence or..."

At first, Jorge and Nikolaos offered shrugs until Jorge finally answered. "We have our eye on many Rizick members. And we do what we can to make contact, in the event anyone is willing to help." Jorge held direct eye contact when he spoke. "We can't leave anything to chance."

Nikolaos quickly interrupted. "Speaking of which, what do you think happened with the sample you procured?"

Max shook his head. "We were talking about that earlier. Maybe it was their breach because I'm pretty sure I followed protocol. Or I fucked up, I don't know." Max thought about his mother and the file he had seen on her. "To be honest, there were things going on down there that got me kind of frazzled."

Derrick placed a hand on Max's shoulder. "He's had a rough time tonight, you guys. Let's take it easy. If nothing else, I think reality's hit home for Max that there's a war going on. People like us have been fighting Rizick for a long time." Derrick turned to Max. "Your father and his cabal are extremely serious about everything they do. We need the same resolve."

Nikolaos sported a smirk, expressing his regret. "Collateral damage is not what we seek, but there's something poetic about it too. Whatever happened down there forced those people to the surface."

Max's face turned apologetic. "But people are dying up here as well."

Genet swiped several strands of hair from her face, riddled with concern. "A lot of lives were saved too, Max. Don't lose sight of that."

Missy, who had remained silent until now, finally spoke. "Max is right, guys. If he had done something wrong down there, we probably wouldn't be here."

Nikolaos nodded in agreement. "Whatever it is they cooked up can kill in less than twenty-four hours. It stands to reason that none of you were exposed."

Jorge fumbled in his pocket and removed a smartphone to conduct a search. He read briefly before he spoke. "Looks like the death toll's still at twenty-five. I agree with Niko, though. It's karmic, somehow, that they suffered the release of their little beast."

Max mulled over Jorge's statement and the fatal contagion. "I'm not sure what I think of any of this, but you guys are right. My dad's always shown conviction. I assume it's the same for you. Now, I understand what I have to do." The more he spoke, Max's voice became infused with enthusiasm. "If we're going to stop Rizick, we need to do it right, and why not start with my dad? I believe these documents can help bring him down. When we're finished with him, we'll move on to the next. Then we'll go one by one until the house of Rizick tumbles."

Nikolaos, Derrick and the others listened intently. Derrick moved his dreadlocks to the side. "I like it. It's a great idea, but are these documents enough to accomplish that?"

"Absolutely. That's why they were down there. Those files contain things my father doesn't want anyone knowing. They'll need to be handled with care. I'm guessing most people will be too scared to tackle them. I guarantee my father'll sic his best lawyers on whoever." Max removed three files from his bag and handed them to Derrick. "These are just copies. When you find the right people, I'll provide the originals."

Derrick and Nikolaos sat riveted as chills ran up their spines. Although he didn't realize it, Demetrius had finally succeeded in doing what he had tried for years to accomplish: he had motivated Max. Now, a small spark had transformed into a blazing fury. Max sank deeper into thought. "It's taken me until now to realize that people like my dad are ill. Like those hoarders you see on TV who can't dispose of anything, even garbage. How are Rizick members any different?" Max appeared to be thinking out loud. "Yeah, their houses may not be filled with trash, but their need to amass things and money is the same. We have to rip some of that stuff away. That's what'll throw them off kilter." Max felt his confidence growing. "Don't you think we should get started?"

Too curious to wait a moment longer, Derrick opened the first file. He scanned several lines, and his eyes grew wide. "Oh, fuck. This is big, Max." Derrick read further before looking up. "It's a memo listing pharmaceuticals that his father's company knew were dangerous, but they released them anyway." He closed the first file and opened the second to skim its contents. "Bank fraud, too."

With a nod, Max added, "There's another file detailing some pretty compelling cases of insider trading."

Derrick's face lit up. "He's right, you guys. We're definitely gonna need the right people for this."

At the impromptu meeting's conclusion, Derrick located an empty office and allowed Max to sleep on a cot inside of it. The irony was hardly lost on Max. He had fled his luxury, upscale home only to find refuge in a homeless shelter near dozens of displaced men and women.

CHAPTER 51

The next morning, Max awoke to the ringing of his cell phone. Disoriented, he took a moment to recall... *I'm at the shelter*. The phone carried on until he grabbed it and saw Ted's name flashing. He tapped the talk button and placed the phone to his ear. "Ted... what time is it?"

"Sorry, dude, sorry..." Ted had hardly completed a full sentence, but his voice seemed frantic. "I just came from the hospital, and Brigitte's gone. I've been trying to figure out where she is, but they won't tell me anything. I thought you might know if they moved her."

"I don't know, Ted, I don't know." Max's heart dropped as he sat up. *What could possibly go wrong next?* "Are you at the hospital now?"

"Yeah, I just got here, but her room's empty. All her stuff's gone, too."

"What about her brother, did you call Bertrand?"

"He's not answering, and her cell's off."

"I just spoke to her yesterday. She said they might release her. Maybe she's at home."

An uncomfortable silence dragged out, since neither of them believed this was the case. Finally, Max asserted, "I'll head over there now. If you want, meet me in fifteen, okay?"

Ted exhaled with a moderate sense of relief. "All right."

Both men hung up, and Max gathered his things. Without hesitating, he slipped through the shelter's back door and jumped behind the wheel of his car. Max skidded from the lot and rushed across town to Brigitte's house. When he arrived, Ted was already waiting in her driveway, sporting a peculiar expression. He looked at Max and the Pontiac Aztek, which he did not recognize.

"Dude, what's with the car?"

"It's a long story. Is she not here?"

"I don't think so. I rang the bell and knocked, and her phone's still off."

Max fumbled with his key ring and clutched Brigitte's key.

"C'mon, let's go." He led Ted to the front door and opened it. They stepped inside and Max closed the door behind them. "Bridge, are you here?"

Ted pursued Max through the house as they checked every room. They also checked bathrooms and found them empty. Max's worst suspicions began to take shape. Had Demetrius played yet another trump card?

"Where do you think she could be?"

Max shook his head, unsettled by the circumstance and further thrown by the distress in Ted's voice. "I don't know."

"Max… for the last week you've been ranting about all types of surreptitious shit, telling me that I could be in danger and that people around you are in danger. Now Brigitte's gone, and you don't have any idea where she is?"

Max gazed around Brigitte's living room as if some secret hiding place might reveal itself. While he attempted some form of response, a floodgate of emotion unleashed itself upon him. *Not now.* Max did not wish to reveal how vulnerable he felt, but it was too late. Tears were already escaping his eyes. "Fuck."

"I know you have some idea where she is. All these spy cameras and recording devices… you have to."

While he may have wanted to share his suspicions, Max swiped at his tears instead. "I'm not sure, Ted. I need to see what I can find out."

"They said they can't release information at the hospital unless we're family."

Max tried to corral his emotions. "Like I said, I saw her yesterday. She said they might release her."

"They didn't, dude, otherwise she'd be here. She was moved. It has something to do with this espionage shit you keep talking about, I can feel it."

Max wished he had a better poker face, but his growing concern for Brigitte was already out in the open. He could not recall Demetrius ever having shown a particular interest or concern in Brigitte until the mention of her pregnancy. He knew that if his father had her, there were an infinite number of possibilities as to where she might be. *In the Spire. Perhaps in some pyramid somewhere, or deep underground. But why hold her captive?*

"Ted," Max paused, trying to carefully choose his words. "I hate saying this, especially because I can see you're freaked out. But I have to, out of concern for you…"

"Fuck, dude, please don't tell me I shouldn't look for her."

"You can't, Ted. You have to leave this to me. You're already in over your head. And whether you want to believe I'm crazy or not, you need to look at the big picture. I'm even gonna need to disappear for awhile until I can figure this out."

"You gotta be kidding, Max. So, what, I shouldn't contact you either, then?"

Max took a moment before he nodded deliberately. "I'll get in touch when I can, but I wouldn't fish around in any of this, okay?" Max burned a hole in Ted with his gaze. "I can't force you to do anything you don't want, but I hope you believe in me enough to follow my advice."

Ted studied Max's face as if some answer might arise there like childhood acne. "Shit. If you're fuckin' worried, dude, that doesn't make me feel the least bit better."

Max nodded, affirming Ted's concerns. "I don't know where Brigitte is, but we can't panic yet. I'll keep calling Bertrand. He has to know something."

"So, that's all you want me to do, sit back and do nothing?"

"That's my suggestion, Ted, that you do nothing. And understand that no news is good news until we hear otherwise. Can you do that?"

"Fuck, Max… So you'll keep me posted, then."

"Of course."

"Shit, man. I hope one of these days you're gonna be able to explain this shit."

"We should probably get going." Max led the way outside onto Brigitte's porch, where he locked the door. "Just give me time. I'll figure this out, I promise."

Ted felt speechless, but Max had no other choice but to offer an awkward goodbye. Ted watched him with ever-growing curiosity and angst. Then, Max climbed into the Pontiac and quickly drove away.

Max tried many times to reach Bertrand, but he continually got voicemail, just as Ted had predicted. The instinct to phone his father stirred in him, but he did not want to give in to the urge, at least not yet. Unable to do much more, he took his car and circled through various parts of Chicago. He passed through nicer neighborhoods and sketchier ones, too.

He needed to follow Aurelia's advice and disappear to a safe space. That way, he could regroup in a non-hostile environment. After a 45-minute drive, he pulled onto a street he had visited only months before. When he spotted the Aragon Ballroom, he remembered it was the venue for Marilyn's birthday party. Located in Chicago's historic entertainment district, the building was only two blocks from the Lawrence Street metro station. In recent decades, the area had lost much of its original shine.

This is perfect, Max thought. If need be, he could access public transport. Max also figured no one would look for him in an area that was no longer trendy. He considered the option but continued his search for several hours more, to be sure. In the end, he returned to the Aragon and parked. Still wrought with anxiety, he closed his eyes and placed his head against the steering wheel. After a long while, he got out and leaned against the car, taking in the neighborhood.

Max stepped away from the car and strolled down the cracked sidewalk before a series of abandoned storefronts. His entire life he had lived in nothing less than luxurious homes. Max felt frightened leaving all of that behind to take up residence in what was, for him, one of Chicago's unlikeliest neighborhoods. Swallowing his concern, he circled around several blocks. He finally came across a refurbished building, which were peppered throughout the area. Every now and again he could see into several large warehouses, where he spotted large canvases or sculptures. Several artists had set up shop, and it was Max's intention to join their ranks.

Satisfied of his bearings, he doubled back a few blocks to revisit what appeared to be a rare find. A three-story brick building had a dilapidated sign in front, indicating it was a "hotel." Several ground-floor windows faced the street with penitentiary bars on them. With some level of unease, Max noted three weathered men holding court on the front stoop. Two of them nodded, flashing stained or missing teeth. He smiled to acknowledge them as he entered the building.

Max understood that in order to stay off the radar, he would need to use cash for his expenses. He approached the front desk and inquired about available rooms. There were several, but he requested to see the most expensive one first. The manager escorted him to a large studio on the top floor at the back of the building. A large window in the main room looked down into an interior courtyard that appeared more like a jungle than a garden. A decrepit old tree, surrounded by overgrown weeds and grass, stretched from the ground toward the sun. At its base, clusters of wildflowers added splashes of untamed, asymmetrical color.

It wasn't much to look at, but Max could see potential in the space. More than that, he felt encouraged by the unit's location in the building's rear, which precluded anyone spotting him from the street. The top floor was also an added benefit as it prevented most neighbors from spying into the space. Max crossed to another window that offered a direct view of the Lawrence Street station. The ability to flee, Max felt, was an added benefit. He turned to the hotel manager, resolute. "Will you accept cash?"

Nodding with a smile, the hotel manager took Max's hand and shook it. He accepted the requisite cash for the keys.

Max experienced some satisfaction with his lodging choice, but he wasn't quite ready to live there. For several more days, he slept in the homeless shelter office, during which time, he was unable to unearth even the slightest clue about Brigitte's whereabouts. Bertrand's phone rang every time he called, but her brother never answered or replied. Her phone, on the other hand, appeared to be powered off, as his calls consistently went to voicemail.

In an effort to pass time and keep his head clear, he visited his new digs daily to prepare an adequate living space. In his ideal world, he would have loved a contractor to gut and refurbish it, but it was not an option to invite anyone inside of the new refuge. Max simply felt safer knowing no one knew where he lived, and that included Derrick, Missy and Genet.

Even though Demetrius had cut him loose financially, money was not a concern for now. In the shuffling of his accounts, Max had put more than enough aside.

On his third night in the shelter, Derrick, Missy and Genet appeared at the door of the small office where he had spent his last few nights. It was minutes after 11:30 p.m., and lights out had officially been announced an hour and a half before. Missy placed a finger to her lips and beckoned Max to follow them. He pursued them into the hall and together they made a beeline for the office where they had convened a few days before. Once they were safely inside, Genet closed and latched the door.

"Darling, have you heard today's news?"

"You mean about the Smithsonian outbreak?"

"It's finally been contained. They announced it this morning. We thought you should know."

"I still haven't gotten a TV, but I saw the headline earlier today. It is good news."

Somehow, Derrick did not seem quite as pleased. He bundled up his locks and fastened them behind his head. "It's only been a few days, but apparently, the Battenberg pharmaceutical arm has an inoculation that's an effective safeguard against that particular strain of virus. How coincidental is that?"

Despite the good news, Missy appeared equally disheartened. "The CDC just announced their recommendation that everyone get the shot. Whatever happened down in that facility has now become yet another money-making prospect for some pretty wicked people."

"What's a few dozen deaths," Derrick jeered, "and an entire hospital shut down? Your father, it appears, stands to make a windfall from whatever breach happened down there."

"As usual, Rizick keeps getting wealthier and wealthier," Genet chimed in, but Derrick completed her thought.

"All off the suffering of others."

Max remained contrite. "I'm sorry, guys. I swear I didn't know any of this was going on before a few months ago. They prefer that we blend in, so we're kept in the dark until we're twenty-five. Somehow, I understand that it's easier for us to just accept everything once we've been initiated. But I promise I will help in any way I can."

While they did not intend to do so in unison, the three of them offered Max simultaneous thank-yous. Derrick took a hand and amicably patted Max on the shoulder. "We just thought you should know."

"Yeah," Max agreed, "I'm glad you did. And I'm grateful that you've let me stay here. This will be my last night, though. I found a safe spot to regroup."

Derrick shared looks with Missy and Genet. "Will you keep the radio then, so we can get in touch?"

"Sure. But I'm not likely to reach out any time soon. I need time to clear my head, get things in perspective."

"All right, Max." Missy extended her hand. "Get some rest."

Genet stepped to Max, also to shake his hand. "And don't be a stranger."

"I won't." Max shook Derrick's hand with a weary smile. After some final pleasantries, he retreated alone to the small office for several precious hours of sleep.

CHAPTER 52

The next day, and for several weeks thereafter, Max began working on his own home space. For the first time in his life, he would tackle a small renovation. After researching multiple how-to and DIY sites, he lavished the dilapidated studio space with the deepest cleaning it had seen in years. He stripped layers of paint and varnish from the walls and floors, at times uncovering wood in its original glory. He refinished the floors with a layer of clear coat that made them sparkle. Max primed the walls, then opted not to paint them. At the finish, he converted the space into a bright and rather livable environment that held no resemblance to its former self. The task wore him out, but it also prevented the extreme stress from preying on his mind.

Max had no idea how long he might reside near the Aragon, but, for now, the quarters were more than adequate. If and when the time presented itself, he would certainly relocate to a more suitable address. Until then, he planned to hang around and monitor whether or not Brigitte resurfaced. Her disappearance disturbed him, but he intuited that Demetrius would not harm her. He still possessed a strong desire to participate in the birth of their child, a bargaining chip that Demetrius surely planned to use against him. It was hard to conceive that weeks had passed since she had dropped off the radar. Despite his efforts, he still had no clue about her actual whereabouts, let alone a viable rescue plan. In addition to his concern for Brigitte, he also believed it necessary to remain in town until the documents from his father's vault could properly be curated.

With each passing day, it grew increasingly difficult for Max not to contact Demetrius. There was no doubt in his mind that his father had been behind Brigitte's vanishing act. In the end, though, Max became even more obstinate and resolute that he would not give in to such urges. In all likelihood, this had been Demetrius' goal, to use Brigitte as a bargaining tool to flush him out. *Or might there be some other plan? Grooming my son to do what I would not. Fuck!*

He prayed Brigitte still had the number to his burner phone, but she had not gotten in touch thus far. He did not believe she was so unhappy that she would intentionally remain out of contact. But Max also understood this was a possibility. As a precaution, he double-checked the phone each day to assure it was properly charged. When the time arrived, he wanted to be sure he could receive her call. Either way, he would eventually have to confront his father if she did not reappear. But he would only do so when the correct time presented itself.

During the first month in his rental space, Max felt out of place and sometimes ill at ease. The plumbing and heating were minimally functional. The tenement walls, it turned out, were thin, and the noise and chatter of his neighbors felt intrusive. Each day, he had to remind himself of the danger he faced should he ever decide to resurface. In the second month, however, Max began acclimating to his new surroundings. Several neighbors even made the effort to befriend him, but Max held them at bay, for both their safety and his own.

After eight weeks in the building, he finally picked up the walkie-talkie to arrange a rendezvous with Derrick and the others. Until now, no one at all knew were he was living, and for the time being Max wanted to keep it that way. For this reason, they agreed to meet later that night at the nightclub location of their first encounter. At the appointed time, Max made his way across town for an update with Derrick and the crew. When they were finally assembled, Derrick grabbed Max's hand and briskly shook it.

"How've you been, man?"

"Good, I guess." Max hugged them all affectionately. "How is everyone?"

Genet had her hair down again, only this time it framed her face in tight symmetrical curls. She removed a band and used it to tie the hair away from her face. "Lots of updates, darling. I know it's been awhile since we spoke."

Derrick nodded, interrupting Genet. "I have to be honest; you were dead on about those documents. It wasn't easy finding someone brave enough to tangle with them. I think we finally got the right people, though."

"That's fantastic," Max extolled. "Do you have a time line?"

Missy smiled, then took charge of the conversation. "It's like providence that you chose today to get in touch. If all goes as planned, we'll need the original documents at the end of the week."

"That soon, huh?" Max seemed pleased.

"Once we hand over the originals, it should be a matter of days. I'd keep my television tuned, if you have one."

Max frowned. "I don't, but I can figure something out." With mounting enthusiasm, he pulled a stack of files from his bag and handed them to Derrick. "Here are the originals. It's been a while, so I figured you might need them. I made another set of copies, by the way." He reached in the bag again and pulled out another deck of papers. "I also forgot about this. It's a list of people I was told not to associate with. We should look into why. Some of them might know things that'll work in our favor."

Genet took the latest document and thumbed through it. "We'll look into it." She placed the pages in her bag and fastened it. "So, where've you been, darling? We've had our eyes peeled, but it's like you became a ghost."

Max, while he had not found it easy, had used the last months to erase practically every vestige of his existence. In a peculiar way, he found cool comfort in his new anonymity. "I've been around, I guess. I'll be there when you guys need me, though."

There was a modicum of truth in Genet's assertion that Max had become a ghost. Even though Demetrius' plan to assassinate him had failed, in the end, his father still made him disappear. In a matter of weeks, he had vanished from his previous life, and no one he knew had a clear idea of his whereabouts. He had closed his bank accounts and credit cards, and the SUV had eventually been impounded for failure to pay insurance and registration. Max held on to the throwaway cell phone that he charged with a prepaid minutes card. Life in his new building ultimately permitted him to remain off-grid since he could pay cash with no questions asked.

Genet, Derrick and Missy observed Max with a special sense of awe. Whenever they required his assistance, he always seemed to appear. In the weeks since his procurement of the virus, his importance in the resistance had grown, and they expected him to become even more integral as time passed.

A week after he handed off the original documents, Max awoke in his studio. He crossed to the large window and took a seat on a large cushion situated in the center of an empty floor. Over time, the unkempt courtyard had appreciated in beauty to Max. Once he took the time to notice, he had discovered birds and squirrels in the tree. In the early morning, the sun peered over the courtyard roof, illuminating the little shabby quad.

Suddenly, his walkie-talkie came to life, jarring Max from his reverie. He recognized Missy's voice coming through the receiver. "You there, Max? The documents have been procured; it's happening this morning."

Max rose from his cushion and went to the table. He pushed a button on the walkie-talkie to offer his response. "Okay, thanks."

Crossing to his chest of drawers, he dressed in a pair of gray sweatpants that he had worn while refurbishing the space. The athletic pants appeared soiled and stained with varnish and primer. He decided not to shave and stealthily made his way to his father's neighborhood. Max located a rare payphone several blocks from the Spire. He removed the receiver and dialed Rosalee's number. After several rings, she picked up.

"Battenberg Industries, this is Rosalee."

"Good morning, Rosalee. It's Max Battenberg."

Rosalee paused briefly before she spoke again. Max imagined she might be gathering herself so as not to sound too surprised. "Good morning, Mr. Battenberg. How are you?"

"Couldn't be better. Thank you for asking. If possible, I'd like to speak with my dad."

"He has been traveling, but he landed not too long ago. He's on his way back to the office now. Let me see if I can get him."

In the past, it rarely happened that Demetrius would take unprompted calls, even from Max. But this day, he was sure it would be different. After only a few seconds, indeed, Demetrius came on the line. "Good morning, Max."

"Good morning to you. I figured it was about time you and I checked in."

"I felt certain you would've done so sooner, to be honest. Where have you been?"

"Come on... First you kill Mom and Christian, then you send

assassins to get me. I hope to God you haven't done anything to Brigitte, or my child—your grandchild. Because if you have…"

Demetrius sighed into the phone. "I've explained already that Christian was an accident. Your mother was a different story. She was a betrayer, much like you turned out to be. She had to be dealt with."

"If you touch even a hair on her head—"

"Now, why would I do that, Max, when she's carrying my grandchild? She's not in danger, at least not until after she gives birth, and maybe even then."

"Don't fucking say that! I haven't figured out where you have her, but I'm coming for her and my child. You can bet on that."

"I admit you've proven resourceful these last weeks. But I highly doubt you'll find the girl."

"You're not so untouchable, you know. Brazil showed you that. I've also arranged another little reminder to reiterate it. That's why I'm calling, in fact, so you can see just how resourceful I can be."

Demetrius felt the tickle of intrigue. "What the hell are you talking about?"

"When we last talked, both of us said things that can never be unspoken. Somehow, hardly any of it registered until I woke up to those men at my house. And taking Brigitte… let's just say I understand now how the game is played."

A moment of silence played out on Demetrius' end before he replied. "I know you've put resources aside, Max, but they can't last forever. You never learned self-control. Sooner or later you'll have to come up for air, and I'll be right there waiting."

"Maybe, Dad, but that won't be today. Today, it's your turn to be the one needing air. I just figured I'd give you a heads up, that's all."

Demetrius spat out a hearty laugh, as yet unable to feel any threat in his son's words.

"You think this is a game, taking Brigitte and sending those men to my house?" Max could hear his father snickering on the other end. "Well, I've made the last fucking move, okay? Let's see how you feel about it."

"This *game* you've known for months I've been playing for

twenty-plus years. Do you really think you can challenge me?"

"Who knows?" Max said, delighted at connecting with his father. "One of these days you'll let me know. Perhaps the events of today will even bring us closer."

"You should swing by the office so we can talk in person. Maybe I'll even let you see Brigitte."

"Tell her I'm coming for her — I will get her back. And know this... Today, you're the one I'm coming for!" Max took the payphone receiver and slammed it in its cradle. With a smug sense of satisfaction he made his way to the corner, where he spotted a black Mercedes Benz Maybach with midnight-tinted windows. The top-of-the-line limousine approached on its way to the Spire. Within seconds, it shot by and continued toward Battenberg Industries.

Seated in the Maybach's rear, Demetrius still had the phone pressed to his ear. "Max? Are you there?" He examined the phone to confirm that the call had dropped. "Rosalee, did we lose him?"

"Yes, sir. It looks like he hung up."

"What about the trace?"

"Yes, sir, it appears he was at a payphone just a few blocks from here."

Demetrius spun around and peered through his rear window, but he did not recognize anyone he saw. He failed to notice Max standing at the opposite end of the block, unshaven and dressed in shabby sweats. "Send someone to see if they can find him. And have him brought to me. What was that nonsense he was talking about?"

"I'm not sure, sir. I will look into it."

Demetrius could not be certain how or why, but Max had gotten to him. He barked his irritation at Rosalee. "I'm almost at the office. I'll see you in a few." Without awaiting a response, he hung up and gazed through the window. With a deep exhale, he settled deeper into the garment leather of the limo's rear bench.

The car slowed upon its approach to the Spire. As the chauffeur maneuvered into the underground parking structure, Demetrius spotted it on the wall that descended underneath the building: a single piece of stenciled graffiti stood out like an unfortunate tattoo. He narrowed his eyes at the tag that appeared to have recently been sprayed on. The image, in black paint, was his own likeness with the word "RIZICK" written above it. Demetrius stared while the paint still dripped in places.

Seething, he slammed his hand down on the intercom button in the door console. "I want that graffiti removed immediately, and make sure there aren't any others."

"Of course, sir." The driver's response piped through the car's speakers.

A moment later, Demetrius stomped through Battenberg Industries' front office. Under normal circumstances, his presence would have prompted people to scramble about, trying to appear productive. But this day, that was not the case.

For reasons he did not yet understand, a large cluster of employees had converged on the largest conference room, which was abuzz with commotion. He made his approach and noticed everyone turned toward an enormous flat-screen monitor. His employees had their eyes glued to a popular news station. On screen, a large caption read, "The Improprieties of Battenberg Industries." Demetrius spotted his own photo on display behind the anchor. His staff of onlookers barely noticed him enter, while the anchorman delivered his story:

"This morning, Battenberg Industries suffered not one but two major blows. It appears whistle-blowers have released incriminating documents, revealing multiple improprieties and illegal actions of the company's banking and pharmaceutical arms. This morning, markets are a frenzy as B.I.'s stock prices continue to plunge, and federal fines are certain to be steep if the allegations being made are proven true…"

Demetrius turned and stormed to his office, where he slammed his briefcase down on a $45,000 couch. He continued to his desk and punched the intercom button.

"Rosalee, can you please tell me what the hell's going on?"

"Big problems, I'm afraid, sir. It seems a series of internal documents has been leaked. I'm working now to confirm their authenticity. Everyone's been calling to request a statement. What is it you'd like to do?"

Filled with scorn, Demetrius gazed through his office window. "You know it's Max who did this. Have you dispatched someone to find him?"

"Of course, sir. They're looking for him now."

Less than a mile away, Max strolled up to a nearby Chicago Transit Authority station. In plain view, he took the cardboard cutout of his father's likeness and the word "RIZICK," and he spray-painted another tag against the metro station wall. He pulled the cardboard away and watched paint dripping down. Satisfied, he placed the stencil and paint in a bag, then mounted the stairs to the train platform.

Two of Demetrius' security guards marched toward the station, each holding photographs of Max. One spotted the dripping graffiti and shared a glance with his accomplice. They heard a train arriving and scurried up the steps toward the station's turnstiles. At the top of the stairs, a horde of disembarking passengers blocked their entrance onto the platform. In a desperate attempt, they pushed and shoved to penetrate the crowd.

Max calmly took a seat on the train with his back to the window. He placed his bag at his side as the electronic bell chimed, signaling the train's departure. All sliding doors slid shut, and the train jerked forward. Max didn't notice his father's security detail on the platform, scanning faces in the crowd. But he smiled nonetheless.

CHAPTER 53

For his own safety, Max had become a chameleon. He had learned to disappear in a crowd, and in some ways, every week was like Halloween. For more than a month following the release of his father's documents, he had chosen an array of disguises to obscure his identity. Today, the motif was streetwise chic. Dressed in a satiny royal blue tracksuit, Max allowed his pants to sag in all the right places. With his hair slicked back beneath a baseball cap, he resembled a rap star more than a billionaire's son. It was 9:00 p.m., but Max still had aviator sunglasses on the bridge of his nose, making him look seventeen rather than twenty-four.

An hour before, he had packed a satchel and locked his rented room. With a bag flung over one shoulder, he headed to the Lawrence Street metro station. At first glance, he exuded a strange ethnic appeal that was difficult to identify. He could have been Southern Italian, Latino or even Eastern European. Ear buds snaked from each ear, and Max bopped his head to the beat of music only he could hear.

He walked a block and a half to the station and waited outside at the curb. Roughly fifteen minutes later, a Volkswagen Jetta pulled up. Max crossed to the vehicle as the passenger window descended. He leaned inside, and the bald, freckly-faced driver smiled.

"Are you Ian?"

"That'd be me," Max smiled back.

"I'm John. Sorry I'm late."

"No worries, man."

"Go on, hop in. We've got a 12-hour drive if we're ever gonna get to New York."

Max threw his satchel in the back seat, then hopped in the front. John pulled from the curb and merged into traffic, en route to the nearest interstate. He glanced at Max, slightly amused by his appearance.

"I'm glad you caught me before I hit the road. I can swing a 400-mile drive, no problem. Eight is a stretch, though. Another driver always helps."

Max removed his sunglasses and smiled. "Craigslist is great, isn't it?"

He and John drove through the night, chatting as if they had known each other for years. After roughly five hours, they swapped places, and Max took the wheel, allowing John a break. At sunrise, they switched again. Shortly thereafter, John drove through the Lincoln Tunnel into Manhattan. While he enjoyed Max's company, John still found it peculiar that "Ian" had no landline or cell phone. There was something off about his co-pilot, but he didn't waste much time on the circumstance. He thanked Max and offered his contact information before letting him out at Penn Station.

They had made the trip faster than expected, so Max took to wandering Manhattan before his appointment. He strolled the High Line, reminiscing about New York and reinvigorating his love for the city. After a quick breakfast, he tossed his satchel over one shoulder and made his way to a brownstone in the East Village. Max climbed the steps to a red door with a golden knocker on it. He used it, knocking three times. Inside, he could hear slow but deliberate footsteps coming his way. Finally, someone unlatched the door and pulled it open.

Odeon Rutherford was just as disheveled as he had been in Greece at the Rizick Group meeting. He peered over horn-rimmed spectacles at Max until a look of distrust overcame his surprise. Odeon made every attempt to slam the door, but Max rushed to hold it open.

"Mr. Rutherford, please, I need to speak with you."

"Mr. Battenberg, it was my understanding I was to meet a Mr. Ian Daniels."

"I know. It's an alias I use. I was certain you wouldn't see me otherwise."

Odeon hesitated, clinging tightly to his door. "This is highly unusual. What do you want?"

"I need your help deciphering some artifacts. I hope you'll trust me enough to at least listen."

Odeon remained reticent at first. He stared over his glasses at Max, his eyes unwavering. "If the rumors are true, I take it your father doesn't know you're here."

"I imagine what you've heard is correct, Mr. Rutherford. We'd both be in quite a bit of trouble if my father knew I was here."

Odeon scoffed at the idea, cracking a smile. The mention of antiquities had always piqued his interest. Softening, he pulled the door open. "Come in then." Max stepped inside, and Odeon locked the door behind him. "I have to admit, it's a bit off-putting to find a Battenberg at my door."

"I figured it might be. To be honest, the idea to contact you even spun me out; that's why I used the name 'Ian.'" Max surveyed Odeon's home, which appeared tastefully conservative in decor with ample wood and brass furnishings. "I realized I needed an expert on Sumerian text. It didn't take long to figure out you're that guy."

Odeon studied Max, full of awe. "Fascinating. Come, let's have a seat in the study." He led Max into a library packed with books. Three of four walls were crammed with bookshelves built from floor to ceiling. In addition, several tables and a desk were piled high with volumes of books in first, second, third and fourth editions. He motioned toward a series of four armchairs that were crowded around a circular coffee table also covered with books. Max took a seat, and Odeon sat in the adjacent chair.

"I'll try not to take much of your time. It's just, there's something I've been trying to translate." Max reached in his bag and removed a large color print of the Table of Destiny, the one he had taken in Demetrius' vault. He placed it on the table before Odeon.

Rutherford gazed at Max a long moment before picking it up. He adjusted his glasses before taking a solid look. Suddenly, his eyes grew wide with amazement. "Where did you get this?"

Max struggled, trying to decide whether or not he should confide in Odeon. After a moment's hesitancy, he continued, "It's hidden away in a secret vault that belongs to my dad."

"And you've seen it? The tablets, I mean, not just the photograph?"

"I took the photograph."

Odeon studied Max again before shifting his gaze back to the photo. His excitement was unmistakable. "This is the Table of Destiny. I've heard rumors of it, that it was left behind, but I was having none of it. I would love to know how your father gained possession of it. This is the Holy Grail, son: the Table of Destiny. It holds the key to cosmic knowing."

"I touched it, and something crazy happened."

"But of course. Whoever becomes its steward gains incredible understanding of things normally not understood. No wonder your family has flourished so." Odeon adjusted his glasses again, then studied the plaques that depicted images of Enki and Enlil. "They're as beautiful as I imagined."

Max admired the photo with Odeon, completely aware that his tablet camera had in no way captured the etching's true beauty. The brothers' faces, although very different, were incredibly stunning and symmetrical. While gazing at the photo, something further piqued Odeon's interest. He shifted forward, peering closer at the print. "These symbols are strange beneath the carvings…" A look of utter bewilderment fell like a veil across Odeon's face. "Son, these markings…"

Max waited for Odeon to continue, but he didn't. The old man leapt from his seat and grabbed a book from a shelf behind them. While the room felt cluttered, Odeon appeared to know exactly where everything was. He flipped through the volume and frantically ripped a page from it.

"What is it, Mr. Rutherford?"

Odeon didn't respond. Instead, he scribbled something on the page he had torn out. He looked from the photograph to his own writings. Then he pulled down several other tomes, searching for something, but Max had no idea what.

"While I understand the Battenbergs hail from Enlil's bloodline, I'm rather happy to report that my family are descendants of Enki. If it weren't for his records, so much history would be lost." Odeon located a large coffee-table book and flipped through it until he found a page depicting clay tablets engraved with cuneiform. "At one point, a discovery was made of fourteen tablets. The story engraved upon them appeared to be in the first person. Its best translations, including mine, recount a tale from Enki's point of view. He had been careful, you see, to record everything that happened all those years ago."

"Until the flood?"

"Oh, no, my dear boy. Quite a bit occurred after that. They

returned rather quickly to Egypt and the Yucatan." Odeon continued flipping through the collection of books on his table, only stopping intermittently to describe little bits of knowledge. "You see, all those years ago, Nibiru's approach was quite damaging to the atmosphere here." Odeon located a page in one of his books. He pointed to a series of cuneiform. "It's all right here. A tsunami, a massive flood swept the region."

"Killing everyone, right? Including the workers they created."

"Which was Enlil's wish. Quite a nasty man he was. They presumed their work with the hybrids was done and that their atmosphere had been healed. That's why they packed up and left. But the detriment to Earth's atmosphere, you see—they didn't know this at the time—it was reciprocal. Even Mars was involved in the equation. All three planets engaged in an atmospheric duel of sorts. Of course, Mars was the one who suffered the most. Both Earth and Nibiru literally shredded her atmosphere away."

In recent months, Max had discovered knowledge of the universe that very few others knew. How many other planets sustained life he couldn't say for sure, but he did know of three others besides Earth that science refused to acknowledge: Mars, Nibiru and some other unnamed world in the Pleiades. As it turned out, movies like "Star Trek" and "Star Wars" didn't have it so wrong.

"It didn't take long to figure out," Odeon continued, "that their repairs to Nibiru's atmosphere had in large part been in vain. This planet we grew up on, while small, has much spirit, and she'll never go down without a battle. She struck back at Nibiru with surprising efficiency. So, you see, my young Battenberg, it was all very necessary that the operation, the one they called Gold Dust, continue."

"So, what, they came back?"

"Absolutely. They had to. All their work, all the repairs had been stripped away. Mars, or Lahmu as they called it, had become uninhabitable. But they camped out there until the waters here receded. It was there on Mars that Enki's son, Ningishzidda, first saw the monument to Alalu."

Max looked from the photograph back to Odeon. "The face on Mars, you mean?"

"It's called Cydonia. No one in government was pleased when that obscure photograph was captured. But the public at large demands so little on that topic, even after multiple Rovers have been dispatched to see what's up there. From what I understand, it was a gorgeous monument before the catastrophe laid Mars to waste. The minute Ningishzidda laid eyes upon it, he demanded a similar one be constructed in his likeness."

Max felt Odeon was rambling, and he still hadn't figured out his point.

Odeon stared back at him, aware of his bemusement. "Have you learned so little since your initiation? Ningishzidda's monument is one of Earth's seven wonders, Mr. Battenberg. I'm sure you've seen it many times. Even with its nose blown off, it remains one of Cairo's most impressive sites."

Max narrowed his eyes at the eccentric Rutherford. "You mean the Sphinx?"

"Bingo."

Max felt Odeon might finally be warming to him. Either way, his father's nemesis was immensely enjoying the history lesson.

"Eridu and the Abzu," Rutherford continued, "and countless other settlements were destroyed during the floods. It's likely they would've rebuilt, but the landscape had changed. Rivers that had been no longer existed, and much of the land ideal for mining remained under water. So, they traveled to Kemet." Odeon spotted the blank look on Max's face. "Egypt. Yes, they went there. Then to Mexico. Chichen Itza, Cholula, Teotihuacán. They went to Belize, Guatemala, Honduras and Peru. Caracol, Lamanai, Xunantunich. Mixco Viejo, Tikal and Copan. Oh, and don't forget Caral and El Paraiso." Odeon seemed to be losing himself in the account. "Oh, yes, my friend, they came back in full force." Odeon readjusted the glasses on his nose and proceeded to reexamine Max's photograph of the Table of Destiny.

"I also have video, Mr. Rutherford, if you'd like to see it."

"Oh, you do?" Odeon peered once more over his glasses at Max. "By all means I should like to."

Max removed the electronic tablet from his bag and pulled up the footage. He launched it and handed the device to Odeon. The old man fixed his gaze upon it until his eyes grew wide.

"Oh my Lord. Have you seen this?" Odeon restarted the video. "Look at the symbols! They are changing, melting somehow and reforming."

Max studied the screen. He hadn't noticed it when he shot the video, but the symbols were morphing before their eyes.

"It's fascinating, is it not?" Odeon replayed the footage multiple times before he finally looked up. "Without benefit of the artifact before me, I can't say for sure. If I'm not mistaken, though, these symbols speak of a return."

"What do you mean?" Max demanded, unsure if he should be intrigued or frightened.

Odeon replayed the footage again. "They keep morphing… If I'm reading it correctly…" He pressed pause and looked up in shock. "It can't be."

Max studied Odeon, his face questioning. "What is it?"

"The brothers, Enki and Enlil… How can it be that all these years later, they may be returning?"

Max could hardly believe Odeon's words. "Wait a minute… How is that possible?"

"All we have are theories, Mr. Battenberg, but it certainly is a possibility. Time here is accelerated. Or it's slower out there. Or both."

Max didn't know if he should put faith in the old man's translation, but Odeon's enthusiasm was convincing. "Does it say when?" As hard as he tried, Max couldn't fathom the idea of the brothers still being alive, not when they had lived thousands of years earlier during Earth's prehistory.

Even so, Odeon appeared like a child on a roller coaster, his face a mix of fear and excitement. "It makes perfect sense. The end of the Mayan Calendar has already occurred, and the galactic alignment…"

Max stared at Odeon in disbelief. "Mr. Rutherford, what are you saying? Is what you describe good or bad?"

"Oh, Mr. Battenberg, must everything be about duality? Not everything is good or bad. Some things just are. As I mentioned, I cannot be sure, but there is a possibility our Nibirian ancestors are once again on their way here. In fact, they may have already arrived."

Max pondered the possibility. However far-fetched, he considered his paternal roots, how they traced back to Nibiru, and his maternal ones, likewise to the Pleiades. Suddenly, the idea of Enki and Enlil walking the planet again didn't seem so fantastic or implausible.

Odeon placed Max's electronic tablet on his coffee table. "It's difficult to know for sure, unless we ask your father. The Table of Destiny could reveal such a thing with certainty. Do you believe it is still in his vault?"

"I can't say for certain, but I would guess so."

In no other circumstance would Odeon have trusted a Battenberg, but a chance at the Table of Destiny presented opportunities he could hardly ignore. He smiled gleefully. "We need to get our hands on it, then."

Max considered the idea, but such a task seemed utterly hopeless. "I have no idea how to do that, not after what happened. Unless…" Max thought of Aurelia and her small cohort. They had successfully circumvented every security measure he knew. A smile slowly crept onto his face. "There might be a way."

"Trust me, young man, it would behoove us to uncover the precise time of their return. If indeed they do come back, there is no guarantee they will be pleased with what they find."

Max looked at Odeon, studying his stern expression. "And what if they aren't?"

"Your guess is as good as any. It's not beyond the realm of possibility that they might finish what they started and raze everything we've built. They must have the technology to do so if that's their desire."

Max contemplated everything stored in his father's vault. He had barely touched the Table of Destiny, and an avalanche of knowledge had overflowed within him. To remove it from Demetrius' custody would no doubt deal his father a blow. "I can't imagine either of us have a real shot at getting in my father's vault. Maybe if we work together…" Max silently weighed the pros and cons. "With a few of my friends and some of yours. There just might be a chance."

Odeon removed his spectacles and fixed Max in his gaze. "Battenberg against Battenberg, huh? Perhaps we are not destined to repeat the mistakes of our fathers after all. Okay, then. When should we get started?"

Max smiled at the prospect, feeling empowered for the first time. "We need to figure that out. But there's something I'd like to do first."

Odeon nodded, urging Max to continue.

"It's my girlfriend. She disappeared almost two months ago. My father has her somewhere. I have no idea where, or if she's okay." Max felt volcanic emotion welling inside of him. An eruption, however, was the last thing he wanted in front of Odeon. "She is pregnant, and the baby's due any day now."

"An heir apparent. Could be very valuable to your father."

"Yeah, I know."

"And you want me to help rescue this woman and your child?"

Max could practically see his father's rival performing mental gymnastics as Odeon pieced together the bigger picture. "I have to find her first and make sure she and my child are okay."

Odeon mulled over Max's proposition, and the gears of his mind began grinding with possibilities. "I'll do some checking and see what I can find out."

"Thank you. I'll be better… more focused if I know she and the baby are fine."

"Understood." Odeon lifted the photograph of the Table of Destiny and gazed at it once again.

"I'm sure you're aware, it won't be easy to get in my father's vault."

"Oh, please…" Odeon waved a hand dismissively. "Nothing in life is easy, Mr. Battenberg, but this doesn't mean we shouldn't task ourselves to try."

"There's nothing I'd like more than to get my hands on that thing, but I need to find Brigitte first."

Odeon cracked a smile. "Very well, Mr. Battenberg. I say drinks are in order. Would you like one?"

Max glanced at a clock above Odeon's window and noticed it was only minutes after 10:00 a.m. "It's a bit early for that, but why not?"

Odeon reached out and shook Max's hand before rushing to a wet bar in the corner of the room. He filled two snifters with brandy and returned to hand one to Max. "I don't usually drink this early either, but in this case, I think a toast is in order!" Odeon raised his glass and clinked it against Max's. "To the Table of Destiny and an unlikely partnership."

Max lifted his glass a second time. "To Brigitte Sturdivant and my unborn child. And to the brothers' return. May we all survive it."

"Here, here," Odeon cheered.

In spite of the early hour, Max and his new accomplice turned up their glasses and drank.

Here ends Volume 2.0 of The Unveiling.
To uncover the series' dramatic conclusion, please
stay tuned for the third and final volume,
The Unveiling 3.0.

Coming soon

THE UNVEILING 3.0

Abgal – Sumerian character, assigned to be Enki's pilot.

Abzu – This region, as told in Sumerian mythology, is believed to be the area known under modern appellation as the southern coast of South Africa.

Adamu – The very first man of a genetically created race of hybrid workers.

Adapa – Sumerian character, illegitimate hybrid son of Enki, who would eventually become the father of twin sons Ka-in and Ab-el.

Akasha – Sanskrit word meaning ether, the fifth element after air, fire, water and earth.

Akashic Record – Believed to be a library of everything ever created in human existence as well as the history of the cosmos. The Akashic record does not exist in the physical plane, but is found in the ether.

Anunnaki [Best translation = "those of royal blood"] – A race of beings that came to Earth from the planet Nibiru as described in Sumerian mythology.

Antikythera Mechanism – An ancient device discovered in 1901 in the Antikythera shipwreck off the coast of Greece. The mechanism, believed to have been constructed between 100 and 150 BC, is historically out of order, as its technology was not considered existent before the fourteenth century.

Anu – Sumerian deity considered to be the Supreme Leader of the royal race of Anunnaki. **Chakras** – Concepts that originate in Hindu text; there are seven power centers or vortices that exist along the spine, and each are considered portals that channel energy from the spiritual world into the physical world.

Enki – Sumerian deity, considered a prince, as the first-born son of Anu and his second wife, Antu, and half brother of Enlil

Enlil – Sumerian deity, considered a prince, as the second-born son of Anu and his first wife, Ki, and half brother of Enki.

Eridu – The first city on Earth to be created by the Anunnaki. Eridu is believed to be in ancient Sumer or what is also known as Mesopotamia. Today this region is known as parts of Iraq, northeastern Syria, southeastern Turkey and southwestern Iran.

Galzu – Sumerian character, emissary sent from Nibiru to inform Enki, Enlil and Ninmah that they should leave Earth and return home.

Hatha Yoga – In Sanskrit, the word "Ha" translates to sun and "Tha" to moon. As with night and day, Hatha is a system of yoga that unites opposites.

Igigi – The Anunnaki workforce brought to Earth from Nibiru.

Ka-in and Ab-el – Hybrid twins, sons to Adapa and Titi (to be compared to Cain and Abel in the Old Testament).

Ki – Sumerian deity, first wife of Anu and mother to Enlil.

Kundalini Yoga – The yoga of awareness. Kundalini is a practice that attunes the physical body with spiritual awareness. Kundalini activation is the process of fully activating each of the seven chakras.

Marduk – Sumerian deity, born on Nibiru, first son to Enki.

Money Pit – The site of the world's longest running hunt for lost treasure. The booby-trapped pit has drawn treasure hunters to Nova Scotia's Oak Island for nearly two centuries.

Nibiru (or Marduk) – Believed to be the twelfth planet of our solar system, as referred to in Zecharia Sitchen's book "The 12th Planet." Modern appellations include Planet X, Eris.

Ningishzidda – Sumerian deity, born on Earth, second son to Enki with mother Ereshkigal. Sumerian mythology alleges that the Egyptian Sphinx is Ningishzidda's likeness.

Ninmah – Sumerian deity, daughter of Anu and his first wife, Ki; full sister to Enlil; half-sister to Enki.

Ninurta – Sumerian deity, born on Nibiru, first son to Enlil and Ninmah.

Sud (aka Ninti) – Sumerian deity, former assistant to Ninmah, wed to Enlil after his sexual assault against her and bestowed with the royal title Ninti.

Sumerian Mythology – In the vein of Greek mythology, Roman mythology and Egyptian mythology… Sumerian mythology recounts the story of gods from the planet Nibiru as told by the culture that is modernly known as Iraq.

White Powder of Gold – The byproduct of gold that has been vaporized by heating it to the temperature of the sun. It is a super-conductor with monoatomic properties.

Ziusudra – Earthborn hybrid who was given plans for a submarine in order to survive the Great Flood. His role should be compared to the role of Noah in the Old Testament.